The Painted Lady

Françoise Sagan achieved international acclaim with her first novel, *Bonjour Tristesse,* published in 1954 when she was only nineteen. Her life since then has been as eventful as her literary career has been successful. She has written many novels, some of which have become films, and several plays. *The Painted Lady* marks a new departure for Sagan and has been greeted with great enthusiasm by the critics in France, Britain and America.

'Sagan's richest and most masterly book'
Jacques de Decker, *Le Soir de Bruxelles*

'Sagan has taken on a new challenge — and emerged victorious'
Nouvelles Littéraires

'Sagan has become expansive, gossipy, generously nostalgic . . . *The Painted Lady* is great fun, and guaranteed to outclass the Krantzes and the Conrans on the right beaches'
Lorna Sage, *The Observer*

'Partners are swapped like colourful cigarette cards, passions are spent like wads of franc notes and pretensions and illusions of the French rich are pricked with glinting pins. Throughout the goings and comings are observed with the wry mordant wit of Ms Saga'
Liverpool Daily Post

'Entertaining throughout'
Birmingham Post

'Sly and ironic'
New York Times Book Review

'Proustian in its richness and texture'
Harper's Bazaar

Françoise Sagan

The Painted Lady

Translated by Lee Fahnestock

A STAR BOOK
published by
the Paperback Division of
W. H. ALLEN & Co. Ltd

A Star Book
Published in 1984
by the Paperback Division of
W. H. Allen & Co. Ltd
A Howard and Wyndham Company
44 Hill Street, London W1X 8LB

First published in Great Britain
by W. H. Allen & Co. Ltd, 1983

Copyright © Françoise Sagan, Jean-Jacques Pauvert et
Editions Ramsay, Paris 1981

Printed and bound in Great Britain by
Anchor Brendon Ltd, Tiptree, Essex

ISBN 0 352 31483 4

FOR JEAN-JACQUES PAUVERT

*thanks to whom
the story of this book
is a happy one,
from his friend*

What importance can we attach to the things of this world? Friendship? It disappears when the one who is liked comes to grief, or when the one who likes becomes powerful. Love? It is deceived, fleeting, or guilty. Fame? You share it with mediocrity or crime. Fortune? Could that frivolity be counted a blessing? All that remains are those so-called happy days which flow past unnoticed in the obscurity of domestic cares, leaving man with the desire neither to lose his life nor to begin it over.

CHATEAUBRIAND, *Vie de Rancé*

*I*t was the last of summer, a summer that had been yellow and raw, violent, one of those summers that bring back thoughts of wartime or childhood. But now a pale burnished sun rested on the calm blue waters of Cannes harbour. It was the end of a summer day, the beginning of an autumn evening, and there was something languorous in the air, something golden, superb, and above all perishable, as if all that beauty had been condemned to death by its very excess.

Beside the quay the *Narcissus*, pride of the Compagnie Pottin, was readying to weigh anchor for its celebrated autumn music-cruise. Stationed as if at attention at the foot of the gangway, Captain Elledocq and his purser, Charley Bollinger, seemed unaware of the beauty of the moment. They were greeting the privileged passengers of an ocean liner luxurious enough to justify the exorbitant price of the cruise. The poster, displayed in travel agencies around the world every year for the past two decades, was enticing. Its slogan, five words inscribed against a blue blackground, encircling an Aeolian harp of uncertain date: '*In mare te musica sperat*,' which for not overly exacting Latinists might be translated as 'Music awaits you at sea.'

Indeed for ten days, if you had the taste for it and the means to indulge your tastes, you could make a brief tour of the Mediterranean in elegant comfort and in the company of one or two of the musical world's greatest living performers.

The Compagnie Pottin had planned the trip so that, ideally speaking, the port of call determined the musical work, and the musical work determined the menu. These delicate musical relationships, hesitant at first, had gradually evolved into invariable ritual, even if it occasionally happened that the sudden decay of a *tournedos* necessitated the replacement of Rossini by Mahler, and the *tournedos* by a Bavarian pot roast. Often advised at the last moment by the steward of the latest caprice of the ship's deep freeze or of Mediterranean markets, the performers were prey to slight attacks of nerves; this added spice to an existence that was otherwise rather monotonous, if you overlooked the price. The cost of the cruise was, in fact, ninety-eight thousand francs in de luxe and sixty-two thousand in first class, second class having been forever banished from the *Narcissus* in order to spare the sensibilities of those among the privileged who were less privileged than the rest. No matter; the *Narcissus* always set out with every berth filled. People fought for cabins two years in advance, and they returned regularly to the rocking chairs of the upper decks as others did to the tiers of Bayreuth or Salzburg—among fellow music-lovers, among the wealthy, whose eyes, ears, whose sense of smell and taste were richly gratified day after day. Only the satisfaction of the fifth sense remained optional—which, given the average age of the passengers, was on the whole a good thing.

At five o'clock, departure time, Captain Elledocq grunted, drew his watch from his waistcoat pocket and dangled it before his eyes with disbelief before waving it in front of the patient and less surprised Charley Bollinger. The two men had been sailing together for ten years and had picked up quasi-marital habits which, given their appearance, seemed quite preposterous.

'Want to bet, no Bautet-Lebreche before seven?'

'Very likely,' answered Charley Bollinger in his pleasantly reedy voice. Over the years he had grown quite accustomed to the commanding officer's telegraphic style.

With his colossal stature, his beard, beetle brows and rolling gait, Elledocq looked so much the part of an old sea-dog that he had worked his way up through the ranks of the Compagnie Pottin despite a singular inaptitude for navigation. After a couple of shipwrecks and no little damage he had been taken off the high seas and entrusted with peril-free runs, from one coastal port to another where, from the bridge of a solid and well-equipped steamer and aided by a first officer with a fair command of navigation, nothing untoward could ever happen to him. The conceit that Elledocq had developed since his earliest youth for reasons no one could understand bordered on paranoia and made him automatically equate the lack of responsibility in his post with complete confidence on the part of his employers. But he dreamed of Conradian adventures, a life à la *Captain Courageous*. And the impossibility, in these waters, of sending out romantic distress signals or a heart-rending SOS delivered in a firm but emotionless voice had never ceased to weigh on him cruelly. At night he dreamed of shouting into a crackling mike from the eye of a hurricane, 'Longitude such and such, latitude such and such and holding . . . Passengers safe . . . No intention abandoning ship . . .' Alas, in the morning he could only send messages like, 'Fish spoiled. Kindly change purveyor,' or at best, 'Provide wheelchair, disabled passenger.' The use of code had become so natural to him that if he used any preposition at all—an *of* or *at* or *for*—his subordinates were plunged into a state of panic, particularly the blond, the fearful Charley Bollinger.

Born in Ghent of a bourgeois family, a homosexual and a Protestant, Charley's life had been a series of affronts endured more with grace than enjoyment, and in Elledocq's hauteur, in his uncompromising virility and intolerant brusqueness, strangely enough, Charley had found a sense of stability, a relationship which, platonic though it might be (and God knows it was), in some obscure way reassured him. As for Elledocq, who hated in descending order communists, foreigners, and homosexuals, it was miraculous, Charley thought, that for some time he should have had some dealings with the latter.

'Of course our dear Edma will be a bit late,' said Charley enthusiastically. 'But I'd like to point out that the great Kreuze himself hasn't arrived yet either. And as for waiting, alas, we're used to that, Captain.'

He gave his companion a sort of thump on the back—or that was what he intended. Captain Elledocq eyed him furiously. He detested the 'we' that Bollinger perpetually imposed on him. It was only three years ago that he had found out about poor Charley's lifestyle. Having gone ashore at Capri to buy a pouch of tobacco (an exception to the rule, for it was a sacred principle that he never left the ship), he had come across his purser, dressed as a gypsy maiden, dancing the cha-cha-cha with a muscular Capriot on the Piazzetta. Though horror had riveted him to the spot, he had never said a word about it to the culprit; but ever since then he had regarded Charley with a somewhat horrified and occasionally fearful contempt. And from that day he had entirely given up smoking, an odd reaction he could never have explained.

'Who now, this Kreuze?' he asked, suspicious.

'But Captain! Kreuze—Hans-Helmut Kreuze! Really, Captain, I know you're not much of a music-lover . . .' Charley could not restrain a giggle at the thought, a small pearl of mirth that further blackened the captain's brow. 'Why, Kreuze is now the world's greatest conductor! And the greatest pianist, they say . . . Last week . . . Well, you do read *Paris-Match*, don't you?'

'No time. *Match* or no, this Kreuze—he's late! May run an orchestra, doesn't run my ship! You know how much he gets, ten days wrecking ship's piano? Heads or tails, three hundred thousand! Not bad, eh, Charley? Wanted his *own*

12

piano. Our Pleyel not good enough! Straighten him out, this Kreuze, I will.'

And with a snort, Captain Elledocq shifted his quid of tobacco and sent a jet of brownish saliva toward his feet. A malicious gust of wind spattered it onto Charley's immaculate trousers. 'Oh, damn—'

Charley's cry of dismay was cut short by a gleeful voice calling to him from deep inside a chauffeured Cadillac. In an instant Charley's expression changed from one of annoyance to joy, as he rushed to welcome Madame Edma Bautet-Lebreche herself. Elledocq stayed put—seemingly deaf to this voice familiar to all the Jet Set, to every opera house and to every fashionable salon in Europe and the States.

So Edma Bautet-Lebreche, followed by her husband Armand Bautet-Lebreche (of Bautet-Lebreche Sugars, among others) stepped from the car, carolling a soprano 'Hello, Captain! Hello, Charley! Hello, *Narcissus*! Hello, sea!' She was playing the 'vivacious stunning charmer', as she liked to describe herself. In an instant all harbour activity was arrested by that shrill but forceful voice: sailors were immobilised at their posts, passengers at the ship's rail, seagulls in flight. Captain Elledocq alone, hearing other voices in the cyclones of his soul, remained deaf to it.

Though Edma Bautet-Lebreche admitted to fifty years (as she had now for a good decade), she was youthfully dressed in a hound's-tooth suit and a white turban, an outfit that accentuated her extremely slim figure, her vaguely equine face with slightly protruding almond eyes, and what she liked to think of as her 'regal bearing'. Her husband's bearing, on the other hand, was that of a bustling accountant. Nobody ever remembered Armand Bautet-Lebreche— except those who had done business with him, and they never forgot him. He had one of the largest fortunes in France, indeed in Europe. Perpetually immersed in a reverie that bordered on absent-mindedness and made him stumble wherever he went, he might have been taken for a poet, but it was figures and percentages that haunted his bald egg-shaped head. But, though master of his fortune and of his

13

empire, 'A.B.L.' was also slave to that frenzied computer that had clicked away unceasingly in his cold brain since earliest childhood, making him one of the thousand martyr beneficiaries of modern mathematics. His own limousine had got lost on the autoroute, so he was settling with the chauffeur of the hired Cadillac—giving him, without even stopping to think about it, a twelve per cent tip, correct to the nearest centime. Charley Bollinger was taking out of the boot of the car an unbelievable stack of black leather suitcases simply marked B.L., but nine-tenths of which he knew would belong to Edma rather than Armand. Two muscular sailors came down the gangway and were all ready to carry them on board.

'It's still number 104?' Edma inquired, in a tone more affirmative than interrogative.

Number 104 was indeed her cabin. It enjoyed what to her eyes was the privilege (to the captain's eyes, the curse) of being next to those of the performers.

'Charley, tell me right away, will I be sleeping next to the diva, or Kreuze? I really don't know which I'd rather hear in the morning when I'm having my breakfast, la Doria's trills or Kreuze's arpeggios . . . What joy, what utter joy! I'm thrilled, Captain, I'm just too, too happy. I must give you a kiss . . . May I?'

Without waiting for a reply, Edma had already leapt like a large spider at the neck of the secretly indignant captain and was dispensing her geranium-red lipstick on his black beard. She had always had a mischievous spontaneity—which apparently delighted Charley Bollinger as much as it annoyed her spouse. What A.B.L. termed his wife's 'provocations'—forty years earlier they had seemed charming enough for him to marry her—were one of the very few things capable of tearing him away from his figures and occasionally causing him to miscalculate. But now that coarse and ridiculous Elledocq was the victim, Armand Bautet-Lebreche appreciated her little game, and for an instant his eyes met with those of Charley Bollinger, above identically conspiratorial smiles.

'And me?' Charley cried out. 'And what about me, Milady? Aren't I entitled to a little reunion kiss too?'

'Why yes, why, of course, my dear Charley . . . I did miss you, you know.'

Red with rage, Elledocq stepped back and cast a sarcastic glance at the tenderly entwined couple. A fag and a madwoman, he thought darkly. Now I've seen everything.

'You're not jealous, Monsieur Bautet-Lebreche?' he asked in an ironic, virile voice, man to man—since, after all, this sugar baron, even if he looked like a piece of badly cooked veal, was still a male.

But he got no acknowledgement of their affinity in return.

'Jealous? Oh no,' mumbled the complacent husband. 'Let's go on up, shall we, Edma? I'm a bit tired. But it's nothing, no, nothing, don't worry,' he continued hastily as Edma, whipping about on the wind of anxiety, turned back to pat his cheek and loosen his tie, fussing over him as she did each time she was reminded of his existence. Taller than Armand Bautet-Lebreche by a good two inches at the time of their engagement, Edma now topped him by four. She was still amazed to have married an immense fortune—her ambition all through her youth—and from time to time she liked to reaffirm her rights over her spouse, this taciturn little man who belonged to her alone and who alone owned all that sugar, all those factories, all that money. Meanwhile she ran her hands over him and fussed at him with a worried smile, like a little girl with a bald doll. Armand, whom the shrill vivacity of his wife had quickly reduced to impotence, attributed this occasionally frenetic behaviour in the otherwise haughty Edma to maternal instincts that he had frustrated. So he dared not protest too much. Though with the passing years she forgot his existence more and more often, thank the Lord, the moments when she did remember him were all the more demonstrative. Perhaps it was owing to Armand's desire that his wife should forget him that everybody else did so with such ease.

His unwary invitation to 'go on up' unleashed a whole conjugal memory in Edma's mind. Armand fled toward his cabin, knowing that once stretched out on his bunk he would be safe from her solicitude. And indeed Edma—who early in their marriage had become irritated by her husband's embraces and who believed she still had to fear them, despite the fact that any physical intimacy between them was virtually past history—imagined he found her 'tempting'. Refusing to play with fire, she normally approached Armand only when he was seated or standing—sensual pleasure for her being linked to the supine position. This fact Armand, that heap of living ash, was able to exploit shamelessly, by lying down for no reason at all on the first divan in sight.

The Sugar Baron reached cabin 104 first and threw himself panting onto the first bunk. Edma came in a half-length behind, followed in turn by the devoted Charley Bollinger.

'Well then . . .' whispered Edma, whose ladylike gasps suddenly caused a dog in the neighbouring cabin to bark furiously, 'well then, what's the news, Charley? Do sit down.'

She herself had collapsed into an armchair and was allowing her satisfied gaze to wander over the luxurious décor, so ugly and so familiar. It was a ship's cabin decorated as a ship's cabin by a very well-known Parisian designer—that is to say, with a great deal of teak, brass and objects considered either English or maritime.

'Well then, tell me everything! First, are there any new people? But what in the world is that beast?' she continued in her high, nasal voice, annoyed now for the dog was howling all the louder.

'It's Kreuze's bulldog,' said Charley, not without pride. 'He arrived the day before yesterday, ahead of his master. He's already tried to bite two of the stewards!'

'It seems that Kreuze also barks a lot,' said Edma, who, after a distressing and mysterious incident at Bayreuth, had become a thorough Germanophobe. 'That dog will have to be muzzled by his master,' she said still louder to overcome the racket. 'Or else thrown overboard,' she added, a demi-octave higher. 'Who are the new people? Old Stanistasky died, didn't he, back in the spring, in Munich? Who inherited 101?'

'The Lethuilliers,' said Charley. The dog immediately fell silent. 'You know, Eric Lethuillier? *Forum*, that leftist paper—well, practically communist? The Eric Lethuillier who married the heiress to the Dureau Steelworks . . . Well, we're going to have a man of the left travelling with us, my dear! Music draws everyone together, in the end . . . Thank heavens,' he added sentimentally.

'But that's truly amazing, isn't it?' exclaimed Edma. 'What on earth is wrong with that animal?' Edma was now tapping her foot. 'Perhaps it's my voice that's annoying him? Well, Armand, say something!'

'What do you want me to say?' Armand asked in a spiritless tone which, as if by magic, calmed the dog.

'If it's women's voices that annoy him, la Doria will have an amusing time on the other side. Ha! I'm laughing already! Just think of it! What with la Doria and her temper, there'll be a real set-to . . . Which reminds me, how did you manage to get her?' she whispered, defeated by her canine enemy who, on the other side of the partition, was wheezing feverishly, like an exhaust valve—an altogether demoralising noise.

'They paid her a fortune, I believe,' Charley answered, whispering too, as though it were contagious.

'Her last gigolo must have been more expensive than the others,' said Edma naughtily and with a touch of envy, for the amours of la Doriacci were renowned for their multiplicity—and brevity.

'I don't believe she has to pay anyone,' said Charley, who, like nine-tenths of all music-lovers, was madly in love with Doria Doriacci, in spite of everything. 'She's still splendid, you know, for all her fifty-odd years,' he added, then suddenly blushed.

But Edma was not to be upset over such a trifle. 'Oh, she's well past that!' Edma's triumphant voice again set off the barking next door.

'At any rate,' continued Charley once the storm had abated, 'she's coming aboard alone. But she will, I believe,

17

have the opportunity to debark in company . . . We have two new guests this year. Two young men, one of whom is not bad, actually! An art appraiser from Sydney, Australia, named Peyrat. And a mystery man I haven't seen yet: no profession, single, and only twenty-five. All I know is he's from Nevers. That'll give Doria plenty of choice . . . if they don't succumb to your charms first!' he added flirtatiously, causing Armand, over on his bunk, to clamp his eyes shut again.

'Flatterer!' exclaimed the imprudent Edma with a laugh that reawakened the dog's ire.

But they were not going to provoke the dog any further; he had won. Edma and Charley said goodbye in whispers.

Charley returned to take up his post beside Elledocq, who was just welcoming the renowned Hans-Helmut Kreuze himself. It was from a distance that Charley first observed the confrontation of the two massive figures, these two men who symbolised and controlled, so they believed, two old and magnificent allies—music and the sea; but who, being no more than mere vassals, interpreter and navigator, might well find themselves enemies.

Hans-Helmut Kreuze was a Bavarian, of medium height, stocky with heavy features and thick, close-cropped hair that looked sometimes yellow, sometimes grey, and he bore a striking resemblance to the anti-German caricatures of the First World War—it was easy to imagine him in a spiked helmet, chopping the hands off a babe in its cradle. But he played Debussy like nobody else. And he knew it.

Accustomed as he was to seeing fifty wind instruments, fifty strings, a triangle and whole choirs obeying his merest glance, Kreuze was at first stunned by the unyielding attitude of Captain Elledocq. Then it put him in a rage. Getting out of a Mercedes so new as to be colourless, he marched right up to the old sea-dog and clicked his heels before him, chin slightly raised. From behind glasses his eyes fixed upon Elledocq's epaulettes.

'You are undoubtedly the pilot of this vessel, sir!' he demanded in clipped syllables.

'The captain, sir. I am Captain Elledocq, commanding the *Narcissus*. And you, sir?'

The idea that anyone might not recognise him was so inconceivable to Hans-Helmet Kreuze that he though Elledocq was being deliberately insolent. Without a word he drew his ticket from the right-hand pocket of his coat, which was too heavy for the season, and waved it rudely under Elledocq's nose. The captain remained impassive, hands behind his back. The two belligerents stared at each other for an instant, while Charley, absolutely appalled, tried to slip between them.

'Maestro, Maestro,' he said. 'Such an honour! Maestro! What a joy to have you on board! May I introduce to you Captain Elledocq? Captain, this is Maestro Hans-Helmut Kreuze, who all of us on board have been awaiting with such impatience . . . You remember, of course . . . I was telling you . . . We were so anxious . . .'

Charley floundered, spluttering, while Kreuze walked straight past the still-unyielding Elledocq, and headed resolutely up the gangplank.

'My cabin, please,' he said to Charley. 'My dog has already settled in? I trust you have provided him with some appetising titbits,' he added menacingly, in that mannered yet touristy style of speech which he affected whenever he condescended not to use his mother tongue. 'I hope we shall be weighing anchor soon,' he threw back at poor Charley, who trotted along behind, mopping his brow. 'I tend to get nauseous in port.'

He entered cabin 103, was welcomed with a muted growl of hatred by his pet, and slammed the door in Charley's face.

Slowly and majestically leaving quay and terra firma behind, Captain Elledocq strode up the gangplank, which was instantly raised. Three minutes later, its plaintive horn drowning the dog's barking and the squeals of Edma Bautet-Lebreche as she broke a fingernail on a coat hanger, the *Narcissus* slowly left Cannes harbour on waters as sleek and lustrous as a dream, and Charley Bollinger had to wipe from his eyes the mist that such great beauty brought to them. For in half an hour the sun had reddened. Its haemorrhaging bathed in warmth the waters of the port and at the same time dyed them blood-red. Quickly, all too quickly, despite the fleecy little clouds that pressed against it, their whiteness changing to scarlet, that same sun threw back its head, seemingly resigned to ending all of a sudden its slow, its eternally immobile plunge.

'*I*'m going to go and wander around a bit, aren't you coming? Armand, do get up . . . Dusk will be gorgeous, I just know it . . . What? Already asleep? What a pity! Really, such a pity! Well, then, take a rest. You've certainly earned it, my poor pet . . .' Edma brought to an end her outpouring of tender cautions—the total lack of an audience was heartbreaking—and she was already slipping out of the door that she closed with the greatest of care.

If Edma occasionally performed without an audience, you could not therefore say that she really acted for herself. (It was, she thought, more complicated than that.)

Setting out on tiptoe down the passageway, she found herself—for once unintentionally—being indiscreet. Inside cabin 101, a woman was trying to hum the overture to the last act of Strauss's *Capriccio* in a voice so naked that the intrepid Edma suddenly got goose pimples. It was, she thought, the voice of a child, or a woman on the very brink of despair. And not wishing to know any more about it— unusual for Edma—she fled to the deck.

21

It was only much later, during a performance of *Capriccio* in Vienna, that Edma would recall that moment, that voice, and feel that at last she understood everything about the cruise. In the meantime, burying that moment among other more banal recollections in the catch-all of her memory, she reached the deck in a sheath of banana-coloured surah deliciously set off by a navy scarf encircling her slim neck. She took in at a glance the two decks, the stack, the bridge, the crowd, the rattan chairs, that penetrating glance that was so well known to her little circle—the glance of a proprietor, albeit a sarcastic one. As if mysteriously alerted by what she herself thought of as her aura (and Edma really had acquired one, by dint of willing to set off an alarm by her very presence) several faces turned towards her. A graceful and slender silhouette, so elegantly dressed, so free from all sign of age in the misty soft light, she described herself mentally. And smiling down at her enthusiastic subjects, the good queen Edma descended the steps to the deck.

The first to kiss her hand was a boy in blue jeans, exquisitely handsome, perhaps a little too handsome. And of course it was Charley Bollinger, showing every sign of having fallen madly in love within the past ten minutes, who introduced them.

'Madam Edma Bautet-Lebreche, may I present Monsieur Fayard? Andreas Fayard ... *Andreas*!' he concluded, thereby openly and distractedly surmounting at a single stroke all the barriers that society had so cruelly erected between himself and this unknown young man. 'I don't believe I mentioned him to you,' he added, his pride tempered by apology.

In fact, Charley was apologising for his failure to foresee his own sudden passion for this young man, and for failure to alert Edma in advance—that being one of his duties towards her. She gave him a faint peacemaking smile, and he thanked her with a look—gestures that were at once perfectly understood and perfectly unconscious.

'Ah yes,' she said with an amiable nod (but also a certain reserve which meant, 'Fair enough, Charley, he's yours. So keep him, I won't touch, since you saw him first'). 'Ah yes!

22

Well, then, this is Andreas Fayard from . . . from Nevers? Am I right? My dear Charley, you'll never again accuse me of losing my memory.' She finished with a loud nervous laugh at the young man's evident surprise.

And as for this young man, Edma mused, with his Greek profile, deep-set eyes and puppy-dog teeth, he must be used to having strangers take notice of him. Just so long as Charley hasn't fallen again for a little crook more crooked than the rest.

That was what was so annoying about these young people, all these young people wafted back by the evening breezes year after year to the ever-craving but inexorably united tribe of the truly rich. Yet, that was the most annoying part of all—you couldn't make them understand that if you knew what they were doing, then you knew what they were thinking. By and large one side was just as cynical as the other when it came to the terms of the barter. In the long run it was the profiteers, the pimps who were more insistent on sentimental flourishes than their victims. These young small-time predators had it all wrong; they wasted people's time—including some of their own, short-lived as their attractions were—far more than they did the tears and golden trinkets of their avid, elderly prey.

'You know Nevers?' the young man was asking. 'Do you know the road to Vierzon, near the Loire, where . . .' He paused, and the slightly haggard look of eagerness that made him seem even younger vanished from his face. 'Well, I just came from there . . . ' he stammered as if to excuse his look of pleasure, unexpected in one of his profession; for when these young people spoke of their provincial homes, it was generally to congratulate themselves on having left them.

'But it's very good to love one's birthplace,' she said with a smile. 'It's silly—I was born in Neuilly, in a hospital that doesn't even exist any more—and I can't remember a single thing about the place . . . It's very frustrating and very sad,' she continued with a peal of laugher. 'Ah, yes, yes . . .' she insisted, since Charley and the young man were laughing too, Charley from nervousness and the young man out of goodwill. 'Ah, yes, yes, and it was such a drawback when it came to reading Proust.'

Her eyes swept across Charley's vacantly appreciative face—he naturally hadn't pushed professional conscience to the point of reading *Remembrance of Things Past*—and then equally unexpectantly over the young man's, who to her great surprise, did not assume a vaguely knowing air, but regretfully admitted, 'I haven't read Proust.'

A point in his favour, thought Edma as she turned away from this new couple in search of less difficult quarry, though not without a certain fleeting regret that made her heart flutter. For whatever her best friends—or she herself, for that matter—might say on the subject, there had been men whom Edma Bautet-Lebreche had deeply loved. And though for five years now she had been loudly congratulating herself on having given up, for reasons of aesthetics and possible ridicule, the flesh 'and all its works, the pomps and vanity of the world', still she could not suppress the occasional regrets, fierce to the point of nausea, stirred by certain recollections that were all the more unnerving because she could not put a face or a name to them; and for recalling to mind—had she cared to examine them closely—no more than an empty bed with sheets tinged blue by the sun.

Mercifully, Captain Elledocq now came toward her, rolling as though this were the *Titanic*'s worst hour, and removed at a stroke any longing for the male sex.

'Introduction, eh, new recruit?' he said, vigorously pounding the shoulder of young Andreas, who wavered but did not bend.

Under that schoolboy's blazer he must be solid as a rock, thought Edma. For she knew that a thump of this sort was a favourite game of the slow-witted brute who commanded the *Narcissus*. Poor Armand, subjected for the first time to that fist, had been all but swept away, like a little packet of his famous sugar. In Captain Elledocq's defence it might be said that he had confused Monsieur Bautet-Lebreche with a Central European film director, excuse enough for his breach of protocol.

'Well there, 104? Everything okay?' He turned amicably

24

towards Edma, who drew back a pace, ducking her chin and flaring her nostrils as though he reeked of garlic and tobacco.

For three years running, one of Edma's favourite little torments had been to identify in the unhappy captain all the stigmata of the incurable smoker (which he no longer was, since the memorable incident at Capri). She would discover a pouch of tobacco in some deck chair and bring it to him like a retriever. With a conniving look she would offer him matches while he chewed on a straw, ask him for a light ten times a day with the assurance of a heroin addict looking for a needle in the pocket of a fellow addict. To the furious and exasperated denials of the confirmed non-smoker that Elledocq had become, she would respond with deliberately exaggerated exclamations that enraged him: 'Oh, but that's quite true! My goodness, how can I keep forgetting? I'm too stupid for words. It's just not possible to have such a bad memory . . . But it only happens to me with you, isn't it strange . . .' And so the work of undermining continued. Sometimes Elledocq clamped his teeth onto the stem of an imaginary pipe with a savagery that would have snapped it off had it been there. Now, as she took a cigarette from her purse Elledocq scowled in anticipation. With the perversity always at her command, Edma leaned towards the young man.

'Do you have a light, Monsieur? Since Captain Elledocq doesn't smoke any more, I'm always looking for someone to offer me a match. I'll be pestering you all through the cruise. So now you're warned!' she said, taking hold of the beautiful pale hand that held the lighter and drawing it slowly towards her mouth, where her cigarette seemed for an instant a useless accessory—rather too slowly, so that Charley went pale and the young man blinked.

There's one she'll pick off, the old goat! thought Elledocq, keen psychologist that he was. He grunted scornfully at such wiles. For him all women were either catty bitches or else mothers and wives. He had an arsenal of opinions that had been out of style for two generations, and a wealth of similarly outmoded expressions that enabled him to voice his opinions all the more trenchantly.

The deck was filling up around them. Fresh and rested, tanned by the summer sun but ready to set off for the lights of the city, bored already but resigned to tolerating their leisure, the passengers of the *Narcissus* appeared from all directions, emerging from companionways, recognising and greeting one another, embracing; they criss-crossed the deck in a rhythm, gathering into little groups that fell apart again, scattered to all quarters like a strange legion of insects emanating, gilded, from a faintly repugnant subterranean world.

It's the reflection of gold that gives them that colour, thought Julien Peyrat as he leaned against the railing with his back to the sea, already facing those whom he expected royally to fleece. He was an old and tall young man of forty-five, thin-faced, with a certain boyish, cynical charm that suggested, according to one's point of view, either one of those athletic young American senators described in the newspapers, or a mafioso whose male beauty means violence and corruption. Edma, who had always hated men of that sort, was surprised to find him on the whole agreeable. He looked cheerful, and though his blue wool sweater was a bit casual for the hour and occasion, it was not casual in the playboy sense. At any rate, he seemed more real than the other passengers. And when he smiled or appeared puzzled, as he did just then, he had almost a tender look. She took note of this as she turned involuntarily towards the commotion that had drawn his attention and indeed seemed to fascinate him.

Emerging in their turn from the innards of the ship, a man and a woman moved towards the sort of checkpoint formed by the captain and Charley. After a moment's thought, she identified the couple as the Lethuilliers. For a moment she along with the rest froze before Eric Lethuillier—his perfect profile, his height and dignity, blond hair, the intransigence and genuine violence of his nature which had earned him in the press the name of 'the Viking'. Here he was, the incorruptible Eric Lethuillier, whose weekly paper *Forum* had for almost eight years been striking relentlessly at the same targets—the numerous and varied iniquities of those in power, the flagrant injustices of society and the egoism of the upper class (to which, almost without exception, his fellow passengers belonged). Here he was, the handsome Eric Lethuillier, moving towards them with a firm tread, and on his arm the most beautiful prize of his life, heiress to the Dureau Steelworks, his wife, the mysterious Clarisse. Clarisse, whose mere appearance had a stunning effect on people: tall and thin, defying precise physical description as she was said to evade analysis of her character and personality, with long, tawny blonde hair that fell around her face as if to conceal it once and for all, a face now caked with grotesquely thick gleaming make-up; for this diffident upper-class lady painted herself like a whore and, according to the gossip columns, she also drank like a fish, drugged herself like a Chinaman and was, in short, systematically destroying herself and her marriage. Her retreats to and escape from specialized clinics, the pattern of her nervous breakdowns were as notorious as the extent of her family fortune and the patience and devotion of her husband.

Notorious, to be sure, yet not to the point that all the stewards of the *Narcissus* would have had wind of it. And so it was that one of the unfortunate crew, after offering Clarisse a dry martini which she swigged down, was encouraged to return with a replenished tray and the happy smile of one who has found a good customer. As Clarisse reached out for a glass, Eric's arm swept brutally across the tray, splintering its contents on the deck. The flabbergasted waiter knelt, while everyone turned towards the commotion. Eric Lethuillier seemed unaware of his audience; white with rage and anxiety he glared at his wife, with an expression at once wounded, angry and disappointed, and seemingly oblivious of the witnesses all about him, he said to her loudly and distinctly, 'Clarisse, I beg of you, no! You promised you'd behave like a human on this trip. I implore you . . .'

He stopped, but it was too late. Everyone stood frozen with embarrassment until Clarisse turned without a word and began running towards the companionway. Impeded by her high heels, she stumbled and half-way across the deck she would have fallen—to the further dismay of her involuntary spectators—had it not been for the supporting arm of Julien Peyrat, the art appraiser from Australia. Edma detected in Eric Lethuillier's expression more annoyance than gratitude; a gratitude that would have been only natural towards one who had saved his wife from a humiliating fall—though less humiliating, on reflection, than the public outburst he had just levelled against her, and the tone of which, let alone the words, could hardly be construed as giving the remotest impression of tenderness or concern.

So Edma watched the rest of Clarisse's flight with an uncharacteristic expression of indulgent commiseration. And when, rapidly swivelling her elegant, trim torso, she caught the look which the mafioso senator directed at Lethuillier's impeccably tailored shoulders, she was not surprised to detect in it a sort of scorn. She arranged to cross paths with Peyrat as he moved forward, and after Charley had introduced him as 'the noted art appraiser from Sydney', she caught his sleeve. Possessed of a certain wisdom, but not so much that she could refrain from giving evidence of it, Edma still marvelled, after sixty years, that this could annoy others. With a confiding hand still on Julien's arm, she murmured something inaudible.

He politely leaned towards her: 'What did you say?'

'I said a man is always responsible for his wife,' she told him crisply. As she let go of his sleeve, her interlocutor's slight shrug allowed her to think she had hit the mark. And she went off certain that she had left him gasping at her clairvoyance.

Instead she had only irritated him. Yet this was the sort of woman that he was supposed to cultivate—before embarking he had spent enough time mugging up *Who's Who* and the society pages to know that much. He could still see a photo of Edma Bautet-Lebreche on the arm of the American or Russian ambassador, and the caption below it which noted that *Vogue* had named her one of the best-dressed women of the year. That she was also one of the richest could barely have escaped the likes of Julien. Indeed, he should be gaining admission to her salons, not to mention her cabin, should the opportunity arise. Anyway, the woman was a real terror. He watched her cackling as she perched on the arm of the unfortunate purser. He observed the glitter of her eyes, the agitation of her hands, heard the cutting edge of her voice which proved that, failing a real intelligence, you could still acquire a sort of perspicacity by rummaging in the affairs of others—a perspicacity that could well prove disastrous for him during this cruise. All the same, the eternal lover Julien repressed within himself noted grudgingly that her body must once have been superb, and that her legs still were.

A crowd had now gathered in the stern. From the cries of excitement, it appeared that something was going on back there—something that should not escape Edma's attention, whatever it might be. So she trotted off towards the rear pool deck.

Bounding across the water and raising a wake of immodest pink spray, a speedboat with an outboard engine was about to pull up alongside the *Narcissus*. Astern lay a heap of glistening leather baggage, all in beige—a somewhat vulgar beige, prone to spotting, mused Edma. 'Latecomers!' somebody called out, scandalised—for it was very seldom indeed that anyone boarded this luxurious craft other than at the appointed hour and from the designated pier. You would have to be really dissolute—and exceptionally powerful—to think of boarding the *Narcissus* at sea. Edma leaned against the bulwarks, and between the transparent furrow of the wake and the dark figure of the sailor at the wheel, she made out two individuals entirely unknown to her. 'Well, who is it?' she demanded of Charley, who was calling out orders and looking important. He gave her an excited, raffish look that she found irritating.

'It's Simon Béjard,' he said. 'The producer, you know? He's arriving from Monte Carlo. And the young lady, of course, is Olga Lamouroux.'

'Ah yes . . . ah yes. I see.' Edma Bautet-Lebreche sighed aloud over the heads of the crowding passengers. 'Leave it to film people to make this sort of entrance. But who exactly are they?'

Great, so now she's going to play ignorant, Charley thought as he came up beside her. Edma did in fact make a show of knowing nothing about cinema, television or sport—pastimes she thought rather common. She would gladly have asked who Charley Chaplin was, had she thought she could get away with it without sounding ridiculous.

Charley adopted a noncommittal tone. 'Simon Béjard. Until last May he was a total unknown, but then came *Fire and Smoke*. You must have heard of it, my dear lady? Winner of the Grand Prix at Cannes? Béjard produced it—and Olga Lamouroux is the latest sensation.'

'Well, no . . . Alas, I was in New York last May,' Edma said in a tone of false regret.

Charley was secretly exasperated. Personally he loved the idea of having movie people on board, at last. They might be vulgar but they were famous, and Charley was almost as charmed by fame as he was by youth—though there was little charm to be found in the embarkation of the newcomers, who obviously lacked sea legs.

'I'm terribly sorry, terribly sorry.' Simon Béjard waved his arms as he staggered onto the suddenly stable deck. 'Really sorry I couldn't make it on time. We didn't hold you up, did we?' he asked Captain Elledocq who glared back with a brooding horror—not only was he a famous producer, he was probably foreign, and he was most certainly late.

'It took less than a half-hour to catch up! These things really move!' continued Simon Béjard, casting an admiring eye towards the speedboat, which was already disappearing over the horizon in the direction of Monte Carlo. 'They're really something! Ninety horse! the old pirate said . . . They're really something!'

His admiration found no echo, but the little red-headed man didn't seem to notice. With his loud Bermuda shorts, tortoise-shell glasses and Cerruti scuffs he was a caricature of a Hollywood director, an impression in no way diminished by his wide-eyed little-boy look. The young person at his side, on the other hand, was dressed very obviously à la

Chanel, hair pulled back, large sunglasses on the tip of her nose. She evidently did not enjoy playing the starlet, or anything else for that matter, and she wore a cantankerous expression that for all her beauty made her unpleasant to look at. This demeanour immediately sharpened Edma's unfortunate propensity for teasing. Meanwhile, Simon Béjard, with a promise to return immediately, guiding baggage and companion before him, disappeared after Charley into a companionway. The ironic commentaries clipped along for a minute or two—and then stopped abruptly with the realisation that Doria Doriacci, the diva of divas, had taken advantage of the commotion to make a discreet entrance and was now quietly sitting in a rocking chair just behind Elledocq.

'La Doriacci', as the opera directors called her, 'la Doria', as the crowd called her, and 'Dorinina', as five thousand snobs claimed to call her, was over fifty. All sources of information, for once, were in agreement on that score. Actually at times she could as easily look seventy as thirty. A woman of medium height, she had the robust vitality of certain Latin women, and a rounded body that could not really be called fleshy. What flesh she did have was nicely contained by a superbly smooth, rosy skin, the skin of a young woman; and the body might have refuted her age were it not for what was known as Doriacci's 'mug': a round but deeply lined face, raven hair, immense flashing eyes, and a perfectly straight nose. It was a tragic face, in short, in which the childish mouth, the lips too red and too full, came as a surprise—a turn-of-the-century mouth that failed to overcome the haunted quality of the face (and haunting, too), as if swept by some vague violence. A face like a menace or a permanent temptation. In the end you overlooked the drawn features, the crow's-feet, the lines around the mouth—all the seemingly irreparable ravages that a burst of laughter or sudden desire on her part could repair in an instant. At this particular moment she was staring at the back of Elledocq's head with an intimidating persistence which made even him, as he turned around at an exclamation

31

from Charley, quiver like a skittish horse that has met its master. Elledocq's entire hierarchic nature quavered under that look; he stood at attention, then bent in two and clicked his heels, looking more military than 'cruise ship'.

'Good gracious,' cried Charley, quickly lifting the be-ringed hand of la Doriacci to his lips and kissing it twice. 'Good gracious! To think you were right there all this time . . . How was I to know? . . . You told me you'd be staying in your room . . .'

'I couldn't stay in my cabin,' said la Doriacci, smilingly disengaging her hand and quietly wiping it on her dress without the least show of malice or awkwardness, though Charley was deeply hurt. 'Poor Kreuze's dog just can't get used to the idea of growing old! The same as his papa . . . He keeps howling! Don't you have any muzzles on this ship? You ought to—dog or no dog.'

This last she added darkly, with the wild look of a Tosca. For prevented by the intervening crowd from addressing the diva directly, Edma Bautet-Lebreche had launched an ear-splitting tribute in the direction of the startled Julien Peyrat. 'We heard her last winter, my husband and I, at the Palais Garnier!' She closed her eyes with delight 'She was divine! but then again "divine" doesn't really say it! She was beyond anything human! Better, or worse, than human! I went hot and cold, I lost all notion of what I was saying,' she concluded in the midst of a total silence.

Then pretending to catch sight of the diva, she rushed forward, seized her hand and held it avidly between her own. 'Madame,' she said, 'I have dreamed of meeting you, but I never for an instant dared hope that my dream would be realised! And now here you are! And here I am! At your feet, as is only fitting. Need I tell you that this is one of the greatest days of my life!'

'But why such surprise,' la Doriacci said almost affection-ately. 'Didn't you read the programme for the cruise before-hand? I was there in large type—in very large type, as a matter of fact, otherwise my manager is out of a job!' She withdrew her hand and set it down like an object, this time without preliminary cleaning, on the arm of the chair.

'Captain,' she said bluntly, 'Captain, I'd like to make something quite clear. Life is dear to me, you see, and I loathe the sea. That's why I would like to look at you closely before entrusting myself to your care. Tell me, is life also dear to you, Captain? And for what reasons?'

'But I . . . I am responsible for passengers . . .' Elledocq stammered. 'And . . . and . . .'

'. . . and you'll do your best, I suppose? What a horrible expression! Any conductor I work with who tells me he's going to "do his best", I have him fired! But the sea isn't the stage, is it? So I suppose we can't complain . . .'

Whereupon she whisked out of an enormous satchel a single cigarette and then a lighter, lighting the one with the other so rapidly that no one had time to assist her.

Charley Bollinger was entranced. There was something in her that inspired him with confidence even as it frightened him. He felt that from the moment she had stepped on board, the *Narcissus* was destined to return to port safe and sound—even if it lost keel, rudder or engines. He was almost as certain that by then the supreme authority would have changed hands, that by their return to Cannes la Doriacci would be in possession of the blue cap and the loudspeaker (hardly necessary in her case) while Captain Elledocq crouched in the hold, bound and gagged, with his feet in chains. Such, at any rate, was the apocalyptic vision that crossed Charley's mind, divided as it was between delight and terror. In all the ten years that they had sailed together, nobody had ever treated Elledocq so rudely or with such open scorn.

Charley made another attempt to seize the hand of the diva and this time succeeded in placing his lips between two enormous rings—one of which immediately grazed his nose when la Doriacci, believing the formalities long since over and surprised at this belated gallantry, pulled back her hand with the abruptness of a city-dweller in the countryside who finds herself unexpectedly licked by some affectionate goat. The gash on Charley's nose promptly began to bleed.

'Oh, do excuse me! My poor boy, do excuse me . . .' cried the diva, genuinely upset. 'I'm awfully sorry.

33

You made me jump. I thought all the hand-kissing was over. Let's call it a day, before your nose takes another beating . . .' As she spoke she rapidly patted the wound with a well-worn batiste handkerchief miraculously extracted from her satchel, in the end hurting him as much as she had scared him.

'It's still bleeding. Come to my cabin, I'll put some iodine on it. You know nothing infects the human skin more than a precious stone . . . Yes, yes, do,' she insisted as Charley feebly protested. 'Come and get me settled . . . Settled, that's all!'

'Never fear, Captain Haddock,' she said, as if he had shown some sign of jealousy, 'I set out alone, and sometimes I return less so. But not this time, because I am absolutely exhausted. We did *Don Carlos* at the Met for a full month, and now I have only one desire—to sleep, sleep, sleep! Oh, I'll sing—for ten minutes between naps,' she concluded, reassuringly. Then, directing Charley with a movement of her chin, she said, 'To my cabin, for pity's sake, Monsieur Taittinger! Quick march, if you please.'

Without another glance towards the captain, ignoring him as she had his previous gloomy retort of 'Elledocq! Elledocq!' she rose and elbowed her way through the crowd.

The cabin was vast and luxurious, but still seemed appallingly cramped, and Clarisse was waiting. Eric was whistling in the adjoining bathroom. He always whistled in his bath like a carefree man, but there was something intense, breathless, almost furious, in the way he did it, which suggested anything but insouciance to Clarisse. In his defence it had to be said that a light-hearted mood is one of the most difficult to feign—and Eric simply was not cut out for light comedy. Insouciance presupposes, by definition, a certain forgetfulness; and to remember to forget is in itself a paradoxical and laborious task. At times, when Clarisse forgot that he no longer loved her, that he no longer desired her, that he was contemptuous of her and that he frightened her, she might almost have found him comic. But this was only at rare moments; the rest of the time she hated herself too much for the implacable and unrelieved vapidity of which he tacitly and rightly accused her—a vapidity he had over-looked in the myopia of passion before marrying her, and which even the heaviest make-up could no longer conceal but simply succeeded in making garish.

She was waiting. She had sat down at random on one of the cabin's two berths. Eric hadn't yet chosen his—or more precisely, hadn't yet chosen Clarisse's. Naturally he wasn't going to say, 'I'm taking the berth nearest the porthole because the view is better.' Rather it would be, 'You take the one next to the bathroom, it will be more comfortable.' In fact that was the one she wanted—not for any reason of comfort or aesthetics, but simply because it was nearer the door. Everywhere, in theatres, drawing rooms, on trains, it was invariably the aisle, the door—in short, the exit—that always determined her choice of seat whenever Eric was with her. He had not yet realised this because she always managed to appear vexed by his final decision, knowing all too well that his own satisfaction depended upon her not getting her way. So she had sat down on the berth furthest from the door, waiting, with her arms crossed, like a child kept after school.

'Dreaming, eh? You're already bored?'

Eric had come out of the bathroom and was buttoning his shirt in front of the mirror with the serious, precise gestures of a man indifferent to his appearance—though Clarisse could see the narcissism that peered out from under every glance at his own reflection.

'You'd be better off on the other bunk,' he said. 'You'd be nearer to the bathroom. Don't you think so?'

With a semblance of reluctance, Clarisse picked up her purse and went to lie down on the bunk by the door. But in the mirror Eric saw her smiling, and immediately a gust of cold rage swept over him. What was she smiling about? What right had she to smile without his knowing why? He knew that this voyage together, this sumptuous conjugal offering, was going to be—was already—a torture for her. He knew that very soon she would become involved in the tortuous routine of the alcoholic, in humiliating

35

arrangements with the barmen. He knew that this handsome face bereft of animation by guilt and resignation, the beautiful face of a spoiled yet chastised child, concealed a trembling woman, exhausted and on the verge of nervous collapse. She was at his mercy, she was at the opposite extreme from happiness. She was no longer interested in anything. But something in her still indefatigably resisted, something refused to go under with the rest, and in his fury and his jealousy Eric believed that whatever it was came from her money—the money he blamed her for having, but nevertheless he could not think of it except as an attractive quality; the money she had had since childhood and which he had lacked all through his youth.

She was smiling again, her head tilted to one side. After a few seconds he sensed that this time it was not he who was the cause of her customary frightened smile, but the voice of some unknown person humming a waltz tune nearby. And this time it was not, it could not be, fear that lighted up Clarisse's face in this unexpected and intolerable way; it was pleasure.

Julien Peyrat removed the painting with the greatest of care from his suitcase, and found himself once more seduced by the talent of the forger. Marquet's charm was certainly there: those grey roofs deadened by the cold, that yellow snow under the wobbly wheels of the hackneys, and the steam quivering at the horses' nostrils . . . The steam, of course, was a figment of his imagination. But for an instant he, Julien Peyrat, felt he was back in the heart of Paris, in winter, in 1900; for an instant he had breathed the smells of leather and of steaming horses, of the wet panelling inside the black carriage arrested there in the centre of the canvas. And he had followed, with eyes full of nostalgia and disappointed desire, the painted lady in a fox fur who was rounding the corner to the right, ready to leave the painting without once turning his way. For an instant he had inhaled, had recognised that smell of the first frost in Paris, that suspended whiff of smoke, of extinguished wood fires, of cold rain, that aroma in which were mingled the pungent tang of ozone and of the snow above the streetlights, the gentle odour familiar to all Parisians, that remained the same despite the cries and groans of those who consigned the capital first to ugliness and then to destruction, perhaps out of jealousy, owing to the simple fact of their own impending death. For Julien, Paris was an eternal city with eternal charms . . . but expensive, alas! He smiled as he thought of the male passengers aboard the *Narcissus*. Boredom would quickly bring them to bridge, perhaps gin rummy, at any rate to cards and eventually to poker. Julien reached for his pack and practised a few deals that gave him four kings every time.

There was a waltz tune running through his head, which he hummed continually without being able to identify, and which at moments exasperated him.

*B*y now the sun had set on a grey sea just faintly tinged with blue, a murky sea already invaded to the east by a milky haze. On every deck and before every mirror, passengers were readying themselves for the first evening on board. But Edma, who had already spent an hour in her cabin, was champing at the bit with an impatience doubled by the total inertia of her spouse, still absorbed in the stock market. So she left ahead of him and entered the bar, humming off key a Rossini aria, afraid that she might find no one there. Thank God, destiny had seated a block of granite at the far end of the bar that she identified as Maestro Hans-Helmut Kreuze, who was sipping a beer as he mulled over his grievance against that lout of a captain. He was feeling calm and undisturbed, when the voice of Edma Bautet-Lebreche rang out like a tocsin across the evening sky. Outside, a few seagulls took to the air. If, however, Hans-Helmut Kreuze, unable to follow them, was obliged to turn and face her, it was not without a certain satisfaction.

For though Hans-Helmut Kreuze found it absurd that, for a few sordid bank notes, anyone with money, whether music-lover or clod, should imagine themselves entitled to hear Music (particularly as he, Kreuze, performed it), he did not think it contradictory that he should demand gigantic fees, and that he had a fervent respect for cash in hand. And, curiously, scorn vanished abruptly when he came face to face with the owner of a large fortune, so it was with sympathy, indeed with deference, that he greeted the wife of the Sugar Baron. He even got off his stool in what he intended as a gallant gesture—which is to say he dropped heavily onto his well-shod feet, grunting like a lumberjack. The deck trembled. He bent his spine at a forty-five-degree angle to his haunches, and with a click of the heels he bowed across the beringed hand of the imperious Edma.

'Maestro,' she said, 'I could never have hoped for this! This meeting! You! Alone! And in this solitary place! At this solitary hour! I must be dreaming . . . And if I dared . . . or more precisely, if you should ask me'—then and there hoisting herself gracefully onto the neighbouring stool—'I might allow myself a few minutes of your company. But only if you insist,' she added, addressing the barman with a raised finger and 'A gin fizz, please.'

Hans-Helmut Kreuze was about to offer the requisite gentlemanly insistence when he realised that Edma was comfortably seated, with an olive between her teeth, and was already swinging her foot, completely at ease; he abandoned the formality. In fact Edma's air of authority did not displease him. Like many people in his line of business, like virtuosi and celebrities in general, he had a limitless taste for orders, for the cavalier attitude and the *fait accompli*. For a moment they talked music, and Edma displayed her true musical culture—which managed to assert itself for all her snobbery. Hans-Helmut's respect increased to the point of obsequiousness, for in his relations with human beings, unlike musical scores, he played in only two keys: the key of scorn or the key of obeisance. Within ten minutes they had reached a degree of intimacy that Edma would never have imagined possible, or even for that matter desired, and which, assisted by several beers, impelled Kreuze to a confidence.

'I have one anxiousness here,' he told her, lowering his voice. 'One big ugly anxiousness . . .' (Edma winced; despite her poise, she could not quite adapt to his curious way of speaking.) 'Well, you know, usually, women with me . . .' He chuckled suggestively, 'Females usually, at me they look . . .'

Edma realised suddenly what he was trying to say. Ah! So, away from the podium he turns into the big buck! Really these conductors are all paranoid.

'Why, of course, that's to be expected,' she said between her teeth, 'particularly for anyone so well known.'

Don Juan nodded his approbation. He continued, after swallowing huge quantities of beer: 'And even certain well-known females . . . very, very well known . . .' he whispered, a finger to his lips.

(Grotesque, Edma thought. He's actually simpering!)

'But, dear Madame, do not make me to name names. Not a single name. Not one! Let us keep in mind the honour of the ladies . . . I say no! No, no,' he repeated, removing the index finger from his lips to shake it under the nose of Edma, who suddenly took offence.

'But, my dear man,' she said, raising her head and eyeing him. 'My dear man, who in world asked you for a name? The name of whom or what, to begin with? Surely you're not suggesting that I'm pressing you for any such thing?'

'Not precisely,' said Kreuze, craftily narrowing his eyes. 'You were not asking me the name of the lady on this very boat, who one evening, with Hans-Helmet Kreuze . . .' The same coarse laughter convulsed him.

Edma was torn between a really appalling curiosity and a distaste that very nearly got the upper hand—but as always, only very nearly.

'Well, well,' she mused aloud. 'And so who on this boat could it be?'

'You promise me silence . . . Shh, shh, and once again shh? Promise?'

'Promised, sworn, shh, shh and again shh, whatever you like,' Edma chanted, eyes piously lifted skyward.

The virtuoso assumed an air of gravity. Leaning so close that she could see the screws in the hinges of his glasses, he abruptly breathed against her ear and down her neck, 'La Loupa'—and then drew back as if to judge the effect he had produced.

Edma exclaimed, flinching under the gale of beer, 'What? What? La Loupa? La Loupa? Ah! Loupa: she-wolf . . . The she-wolf? . . . Well, all right, I understand Latin! Thank goodness! The she-wolf, but which one? There are a good many of us around, us she-wolves!' She whinnied mischievously, startling the young barman, who dropped his shaker.

'La Loupa. Doria Doriacci,' Kreuze whispered urgently. 'During the entire '53–'54 season la Doriacci was known only as La Loupa, nothing else. La Loupa. In Vienna, she was easy game. Beautiful already . . . And I, poor Kreuze, away from family, long tour, all by myself . . . And La Loupa is looking at me all the time like this . . .'

The maestro, widening the shoe-button irises behind his spectacles, slid a pink tongue across his lips.

Faintly disgusted, Edma Bautet-Lebreche said, 'And what then? Did you succumb? Or resist? It's a charming tale you're telling me . . .'

She could feel herself visibly turning into a feminist. Poor Doria must really have been starving to put up with this baboon.

'Yes, but . . .' the other continued, imperturbable, 'yes, but the end is not nice. You French females, you say hello afterwards, is it not so? La Loupa, nothing! For thirty years, La Loupa makes not one hello, not one little sign, smiling not even one little bit. But you would smile, my dear little Madame, is it not so?'

'Who? Me? Certainly not!' Edma said, abruptly decisive.

'But yes, but yes . . .' Kreuze reassured her. 'But yes, little French females, afterwards, all do like this!'

And while Edma stared in indignation, he gave her a horrid wink from behind his lenses—at the same time lifting his upper lip to reveal a single gold tooth invisible until then but which was perfectly in keeping with his malicious smile. After a moment of frozen horror, Edma quickly recovered. Her face settled into an expression of disdain and lassitude—a maniacally dangerous expression which, alas, neither Hans-Helmut Kreuze at the peak of his imaginative powers, nor Armand Bautet-Lebreche, who had just arrived and had placidy taken an armchair at the far end of the bar, was capable of noticing or understanding.

'You think that is nice?' persisted Kreuze. 'That La Loupa, for whom I paid for a dinner, at Sacher in Vienna on that same evening, thirty years later treats me, Kreuze, like a clod? Well?'

'Well?' Edma gave herself over to the delicious feeling of overwhelming languor, very close to physical pleasure, that swept over her, along with anger, a certainty of the imminence of drama, of explosion, catastrophe. 'Well, exactly! You *are* a clod!'

To persuade him of the strength of her conviction on the subject she poked him insistently in the sternum with a horizontally extended index finger. But, wonder of wonders, Kreuze did not budge. His memory, gorged on recollected demonstrations of admiration, steeped in frenetic bravos and glutted with remembrances of his family's complete subservience to him, could not admit Edma's sacrilege. Everything in him—memory, vanity, primitive self-assurance, even coronary arteries—his entire being refused and rejected what his eyes and ears transmitted to him, this 'Exactly! You *are* a clod!' And he took the hand of this charmingly outspoken woman, who let him hold it for an instant, disdainful but terrified, convinced he was going to strike her or push her off her stool.

'Such a charming little lady,' he said. 'You should not use such language. These are not things a pretty elegant woman should be saying . . .'

Indulgently he kissed the tips of her fingers to her great indignation.

'A thousand pardons, Maestro! But I know perfectly well the meaning of the word *clod*,' she said coldly, chilled by what she considered his hypocritical cowardice. 'I give you my word! And I'll repeat it for you once more: you are indiscreet, crude, vulgar, stingy—the archetypal clod, so there! The big buck clod, in fact,' she added, but to a phantom audience.

For Kreuze had fled towards the exit with a grating unnatural laugh, coughing frenetically and waving his hand back and forth, as though by wishing not to hear Edma's inconceivable words he denied them, and thereby actually did not hear them.

Vaguely uneasy at his exit, which left her voracious fury unsatisfied, Edma moved off in a prancing clatter of heels, blazing eyes and, one might have said, smoking nostrils, to relate this incident to her spouse, whom Edma was surprised to find still sunk deep in his club chair with half-shut eyes, apparently lost in a dream.

'Well, *mon vieux*,' she called out. 'You are about to hear an amazing story.'

Although Armand opened his eyes at the sound of her voice, it was only through a superhuman effort. Edma had sat down next to him, but her voice reached him as if from some great distance, and he could scarcely hear her.

'I just told Maestro Hans-Helmut Kreuze, director of the Konzertgebaum of Berlin, that he was a clod!' she said in a tone of exaggerated though penetrating calm, a tone which caused a momentary quivering deep within the memory of Armand Bautet-Lebreche. For an instant he was the young man he had been thirty years before, in morning coat, standing before the altar of Saint-Honoré-d'Eylau. But the young man quickly vanished, leaving him prey to his current debility.

It sometimes happens that a large ship, at a certain speed and on a certain kind of sea, achieves a gentle roll, a regular rocking motion whose effect on the human being can be irresistibly soporific. Addressed by his wife, the uneasy Monsieur Bautet-Lebreche at first tried to assume the cunning look of a psychologising husband, to observe her through half-closed eyes, smiling vaguely all the while. But to raise his eyelids the slightest degree demanded an effort as great as it took to raise the metal doors of certain garages.

Hard-pressed, Armand then attempted to extricate from the still conscious tatters of his tormented mind some comparison, some image that would force Edma to understand and allow for his unexpected drowsiness. For she was not a woman to let anyone fall asleep at her table, not even her husband. But how could he explain to her? . . . It was as though he were being rocked to sleep by a nurse . . . a muscular nurse, true, but so, so soft . . . a nurse who had just soaked her bodice with chloroform . . . There, that was it exactly . .. But why chloroform? Why would a nurse put on chloroform? . . . No, rather, it was as if someone had hit him on the head with a mallet, just five minutes ago. . . But given the cost of a berth aboard the *Narcissus*, surely no one would brain the passengers with a mallet . . . Unless the captain . . . that boor . . . used . . . chloroform . . . He slumped towards Edma's shoulder, still vaguely aware of the perfume she was wearing.

Thank God, someone answered all the same, in his own voice—grown suddenly gentle and distant, but still his own, the voice of Armand Bautet-Lebreche sedately declaring, 'You did well, my love.' Then he passed out completely against the shoulder of his wife—who with a yelp of surprise and alarm got up, leaving the Sugar Baron with his face in his saucer. The waiters came running to hold him up, but from the deep snoring that issued from the club chair, Edma now understood the nature of her husband's ailment.

A fine start to the trip, she mused, battle-weary, as she settled down to a second gin fizz. An absurd dialogue with an obscene megalomaniac, her own husband snoring at her own table—it all augured a cruise quite unlike the others. And suddenly Edma asked herself whether that wasn't better by far.

The last arrival at dinner that evening was Andreas Fayard. He had fallen back into a daytime nap, awoke with a start from a familiar nightmare. He had gone to sleep in his jeans. Now he undressed and showered quickly. But before getting dressed again, he confronted himself in front of the large bathroom mirror and gave his face and body the cool appraisal of a horse trader. He would have to watch his waistline, take some calcium, have that incisor straightened, and give his always fragile, blond hair a light shampoo. All this if some grateful woman was ever to buy him a Rolls-Royce in return for his amorous attentions, for his gentleness and his passion. And it would have to happen quickly, Andreas told himself, sitting on his bunk on the *Narcissus*— for undertaking this solitary cruise had exhausted the meagre inheritance his two aunts, the librarians in Nevers who had brought him up, had painfully assembled before dying, just two months apart, a year ago. Yes, he would quickly attend to that incisor, to the blond hair, and to everything else. All the same, Andreas found himself close to tears at the realisation that never again would anyone remind him to wash behind his ears, not for years to come, perhaps never again for the rest of his life.

*W*hile those in first class were
having a sumptuous dinner at small tables presided over by
the vessel's lesser officers, the thirty-odd passengers on the
de luxe deck were being divided—temporarily, or supposedly so—between two tables, the captain's and Charley's.
The latter, by far the livelier, was largely occupied by habitués of the *Narcissus*—though this year some were overawed by the presence on the captain's right of la Doria.
Quite a few, in fact—the exception being Edma, who had
that sense of fidelity to the pack found only in certain wolves
and jackals, animals savage enough to finish off the laggards
and chase off the weakest. In similar fashion did the hordes
of the worldly return to the same lairs and take off on the
same yearly migrations, though their members seemed
always on the verge of mortal discord; twenty years later
however they proved either thick-skinned or placid enough
to remain friends forever, forever stripped and depleted,
without real gaiety, kindness, or the slightest confidence in
the human species.

Edma sat next to Charley, followed by several habitués who were reduced by her elegance and shrill voice to a state of thraldom. It was Edma, for example, who would invariably give the signal to begin applauding after a concert, who pronounced the eggs fresh or the weather fine, who decided if someone merited attention.

But the star this year was obviously la Doriacci, already seated on the captain's right when the passengers entered— la Doria, who, with her shoulders covered by a shawl, her face nearly bare of make-up, her expression one of good-natured hauteur, looked so maddeningly like a bourgeois dowager on a cruise, which of course she was not. All her admirers felt a bit disconcerted, even let down, by this first glimpse of her.

For la Doriacci, after all, was a star! A real star of the sort they don't make any more, a woman who faced the flashbulbs brandishing a cigarette-holder—never wielding anything so mundane as a frying pan—a woman famed not only for her extraordinary voice and the art with which she used it but also for her taste for scandal, for men, her scorn for gossip and her excesses, her rages, her extravagance, her manias, her charm. Since that evening already more than twenty-five years ago when at a moment's notice this unknown singer had replaced the renowned and suddenly indisposed Roncani in *La Traviata*, and had brought down the house with applause that went on for over an hour in the world's most blasé opera house. No longer was she 'unknown' to a single member of La Scala. Each and every one, from the lowliest stagehand to the top administrator, had passed through her arms, and all of them remembered it. Since then, whenever she arrived in a city, la Doriacci, like certain Mongol invaders, would ransom off its leading citizens, ridicule their wives, abduct their young, all with a natural ease and gusto that seemed to increase with age. As she herself told the journalists, her principal admirers, 'I have always loved men younger than myself, and I've been lucky: the older I get the more I find!' In short, the great Doriacci bore no resemblance whatever to the placid figure

47

with the tightly drawn chignon seated that evening beside Elledocq.

So Elledocq had at his table the diva; the sleeping 'clown-lady' and her 'well-groomed communist', as he called Clarisse and Eric Lethuillier; two couples of advanced age who were lifetime ticket-holders on the *Narcissus*; the 'dirty Kraut' Kreuze; and the 'picture-pricer' Julien Peyrat. The captain had ordered Charley to take Béjard and Olga at his table, along with several octogenarian music-lovers. 'No travelling circus. Won't have it!' he had declared ill-humouredly. Then his anger had erupted at Charley's outraged protests, and with one of his laconically incendiary messages—'REMOVE THEM STOP YOU HAVE TWO MINUTES STOP MESSAGE OVER STOP ROGER'—he got his way. The winds of his fury may have driven off the travelling circus, but they brought in return the 'young gigolo' from Nevers, even depositing him to the right of la Doria, who in turn was to the right of the captain. Elledocq, taken by surprise, had not been able to react, though he had the consolation of observing Charley's baleful looks in his direction.

At the start of the meal Elledocq, discharging his painful duty, launched into elliptical rumblings, tossed out equably to either la Doria or the 'clown'. Inattentive at first, la Doria in the end listened thoughtfully, her brow furrowed, following his lips with her eyes. Until the salad course all went well; but as the captain mired himself ever deeper in the gloomy future of the French Merchant Marine and the morality of those at the helm, la Doriacci abruptly put down her knife and fork—so abruptly that those at the other table, who up until that moment had been quite animated, turned as one in their direction.

'But really,' she asked in a grave voice, 'in the first place, where do you want me to stash my jewellery? And in the second place, why should I? Is this some sort of den of thieves?'

Elledocq, taken by surprise, blushed beneath his tan and sat there without answering, his eyes fixed on a corner of the tablecloth, his ears ringing, while the others at his table looked at him mockingly.

'This could be as amusing as a detective movie,' la Doria went on in her throaty voice. 'We could each search the other and we'd all be killed, one after another. I'd have to sing Verdi's *Requiem* at every port of call . . .'

Relieved, the crowd burst into laughter except for Elledocq, who was a bit slow at catching on. The 'sad clown', Julien thought distractedly, had pretty teeth.

'Because you, of course, would not die?' Eric Lethuillier inquired with a faint smile.

But he hadn't been laughing a moment before, Julien observed to himself. He had let himself go so far as to smile a bit more openly than usual, as if to show he was willing to amuse himself with the others, but that he was aware of the futility of such form of amusement . . . At any rate he was suggesting, or trying to, that this recess was only temporary and that the class would soon be getting down to business again. At least that was the impression he gave Julien Peyrat. For Lethuillier, class was never over, and no doubt he gave the same impression to his wife, that poor creature disfigured this evening by glittery green eye shadow put on askew; for she abruptly stopped laughing, as if caught at fault, and casting her eyes down applied herself to her lobster once more. Beside her, Julien admired the beauty of her hands. They were long, with an odd swelling at the tips of the fingers, such as sculptors have, like the paws of a cat. From his position at the side, the hands were practically all he could see of her. He didn't dare look at her directly for fear of alarming her. Besides, what more could he have seen under the thick rosy coating of make-up, undoubtedly laid on with a trowel early every morning? She was really ridiculous, and this vexed Julien almost as though it were a personal insult, or an insult against all womankind. He would have preferred the obscene to the ridiculous. Scandal at least didn't kill desire . . . He had the best seat, Julien concluded, since without looking her in the face, he could watch her hands, hear her breathing, smell her warmth, her perfume, first the Dior and beneath it the smell of her body, the perfume of her skin, which despite her Indian warpaint was the perfume of a woman's flesh. He began to delight in her movements as she picked up bread and tore it, as she lifted a glass to her lips—but Julien saw no more than that. The movements of her hands were nonchalant and assured, hands that could be expert, that conveyed authority but were tender and consoling as well. The wedding ring that adorned her hand—the only ring she wore—seemed too brilliant, too heavy, looked out of keeping. She had laid her left hand flat on the tablecloth; then, restless, it moved towards a loose thread and furtively pulled at it, drawing out others in the process, and a lengthy unravelling ensued, the work of nails painted a pink that was almost violet—an atrocious colour. Wearying of this vandalism, which had begun to be obvious, the right hand had moved a salt cellar to conceal the depredations as if the right hand were in the habit of repairing the damage wrought by the left. Its activities checked, that hand now lay with palm open, taking on the appearance of a dog in the sun, turned over on its back to present its throat to the warmth and possibly the fangs of a mortal enemy. As the hand repeatedly flattened, closed up, and opened again, Julien had tried vainly to read something in the lifelines intertwined with the lines of the heart. As he leaned to give her a light, and her shimmering tawny hair momentarily entered his field of vision, bringing with it a cloud of perfume, Julien discovered with surprise that he desired her.

This had taken place during dessert, and from then on he waited impatiently for everyone to get up, so that he could laugh at himself, once and for all, by looking directly into the face he knew to be grotesque.

It was then that another incident occurred—Charley noted that it was the second on the trip.

'You're not going to sit there and tell me, Captain Braddock . . . excuse me, Elledocq,' la Doria was saying, 'that this Desdemona is not a dunce. It's possible to convince a man of one's innocence even if one is guilty. So anyone who isn't . . .'

'Guiltless females are few in number, but many are the females capable of anything . . .' That was Kreuze—who up until then, to no one's particular regret, had been mute as he solemnly gorged himself. 'There are females who can make a man believe that black is white.'

'Well, that's not too terrible, is it?' asked Julien, smiling and ready for amusement despite the length of the meal. Whatever the circumstances, he could not but nurture this perpetual mad hope that there would be fun. And yes, even with this boatload of octogenarians, of snobs and would-be aesthetes, he, Julien Peyrat, who had passed his fortieth birthday, still looked forward to having fun. At times he was desperately annoyed with himself for not being more pessimistic, more clear-headed about human nature . . .

'*Ja!*'

Hans-Helmut Kreuze's peremptory voice exploded like a shot across the dining saloon's varnished mahogany. The waiter, who at that moment was offering Julien a second helping of sherbet, began to tremble so convulsively that the spoon struck against the bowl with the rattle of castanets, and for an instant distracted general attention from Kreuze to the sherbet. Obligingly, Julien served himself and kept the spoon.

'*Ja*, there are females who behave like animals! Except that animals are not ungrateful.'

At both tables there was a slight flurry of surprise and amusement—which the ordinarily inflammatory Edma now unexpectedly sought to dissipate.

'Suppose we strike camp, Captain,' she called out from her table. 'It's a bit warm in here don't you find?'

Perhaps her injunction would have been followed, had the ill-mannered Simon Béjard not registered his curiosity.

'And whom do you have in mind, Maestro?' He pronounced the word 'Maestro' in a tragicomic tone, as if to underline the comic-opera element it suggested—to the musician's evident dismay.

'I was speaking of ungrateful females generally,' Hans-Helmut Kreuze asserted loudly, so as to be heard from where he sat. 'I was just throwing it in the air like that, but if you want to see how it falls . . .'

The others exchanged glances and raised eyebrows, while Hans-Helmut, looking both resigned and victorious, wiped

51

the moustache that he had removed two years ago, and placed his napkin on the table with a conclusive gesture. La Doria opened fire. 'Oh my God!' she said, and she burst into laughter as though suddenly struck by the obvious. 'My God, and there I was, trying to imagine . . . Would you believe it,' she said spiritedly. 'I do believe I now know who it is the maestro has in mind . . . Or am I mistaken, Maestro?. . .'

His face expressed misgivings and fury in rapid succession. Behind her lashes Edma's eyes twinkled with excitement and delight—to the alarm of Armand Bautet-Lebreche, who had suddenly emerged from his prolonged siesta.

'No, I am not mistaken,' the diva continued. 'Would you believe that we met, the famed Maestro Hans-Helmut Kreuze and I, in Vienna . . . or possibly in Berlin . . . or Stuttgart, I forget which, it was . . . during the fifties or sixties . . . No, not the sixties! By then I was famous and I could choose. I speak of a period when I could not choose and when the illustrious Kreuze deigned to notice la Loupa—which was the name they gave me. I looked at the time like a young she-wolf and that is exactly what I was. Alas, such a long time ago . . . I was playing the third soubrette in *Cavalleria*. I only sang with the others. I had no solo part, but I did have nice legs, which I tried to show off in the wings and on stage, just in case . . . We were very, very badly paid in Vienna. Maestro Kreuze, who was already as famous as he is now, deigned to notice my legs and to desire to see more. The perfect gentleman, he made this known to me through his secretary, and to seal the conquest he bought me a sauerkraut and sherbet at the Sacher. That is what it was, a sauerkraut and sherbet, was it not, Hans-Helmut?'

'I . . . I don't know.' The virtuoso had turned scarlet. No one dared budge, or look at him or at la Doriacci—no one, that is, except Clarisse, whom she now addressed.

'Well, anyway!' la Doriacci went on, more gaily than ever. 'It was all rather dull, but the honour I was being paid took care of that . . . Do not suppose I had forgotten, dear

52

Maestro,' la Doriacci said through an appalled silence, leaning forward across the table (and, as Julien noticed, suddenly ablaze with beauty and youth), 'I had not forgotten. But I was afraid it might embarrass you, or that Gertrude . . . as Madame Kreuze is called, I believe? . . . that Gertrude might hear about it. I was also afraid that thirty years later you might be ashamed of having lowered yourself to sleeping with a soubrette, Herr Direktor von Konzertgebaum Berlin.'

Elledocq had followed all this with eyes absolutely popping out of his head. Since he could make nothing of the situation and to be on the safe side, he retreated into a towering silence. With impassive face, wearing his dress uniform as if it were a toga, he felt head and shoulders above this business of sex. At any rate, he seemed to have no intention at all of getting up from the table—which was really the only thing to do, thought Charley, desperately trying to catch his eye. But in vain.

So, for the first time in all their life at sea together, it was Charley who suddenly pushed back his chair and got up, precipitately followed by the others.

'What a delicious dinner,' twittered Edma. 'Is there a new chef? Armand, don't you agree? . . . Armand!' she shrieked at her spouse, who, the storm scarcely over, had relapsed once more into his sickly lethargy.

'Well, I must say that when it comes to shipboard food, I never had better,' commented Simon. 'Don't you agree, my angel?'

As he tried to put an arm around her waist, Olga ducked. Eric Lethuillier walked around the table and took Clarisse by the elbow—as if to prevent her from falling, but quite unnecessarily, thought Julien, who had seen her drink only two glasses of wine. But she made no protest, and this annoyed him; though her outrageous make-up was again visible, he remembered the pang he had felt, and he still had for her a sort of retrospective, surprised admiration. And a beautiful body, too, he mused as she moved off into the giddy commotion that always follows public outbursts.

La Doriacci slowly rose from her place opposite Kreuze,

who still sat there with his eyes on the tablecloth. She looked at him while she gathered up her lipstick, cigarettes, lighter, pillbox, compact—all the paraphernalia which she unpacked and laid out around her, like a gypsy, at every meal.

'Well,' she said in a low voice. 'Well then, my great big wicked Helmut, are you happy now?'

Her voice was inaudible to all except him. Even so, he did not reply, but sat with his eyes lowered, and she went off with a smile, snapping her fingers to a rumba rhythm.

'Hellish woman, eh?' observed the captain, who had returned to the doorway and stood waiting for Kreuze. 'Hellish female, as you would say, Maestro.'

Since the maestro still did not answer, the captain, with his rolling gait, returned to his guests.

'No fun, that Kraut, no sense of humour,' he knowingly confided to Charley Bollinger.

'If we're lucky, this cruise is really going to be something,' Simon Béjard was saying to the Lethuilliers. 'The opening's been pretty good . . . As far as the music goes, their so-called "floating concert" will make something of a noise. Maybe even a few false notes . . .'

He always makes stupid jokes and then laughs until he cries, and he's so pleased with himself, thought Olga looking at him with hatred. What wild notion could have induced her to bring him among these chic, elegant people? How could she have exposed herself to the incessant rebuffs provoked by this vulgar, stupid, joke-cracking boor? And in front of that aristocrat of the intellect, that revolutionary who could have been a marquis, the impeccable Eric Lethuillier, who was loaded with class right down to his fingertips . . . She was crazy about him, with his beautiful Viking profile . . . No, not Viking, that was too much of a cliché. She would tell them it was the profile of . . . an Aryan. That was it!

She was rehearsing a performance for her most appreciative fans, two classmates whose admiration she had carefully cultivated since she was fifteen. For their benefit Olga Lamouroux, wherever she went, mentally recounted the spellbinding details of her daily existence. She could hear herself already, and closed her eyes a second to blot out the too distracting, the (already!) too absorbing presence of Eric Lethuillier. *You know me, Fernande . . . You know how under my bold exterior I'm sometimes just a quivering mass? . . . Well, when I find, when I feel that I'm on the same wavelength as a fellow who cares about the same things I do, I come to life again. Well, I came to life there in that huge room, sumptuous in its austerity, its maritime décor, its masculine good taste. So then, when I suddenly heard Simon holding forth . . .* (no: *Simon trotting out his inanities*), *in the presence of that Aryan with a Viking profile . . . No, of that gorgeous man with the Aryan profile . . . When I saw him just barely . . . almost imperceptibly frown, and then turn away so that I shouldn't detect his instinctive disgust . . . When I saw him, a little later, turn his tourmaline eyes back to me . . .* (she would have to look up 'tourmaline'); *when I saw him turn his blue-green eyes back to me* (no . . . *sea-blue . . .*). *Well, at that point, Micheline! . . .* (no, I was telling this to Fernande), *well, at that point, Fernande! should I admit it? I was ashamed . . . Ashamed of my companion! And that's a terrible thing for a woman . . . But you know that, you're so perceptive about that sort of thing . . .* (the compliment always cropped up, quite unconsciously in these accounts; it kept attention from flagging, though in this case it was hardly necessary, since poor Fernande was in Tarbes with her mother-in-law and the kids). *Good, so now you know . . . I was ashamed of that man. You know I always wanted to keep Simon at arm's length, pretending not to notice the enormous gulf that separates us, the . . . etc., etc.* Her internal monologue trailed off, since the Aryan had begun to speak. *And his voice, a voice like bronze, its warm timbre . . .* (later she would check out that word) *simply reverberated . . .*

'Personally,' Eric Lethuillier was saying, 'I must admit that I hate that kind of scene. There's always an element of exhibitionism in these outbursts that puts me off . . . No? You don't agree? Don't you think so, Clarisse?'

'I found it rather entertaining,' said Clarisse. 'In fact, very entertaining.' And she smiled off into the distance—which humanised her mask for an instant and left Eric visibly annoyed.

'Unfortunately, Clarisse reads nothing but the gossip columns. The private lives of other people have always entertained her . . . sometimes even more than her own, I fear,' Eric added as an aside, but still audibly.

Although Clarisse did not flinch, Simon appeared shocked.

'Well, as for exhibitionism, you know,' he said, 'you too . . .'

'Know what?'

Eric Lethuillier's voice had an edge. Suddenly he appeared to be in a cold rage, and Simon Béjard stepped back. He wasn't going to grapple with this big cantankerous Protestant merely because he'd been odious to his wife . . . That, after all, was no business of his. And with Olga already beginning to make eyes at him! So he said nothing. The trip already promised to be more comical than he had dared hope. The wife of the sugar magnate was coming towards them at full tilt, her eyes popping out even more than usual. *There's* one who probably isn't too unhappy about all the histrionics, Simon thought.

'Ah, my dears!' she said, openly offering relief in the form of a tumbler of whisky to Clarisse Lethuillier, who accepted it with a firm hand under Eric's icy stare. 'Such a meal! My dears, what a session that was! . . . I didn't know where to turn . . . Well, la Doriacci really put that boor in his place! I find our diva absolutely splendid . . . What a performance! She was completely mesmerising. I couldn't take my eyes off her, I must admit. I was totally entranced. Weren't you?'

'Not precisely.' Eric took a tone of raillery.

She broke in, 'Well, that doesn't surprise me. What would it take to make you sit up and take notice, Monsieur Lethuillier? A Trotsky or a Stalin, I imagine? At very least! . . . But how about you, Monsieur Béjard? And you, Mademoiselle . . . uh . . . Lamoureux? And you, dear Clarisse? Don't tell me that you were bored!'

'R-o-u-x, roux. Lamou*roux*,' Olga corrected her with a

frigid smile. This was the third time that Edma had muti-
lated her name.

'But that's just what I said, wasn't it—Lamouroux?' Edma
went on smiling. 'At any rate, I do apologise. Olga Lamouroux, for heaven's sake . . . How could I have made
such a mistake? When I saw you in . . . Oh, what was that
charming film, set in Paris, in the Latin Quarter . . . near
there anyway, with that somewhat intellectual actor, but so
marvellous . . . Georges something or other . . . Come on,
you help me,' she said to Simon—who, stunned by her
temerity, gaped at her open-mouthed, and then, coming to,
hastened to respond:

'You must mean *The White Man's Black Night*, a film
by Maxime Duqueret. A truly, truly beautiful film, very
interesting . . . A bit strange, a bit sad, but very interesting
. . . yes, yes, yes,' he reiterated, as though to convince
himself—and with an anxious look towards Olga, who
seemed to be lost, somewhere else. 'I'm pretty sure, yes . . .
that's it . . . yes.'

'Ah, yes!' Edma agreed. '*The Black Man's* something or
other. It was very, very good. That's when I knew that
Mademoiselle Lamoureux, Olga, would make her mark.'

'Olga Lamou*roux*, Lamou*roux*, my dear Madame.' Now
it was Eric who took up the relay, and Edma gave him a
querying glance that was altogether insulting.

'How good of you to help me out. Let me see if I've got
it now: Lamouroux, Lamouroux, Lamouroux, Lamouroux.
I'll practise, I promise you,' she said gravely to Olga, who
was now biting her lip. 'I hope I won't be like our diva,
with her "Braddock", "Ducrock", "Capock", as she never
ceases calling our poor suffering captain . . . Where is Charley? He is so diplomatic, he must be in a state! At any rate
one thing is certain: the seating arrangements will have to
be changed by morning! They should have separated the
couples—one should always separate couples—musical and
otherwise.'

'You would agree to being separated from Monsieur
Bautet-Lebreche?' hissed Olga, not looking at her.

'Oh, but I already have been.' Edma seemed delighted.

'I already have been—though never for very long. With his fortune, my dear Armand makes an ideal catch for a designing woman, as I know all too well.'

There was a moment's silence as she capered off towards another group, perhaps another victim.

'That bitch!' said Olga Lamouroux who had gone completely white.

'Poor woman, she's a true reflection of her environment,' said Eric in a weary tone.

But he put a hand on Olga's shoulder as a sign that he understood, and she fluttered her eyelids a few times under the stress of emotion. Simon kept his peace, but when he happened to catch the look in the clown-woman's eye, he was stupefied to see that this zombie was fairly ready to explode with laughter.

Julien Peyrat leaned against the bar along with Andreas, and the two of them roared with laughter as they went over the showdown at dinner. They looked like two college boys sharing a rather tasteless private joke, and knowing this added to their hilarity. Charley watched them with a look that was reproachful but jealous.

'But did you see how beautiful she looked just then?' said Andreas, serious once more. 'Did you see those eyes! And that voice! . . . God, what a woman! For just an instant she could have been twenty—did you see that?'

'Now hold on a minute! Looks like you could be falling in love, my friend . . .' Julien spoke without malice. 'Could it be you have designs on our national—I mean international—celebrity? You know that it's not impossible that she might succumb, don't you, at least if you can believe the rumour.'

'What do you mean?'

Andreas was no longer joking in the least, and Julien looked at him with surprise. He could not quite figure out this boy. At first, because of Charley, he had taken him for a homosexual, but obviously he was not that. He had taken him for a gigolo, but that did not seem quite it either. On the other hand, Julien shrank from the classic question,

58

'What do you do?' It was a question that had made him suffer all his life until he discovered the vague and splendid profession of 'art appraiser'.

'I only meant,' he went on, 'that Doriacci's love life is famous for being tempestuous. I must have seen thousands of photographs of her with fellows a lot less attractive than you. That's all, old man . . .'

'People will say anything about celebrities,' Andreas declared hotly. 'I happen to believe that she is a woman who lives life to the full. I do not believe, Monsieur Peyrat, that la Doriacci is easy prey.'

'That too is notorious,' said Julien gaily, dropping all caution. 'She is also noted for being very, very difficult to live with. Just ask our friend Kreuze for his view on the subject. That sauerkraut is going to weigh heavily on this cruise . . .'

'Ah! the Sacher sauerkraut,' said Andreas, and once more they were off into gales of laughter.

But Julien was puzzled, all the same.

*T*he ship was slowing down, and already the lights of Portofino were more distinct. It was the first scheduled stop, and Hans-Helmut Kreuze was to open fire with a programme of Debussy. Three white-clad sailors arrived to push the big Steinway, which until now had been stored in the bar under three covers and a tablecloth, out onto the deck. They spent some time undressing it and attaching chains to the legs to make it fast. The gleam of dark wood in the dim light hinted at its shape, but a respectful hush still lay over the crowd after the sailors had gone off with the covers and someone tried the lights. These consisted of four very white overhead spotlights which lividly defined a square performance area, a sort of theatre-in-the-round at whose centre the instrument, with its chains, took on the proportions of an allegorical image. Squat as a bull and gleaming like a shark, the animal clearly awaited its tamer—its torero, its musician, its murderer—and awaited him with hatred. The glittering white teeth seemed ready to snap at a man's hand, ready to draw him shrieking into the depths of its empty body where his cries would echo on and on, before fading away.

Under the lights there was something tragic about the piano, something brutal that was at odds with its Mediterranean surroundings. The sea exuded an overwhelming, sensuous romanticism, at once pitiless but flawlessly gentle. It clasped the hips of the *Narcissus*, at once caressing and violating her, and the soft, incessant pressure of the warm waves was insistent enough to sway her the breadth of a millimetre, enough to make her twenty thousand tons whimper with pleasure. The ship grated at the anchor only just dropped but already hooked onto the ocean floor, and she detested this iron fetter which prevented her from moving about, from abandoning herself in the dark to that voluptuous expanse, so cool-seeming where it foamed at the shoreline, but impenetrable and fathomless farther out, here where the *Narcissus*, immobilised at the end of its tether, had given up all hope of escaping.

*T*he first-class passengers had come up to the de luxe deck. The first thing they did, as always on finding the same privileged people on the same deck, was to launch into an explanation, once again, of how they had left it too late to change their bookings as they would have preferred. This was actually the only humiliating moment for these happy music-lovers, who would have all the rest of the year to make much of their cruise. Julien, approached by a voluble couple who thought they recognised him, fled. Climbing over cables, he hurried up the aisle between the seats and armchairs around the piano and escaped the illuminated area. Only the way back to the cabins was lit; Julien took another route and collided with the door of the bar; there were no lights on in the bar, but the door was open. It was a few seconds before he made out the glow of a cigarette in the darkness, where Clarisse Lethuillier sat alone at the far end of the room.

'Excuse me,' he said, moving a step forward in the gloom. 'I didn't see you. I was looking for a place to hide, to get away from all the traffic. It's a madhouse out there. The concert's about to begin. Would you rather be alone?'

He spoke disconnectedly and felt strangely intimidated. In the darkness Clarisse Lethuillier ceased to be a clown and became a woman, prey of the hunter.

Finally she spoke. 'Sit down wherever you like. The bar's out of bounds in any case.'

Perhaps because of the darkness her voice was unguarded, neither naive, nor precise, nor weary, nor young, nor feminine, nor anything else. It was a voice without pretension, quite unselfconscious, a voice naked as an electric wire— and perhaps just as dangerous were one to approach her.

Julien groped his way to a chair. 'You're not going to the concert?'

'Yes, but later.'

For no good reason, they were whispering. In fact, this bar was another world, where everything was frightening and pleasant all at once: the massed shapes of the armchairs, the outline of the tables, and out there in the distance the agitated spotlit crowd which was getting ready far too early to applaud Kreuze's appearance on stage.

'You like Debussy?'

'Yes, suppose so.' It was the same voice, this time frightened, and Julien guessed the fear was that they would be discovered alone, in this place that was 'out of bounds', as she had put it. But for all his habitually accommodating nature, he had no desire to leave. On the contrary, he would have liked Eric Lethuillier to arrive, discover them there doing nothing, and behave just odiously enough—anything at all would give him an excuse—so that he, Julien, could punch him in the jaw. He hated his sort, and to his surprise Julien suddenly realised that he could not put up with him, that he would not be able to spend a week in Eric's company aboard this ship without tangling with him one way or another, without at least one good chance to punch that arrogantly self-assured face. The urge to strike was so acute that all of a sudden he was trembling with thirst.

'Isn't there a single bottle in this place?' he burst out. 'I'm dying of thirst, aren't you?'

63

'No,' Clarisse said, in a dejected voice. 'It's all locked up. You can bet I've already tried.' That 'You can bet' meant . . . 'They must have told you? You can bet on me, Clarisse, the alcoholic! Sure, I tried to find something to drink, for heaven's sake . . .'

But Julien didn't pay any attention. 'That'll be the day when a lock can get the better of me,' he said, stumbling through the furniture.

He went behind the counter where it was pitch black.

'Do you have a lighter?' he asked, and instantly she was on the nearest bar stool, lighter in hand. The locks were childishly simple, and Julien quickly mastered them with his boy-scout knife. He opened a cupboard at random and turned back to face Clarisse. In the glow of the lighter her greasepaint made her look like something out of the Grand Guignol. He felt for a second like asking her to take off the mask, but caught himself in time.

'What would you like? There's just about everything, I think. Port, whisky, gin? I'm going to have some whisky.'

'So will I,' she said. The assurance had returned to her voice, perhaps, Julien thought gaily, in anticipation of the unexpected whisky. Unquestionably he was the evil genius of this ship. He was going to ruin a music-lover at cards, defraud an art collector, and inebriate an alcoholic.

As usual, Julien reacted gleefully to finding himself fall into this role. Something in him was so thoroughly accommodating that all the cynical roles he ended up playing never seemed real to him. They were part of a vast fiction, a series of short stories by some Anglo-Saxon humorist entitled *The Life and Adventures of Julien Peyrat*. He half-filled two glasses, held one out to Clarisse, who had gone back to her table, and deliberately sat down beside her. They clinked glasses and solemnly drank. The liquor was strong and burned his throat. Coughing a bit, he noticed that Clarisse hadn't turned a hair. The sudden warmth and ease that immediately coursed through him left no doubt that his burglary had been worth while.

'That's better, isn't it?' he said. 'I was tense and uncomfortable. Now I feel revived—how about you?'

'Oh yes!' she breathed. 'I really feel revived . . . or rather, I simply feel alive.'

'It doesn't happen for you without help?'

'Never,' she said. 'Not any more. Did you keep the bottle?'

'Of course,' he said, and leaning across, poured her another drink. He saw her white hand as it lifted the glass towards her face, and he recalled the effect that hand had had on him during dinner, and was annoyed with himself. The situation seemed just a bit too promising. He poured another drink for himself. At this rate they would both be dead drunk before the start of the concert. He imagined himself turning up with Clarisse on his arm, both of them stumbling in during one of Kreuze's arpeggios, and began to laugh.

'Why are you laughing?'

'I was just thinking about the two of us showing up dead drunk in the middle of the concert,' he said. 'It doesn't take much to make me laugh. That's not true of your husband, is it? I get the impression he doesn't laugh easily.'

'For Eric, life is a serious matter,' she said flatly, as she would have stated a fact. 'And I can quite see how a person might want to take life seriously, given you have enough strength to take it one way or another . . . Right now, I have it. I'm breathing again. I can feel my heart beating. I feel I'm alive inside my body, things are becoming real . . . I'm even aware of the smell of the sea, or the way this glass feels cold between my fingers. Can you understand that?'

'Of course,' said Julien.

Above all, he thought, she shouldn't be interrupted. She had to talk, whether it be to him or someone else. He felt great pity for this woman, almost as great as the hatred he felt for her husband. But what was he doing involving himself with these Lethuilliers?

'All day long I had the feeling I was wandering in a desert full of obstacles that at the last moment I could not see. I felt as though nothing I said was right, that everybody noticed, that I was ridiculous. I felt as though I could only think in platitudes. I felt that any minute I would drop my fork, that I would fall off my chair, that once more I was going to shame Eric, to embarrass other people or make them laugh . . . I felt that I was going to die of asphyxiation in that cabin. I felt that this ship was either too big or too small, but that anyhow I had no business being here . . . I felt that these nine days would never come to an end and yet that this was my last chance. But my last chance for what? . . . I was caught up in such disorder, in confusion, in boredom . . . and the self-doubt was such a torture . . . a torture . . .' Her voice rose. 'I've spent hours and hours feeling tortured. And now, thanks to this,' she tapped her nail against the glass. 'I am at peace with Clarisse Lethuillier, *née* Dureau, thirty-two, pale and wan of visage. Clarisse Lethuillier, alcoholic. And not even ashamed of it!'

'Well, you're not strictly speaking an alcoholic. And as for the pale face, I'll have to take you at your word . . . your pallor is so painted . . . Madame Lethuillier! But at any rate, Clarisse Lethuillier, a lonely woman . . . that much I believe.'

'The poor little rich girl . . . it has the ring of a cheap romance, doesn't it, Monsieur Peyrat? In any case, I can't thank you enough for picking that lock . . . and if I could count on you also to hide a few bottles in your cabin, and if you'd be good enough to tell me the number, I'd be eternally grateful. You're not the sort who locks his door, I imagine?'

The voice was now hurried but clear, crisp, almost arrogant. Still the voice of Mademoiselle Dureau, no doubt. He prefered her unfriendly to unhappy.

'Why of course,' said Julien, 'I'll lay in a supply first thing tomorrow. And I'm in cabin 109.'

A silence ensued and then she asked in the other voice, the one that had preceded the whisky, 'You won't regret it? Or . . . would you want me to repay you?'

'I never have regrets,' said Julien. 'And I never ask a woman to pay me for anything.' And there he was telling the truth.

He sensed rather than actually saw Clarisse hold out her

glass, and he refilled it for her without comment. She emptied it, got up and went out, walking with a firm step it seemed to him, in the direction of the lights. He waited for a moment, then finished his drink and followed her.

Clarisse barely had time to sit down beside Eric and hear him run through his customary exaggerated courtesies, when Hans-Helmut Kreuze arrived in a storm of applause. His evening clothes made him look all the more Prussian. The stiff collar seemed to scrape against his neck when he bowed. But from the moment he sat down and began to play, the musician completely took over his personality. He played Debussy with the light touch, the tact, the gentleness that he himself lacked. He made it flow like liquid, like rain falling on the deck, and Clarisse sat with open eyes, feeling once again, as she drank in that cool water, young, inviolate, invulnerable, totally cleansed. She was in the woods, in the meadows of her childhood, knowing nothing of love, of money, of men. She was eight years old, she was twelve, and then again she was sixty and everything had the same limpid perfection. The meaning of life was there in that inviolable innocence of the human being, in the accepted but fleeting course of life, in the merciful inevitability of death, in something else which for her was not God, but about which at this precise moment she felt just as certain as those who apparently believed in the existence of God. It did not even surprise her that Kreuze should play this way, in complete contrast with his personality and his appearance. What did surprise her, when it ended, was that the blond stranger at her side should nudge her elbow and tell her to applaud. Eric was nodding gravely and with a certain sadness, as he did whenever he found himself in the presence of undeniable talent.

'You cannot deny that he has genius,' he said, as if his first impulse had been to deny that same genius, and as if the impossibility of doing so were painful. But suddenly she didn't give a damn about Eric. It even seemed an enormous futility, the great stupidity of having loved him so long and suffered so much through him. Of course someone whispering inside her was telling her that this liberation, this ceasing to care, would be drained away from her spirit along with the alcohol in her bloodstream; but someone was also telling her that the truth was right there in that perception, however deceptive, falsified and perverted by alcohol it supposedly was. This voice which told her she was right when she was happy and wrong when she was not, this same voice had been the only one since childhood, of the countless throng within her, whose advice had never changed. She had applauded a bit longer than the others, people were looking at her and Eric's face was flushed, but that made no difference to her at all. On the far side of the piano stood Julien Peyrat, her accomplice. He smiled at her and she returned his smile openly. Her saviour was also a handsome man, she noted with some amusement and a sort of satisfied anticipation of a kind she had not felt for years—for centuries, it seemed. Few men, it was true, measured up to Eric Lethuillier.

Simon Béjard, who had taken his seat in his new dinner jacket with the same sense of peril and boredom, found he had tears in his eyes—all because of this fat lump of a Kreuze whom he found unbearable, and because of Debussy, whom he had always considered impossibly boring. In fact, this was the first time that he had felt

69

genuine pleasure, the first time in years. Years during which whenever he saw a film it had been to discover new actors, to see what kind of job someone else had done on it, just as he had read novels only in search of scenarios—aside from those whose success, whose crazy popularity did away with the fatal requirement to be thrilling. But in those cases, Simon couldn't acquire the rights anyhow.

He had seen his first movie on the occasion of his sixth birthday. And throughout the forty years since then all landscapes had been no more than scenery, all human beings characters, all music no more than background.

'That was terrific, wasn't it?' he exclaimed enthusiastically. 'Well done, Helmut! Did the same things to me as Chopin.'

At the age of fourteen he had cried over the strains of the 'Polonaise' which featured in a colossal technicolour flop made in America. A tanned, curly-haired, cowboy Chopin began spitting blood over the white keyboard while George Sand wandered about, slim as one of her cigarette holders, through scenery worthy of the Borgias and the Folies-Bergères combined. From this he had concluded that Chopin was a musician capable of moving crowds, even perhaps of providing the musical background for impending masterpieces of his own. But his musical education had gone no further.

And here with Debussy, now that he was rich, a new world was opening for Simon. He suddenly felt an immense hunger and a vast humility towards these towering peaks of Art, living monuments, these fabulous treasures he had had neither the time nor the opportunity to discover. He felt starved of literature, of painting, of music. Indeed everything seemed infinitely desirable to him, for it was only to the extent they could be realised that Simon gave way to his desires. He had to have the means to possess, that was all. And in fact, he could buy tomorrow the best Japanese stereo-system; one, possibly two or more Impressionist paintings, more or less authenticated—and why not a first edition of Fontenelle (about whom he actually knew nothing). Now that he could gratify all these whims, he was entitled to fine books, mini-cassettes, museum visits. As if to gain entrance to the unknown domains of Art there were both a service door and a grand staircase—the first acceptable only if one deliberately chose it in preference to the other. For Simon, the Pantheon and its illustrious dead had finally reached a level of prestige comparable to United Artists and its private dicks. Here, at any rate, was proof that he had grown sensitive to matters of Art, and it was with a certain pride in his tears that he turned his large, humid eyes towards Olga. But she seemed to want no part in it; on the contrary, she seemed in fact quite put out.

'Oh, Simon, don't be ridiculous,' she hissed.

Olga had cast a furtive look towards Eric Lethuillier sitting in front of them, and Simon had seen in profile his long-suffering smile.

'I said something wrong?' he asked in a rather loud voice.

Somehow he felt wounded in his sincerity, his goodwill. She was, after all, the one who only yesterday had been seeking in him the very emotion she now seemed to find ridiculous; she was the one who had then seemed to fear that he was incapable of it.

'Why no,' Olga said, 'for heaven's sake. Chopin! . . . Debussy! My poor Simon, you just can't go mixing sheep and goats.'

'So Chopin is the sheep and Debussy the goat? Or is it the other way around?' Simon demanded. After his experience of artistic emotion, he was now seized by fury—two violent, bizarre feelings he had never known until now.

'Oh really!' said Olga, startled by his sudden anger. 'That's not it at all. Let's just say it's a bit too soon to be throwing yourself into comparisons.' She hesitated, glancing towards Lethuillier, who did not turn around.

'But for three whole months,' Simon told her, 'you've been saying it's too late for me. Now suddenly it's too early! You'd better get your pianos tuned,' he said, making a joke in spite of himself, which gave Olga the chance to laugh out loud and pretend she was unaware of his anger.

'Well then,' Simon persisted, 'perhaps you'll explain?'

'Oh, come on, Simon . . .' She had gone strident with

exasperation. 'Well, let's say it just isn't exactly your sort of subject.'

'If it isn't exactly my subject, then this isn't exactly my sort of cruise either,' he said.

He glared at her, furious, while she threw desperate glances towards Lethuillier. But now it was as though the back of his neck were fastened to his shoulders and his ears were attached to either side of his skull for purely decorative purposes. As Olga grew frantic, and Simon was on the point of turning crude, it was the clown-woman who unexpectedly saved the day: she turned towards them, smiling at Simon with such evident kindness that he was instantly mollified. Suddenly this Clarisse Lethuillier was warmth and reassurance; above all, and despite the war-paint, she was genuinely friendly.

'It's odd what you were just saying, Monsieur Béjard,' she said, 'that's exactly the feeling I had! I thought, too, that Kreuze played Debussy in a way that was so . . . tender . . . so sad . . . so flowing, like Chopin. but I didn't dare say so; we're surrounded here by such connoisseurs. It's not my strong subject either.'

'Oh, come on, Clarisse, you know a great deal about music!' said Eric, turning. 'Don't always be running yourself down so—it just doesn't ring true.'

'Running myself down? But how could I run myself down, Eric? To do that I'd need to be worth something, wouldn't I, when the truth is that I still haven't proved myself, don't you agree? In music any more than in anything else.'

Her voice was so gay and insolent that Simon Béjard started to laugh along with her, all the more gaily because he saw that her handsome Eric seemed furious. His eyes fixed on Clarisse were the same cold chlorinated blue as the shipboard swimming pool.

'In my eyes, yes,' he said, 'you have proven yourself! Isn't that enough?'

'Yes, but should the opportunity arise, I would rather your ears were the judge . . .' Clarisse laughed, suddenly released from her melancholy. She needled her master, 'I would have loved to play the harpsichord for you, Eric, a little Handel, in the evenings by the fireside, while you corrected proofs for the paper.'

'A little Handel, and a fine old Armagnac, I suppose?'

'Why not? Or if you'd rather, you could sprinkle your proofs with barley water! . . .'

Simon had been forgotten in the squabble, but he was quite taken at the thought of having started it. He raised Clarisse's right fist, intoning with a heavy Marseilles accent, 'Clariss-eh Le-thui-lliair, ze winnairre, by tech-nee-cal knock-out!' He was smiling, but the look he got from Eric was glassy with hostility.

Simon dropped Clarisse's hand with a shrug, by way of excuse to her. But she smiled back without the slightest trace of alarm or embarrassment.

'How about going to the bar for a drink?' said Simon. 'After all, you two concert buffs could give us two ignoramuses some lessons.'

'I personally give lessons to no one,' said Eric, in a tone that completely belied his statement. 'What's more, I think la Doriacci is about to begin.'

Clarisse and Simon, who were already getting up, obediently sat down again. For just as Eric had said, the four spotlights went on and off, then on and off again, the signal that the programme was to begin. Olga leaned across from her seat and murmured in Eric's ear, 'Sorry . . . sorry he . . .' The supplication was slightly theatrical, as even she realised. But she had been utterly horrified. How could Simon suggest a drink to that Clarisse Lethuillier, knowing her to be an inveterate alcoholic? An inveter . . . well, notorious! How had he dared speak in that tone to that marvellous Viking, an individual with such class, who had renounced the caste system? Because after all, you didn't have to be hypersensitive to see it: Eric Lethuillier was a man who had been flayed right to the heart . . . no, flayed to the bone . . . no, no, no . . . to the very soul, that was it! No! What was really getting silly was for her to stay on. *To stay with a man I didn't respect any more. I couldn't assume responsibility for Béjard any more* (Micheline version), or *I couldn't stand Simon any longer* (Fernande version).

'What's on your mind?' the soon-to-be-excommunicated Simon asked sourly. 'You don't look very chipper. Tummy trouble?'

'No, I'm fine! Everything's fine, I assure you,' she said hastily, horrified.

How could anyone be so vulgar, so crude? Olga, about to draw a poetic, musical comparison to describe her feelings, stopped short. It's enough to make me lose my head, all this, she thought. *There you have it, I lost my head, Micheline, and* . . . But the last time she used that expression, Simon had got down on all fours and pretended to be looking for her head on the carpet, roaring with laughter, for that was the kind of thing that made him laugh. There was a certain breed of man who laughed at things of that sort, practical jokes. A lot of men were like that, in fact. On this ship, for example, she knew at least three who had come for the laughs, who subscribed to Simon Béjard's proud (but false, as she would prove) motto on the subject of love: 'I laugh or I leave.' There was Julien Peyrat, who was charming but so irresponsible, and in any case evidently not to be caught. There was puffball Charley, who'd have a laugh with the men no matter what his other habits; and so, too, would that blond gigolo Andreas.

Olga already detested Andreas for one excellent reason: his youth. She had expected to be the only person aboard under thirty, the sole representative of youthful ardour, and now this little blond pipsqueak who looked so naive and inexperienced seemed almost as young as she, maybe even younger, at least if that cretin of a Simon was to be believed . . .

'That whippersnapper,' he had said when she pointed him out, 'he's still wet behind the ears.'

Instead of reassuring her as Simon had intended, he had simply exasperated her.

'I certainly hope I don't give any such impression,' she had said.

'Not in the least, you can rest assured. You have nothing in common with that kid.'

'Nothing except for age,' she had corrected.

'It wouldn't cross anyone's mind,' Simon, that lout, that boor, had tactlessly concluded.

That evening Olga had put her hair in a pony tail.

Her brooding was cut short by the arrival of the diva. Doria Doriacci made her entrance to applause, and immediately everything—the circle described on the deck by the spotlights, the spectators, the ship itself—took on a theatrical air. For wherever she went, her wild appearance, her make-up, her rhinestones created a delightful dramatic atmosphere. La Doriacci, typically capricious, had disregarded the programme and decided to sing one of the great arias from Verdi's *Don Carlos*.

Slowly and deliberately, her long black dress shimmering, she took her place behind the microphone. Gazing over their heads towards an imaginary point in the direction of Portofino, she began to sing in a low, legato voice.

Sitting before her, Julien was at first perplexed and then disturbed by the physical proximity of that voice. Before he had quite had time to be calmed by her restraint, he suddenly gasped and tensed in his seat. From la Doriacci's imposingly black-bound bosom, quite unexpectedly, there suddenly emerged a savage and desperate cry of one at the peak of fear and rage; Julien felt chills along his spine, then the voice relaxed, extended itself on a single note, becoming hoarse, far too hoarse, with a lyrical indecency. It was the cry of a lovesick animal that now tightened the cords of that neck, modestly encircled though it was by a string of pearls, and Julien perceived beneath her regular features, beneath the discipline of her breathing, beneath the bourgeois coiffure, the blind transports of an unbridled sensuality. He felt a sudden desire for this woman, a desire that was completely physical. He turned away, and it was then that he saw Andreas. The expression on the face of that youth told him what his own expression must be, and gave him pause. From hunter, young Andreas had turned into hunted,

already fervour mingled with covetousness. Julien pitied
him.

For Andreas had forgotten his ambitious plans and, with
eyes fixed upon la Doriacci, repeated to himself over and
over the leitmotif that he must have her, have her, have her,
at any price. This woman had suddenly become romance
incarnate—the madness, the night, gold, violence and peace,
and all at once there was nothing left but Opera, its pomp
and its works and its vanity, which always before had seemed
to be lacking in truth and vitality. Listening to la Doriacci,
he told himself that one day he would wrest that cry from
her by other means, that he would make that deep voice
reach a note deeper than any yet reached. He even told
himself, in his frenzy, that if need be he would go to work
for her, that if she did not wish to support him, then he
would support her: he would write for a newspaper, under
a pseudonym. He would become a music critic—he would
be ferocious, feared and even hated for his severe and exacting arrogance, for his apparently untried youth and
beauty that would make people talk. Yes, all of Paris would
be talking, wondering in vain, until one day la Doriacci
would appear in Paris, just back from a tour, and there and
then would appear the wildest and most passionate of commentaries, and the truth would burst forth into the light of
day. From that day on he would go about on the arm,
having come from the arms, of la Doriacci, bleary-eyed but
happy, and Paris would understand.

*L*a Doriacci had not yet made an exit, despite the ovation of a deliriously enthusiastic crowd. And this time it was truly delirious, even admitting that any passenger who was not delirious every evening would have felt cheated, by himself no less than by the Compagnie Pottin. So they had shouted 'Bis, bis,' 'Encore, encore . . .' while the diva, with a shake of the head, smilingly refused, coming down from the platform to mingle with them, poor mortals. It was a manoeuvre to which she habitually resorted, and had the virtue of saving her from further encores. La Doria knew from experience that in so elegant and gracious a gathering, nobody would have the heart or the gall to call out 'bis' right in her face, and less than a yard away from her. She sometimes regretted that she could not come down this way at La Scala in Milan and wander through the audience as Marlene Dietrich had done with Gary Cooper's Algerian troopers, but it just wasn't done. There was a note of indestructible solemnity in the personality of the diva, a trait she had thought she could ignore at twenty-five, but which at fifty-odd she congratulated herself on having accepted. God knows she was no hypocrite, but her little nocturnal pursuits would undoubtedly have lacked some savour if the iron curtain of celebrity did not infalliby descend upon the coat-tails of her latest lover, pinning him to the ground while she took off for other lights and other lovers.

Actually, she was hungry, she felt like some duck à *l'orange* and a slice of cake with icing, all washed down by a fruity red Bouzy. She also felt a yearning for the handsome blond youth who smiled at her from a distance, shifting from one foot to the other without daring to approach. La Doriacci decided to appeal to the clown-lady, who was sitting nearby. She was about to ask for her help when Clarisse, through a supreme effort, managed to speak up. She had a pretty voice, and without the palette scrapings smeared across her face she would certainly be very attractive. And now that she was talking to her about music, the one subject that Doria Doriacci dreaded above all others, as she described how happy she had been listening to her singing, her voice was a little hoarse, her eyes still moist; and as she thanked her, the diva realised that she was no longer so much alone on this ship. Because someone else, this ridiculous woman, had also experienced what Doria Doriacci called the Great Joy, something she and only a few others were privileged to experience; it was not a privilege of caste or education, but almost a chromosomic privilege that led one to feel Great Joy in the presence of Music, at such times as it chanced to keep the rendezvous. It was this element of chance that engraved it in the memory, labelled and tucked away in the ever half-empty drawer of Great or Perfect Joys, recollections that became vaguer and vaguer about the origin of the Joy, but clearer and clearer about its reality.

This young woman understood Music, and that was a good thing. But the blond lamb over there was already trembling on his beautiful legs in unconscious anticipation of the sacrifice. It was a sacrifice that could not be postponed, because, prancing about at the door of the bar, her dyed ringlets entangling her antique earrings, her high heels tapping the deck smartly as though readying to charge, Madame Bautet-Lebreche was about to head in the diva's direction. Indeed Edma had singled them out and was now cantering up to their table. Flabbergasted, Clarisse watched while the massive, imposing figure of la Doriacci literally squeaked between two tables that would hardly have allowed passage for a sylph—having swept up from the table with the gesture of a pickpocket her purse, cigarette holder, lipstick and lighter, along with her fan—and was already bearing down on the bar, all without for an instant dropping her tragic hauteur.

What Clarisse did not know was that la Doriacci, when she had chosen a man for immolation on the high altar of her canopied bed, endowed her whole person with a certain funereal pomp, a sort of mutely tragic sorrow befitting a Medea more than a Merry Widow. Frozen in alarm, Andreas was heartbroken to observe the majestic flight of his beloved from the small gathering. Already resigned to seeing her disappear without a word or a look into the deep meandering corridors of the ship, he suddenly caught a slight turning of her head in his direction. And then, like a big three-master borne along its course by the wind and unable to slow down in order to spare the little sloop that will soon be dancing in its wake and very likely founder—like a proud but compassionate ship dropping off a few lifeboats for the rescue of its victims—so la Doriacci with a glance drew Andreas's attention to her side; by her side was her hand, single fingernails crooked inwards. And one of these beckoning fingers gave him to know in the most suggestive, most eloquent manner, that his misery was far from over.

$\mathcal{S}$imon Béjard entered the cabin first, forgetting his good manners such as they were, noted Olga with vague anxiety. He sat down on the berth and began to take off his new patent-leather shoes and his tie at the same time, the left hand tugging at the bow knot, the right hand at the laces in a faintly simian posture. It was only after his feet and his scarlet neck emerged from those instruments of torture that Simon stared at her with a look of rage. Olga walked around the room, her eyes closed, her back arched, lifting her arms and running her fingers through her hair. The allegory of desire, she said to herself. But then, she was not sure that *allegory* was the right word. It should have been Simon, the allegory of desire. But neither his grumpy look nor his balancing act suggested that. She arched her back a bit more.

Of course Olga lived by her talent and not by her body, as she was quick to remind him, and as she very nearly convinced herself. That did not prevent her from falling back on the charms of her person when those of her mind proved inimical to her career.

'Come on, Simon,' she said amiably, even affectionately, with the tender little laugh that marked her voice at its most gracious—but which the churl appeared not to notice. 'Come on, Simon, don't be angry at what I said. It's not your fault if you have no musical training. You're not going to sulk all night with your bird of paradise . . .'

'My bird of paradise . . . My bird of paradise . . . My little goose would be more like it. Yes, that's it, my sour-tempered little goose,' Simon grumbled before looking up at the youthful body of his mistress, lithe as a sapling, before admiring with something of a wrench the back of her long smooth neck with its all but imperceptible blonde down.

Now Simon's vague anger was transformed into a ripple of tenderness, a tenderness so acute and so sad that he felt tears rising to his eyes. And, lowering his head, he turned savagely back to his shoelaces.

'You have so many other cultural attributes. You're so far superior to me, for heaven's sake. What about the Seventh Art, for instance . . .'

Simon Béjard felt ill. He was angry at her for having opposed his newly discovered self who was ready to love passionately, piously and freely the entire universe which, under the name of Art, had first been unknown to him, then inaccessible and finally hostile, to judge from the frequent mention it was given by film critics at his expense. Art was the private preserve of a social class that he scorned but at the same time dreamed of conquering. All those paintings, all those books, all the musical compositions, fragile pieces of paper or canvases, were above all, he knew, the explanations of a brotherhood or attempts to explain an absurd existence in which unknown brothers were linked and all too often crushed—but to which for over an hour now Simon felt himself to be the comprehending and grateful heir. Now it was simply up to him to gain access to that world. He no longer needed the condescending tutelage of all those people, nor Olga's confused and tiresome explanations. Something almost like a secret but unmistakable solidarity now linked him with Debussy, as if they had done their military service together, or together experienced the first pangs of blighted love. He would no longer allow anyone to come between them.

'The Seventh Art,' he said, drawn away from his anger by this new assurance. 'Ah! let's talk about the Seventh Art. Do you know what my favourite movie was all through my childhood? And I saw plenty, as I must have told you, because my father was a projectionist at the Eden, in Bagnolet, all during the war and afterwards too. My favourite . . . you'll never guess!'

'No,' said Olga half-heartedly. She hated him to speak about his family in this offhand way. His father a projectionist and his mother a seamstress! It was nothing to boast about. Nor to hide, of course . . . but still she wished he would be a little less open about it.

Olga herself, after all, so as not to embarrass anyone, tended to turn her mother's haberdashery into a textile mill and their house into a manor. And no matter what Simon might say, it had impressed him. She wondered if it weren't her middle-class style that he valued. Seriously.

'Well, it was *Pontcarral*,' Simon said finally, smiling. 'I was madly in love with the little blonde, Suzy Carrier, who took Pierre Blanchar away from Annie Ducaux, who played her sister. Those were the days when chaste little blonde virgins won out over vamps,' he said without thinking, and then stopped short.

Maybe that explains everything, he told himself. My inclination to fall head over heels in love with virginal young girls who won't give me the time of day, my contempt for women my own age I feel comfortable with and who might love me. Could all that come from *Pontcarral*? That would be too stupid—a whole life based on *Pontcarral*! It could only happen to me! he told himself bitterly, unaware of how few people are proud of their likes and dislikes, how few are really attracted by what they idealise, unaware of how much terrible havoc—and some good literature—the divorce between one's image of oneself and the pleasures one actually enjoys had produced over the centuries.

'But . . . but . . . I've heard of Pierre Blanchar too,' stammered Olga, happy as always when a recollection of Simon's, or of some other lover, coincided with a memory of her own childhood—all the more since she didn't care much for people her own age, who would not have been nearly so impressed by her youth. 'Why, of course,' she said. 'Pierre Blanchar. My mother was crazy about him.'

'When she was a very, very young girl of course,' Simon observed with a shrug.

This time Olga held her tongue. She would have to be careful. She had managed to pry Simon from his vacation at Saint-Tropez, where she would have had competition from ten other starlets. She had managed to get him onto this ship bursting with septuagenarians; now, in the intoxication of success, she would have to take care not to exasperate him completely. Simon was a decent sort, awkward, sometimes naive, but he was a man, as he persisted in proving every night—which Olga found intensely wearisome. For after having so often simulated physical pleasure, Olga could no longer be sure whether she had ever experienced it. But her frigidity worried her only in relation to splendid young men who were reputedly skilled as lovers. Perhaps that was why for the last ten years she had only been to bed with men whose lack of physical appeal or whose great financial appeal permitted her to believe that she was not really frigid, that somewhere within her dwelt a passionate lover thwarted by destiny. As for tonight, the obligatory sham would be less tedious than usual since, as a means of reconciliation with Simon, it lost the futile, gratuitous and transitory aspect that she had always detested in her liaisons.

But for once her planned ecstasy did not take care of everything, since Simon put on a sweater and his tight blue jeans and without another word closed the cabin door behind him.

*A*ndreas had been astounded at
first by la Doriacci's unequivocal pantomime of the commanding index finger as she left the scene, and a slight
feeling of reprobation mingled with his joy. Since the beginning of what he called his 'love story' Andreas had in fact
been uneasy. He was more and more smitten with la Doriacci, and at the same time felt guilty for being so—guilty
of feeling a desire that he had decided in advance to declare
and to prove. In the wildest of his naive if cynical fantasies
Andreas had imagined himself counting baggage in the front
hall of a palace, or laying a mink stole across shoulders
swathed in diamonds, or dancing a slow foxtrot with his
benefactress on the dance floor of a well-known nightclub.
He never thought of himself in bed, lying naked next to a
naked spent woman, or engaged in the act of love, despite
numerous recent experiences of this sort. On that score his
reveries remained as chaste as anything ascribed to a
nineteenth-century maiden. Above all, he never imagined
the slightest glimpse of his own body. But that body, like

a faithful steward, would perform. He was absolutely sure of it, thanks to several exploits carried out coldly and against all his sensual inclinations. It must be said that at Nevers and during his military service, Andreas had more often had to restrain his erotic desires than to stimulate them.

So now the emotion that la Doriacci aroused in him was worrisome. She raised doubts in his mind about his virility, questions which a total emotional indifference had until now oddly spared him. But suddenly he found la Doriacci magnificent: those shoulders, those arms, that voice, those eyes. She must weigh a good deal, though thank God she appeared much smaller standing here in her cabin than while she was singing on stage. As for her eyes, those immense, amazing eyes, in some altogether incongruous way they reminded him of his Aunt Jeanne—though they were rather more made-up, to be sure. He blotted out those dangerous memories, knowing that if he gave them free rein he would find himself cuddled up against this shoulder wheedling for some tin soldiers, when what he needed was a car, a *pied-à-terre* and a few neckties. He had no need to be pitied or cajoled, but to be desired, madly desired by this sublime woman, his first celebrity, a woman, what's more, who travelled continuously and would take him with her, along with her luggage. A woman who was real and vital, if at times a bit too free with her favours, but who was admired all the same, one who would not bring on the glassy stare of headwaiters to which he had already been subjected in the company of an occasional dissolute sexagenarian back in the Upper Loire. No more of that! He was going to be envied rather than scorned. And this was important to Andreas, who had a great concern for respectability inherited from his father, his grandfather, all his honourable forbears. Ah, if only the women who had brought him up, his true and only public, could see him at this moment, at the apogee of his career and their ambitions . . .

All these ideas buzzed about in his head while Andreas gazed at the diva's sumptuous décolletage and she for her part inspected him, though more professionally. She had the practised, shrewd look of a horse dealer, but Andreas knew he was irreproachable: weight, teeth (except for that one incisor), skin, hair, everything impeccable, he had seen to it. And she must have recognised that, for she had invited him into her cabin with an ironic bow and closed the door behind him.

'Have a seat,' she said. 'What would you like?'

'A Coca-Cola,' he said. 'But don't bother, I'll get it. You must have a little bar, don't you, in your cabin?'

The idea of a private bar delighted Andreas, unaccustomed as he still was to luxury. But it didn't seem to have aroused the same enthusiasm in la Doriacci.

'In the bedroom,' she said, settling onto a chaise longue made of fake mahogany. 'I'll have a glass of vodka, please.'

Andreas flew into the bedroom and before helping himself at the little bar he flung a delighted glance at the double bed. The whole cabin was in a state of disarray, a seductive disarray of clothes, newspapers, fans, musical scores, even books—rather heavy ones, it seemed to him, which had quite evidently been read.

He brought la Doriacci a glass of vodka and took a long gulp of Coca-Cola. His heart was pounding, he was ready to expire of thirst and timidity. The thought of desire did not even cross his mind.

'You don't need a drink to warm up?' she asked. 'You start off cold, just like that, on an empty stomach?'

Her voice was sarcastic though affectionate, and Andreas blushed to hear her use an expression so devoid of romance. He quickly changed the subject. 'What was the name of the piece you sang?' he said. 'How beautiful it was.'

'One of the great arias from Verdi's *Don Carlos*. You liked it?'

'Oh yes, it was marvellous,' Andreas said, his eyes gleaming. 'At first it might have been a very young girl singing. Then later a real woman, madly ferocious . . . Actually I don't know a thing about music, but I loved that, it was tremendous. Maybe you could help me learn something about music? I'm afraid you'll find my ignorance very trying . . .'

'In that department not at all,' she said, smiling. 'In

others, perhaps! I don't like to do the teaching. How old are you?'

'Twenty-seven,' said Andreas, automatically adding three years.

'That's young. You know how old I am? A little over twice that.'

'No!' said Andreas, stunned. 'I would have said . . . I would have thought . . .'

He was perched on the edge of his chair in his smart new dinner jacket, his blond hair standing up in tufts; she sauntered around him with an amused but attentive air.

'You don't do anything else in life besides being a concert buff?' she asked.

'No. And then, well, concert buff, that's saying a lot,' he added ingenuously.

She laughed.

'So you're not in public relations or working for the press? You have no professional front in Paris or anywhere else?'

'I come from Nevers,' he said woefully. 'There isn't any paper in Nevers, or any public relations. There's nothing in Nevers, you see.'

'And in Nevers,' she asked abruptly, 'who did you prefer—men or women?'

'Why, women,' Andreas responded artlessly.

Not for a moment did he imagine that this admitted preference could be in the nature of a reference.

'They all say that,' muttered la Doriacci to herself, mysteriously annoyed.

She moved towards the bedroom making the same over-explicit gesture that had already embarrassed Andreas. Kicking off her pumps, she stretched out on the bed completely clothed, arms behind her head, and looked at him ironically—and it was as if she was looking down at him although he remained upright, standing six foot tall.

'For heaven's sake, sit down,' she said. 'Right here . . .'

He sat down next to her, and once again she crooked her index finger in his direction but more slowly. Andreas, bending down to kiss her, was surprised to discover a cool mouth that tasted more of mint than vodka. She let herself be kissed so passively, seemingly inert, that he was doubly surprised when she put a hand on him, deliberately and precisely, and then began to laugh.

'Braggart,' she said.

Andreas was abashed, less by shame than by sheer amazement. And she must have seen this, because she stopped laughing and looked at him soberly.

'This has never happened to you before?'

'Why no . . . and what's more, I find you very attractive,' he said with a passion that was very nearly candid.

Laughing again, she slipped an arm around his neck and drew him close. Andreas relaxed, nestled his head against her perfumed shoulder and was immediately suffused by a sense of well-being. A divinely skilful hand undid his shirt collar, so that he could breathe more easily, then rested on the nape of his neck. In turn he moved a supposedly expert but in fact trembling hand along the warm and comfortable body next to his, seeking a breast, a thigh, a so-called erogenous zone, but gropingly, as if engaged in a mnemonic exercise—when a sharp tap accompanied by a throaty growl next to his ear brought him to a halt.

'*Sta' tranquillo*,' she said severely, but unnecessarily, for of its own accord, Andreas's body had sunk into a beatific but disgraceful lethargy—though it seemed to him more beatific than disgraceful. He tried to tell himself that he was finished, washed up, dismissed. The great chance of his life, the gilded life of Andreas the handsome gigolo was in the process of vanishing. But little Andreas from Nevers felt so comfortable and snug that, though it would leave him defeated on the very threshold of success, he let it all go—the glory, the luxurious life of a dandy, all of it—for this quarter-hour of fondling, this soothing hand on his hair, this innocent sleep, against this all-too-briefly understanding shoulder. Andreas Fayard of Nevers, amorous and impotent, disgraced and enraptured, promptly fell asleep.

As for la Doriacci, she lay there a while in the dark, open-eyed, smoking a cigarette in quick little puffs, frowning, with an occasional tremor of the right foot that eventually disappeared along with the frown. She was alone as usual. Alone on stage, alone in her box, alone on airplanes, still more often alone with one of these young men in bed with her, alone in life as she had been since the beginning—that is if you could call it being alone when your music was always with you, when you had music for a lover. How lucky she had been! And how lucky she still was, to possess this thing—this voice of diabolical power, a voice she had trained to obey her the way you train an unruly dog, the voice she had throttled after great struggle with the help of Yousepov, the Russian baritone; Yousepov who, like her, had been scared of this animal sound to begin with, and who sometimes in the evening, when the exercises were over, would stare at her throat with an admiring fear that was almost comic when you stopped to think about it. It had made her blush as if she had been pregnant, as if what inhabited her below the thorax had been the already stigmatised foetus of some roughneck or criminal . . . Thanks to him she had kept on working until she arrived, achieved this success smelling of patchouli and furs, this success in a career which left her time neither for love nor for listening to music, and from which she would hardly have time to exit one day, dying and knowing it, into some dirty corner in the wings.

'They say the Americans now make a cognac that's better than ours,' said Simon Béjard with a doubtful air, which allowed him to pick up the bottle, studying it severely, as if his only concern were to verify the rumour. He took a good swallow and grew still more certain of French superiority in spirits. 'I'd be very much surprised. Are you really not drinking, Peyrat?'

Pretty soon he'll be drunk as a lord, Julien reflected with annoyance. They had been playing gin rummy for an hour now, and Julien hated to fleece a drunk. It took all the sport out of the thing. And he found Béjard sympathetic, if only because of that peevish chit travelling with him—though she had very pretty breasts, Julien duly noted. What was more, gin rummy was a game for little old ladies, and it took forever . . . In two hours, he would get only fifteen thousand francs out of the poor guy. Julien had arranged things so that it was Simon who suggested the game; he himself half-way refused, in front of witnesses. After all, he was not going to let a few miserable games of cards ruin his Marquet project, which promised much higher rewards. But Simon had latched onto him with the idea of a little game between men. Nobody was left on the de luxe deck but themselves; themselves and the indefatigable Charley, who strode along the bridge, a heavy white pullover thrown across his shoulders, looking more effete than an Irish setter.

'You have all the luck,' commented Simon as he was ginned for the second time. 'If you weren't so far from Australia, I'd tell you to keep an eye on your woman. But that wouldn't be very sporting, since you couldn't check on her yourself . . . Anyway, it's an idiotic proverb, don't you think, Peyrat? "Unlucky at cards, lucky in love"? Do I for instance look as though I'm lucky in love? Would you say I have the face of a guy who's lucky in love? Me? Be honest.'

Oh great, he's going to be an unhappy drunk, thought Julien with dismay. He instinctively detested man-to-man talk, whether coarse or sentimental. Julien believed talking about love and sex was entirely the domain of women, and he plainly said so to Simon Béjard, who did not become angry but in fact enthusiastically agreed.

'You're absolutely right, my friend. And there are times when I think women ought to keep quiet . . . for instance, I don't want to be indiscreet, but since she's the one who's here . . . I'll tell you about her,' he said in semi-apology. Julien stared, dumbfounded by the new rule of discretion just laid down by Simon Béjard. 'Well, Olga, for instance—healthy girl, good bourgeois family, well brought up and all that . . . (and not at all flighty, I must say, not a bit . . .). Well, she talks in bed . . . goes on and on like a windmill. For me that kills it, what about you?'

Julien recoiled, torn between amusement and shock. 'Well, naturally,' he mumbled, 'that could be a handicap.' He blushed, knew it, and felt ridiculous.

'To begin with, a woman who lectures you, that's like a whore from the country, I mean professionally speaking,' Béjard insisted. 'Decent women and high-class call girls keep their traps shut. But me, I always fall for the chatterers . . . magpies, magpies and shrews. It's not much fun being

91

a producer, my friend! All those females running after you . . .'

'What a strange ship,' Julien commented, as if to himself, 'so chic and the women are still called females.'

'That intrigues you, Monsieur Peyrat?'

Something in Simon Béjard's voice revived Julien's sluggish attention. His companion was looking at him with a smile, and his blue eyes were no longer as vapid as they had been a moment before. 'You're an art appraiser from . . . where was it . . . Sydney?'

Oh fine, so they had met before! Julien had thought he recognised Simon at the moment of his triumphant boarding, but then forgot all about it. But the other recognised him and, worse, knew who he was.

'You're wondering, eh?' Simon Béjard was exultant. 'You're wondering where and when? Too bad I've got too good a memory for you, I'm afraid you'll never guess. In any case it wasn't in Sydney. I can tell you that much.'

He dropped the wily manner, leaned across the table and tapped Julien's immobile forearm. 'You can relax, my friend. I'm a discreet fellow.'

'If you really want to reassure me, you might just jog my memory,' Julien said between his teeth.

I'll just have to get off at the next port, he thought. All because of this cretin. And just when I haven't a cent in the bank. Farewell, Marquet, farewell, races at Longchamp, and the smell of Paris in the autumn . . .

'You were on a boat, smaller than this one, in Florida. The boat belonged to someone from MGM. You were there to take care of some sort of life insurance for him. You were working for Herpert & Crook. There, is that right?' he said, as Julien's face lit up with a sudden smile—whereas Simon had expected him to be annoyed by the reminder of such relatively unspectacular work.

'Ah yes, that was a rather difficult period for me,' said Julien, energetically shuffling the cards. 'You scared me, my friend.'

'Scared? Why?'

Simon Béjard had a lousy hand, but he didn't give a

92

hoot. His new companion was damned likeable. Not disparaging or snobbish like the rest of these idiots—la Doriacci excepted.

'Scared of what?' he repeated absently.

'I was once a dishwasher, too,' said Julien laughing. 'I shined shoes on Broadway . . . even less distinguished, wouldn't you say?'

'Go on, you're kidding.'

Simon now began losing again consistently. Someone had told him something about this handsome insurance broker, but he couldn't quite remember what. But whatever it was he was someone worth getting to know, unpretentious but not without distinction.

'You know why I like you, Peyrat? I'm going to tell you why I like you, Peyrat.'

'Go ahead,' said Julien. 'Gin, by the way.'

'Damn,' said Simon, laying down fifty points. 'Still, I'm going to tell you why. In the two hours we've been playing you haven't once suggested a story, or mentioned a subject, or even the name of a book that would make a marvellous film . . . and you know there's no end to it! Ever since I've had cash and people have known about it, they haven't once stopped dragging out stories they want made into movies, their life story, the life story of their mistress, every last one of them! They've all got ideas, great ideas no one's ever had before, that would make a terrific movie! Let me tell you, Peyrat, apart from the tax collectors and spongers, that's the worst thing in my job—when you're successful, I mean. Everyone keeps throwing ideas at you the way you'd throw bones to a dog. Except that with a dog they don't expect him to come back with a gold ingot in his choppers. With me they do.'

'That's the price of success,' Julien said placidly. 'Scenarios by the bucket and pretty little intellectual girlfriends— that's part of life at the top, no?'

'I suppose so . . .' With bloodshot eyes Simon gazed off into space. 'When I think how I dreamed of all this, how all my life I dreamed of this.' He made a vague gesture that included the boat and the glistening black sea that surrounded it. 'And here I am. I won the Grand Prix de Cannes, of all the producers in France I'm the one most in the public eye, I'm on a boat with some smart people and I've got a well-turned-out woman who's got a head on her shoulders as well. I can write cheques for thousands, hundreds of thousands, and my name is Simon Béjard, producer. I should be happy with all this, right, since it's what I wanted?'

Julien looked up, annoyed at the note of pathos that had crept into Simon's voice. 'Well,' he said evenly, 'aren't you?'

'Why yes, not bad, all in all,' Simon Béjard answered after a moment's silence during which he seemed to be listening to his own heartbeat. 'Why yes, I'm more or less . . . fairly happy, yes.'

He looked so bewildered that Julien burst out laughing and called an end to the game then and there. Tomorrow he would let Simon Béjard lose some more. But tonight he found him a bit too likeable to continue.

$\mathcal{C}$larisse sat in the bathtub, her eyes closed, immersed in the double pleasure of hot water and solitude. She was dreaming . . . She was dreaming that she was alone on an island; outside, a palm tree and a playful dog awaited her, and nothing else. Someone called. She stiffened, brought back to sad reality, and turned her head in the direction of the voice. Eric Lethuillier was waiting for her to finish in the bathroom so that he could brush his teeth after her. She glanced at her watch: eight minutes . . . She had been there for eight minutes, eight miserable minutes. She got up, put on the fleecy *Narcissus* bathrobe, despite its ridiculous Napoleonic monogram, and hurriedly brushed her teeth. She had not taken off her make-up before getting into the bath, and the steam from the hot water had diluted the greasepaint and sent rivulets down her face which made her even more grotesque than usual, as she remarked to herself with the bitter pleasure that she experienced more and more often on seeing herself through the eyes of others as she appeared in the mirror.

'Clarisse, I know you're not quite ready, but I'm tired, my dear. This is my first vacation in two years, I'd like to have a bath and get to bed, if that's not too much to ask.'

'I'm coming,' she said.

And without doing anything to her messy make-up, she emerged from the bathroom to find Eric exactly as she had left him, with his hands resting on the arms of the chair, his handsome head thrown back, eyes closed, wearing an expression of lassitude and absolute forbearance.

'Eric,' she said, 'I begged you to take your bath before me. Why didn't you?'

'A question of courtesy, my dear. The fundamental rules of civility . . .'

'But Eric,' she broke in, 'the rules of civility do not oblige you to turn my evening bath into a relay race. I love to stretch out in the bath, it's the height of luxury, it seems to me, every time . . .'

'So long as you're stretched out you're happy. I suppose that's something. But I wonder if this trip is really giving you any pleasure, or if I haven't wasted my time making the effort of going on this cruise with someone who doesn't enjoy it . . . You look sad, you look bored. Everyone can see it, and what's more, everyone finds it embarrassing. Don't you have any love for the sea any more, or for music? I thought music at least was your great passion—the only one you had left, in fact.'

'Of course you're perfectly right,' she answered in a life-less voice. 'Just don't be so impatient.'

She sat down on her bed and drew up her legs so that Eric would not bump into them as he walked up and down undressing.

He was on her right, and then on her left, behind her, in front of her, he was everywhere. And everywhere she was at the mercy of his disparaging and malevolent gaze. Besides, he was making her dizzy.

'Eric, would you please stop walking around?' she said. 'Tell me, why are you so much against me?'

'Against you? Me? You're incredible!' And he burst out laughing. He was laughing, he was delighted: once again she had opened up the bitter subject of their relationship, and if she brought up the subject, he was even more thrilled, since it was ultimately the one that enabled him to land the most blows. For this reason it was a subject she systematically avoided and broached only when she was on the verge of total panic, without friends, without a place to retreat, a space of her own. She would never hold out for ten days with this hostile stranger. He would have to promise to spare her during this cruise, at any rate not to flaunt his unfailing scorn quite so openly—a scorn so genuine that she had ended up sharing it.

'Against you? That's the limit!' he said. 'I offer to send you on this marvellous cruise—for I would like to point out, it is I, Eric, your husband, who am financing this expedition, not the Dureau family. I bring you on this boat so you can hear your two favourite musicians, if I remember rightly. I even arrange at the last moment to join you on the cruise, to keep you from being lonely or making blunders, and after all to share something with you—something besides money and the objects it can buy. And you find me ill-willed!'

She listened to him with a sort of fascination. They were alone, though. They were alone and there was no one there to witness yet another example of his perfect conduct and her ingratitude. But Eric no longer lived a single moment of his life without a public and without commentary: he was always playing to the gallery. Soon he would be unable to say 'Pass me the bread' without asking her the price of the loaf. Why was he unable to tell her what he had to tell her— to tell her, straight out, that he hated her? And if he hated her, why at the last moment had he come with her? Was it the simple certainty that his company would spoil the trip for her—for surely he realised that it would—could that sad fact alone have decided him, persuaded him to leave behind his newspaper, his colleagues, his political associates, his court, the smug assembly without whom, for years now, he had hardly been able to function?

'Why did you come, Eric? Tell me.'

'I came because I adore music. You have no exclusive rights to those pleasures. Beethoven, Mozart, these are popular composers. Even my mother in her total lack of culture loved above all to listen to Mozart. She could always recognise him, better than I—even from Beethoven.'

'I would really like to have known your mother,' Clarisse said feebly. 'That is one of my regrets. You will tell me that all I need to do is add it to the others, and it will be lost in the crowd!'

'But you needn't have any regrets!'

Dressed only in his underpants, Eric was wandering around the room, picking up his cigarettes, his lighter, his newspaper in preparation for a delicious half-hour in a hot bath, the hot bath from which he had dragged her away under the pretext of courtesy. There was no reason at all why he should have that pleasure any longer than she did. A blazing current of anger ran through her at the thought, and she gave in to it with a satisfaction and a fear that were equally strong. Now it was the little girl of ten, the teacher's pet at school, the spoiled child at home, who confronted Eric. It was she who was clamouring for her bath, her snack and her creature comforts with enough single-minded determination to resist the fatalism and resigned submission of the adult Clarisse. It was she who now fervently and contentiously resisted. For these were the only defences which the unquestionable loyalty, the sense of propriety and justice that Eric flaunted night and day could neither over-come nor alter, much less render culpable. She was no longer the loving woman who was floundering in the throes of a cruel passion, no longer the young girl rejecting the lessons of her Pygmalion turned to pitiless sadist, this was the wilful and selfish brat that she didn't remember even having been, who now rebelled.

'You have no reason to feel any remorse,' Eric repri-manded. 'Rather it is I who should. I was stupid enough to suppose it might be possible to change one's class, that through love one might give up certain privileges and choose others that seem more precious to me. I was mistaken. You have nothing to do with it.'

'But in what were you mistaken? Why did I disappoint you, Eric? Do please make it clear to me.'

'Make it clear? The complacency, the cowardice and the brutality of the French upper classes, traits that you inherited from your grandparents, are not conscious in you—they are instinctive. You ask me to bring my mother to visit your family for instance. When, as I've told you, my mother was a maid, a housekeeper if you prefer, for a lower middle-class family in Bordeaux all her life, all through my adolescence, so that I could eat, so that she could eat. And you want me to bring her to your house, where just one of your paintings would have paid to feed us for a hundred years? My mother is the only woman whom I genuinely respect. I don't wish to have her humiliated by your ostentation.'

'By the way, Eric, why do you always say that your mother was a maid in Bordeaux? I was told she worked at the post office.'

Clarisse had asked the question ingenuously, but Eric took it as an insult, paled and turned on her, his face convulsed with rage. There were moments when he could be ugly, she thought to herself—when even she found him ugly. Which was progress of a sort!

'Oh yes? And who, may I ask, told you that? Your uncle? Somebody in your household who considered it more chic, after all, than being a maid? Somebody who knows my life and my childhood better than I do? I really don't believe it, Clarisse.'

'But it was your editor-in-chief, it was Pradine. He said it the other day at dinner. You didn't hear? I'd sent him to Libourne to deliver our Christmas present to your mother, since you didn't want to invite her. He was going near there. He found her at the post office at Meyllat—some name like that—where she actually seemed to be running everything, masterfully. He thought she was charming.'

'That's an insult,' said Eric, and to Clarisse's astonishment he brought his fist down on the table. 'I'm going to kick him out. I will not tolerate anyone trying to criticise my mother.'

'But I can't see,' Clarisse said, 'how it could be a disgrace to work at the post office, or why it should be more

99

honourable to be a housekeeper. Sometimes, Eric, I don't understand you at all.'

She tried to look him in the eye, but for the first time in a long while he evaded her. Usually he would stare at her, look intently into her face, appearing to discern the all-too-evident marks of corruption or stupidity so that she had to look away very quickly, humiliated, before he so much as opened his mouth. A vein stood out on his right temple, setting off a flat brown mole, Eric Lethuillier's only flaw on the aesthetic level. He sat down again. 'I won't try once more to impress my sense of values upon you, Clarisse. But you must know that they are quite different from yours. And I would ask you not to interfere with my family, just as I don't interfere with yours.'

'Eric . . .' Clarisse suddenly felt weary, worn out, submerged in a hopeless sadness, as she lay on the narrow bed with its tightly drawn sheets. 'Eric . . . You spend a part of your life with my uncles—or if not with them, then with their lawyers. And you are so polite to them, so agreeable, it seems, regardless of your declarations of principle, so accommodating even . . .'

'Accommodating? Me, accommodating? That is really the last adjective that I would have used to describe myself!— or that anyone else would have used, for that matter, in Paris or elsewhere.'

'Oh, I know,' Clarisse had closed her eyes. 'I know how principled you are, and I also know that it was to please me that you paid for this cruise and came on it with me. I know all that. You're always right. I believe that sincerely. It's just that there are moments when I don't care in the least that I'm wrong.'

'That, my little Clarisse, is the privilege of the rich. When one is rich, one can afford to be in the wrong, and even to admit it. How could I have imagined that you might escape from all that?'

'How could you have believed that I would change my class? Is that what you mean? But at the time didn't you know that one can never change one's class?'

She was mimicking him, mimicking the tone of his

voice—and was almost laughing. 'But then, what about you, Eric? How did you manage to change?'

He slammed the door behind him.

When he came out of his bath half an hour later, he was ready with a stinging reply. But Clarisse was sound asleep, her face stripped of all make-up, relaxed. She lay on her right side, facing the door, looking suddenly childlike and peaceful. She was almost smiling in her sleep. There was something in her that he was unable to destroy. At such moments as this, he sensed that he would never be able to destroy something that she had acquired at birth, something he was seeking desperately to link with her fortune but which, he was well aware, had nothing to do with it, something that strangely resembled virtue. She defended herself with it, she struggled on. And yet she had nothing at all to fall back on. He had dispossessed her of everything— friends, lovers, family, her childhood and her past. He had dispossessed her of everything, even of herself. And yet from time to time she smiled mysteriously, as if for the first time, at some unknown being invisible to him.

A grey sun rose on the third day of the cruise, veiled in clouds of metallic, suffocating white. Having decided the night before at Porto-Vecchio in a great athletic impulse to try out the swimming pool, Julien found himself there alone at around two o'clock, pallid and shivering in his bathing trunks. What made him all the more miserable was finding himself scrutinised, and no doubt ridiculed, by the Bautet-Lebreches and their followers, all fully dressed and lolling in the rocking chairs above him, by the swimming pool bar. He was in a quandary: to go into the water through the wading pool was beneath his dignity, and to go in through the big pool would be a similar affront to his shivering body. So he sat on the side, dangling his legs in the beautiful blue chlorinated water, lost in contemplation of his own feet. The water's refraction made them seem strange to him and pitiful, as if added to his ankles as an afterthought. By way of reassurance, Julien tried to wiggle his toes one by one, but realised that he couldn't. This little toe remained immovable despite all his mute exhortations while the big toe stirred and bobbed about as if Julien could be fooled by this diversionary manoeuvre. For a moment he struggled against this anarchy and then gave in; after all, it was quite normal that these miserable toes, confined all winter in shoes, holed up all winter in the dungeon of his socks—these toes which he never looked at, which he let out of jail only to plunge right back into the darkness of sheets, to which he gave consideration only when comparing them with those of some new conquest, and then always more or less to their disadvantage—it was natural that these slaves, having been subordinated to the group under the single name 'foot', should prove, on being exposed to the sun, incapable of any individual initiative. It wasn't exactly a brilliant meditation, Julien told himself, but on the whole it was up to the level of the energetic conversation taking place above him.

Madame Edma Bautet-Lebreche, dressed like Piaf in the thirties, her hair even redder in daylight than by lamplight, led the debate with her customary verve. Facing her were Eric Lethuillier, elegant in an old cashmere sweater and beige trousers, Olga Lamouroux, detectably tanned under her Indian silk, and Simon Béjard, trying in vain to subdue the red of his hair and nose with his crimson pullover. The arrival of Hans-Helmut Kreuze in a white sports blazer with gilt buttons, cap and a sort of horrid bulldog at the end of a leash, added a final touch to the elegant eclecticism of this assembly.

Looking rather shaken, Edma was saying to Eric Lethuillier, who had just described the Vietnamese exodus and the massacre of the refugees in particularly atrocious terms, 'I find you hideously pessimistic.'

'He is right, alas, more's the pity,' said Olga Lamouroux, mournfully shaking out her beautiful hair. 'I'm afraid that he hasn't actually told us the worst of it.'

'Rubbish,' mumbled Simon Béjard who with the aid of two martinis felt disposed to optimism. 'Rubbish, all that is happening far away from here. We're in France, and in France when business is okay, everything is okay,' he concluded good-naturedly.

But a disapproving silence followed this intelligence, however reassuring, and Olga gazed with a distressed air towards the horizon. Despite her fervent desire she had not dared give Eric Lethuillier the pained smile or the suggestion of a wink that would have conveyed to him her indignation; quite to the contrary, she had avoided his glance. The role of the stoically loyal woman suggesting a sense of 'fair' play' should raise her in Eric's eyes; to betray Simon would not. Anyway it wasn't necessary, since Eric had effectively followed the drift of her thoughts. The little cretin really wanted him to pay attention to her, he thought, all the while envisioning in the East the smoking ruins of Indochina.

'I haven't yet seen la Doriacci out in the sun,' said Edma, who had long since assigned the varied atrocities perpetrated amongst the lower orders to the area of 'political topics', and deemed the aforementioned political topics deathly dull. 'I must admit it intrigues me. After seeing la Doriacci singing Verdi, *Tosca*, or even, as she did last night, Electra, one can only imagine her enraged and flamboyant, like a torch in the darkness, with her jewels, her cries, her rages, and so on. Not for one second can I imagine her in a swimsuit, sunbathing.'

'La Doriacci has a beautiful skin,' Hans-Helmut Kreuze said absently. Then immediately nailed by an ironic look or two, he blushed and stammered, 'Well, a very young skin, considering what we know to be her age.'

Edma was quick to react. 'Well, you see, dear Maestro, I believe, in fact I'm certain . . . yes, certain'—she added not without some visible surprise at finding herself certain of something—'that when one passionately loves one's art, for instance, if one has the good fortune to practise an art, or when one loves someone really worthy of it, or even when one is just foolishly in love with Life with a capital L, one cannot grow old. One never grows old. Except physically! And that . . .'

'There you're right,' Simon cut in, and this time Eric and Olga exchanged a glance. 'The cinema has always had that effect on me. When I see a beautiful film, I feel thirty years younger. And here too, I don't know if it's the sea air or the atmosphere of the *Narcissus* . . . but this morning, for instance, I haven't even read the papers. We're so nicely cut off from everything.'

'Yes, but nonetheless the world keeps on turning,' Eric said coldly. 'On this ship we are coddled, but there are thousands of other people, less comfortable by far, and far more crowded, who are going to the bottom of the China Sea at this very moment.'

His voice was so toneless, so subdued by a sense of shame that Olga let out a little gasp of dismay and horror. Hans-Helmut Kreuze and Simon Béjard both looked at their shoes, but after a moment's hesitation Edma decided to fight back. Yes, this Lethuillier owned a leftist newspaper, but he had never been cold, or hungry, or thirsty. Here he was, embarked on a luxury pleasure-boat, and he was simply not going to throw the horrors of war at them every morning of this cruise. After all, Armand Bautet-Lebreche worked hard all year and he was here for a rest. So, stopping her ears with two fingers in a dramatic gesture, she levelled a severe eye upon Eric. 'No, no,' she said. 'Dear friend, I beg of you! You're going to accuse me of selfishness, of cruelty, but who cares? We're all here to rest and forget those horrors. We can't do anything about them, can we? No, we're here to appreciate all of this . . .'—with her hand she described a broad parabola in the direction of the open sea—'and also this . . .'—she concluded the gesture by pointing the finger she had just removed from her ear at the chest of Hans-Helmut Kreuze, who started a little in myopic surprise.

'You are right, quite right.'

It was Eric who unexpectedly gave in to Edma's injunctions, deliberately looking off to the northwest as if to leave the field open, one would have said, to all the futile witless forms of occidental amusement. Olga darted a surprised glance in his direction and was worried that he looked so pale. Eric Lethuillier's jaw was clenched, with a light trace of perspiration along the upper lip, and once more Olga was moved by admiration for him. This man had such control over himself, such courtesy, that he managed to stifle that

105

inner cry, that indignation at the egotism of the upper class. Olga would have been less wholehearted in her admiration had she, as Eric had the moment before, felt the searing breath of the bulldog upon her ankles. The animal, until then peacefully sitting at the feet of his master while he rested his old muscles after a little walk, was beginning to get bored. He had decided to make a tour of these unprepossessing individuals and had begun the inspection with Eric. There he was, sniffing with eyes half-closed, his muscles visible under a pelt what was already moth-eaten in places, drooling, and looking ferocious by heredity, training and because he preferred it that way. And he wheezed away, interspersing his grunts with a menacing little whistle like the sound that precedes the final explosion of a falling bomb.

'I'm so pleased we agree about that,' said Edma Bautet-Lebreche, soothed but at the same time disappointed by this lack of resistance. 'We'll talk only about music, if you like, dear friends. Yes, we'll take advantage of our artists.' With a coy gesture she slipped her arm through that of Hans-Helmut—who, in surprise, dropped the dog's leash.

Now it was Simon's turn to go pale. Kreuze's horrible beast was gently tugging at his trouser leg, and the dog's few remaining fangs, though yellow with age, were still enormous. What's more, the beast was almost certainly drugged, he told himself. These Germans were incorrigible! The filthy dog was going to ruin his new trousers. While maintaining a stoic immobility, he cast a pleading glance toward Kreuze. 'Your dog, Maestro,' he said. 'Your dog . . .'

'My dog? He is a bulldog from East Pomerania. He has won fifteen cups and three gold medals at Stuttgart and Dortmund! They are very obedient animals, very good bodyguards. Is it true, Monsieur Béjard, that last night you compared Chopin to Debussy?'

'Me? But . . . oh no, not at all. Absolutely not!' Simon declared. 'No, but right now, I believe your dog—' he indicated with a jerk of his chin the monster attached more and more firmly to his leg—'is getting much too interested in my tibia, no joke . . .'

He was whispering in spite of himself, but without managing to interest Kreuze.

'Do you know that there is as much difference between Chopin and Debussy as between a film by . . . let me see, let me see . . . Ah, I can't find the name I am looking for . . . Help me. Uh . . . Becker . . .. uh, a French director very light, very diaphanous, you know?'

'Becker?' whispered Simon, hard-pressed. 'Becker? Feyder? René Clair? . . . But in the meantime your dog is about to rip my trousers!' He muttered rather than spoke his last phrase, for the dog had begun a low growl at the resistance of his leg to being carried off and torn to shreds, and was now pulling with incredible strength.

'No, no, that is not the name,' said Kreuze looking displeased.

There he was, insisting on the idea of lightness—couldn't be further from what he himself was, of course. With a violent shake, Simon brought his right leg up to the level of his left, and the dog let go with a spiteful yelp, before making his next assault. Fortunately for Simon the animal was almost blind, and the nearest trouser leg turned out to belong to Edma Bautet-Lebreche: perfectly cut, white gabardine slacks, of which she was very fond. Lacking masculine stoicism, she let out a piercing cry.

'Filthy dog!' she cried. 'Let go of me! *Quelle horreur!*'

But it appeared that his jaws were closing once and for all on the fine white fabric, missing by small margin the emaciated calf of the fair Edma who, no longer the centre of a devoted little group, had become a pariah amongst strangers bent on saving their own calves. Simon, seeing himself out of danger, gave way to a laugh.

'But can't you *do* something!' shrieked Edma, beside herself. 'Do something! The dog is going to bite me, in fact, he's already bitten me. Charley! Where is Charley? For heaven's sake, Monsieur Kreuze, control your beast!'

The beast was now growling ferociously, making as much noise as a high-powered vacuum cleaner. Kreuze himself looked on with an expression of helplessness.

'Monsieur Béjard, do something,' begged Edma, aware

that she could expect nothing from either Lethuillier or her own husband. 'Can't you get somebody to help!'

'I think it's up to the big clod to do something,' Simon protested.

'Fuschia!' roared the big clod himself, now crimson, stomping his foot on the deck but without success. 'Fuschia, *komm schnell*!'

For Edma Bautet-Lebreche, anger had overtaken fear. She would no doubt have ended by throttling the helpless Kreuze with her bare white hands—with Fuschia still appended to her trouser leg—if Julien had not arrived on the scene wearing a beach robe and an expression of sheer delight. He had followed all the ins and outs of the incident and, with a fearlessness more unconscious than courageous, he grabbed Fuschia by the scruff of the neck and, drawing on the nervous vitality of a racetrack habitué, hurled him five paces and left him grunting with indignation and surprise. Fuschia was astounded. Accustomed to the most level respect or servile fear—even from his master, so authoritarian in all other respects—he could not understand what had just happened to him. Just as the idea of being called a 'big clod' totally exceeded Kreuze's powers of comprehension, so being mistreated by a two-legged creature exceeded those of the bulldog. He stood there for one brief second, slack-jawed in wonder, a scrap of white gabardine signed by Ungaro hanging from his fangs, and immediately fell asleep.

Edma, on the other hand, was poles away from such drowsiness: her red hair bristled, and her shrill voice broke the sound barrier; a hundred yards away on the bridge, the man on watch froze, looking up at a seagull passing overhead with mingled amazement and respect. Armand, who as usual had intervened too late, gripped the agitated arms of his wife with such strength as his small stature permitted, trying to calm her by a slight but obstinately intermittent tug on her forearms whose muscles were clenched in rage.

He looked rather like Fuschia a little while ago, noticed Julien inadvertently. But there was no question of putting him through the same trajectory, whatever instinctive distaste Julien felt for big financiers, for huge success, particularly success that was the fruit of determination and practical intelligence. He was more at ease with fortunes acquired through opportunism or luck. On that score, and rather oddly for a professional cheat, Julien had great respect. He was strongly attracted by Lady Luck. Regularly every year, after forcing her hand through countless evenings, he submitted himself to all her caprices—from roulette to chemin de fer—suddenly, as though she were a great lady, deferring to her whom he had treated all year as a whore. By consenting to stake on a single card or spin of the wheel according to her wishes, the sums he had laboriously amassed in defiance of this blind goddess, he felt somehow that he was doing homage, repaying debts, salving his conscience. And even then he might double his stake, so little was she prone to hold a grudge.

His bravura had at once turned him into a Robin Hood in the eyes of the women on deck and a swaggerer in the view of the males, who considered him either imprudent or a show-off, apart from Simon, who was simply bowled over. This Peyrat was really something! Too bad he was such a poor loser. For Julien, after starting out by winning some fifteen thousand francs from Simon on the first night at Portofino and thinking it was a miracle (so Simon thought), had on the following night at Porto-Vecchio lost almost twenty-eight thousand francs in hard cash. And now he was obviously taking it badly. Today Simon had had to plead with him to even consider the game of five-card stud that had become objective number one for Simon Béjard, producer. In short, Peyrat was hopeless at cards but not in real life—if such a term could be applied to the musical *Hellzapoppin* this cruise was fast becoming in Simon's eyes. Before boarding he had never expected it to be such fun! Among all these doddering concert buffs! Nor had he expected that Olga would be such a shrew, such an idiot sometimes, or that she would think him so stupid. It was a shame, because he really did like the tilt of her head, her smooth skin, the way she slept, curled up like a kitten. When he saw her at dawn, stretched out on that austere berth that belonged in some boarding-school dorm (at ninety thou' a week), looking so innocent, so pure, such a sweet little girl, he could easily forget the bitchy starlet, ambitious, narrow-minded, basically hard-bitten vixen that he knew her to be. He loved Olga; in a way she had him cornered, and he was terrified of admitting it to himself. For a long time the pressure of daily or weekly finances had prevented all sustained dialogue between Simon and himself. For years he had given himself no more than the instructions a trainer gives an exhausted boxer: *Go on! Don't give up! Now you've got it! Careful!* and so forth. To find himself in love and a devotee of fine music all at once seemed to him a bit more than he could handle, and at any rate a good deal beyond his expectations. He pulled himself together and caught Julien by the elbow, drawing him aside.

'Well, how about that poker?' he said in a low, urgent voice. 'Are we on, pal? You and me take on the sugar king, the gigolo, and the egghead for a thousand apiece? You for technique and patience, me for intuition, luck, right? Afterwards we split it fifty-fifty, okay?'

'I'm terribly sorry, but I don't go partners, like that, at poker or anything else,' said Julien with an embarrassed look—not disapproving, only embarrassed, and somewhat abashed to be admitting to this bourgeois morality.

He was definitely a gent, this one, Simon thought with condescending and theatrical scorn. He began laughing so hard that his shoulders shook—which didn't make him any prettier, Julien thought.

'If you mean you won't go halves, fine, I agree. I meant it lightly, that we'd back each other up, you know, soften the blows. I didn't mean anything underhand, Monsieur Peyrat,' said Simon with a loud laugh. 'No, just a little fun . . . everyone on this boat seems to be loaded except maybe our blond hustler? The diva will take care of him, anyway, don't you think?'

'I rather think he'll be paying for her,' said Julien with a smile and a raised eyebrow, looking mollified.

He cuts a handsome figure, thought Simon suddenly; might even do pretty well for a certain kind of part. The kind of guy who's about forty, disenchanted but reliable, tough but gentle with women. That sort of thing goes over pretty well nowadays. Except he's got the build of an American . . . that's it: he looks like Stuart Whitman!

'Do you know, you look like Stuart Whitman?' Simon asked.

'Stuart Whitman? What does that have to do with poker?' Julien was surprised.

'You see? You can't think about anything else either! And those three who sit gaping at the moon all through the adagios, they'd be mighty glad to be among men for a change, let me tell you, without their womenfolk. And there's one lady who'd be mighty glad to be without her man. Clarisse.' He had hesitated over the name. In fact he had hesitated between 'the wife of Lethuillier', 'the lady-clown', or 'the alcoholic'. Opting finally for 'Clarisse', he had unwittingly pronounced it as a word of love. He realised it and blushed.

'Well then, let's have your poker game,' said Julien, suddenly affectionate.

And in turn he gave a dry laugh that shook him right down to the Gucci moccasins pinching his toes.

They began the game at three o'clock and played until seven. By then Andreas, who had been winning from nearly everyone, had sixty thousand francs, and had drawn upon himself the hatred and suspicion of all except Julien. They stopped for a drink and began a final round at seven-thirty. In three hands Julien, who held four sevens in the last round, took the sixty thousand from Andreas, who had a full house with aces over kings. The whole thing was carried off with impeccable mastery. By eight o'clock it was all over. The gulls had not had time to shift the object of their displeasure and although he had lost five thousand himself, it was Andreas who drew their rancour, while Julien played the part of the lucky fool. At any rate he told himself he wouldn't play with them again this week. Not one of them was possessed of appropriate sang-froid. Andreas played to earn money to live on. Simon played to prove to himself that he was indeed Simon Béjard, producer—a role too recently assumed not to require occasional certification. Armand Bautet-Lebreche played to verify the possibility of 'playing' with money—and found the whole thing nightmarishly abnormal. As for Eric Lethuillier, he played to win, to prove to himself that he was the winner here as elsewhere, and his fury was the most burdensome of the four. Possessed of a livelier intelligence than the others, he had instantly transferred his animosity from Andreas to Julien. And it was with the knowledge of his hatred and scorn, of his determination to gain revenge one way or another, that Julien watched Eric go off in the direction of his cabin.

*W*hile the men were battling away astutely at cards, or at least thinking they were, the women, along with Charley Bollinger, seemed to have succumbed to the influence of the alcoholic Clarisse Lethuillier. Edma Bautet-Lebreche and Charley, absorbed in a game of Scrabble, filled the bar with girlish laughter, peals of giggling that brought a deep frown to the brow of Captain Elledocq—as well as to that of Olga Lamouroux, the sworn enemy of alcohol, amphetamines, tranquillisers or any other drug capable of altering the personality, particularly her own. At this very moment she sat down near the diva, who with her usual hauteur was sucking a jet-black length of licorice with absolutely no indication that she had downed an entire bottle of Wyborowa vodka. Indeed, she seemed to Olga, who had just come from her cabin where she had been reading about the appalling conditions endured by actresses through the ages, to be the only sober person, the one untainted spirit in the room where the men besotted with their game and the women with alcohol made an ugly spectacle.

'I'll just have a lemonade, thank you,' Olga told the blond barman who had hurried over, and she cast an indulgent eye—ostensibly indulgent—towards Clarisse and Edma, both convulsed by the apparently irresistibly funny word that Charley had put down on the board in a great state of hilarity.

'I fear I'm not up to the mark,' Olga added with a pretence of sadness directed towards la Doriacci.

'I fear it too,' said the latter without stirring.

She was a bit rosier than usual and for once kept her lids lowered across her great ferocious eyes. Olga, deceived by her calm, grew bolder. 'I do not believe you and I are fundamentally capable of any intoxication other than that provided by the stage,' she said with a smile. 'Of course I'm not comparing the two of us, Madame, but all the same we do, you and I, sometimes have to enter the arena of lights, before an audience that expects us to create an illusion . . . That is the one real point of comparison, of course . . .'

She was stammering a little from youthful modesty, from devotion. She felt her cheeks go scarlet, the whites of her eyes almost blue with naive admiration. Though the diva didn't quiver an eyelid Olga knew she was listening, avidly listening to the sincere young voice that told her these touching things, and her impassivity was more revealing than any answer—revealing of la Doriacci's character: the silence was one of emotion, the emotion that of a great lady. Olga felt she was at her best: her throat was choked with humility, all the more so since after all, over the past year, she had played the lead in three little films and received ecstatic reviews for her role in the Klouc play, a role she had created and which had been the sensation of Café-Theatre 79.

She went rushing on: 'When I was a little girl, and I heard you on the radio and on my father's old record-player—Papa was crazy about the opera and my mother was almost jealous of you—when I heard you sing, I told myself that I would give my life to die the way you did in *La*

114

Bohème . . . The way you had of saying that last phrase . . . Now how did it go?'

'I don't know,' said la Doriacci in a hoarse voice. 'I never sang *Bohème*.'

'Oh, but how stupid of me . . . of course, of course. I heard *La Traviata*.' Ouf! That was close! What rotten luck. Every singer had done *La Bohème* except for la Doriacci, of course. It was lucky, on the other hand, that la Doriacci was in such a good humour and so placid. In some circumstances she would have blown up at such a gaffe. But in this case she seemed literally bewitched by Olga's clever compliments. After all she was an ordinary warm-hearted woman—a theatre person . . . Waving her hands above her head as if to dispel the muddling flies in her poor memory, Olga took up again.

'*La Traviata*, naturally . . . goodness. *La Traviata*. I cried like a calf when I listened to it . . . and a great big calf at that! I was at least eight, when you said to him, "Addio, Addio" .'

'A great big calf of twenty-eight, then,' la Diva abruptly thundered. 'I recorded *La Traviata* only last year.'

And throwing her head back, she gave way to a fit of stentorian laughter which was apparently quite contagious, since it was quickly taken up without any knowledge of what prompted it by the three playing Scrabble.

In the grip of her uncontrollable mirth, the diva had taken out her batiste handkerchief, now dabbing at her eyes with it, now waving it about as if calling for help, now gesturing with it towards the petrified Olga. She sobbed more than spoke her indistinct phrases. 'It's this child . . . he, ha, ha! Her father crazy for me . . . Puccini, Verdi, *tutti quanti* . . . This child and her record, ha, ha, ha! A great big calf of twenty-eight, hee, hee, hee! . . .' And when she had repeated for the third time in ringing tones, 'A great big calf of twenty-eight,' she finished in an exhausted voice, 'She said so herself!' At first Olga had laughed nervously, but as the awful explanation progressed, she caught a bitter whiff of vodka, finally saw the huge dark eyes set ablaze by alcohol, recognised the trap she had set for herself. She tried to face it out, but when the three degenerate zombies in the far corner collapsed at their table, hiccupping wildly while the wooden letters rolled onto the floor and their heads rolled against the backs of their chairs; when at that fishwife's last phrase, 'She said so herself!' Edma sat up straight in her chair as though struck by electricity; when the alcoholic wife of that poor Eric Lethuillier hid her face in her hands with a pleading babble, 'Oh no, oh no, oh don't'; when that old queen in uniform hugged his sides as he sat there shaking—at that point Olga Lamouroux, with dignity and without saying a word, simply got up and left the table. She paused for an instant in the doorway and gave the poor drunken derelicts a single pitying glance, whose effect was to double their hilarity. So she was trembling with rage when she entered the cabin. There she found Simon sprawled on his bed in his stocking feet, chuckling because, as he put it, he'd 'lost a few thou at five-card and had a high old time doin' it.'

Eric, on returning from that inauspicious poker game, found the cabin empty, and sent a steward off to find Clarisse. 'You will tell Madame Lethuillier that her husband is waiting for her in his cabin,' he ordered without further explanation, and the steward seemed slightly shocked by his imperative tone. But Eric didn't give a damn. This was not the first time that he had felt and believed he had seen Clarisse slipping away from him, physically as well as mentally. Physically, at any rate, it seemed to him that she was forever disappearing on the pretext of going out for a breath of air, or to look at the sea. And since Eric had arranged with Elledocq—to the delight of this adjutant at heart—to have the bar watched so that Clarisse's presence there would be immediately made known to him, he was ready to believe that she had a lover. It seemed all the more likely when she returned from one of her little walks with heightened colour, looking cheerful, everything about her radiating a sense of feeling carefree, a sense he had spent years in eradicating, or more precisely undermining by making her feel guilty and irresponsible.

At that very moment she came in, her hair in a mess, her make-up smudged by tears of laughter, and the colour of her cheeks confirmed all too clearly her light-heartedness. She stood straight and supple in the doorway, eyes wide and teeth gleaming in a face that was tanned despite the make-up. She was beautiful, thought Eric with sudden fury. It had been a long time, a very long time, since he had seen her as beautiful as this. The last time had been on his account. Who in the world on this ship could have restored her self-confidence if it wasn't Johnnie Walker? Could it be that fellow Julien Peyrat, whose masculine charm seemed rather common? If Eric hadn't seen for himself that Clarisse's escapades coincided with Julien's presence on the sports deck or in the swimming pool, or in the bar, he would have thought so. These ladies' men were very clever. Or else it could that two-bit gigolo, Andreas something-or-other . . . But for all his endlessly nurtured contempt of Clarisse, he knew she had little interest in going to bed with youngsters, particularly one so clearly available.

She gazed at him: 'You were looking for me?'

'Have you been having a good time with your friends?' he asked without replying. 'We could hear you laughing all the way up in the main saloon!'

'I hope we didn't disturb your poker,' she said with an oversolicitous expression.

He shot her a quick glance, which she met with a sleek and civilised look, her 'Dureau daughter' look—the one he had had such difficulty in breaking down, that smoothly impeccable face, so indifferent to anything that did not concern her own comfort, her own ways; the look of the pitilessly triumphant bourgeoisie which he thought he had little by little been teaching her to hate, with a loathing that extended to her own family.

'No,' he said, 'you didn't disturb us. Or, I should say, you didn't disturb the manoeuvres of that pair of cheats.'

'What pair?'

'That cowboy of a trimmer and the gigolo who's with him. They must work the cruise ships together! Why are you laughing?'

'I don't know,' she said, trying to keep from laughing. 'But the idea of those two men as a couple strikes me as funny . . .'

'I'm not saying they sleep together.' Eric was growing irritated. 'I'm telling you that they cheat as a pair. They've actually perfected an unbeatable technique.'

'But they don't even know each other!' said Clarisse. 'I heard them talking about which schools they went to and last night at Porto-Vecchio they even discovered some country place they both knew.'

Eric's laugh betrayed his exasperation. 'Naturally you were right there, weren't you?'

Clarisse suddenly blushed, as though ashamed for them— for Julien in particular, she said to herself. Had it been in order more easily to fleece Eric that Julien Peyrat had left his cabin and liquor supply open to her? This possibility made her disagreeably uncomfortable, almost physically embarrassed, and at the same time vaguely sad. She was sitting on her bed, absently combing her hair in front of the mirror on the closet door, which was open before her. As she arranged the strands of her hair, she scrutinised herself with no apparent pleasure, but with no embarrassment either. Suddenly Eric had a desire to strike her, or to make her get off at the next stop. Yes, she was slipping away from him! She was slipping away from him, but into a void. That was the danger. If there were another man involved, he could have quickly settled it, demolishing him before her eyes. But he really couldn't see who, on this ship, could have reawakened the woman within the somnolent and terrorised creature she had become. Unless perhaps it was Andreas . . .

It seemed impossible, but with a neurotic anything was possible. He tried it out: 'You know you stand absolutely no chance with that sort, my sweet. Don't wear yourself out making all those passes—I know they're modest, but they're ridiculous all the same, and in any case futile: he's busy with other things more profitable or more tempting.'

'But who are you talking about?'

Eric laughed. This was not the first time that he had made a pretence of contempt and exasperated jealousy. To humiliate her further, occasionally he had even pretended to believe she was in love with such pathetic individuals that to pay them any heed whatsoever would have been shameful. And every time Clarisse had panicked and floundered. In the past she had denied his charges with hopeless indignation. She had not been capable of the pleasant, slightly weary tone in which she answered today, 'I don't see who you could be talking about.' All the same she had gone pale. She raised a hand to her throat in a familiar gesture, looking at him with uncertainty, resigned and ready for some new blow but not understanding the reason for it.

No, he was clearly mistaken. She had no interest in that gigolo, that was something. Reassured, he flashed a little smile that was calculated to reassure her as well.

'So much the better,' he said. 'After all, he must be nearly ten years younger than you. Much too young,' he added before burying himself in his newspaper, not overly proud of what he had said.

He would have been even less satisfied had he seen the expression of relief on the face of his clown-wife, and the bloom that returned to her cheeks along with the oxygen, the blood, the hope.

In the bathroom ten minutes later, Clarisse violently doused her face in cold water, trying to forget that instant of happiness, or to give it another name. She was trying to deny that in some way she had been close to despair at the idea that Julien Peyrat had been attracted by another woman, for whatever reason, even though he barely looked at her when they were face to face. That very morning there had been a red rose awaiting her in the glass beside the bottle of Haig in Cabin 106—and now, thanks to Eric, she was surprised at having found that simply charming.

*T*hey had almost reached Capri where, according to the programme, the passengers were to have a *vol-au-vent* Curnonsky, two Mozart sonatas and several Schumann *Lieder*, and later that evening, for the more adventurous, a tour of the island. It was the general rule aboard the *Narcissus* not to go ashore at ports of call. Everyone was assumed to be already familiar with the celebrated ports, perhaps even to have explored them by private yacht—as Edma Bautet-Lebreche was in the midst of explaining to Simon Béjard, still green enough to profess to some enthusiasm for these splendid towns. He had hoped that his interest in culture—or at least for cultural matters—would be seen in his favour, whereas in fact it should have discredited him because it implied the resolute non-culture of poverty. But oddly enough this thought process had become so prevalent and was so automatically taken for granted on this ship that Simon struck Edma as naive and original, a good sort.

'You don't know the Mediterranean basin at all, Monsieur

Béjard?' Edma Bautet-Lebreche inquired with an astonished solicitude—as if he had declared that he had never had appendicitis. 'Well, then, you will discover it all at once!' There was a note of envy in her voice, mixed with overtones of pity. 'You know, the Mediterranean is really wonderful,' she assured him, stressing the word with light-hearted affectation. 'Altogether wonderful,' she repeated more quietly, in a tone that was almost tender.

'Well, I'm sure it is,' said Simon, an indefatigable optimist. 'After all, it must be, mustn't it? Pottin didn't put together a cruise at these prices to show us derelict gas plants, eh?'

'Of course not,' admitted Edma, a little disappointed nevertheless by such down-to-earth logic. 'Of course not . . . Tell me, dear friend . . . May I call you Simon? . . . Tell me, Simon,' the impatient Edma began once more. 'What did you expect to get out of this cruise? I mean, why are you here? That intrigues me.'

'Me too,' said Simon, suddenly pensive. 'I really don't know what I'm doing here . . . To begin with it was to . . . to . . . well, I guess Olga didn't like Eden Roc or Saint-Tropez, so . . . And then after all, it's strange, I didn't think I'd enjoy this cruise, but when you come down to it, it isn't bad, is it? Not bad, what they play in the evenings. Really not bad at all . . .'

I was both amused and appalled, Edma would later recall in her drawing room on the avenue Foch. But I was also vaguely touched, I admit. Yes, yes, yes . . . (Edma often found herself countering nonexistent objections.) Yes, yes, I was touched. Because, well . . . there he was, a simple man actually, a little *arriviste*, living for money, by money, with money, a peasant, you know? And quite by chance, or rather thanks to the snobbery of the starlet who was taking advantage of him, there he was discovering music . . . great music. There he was, somehow moved, glimpsing a sort of *terra incognita* . . . a port of call he hadn't foreseen . . . Here Edma's voice would drop to a whisper, and a far-away look would come into her eyes as she gazed at the glow of the hearth fire—if, of course, there happened to be one.

At the time, however, it was not just understanding that prompted Edma, but also a talent for irony, and she

122

regretted there were not more spectators to witness her performance.

'So at first you thought you would prefer Saint-Tropez, Simon dear? You must be a little bored on this ship. After all, without your own set . . . And I don't mean to be insulting, believe me. Each of us has his or her own set.'

'I can imagine . . . You can't be much better off than I am on that score,' said Simon with what, to Edma's way of thinking, was excessive conviction.

'Then it's your little Olga who loves classical music, if I'm not mistaken? At her age, I too felt these cravings, these desires for everything, like all young people, but I didn't struggle against them. I even felt a sort of pride in my desires, my fantasies. And God knows . . .'

She fluttered a hand exhausted by forty years of revelry and debauch. She could not thus demur or take offence when Simon exclaimed with the same conviction, emphasised by a faint suggestive whistle: 'Ah, I can well imagine!', leaving Edma astonished, suspicious, but vaguely flattered.

At this point Charley arrived under full sail—which is to say his silk shirt spread to the wind. For as the ship progressed across the longitudes he relaxed and his nature blossomed with the heat; having begun the journey wearing stiff collar and navy blue uniform, he generally arrived at Palma, the last port of call, wearing a striped shirt and espadrilles, indeed with a single gold ring in his left ear, for piratical effect.

But this was only the third stop, and he limited his extravagance by exchanging his blue blazer for a jacket of off-white surah. He was obviously overjoyed.

'And here we are in Capri!' he said. 'Monsieur Béjard, are you going ashore too? I think that practically the whole ship will go dancing for a while, just this once . . . after the recital, of course,' he added piously.

Indeed, unlike other excursions to shore which the passengers generally shunned, Capri conferred a sort of licence to 'go native' of which they discreetly took advantage, each pretending to go, for fun, in search of a body-mate—a body-sister, brother, or cousin—as if admitting their

123

purpose were enough to negate it from the start, as if each one of those still of an age to do so were not dreaming, before facing dangerous Arabs or ferocious Spaniards, of an Italian idyll. Capri was where civilisation ended and debauchery began—but a decent sort of debauchery nevertheless. So at Capri it was not unusual for the ship to be quite empty at night, or nearly so—there were always a few elderly passengers being watched by nurses, a few sailors confined to ship. Like children being punished, both categories were obliged to stay on deck and see from a distance the bright lights of the town and its pleasures. They also had to put up with the heavy tread of Captain Elledocq who throughout the stopover paced up and down the deck in a state of rage and anxiety, still devastated, like the ghost in *Hamlet*, by a remote but distinctly remembered image. Were he to set foot on the Piazzetta he was absolutely certain that he would always be confronted with the image of Charley: Charley in a gypsy skirt, a carnation between his teeth, bending to the embrace of a rough Capriot!

'You bet I'm going,' said Simon Béjard, all the more firmly since for two days running Olga had insisted that he do nothing of the sort. 'Of course I'm going. I've never been to Capri! But before the fun begins, I'm going to get some chow,' he added, jovially patting his belly, while elegant Edma and sensitive Charley averted their eyes. 'After all, it could turn out to be quite a lark,' he said as he got up.

Against the setting sun, the pinks of his shirt and on his sunburned cheeks made an arresting cameo that bordered on the tragic.

'Why particularly larkish?' inquired Edma whose curiosity always outdid her disdain and who always reproached herself afterwards for her trivial questions—though less so than if she had not secured a reply.

'It could be a real farce,' explained Simon cheerfully. 'Since with nearly all the couples aboard, there's one partner who wants to go ashore while the other doesn't. And what's more we're all eating at the same table tonight, so there could be quite an uproar . . .'

In fact since the first night the guests had automatically

124

sat in just about the same places. But this time they were to be around the extended table of the captain since Elledocq's table had suddenly risen in prestige, outclassing Charley's, thanks to the Doriacci/Kreuze fracas.

'But,' said Edma, 'you are quite mistaken. Armand Bau . . . my husband is altogether delighted to be seeing Capri again.'

'Your husband is a different matter,' said Simon with a comic bow. 'Your husband never takes his eyes off you, he's mad about you . . . He's Othello, that man. Understandably, eh, my friend?' he added with a mighty clap on Charley's back, which jolted him painfully, while Edma Bautet-Lebreche appeared disinclined to take the compliment at its full value. 'But leaving aside you two, the leftish intellectual wants to go, but Clarisse isn't interested. I'm going and Olga doesn't want to. La Doriacci is on her way and her kitten seems to be hesitating. Elledocq isn't going and Charley can't wait to get there!'

He hadn't noticed the little grimace of pain, this time genuine, that had twisted Charley's upper lip at the mention of one of the couples, but Edma—sharp-eyed and kindly—hastened to make amends for the gaffe. She could see that Charley Bollinger had got off to a very bad start on this cruise. Beautiful Andreas, the handsome gigolo—who became more and more handsome every day—was literally fascinated by the diva, her extravagance and her excesses. He trotted along behind her like a pet tomcat, carried her bags, her fans, her shawls—and she didn't seem to be in the least bit aware of him. As far as being a gigolo was concerned, it looked as if he had got off to a bad start, and Charley was no more successful as the satisfied lover.

'Come now,' she said. 'Don't make yourself out to be more naive than you are, Monsieur Béjard—Simon, I beg your pardon. You know very well that the heart of young Andreas is guided by professional motives, and you're not really going to describe that wild beast Elledocq and our sweet Charley as a couple, are you?'

'But that's not what I meant . . .' said Simon, turning towards Charley with a worried look. 'I didn't mean to suggest that!' he repeated warmly. 'You know that, my friend . . . All the women on board are mad about you, so I have no need to defend myself. Ah, how lucky you are to be the purser on this ship full of women with too much leisure on their hands. I wouldn't know how high your score is, old man, but I bet it's good, eh? Am I wrong? You're quite a guy, aren't you?' he added with another vigorous slap.

And he went off laughing—to change, as he announced with an importance that left his auditors perplexed.

'I only like spaghetti cooked *al dente*. How about you, my dear?'

'So do I.' Armand Bautet-Lebreche barely had time discreetly to adjust his dentures before sadly concurring with la Doriacci.

For the past five minutes she had been watching him eat with alarming concentration—or it would have been alarming to anyone else, anyone who had not, like Armand, been immersed for the past three hours in a comparative evaluation of the fluctuating stock prices of Engine Frères, Inc. and Mech-Tech Steel Corporation.

'*Al dente*, does that mean uncooked?' Simon Béjard enquired in a triumphant voice.

By some miracle of hair lotion he had impeccably flattened his stubborn red hair onto his pink skull; he was at his most elegant in a dark-blue and sea-green plaid dinner jacket, and he smelled at ten paces of Lanvin aftershave. Even the discreet Clarisse, who was sitting next to him, seemed somewhat put off. On the positive side, it must be said that Simon's very personal and very prized triumph did have the advantage of preventing him from seeing the looks that passed at table between Eric Lethuillier and his beautiful Olga. They had met up at the door to the bar an hour earlier, and Eric looked irresistible in his beige linen jacket, his shirt and trousers the pale blue of faded jeans, his handsome face tanned by the sun and his Prussian blue eyes at once amused and authoritative. 'I'll see you again ashore tonight,' he had said between his teeth, taking her by the

126

elbow and pressing her arm in a grip of such virile strength that it hurt. *Desire made him clumsy*, Olga told herself, immediately in gear. *He smiled, but he was trembling, he had that awkwardness, so touching and at the same time so troubling, that ill-restrained ardour prompts in mature men.*

That last sentence had so captivated her that she hurriedly went down to her cabin and committed it to her diary, a fat journal with a lock which she hid in her suitcase and which she mistakenly imagined to be the object of countless searches on Simon's part. Consequently she had arrived late for dinner, out of breath, her hair a little untidy and under her tan a slight look of guilt that emphasised her youthfulness. Her dining companions had looked at her with admiration—an admiration of varying degrees, to be sure, but quite genuine. 'A fine slip of a girl, that wench,' Elledocq muttered between his teeth, yet loud enough so that la Doriacci heard it and, with the sole aim of annoying him, asked him, at the top of her lungs, to repeat it. He blushed, and his bad temper worsened when Edma Bautet-Lebreche, with a sly and conspiratorial look, asked him for a light.

'I don't smoke!' he thundered in the midst of an untoward silence, drawing upon himself several glances of ironic severity. He had to make the best of Edma's gracious reply.

Ostensibly taken aback, but smiling all the while, she murmured in a disarming voice: 'That doesn't prevent you from offering me a light!'

He grimaced once again while the swashbuckling Julien Peyrat held out his lighter to the poor victim of his aggression. With that, the conversation took off in diverging directions, all of them incomprehensible to the captain. They touched on the intelligence of dolphins, the arcana of politics, the bad faith of the Russians and the budget scandals at the Ministry of Culture; the conversation was scintillating right through dessert. Thereupon, under whatever pretext, they all went down to their cabins for a last touch of the comb so that they could dash off right after the concert to that carnal isle known as Capri. To Elledocq's great surprise, the only man left at his table who had apparently decided not to join the libidinous band was Julien Peyrat. He asked the captain several pertinent questions about navigation, about the *Narcissus*, about their ports of call and so forth, thereby rising remarkably in the esteem of the ship's master. Naturally this manly conversation, for once of some interest and stripped of hypocritical nonsense, had to be interrupted by the concert. But the captain's scarcely veiled allusion to the 'forced labour' side of this recital seemed to fall on deaf ears. Either this sympathetic and apparently normal fellow really liked music—in which case he ceased to be normal in Elledocq's eyes—or else he was playing an odd sort of game. Half won over, half distrustful, Elledocq followed him with a heavy heart to the place of sacrifice.

La Doriacci began the concert with an air of haste, sang two or three arias at top speed but with incredible technique and vivacity, came to a dead halt in the middle of one *lied* and went onto another without so much as an excuse, but with a small, conniving smile that earned her more applause than all the preceding demonstration of her vocal art, dazzling though it had been. Kreuze followed with a seemingly interminable work of Scarlatti, impeccably played but to so little effect (however commendable) that, to his unexpected indignation, Elledocq's passengers began stealing away one after another, until just those from first class were left. The other confirmed concert-goers had deserted this high altar of music. Saluted by meagre applause, Kreuze bowed as though to a throng, his haughtiness for once justified, and disappeared in the direction of his cabin, followed by Armand Bautet-Lebreche, who seemed quite overjoyed to be on his own. After Elledocq in his turn had wandered off, there remained at the edge of the glowing arena only two pensive silhouettes, separated by a few rows of chairs—those of Julien Peyrat and Clarisse Lethuillier.

*J*ulien sat immobile in his chair, head thrown back to watch the stars overhead, their twinkling, and then from time to time their sudden, beautiful tumbling descent, absurd and unexpected as certain suicides. Without looking he saw her get up after the barman had put out the four glowing spotlights. He followed her with his eyes as she moved towards the bar. He did not move, but he was waiting. Without the slightest premeditation, it seemed to him that their presence on the deck alone at this hour had come about by long-standing agreement, that there was something fateful in the solitude of the deck and in their silence. They were headed somewhere together; where, he was certain she knew no more than he. Perhaps towards a brief and abortive adventure, punctuated by frantic sobs and protestations, perhaps towards a shamefully savage act, perhaps towards silent tears on his shoulder. At any rate ever since the cocktail party on arrival they had had some hazy appointment—ever since he had seen her stumble, looking ridiculous, grotesque in her garish make-up, leaning without confidence on the arm of her too-handsome spouse. She was scared, that much he knew. But he also knew, with a certainty untainted by the slightest arrogance, that she would return to sit beside him. It was not even a need for him, Julien, that would bring her to his side; it was the need for someone, anyone at all but the civilised brute she had married. He breathed slowly and deeply, as he would before sitting down to a table of chemin de fer or beginning a dangerously rigged game of poker, as he would before deliberately driving too fast or introducing himself under an assumed name to people who might well recognise him and call his bluff. He was breathing as though in the face of danger, he thought, and this made him laugh. No woman had ever seemed a danger to him before now—not even those who later turned out to be just that.

It was half an hour before Clarisse came and sat next to him—a half-hour she spent drinking, silently and intently, in front of a waiter who was intimidated by her. Surprisingly so, for Clarisse Lethuillier generally caused bartenders to smile either ironically or with pity, depending on the place, the time, and the number of drinks she had been served. She was smoking too, in great violent puffs which she exhaled immediately in long childish jets, as if she had learned to smoke only that morning. But she put out each of the cigarettes with a look of annoyance after three or four of these quasi-inhalations. She had ground out twenty of them and drunk three double whiskys when she left the bar, leaving a much too generous tip for the waiter, who was strangely worried about her. He liked Clarisse very much, as did the other members of the ship's staff for that matter. Like themselves, she seemed to exist in a state of official inferiority to the rest of the passengers. She stumbled slightly against a chair in the semi-darkness as she reached Julien, and he got up instinctively, more out of concern to hold her up than out of courtesy. She collapsed onto the chair next to his, looked him in the face and suddenly began to laugh. Her hair was a mess, she was even a bit drunk, he thought with a moralising sadness that he didn't recognise in himself.

'You didn't go to Capri with the others? It didn't sound like fun?' he asked softly, as he helped her pick up her purse and the various objects from the jumble within it that now lay gleaming at their feet: a gold compact that must have cost a fortune, too heavy for her, with her initials inlaid in small gems on the lid, a matching lipstick case, some keys from who knew where, a few crumpled franc notes, the photo of an anonymous chateau on a postcard, a tin of cigarettes, a crushed packet of Kleenex, and the inevitable box of mints, the only thing she tried to hide from him.

'Thank you,' she said, sitting up again very quickly, though not quickly enough to prevent him from catching along with her perfume—a persistent, lively one—the fragrance of her body, warmed all day by the sun, and as if spiced by the faintest odour of fear, that Julien instantly recognised as it was familiar to gamblers.

'No,' she said, 'Capri doesn't amuse me . . . Well, it doesn't amuse me any more. And yet, I did have a very good time there once, long ago . . .'

She was looking straight in front of her, and she had demurely crossed her wrists on her knees, as if he had invited her to a conference and she would be in her seat for several hours.

'I've never been there,' said Julien. 'But it was one of my abiding dreams when I was eighteen or nineteen. I wanted to be decadent . . . That's odd, isn't it, for a boy of eighteen? I wanted to live like Oscar Wilde, with Afghan hounds, never-ending De Dion-Boutons, and to race Italian horses in the hippodrome at Capri.'

Clarisse began to laugh just as he did, and he went on, encouraged. 'Of course I didn't know that Capri is a sugar loaf with no flat surfaces, and I didn't know either that Oscar Wilde didn't like women. I think it might be that double disappointment that has kept me from coming here until now, and perhaps the memory is what prevents me from going ashore today.'

'For me it's the memories,' she said. 'I was a great success here socially when I was nineteen or twenty. Even here in Italy everyone knew about the Dureau fortune, and

131

everybody courted me constantly. And at that time there was nothing shameful in being an heiress . . .'

'There isn't now, I trust,' said Julien lightly. 'It is no more shameful to be born rich than poor, so far as I know.'

'I believe it is,' she said seriously. 'For instance,' she said, suddenly voluble, 'you who are an art appraiser, you must like paintings, don't you? Doesn't it break your heart to sell masterpieces to people who are already rich but who dream only of becoming still richer by buying those canvases? And who will lock them up in a vault as soon as they get them home, without even looking at them?'

'They don't all do that,' said Julien.

But she cut him off without listening. 'My grandfather Pasquier, for instance, had a superb collection of Impressionists. He brought them all for a song, naturally—Utrillos, Monets, Vuillards, Pissarros . . . all for three francs, so he said. The rich are always getting bargains, have you noticed? They practically get away with paying less than the concierge for bread. And what's more, they're proud of it.'

She began to laugh, but Julien was silent, and she turned to face him directly, as if irritated. 'You don't believe me?'

'I don't believe in generalities,' said Julien. 'I have known some charming rich people and some infamous ones.'

'Well then, you were lucky,' she said, her voice harsh with anger.

She got up and went towards the ship's rail, standing a bit too erect as if to compensate for her alcoholic unsteadiness. Julien automatically followed and leaned against the rail next to her. When he turned towards her he realised she was crying openly. Great tears ran down her cheeks apparently without her noticing—tears that, oddly, he guessed to be hot merely from their form: drawn-out tears, trickling, oblong, tears of anger that resembled the puffs from her cigarettes, tears that lacked roundness, that full and almost serene quality of studied smoke rings or the tears of children who have been disappointed.

'Why are you crying?' he said.

She settled against him, with her head on his shoulder,

as she might have leaned against a tree or a lamp-post or whatever happened to be there.

Except for the light from the bar that shone onto the deck where they had been a moment before, an oblique light that was blurred, furtive, and uncertain, they were in darkness. Only the beam from the lighthouse on the island occasionally cut through the dark, resting on their faces for two or three econds before continuing its maniacal revolutions. But each time it showed Julien no more than the top of Clarisse's head, so obstinately, with such goatlike stubbornness did she keep it lowered against his shoulder, while her own shoulders shook with small periodic spasms almost serene in their regularity. It was both a bewildered and a peaceful sorrow, a sorrow that came from the depths of time, and also a sorrow without cause. It was a purposeless and inextinguishable sorrow, a madness and a resignation. And to his surprise, Julien by degrees felt imbued by the calm shamelessness of it, by her not trying to explain it while she went on sobbing against his shoulder, he who was a stranger to her. There was a silence, finally, worse than any possible explanation, broken only by her sniffling and the sound of the Kleenex being pulled out with the rough gesture of an adolescent to mop up her tears.

'Come on,' he said, disturbed, leaning towards that over-burdened head. 'Come on, you mustn't cry like that. It's idiotic, it's not good for you,' he added stupidly. 'Why are you crying like this?' he insisted in a whisper.

'It's . . . totally idiotic . . .' she said, turning her face towards him. 'Idiotic . . . But I am idiotic.'

Just then the beacon from the lighthouse crossed her face and the effect on Julien was devastating. Her make-up had succumbed to the tears and Kleenex, and like the ramparts of a city it had crumbled and fallen away. From behind the thick, baroque, almost obscene greasepaint emerged a superb new countenance, until now unknown, outlined and highlighted by the blurry bar light in an implacably tragic way that few faces could have withstood. It was the face of a Eurasian, with perfect bone structure and enormous eyes, even without mascara extending from the nose to the temple, their colour the pale blue of a pack of Gauloises. Beneath them he made out a strongly defined mouth, the top lip beautifully arched, the bottom lip full and sad, a mouth moist from crying. Julien found himself kissing that mouth, bending over it, nuzzling the hair of this mad and drunken woman whose madness was all of a sudden completely immaterial so engrossed was he by the mouth. It was such a determined accessory to his own—so friendly, obliging, generous, demanding, artful. A real mouth, he said to himself in the darkness, the way they were twenty-five years ago when I was twenty and kissed girls through car windows, knowing that things would go no further, that those kisses were the height of all pleasures accessible to me, that in fact those kisses would later leave me no less filled with happiness than sick with longing.

In the years since there had been many mouths and many kisses, kisses of promise spent kisses—kisses before and kisses after, but all of them part of a sequence. Since then there had never been, not once, another of those pointless, gratuitous, kisses, ends in themselves, removed from time, removed from life, removed almost from sex and from the heart itself—those kisses born of the pure desire of one mouth for another. It was the taste of 'the green, confined, greedy kisses of youth'—a description from Montaigne that had once moved him—that he was rediscovering here, tonight, on the mouth of a slightly tipsy socialite. It was laughable, but at the same time he could not tear himself away from that mouth. He tipped his head to the right and to the left following the movements of her neck, and there remained for him—despite his own absurd position, bent over, with a crick in his back—only one idea, one purpose: never again to separate himself from this mouth which he was mentally describing, complimenting, cloaking with epithets—fraternal, maternal, corrupting, confiding, forever his . . .

'Wait,' she said finally.

She tore herself away from him and leaned against the railing, her head back, looking up at him. He could not draw away or take his eyes off her, nor move out of the darkness, for that would have been to shatter something, something infinitely fragile that ought to have been unshatterable. She would regain possession of herself, forget to be beautiful, or else he would forget to desire her so avidly. Something trembled between them in the pale light, something that would vanish if they took their eyes off one another for a single instant.

'Move just a little,' he said. 'Over here.'

He guided her towards the wall outside the bar and leaned her up against it, steadying her in his arms, in effect placing her in the shelter of his body. He felt breathless, his heart was beating too slowly, and it seemed to him vaguely that he could only catch his breath at Clarisse's mouth. But he could no longer move, nor undoubtedly could she, since in the dark she could see Julien offering her, as a blind man or a child might have, his impatient and triumphant face, which she did not push away.

He was gazing at the white blur of this face, at once so remote and so near, now indistinct yet so recently revealed, this face so menacing and so alluring in its proximity, this face already a memory of itself, whose picture he had already filed away forever exactly as he had seen it an instant before by the rail, as he bent towards it, a face seen at precisely that angle, in precisely that light, a face he would never again see just as it was and that already he allowed himself to grieve for, impertinently, furtively, in preference to the thousand other faces that awaited him within that white blur, that indeterminate spot that could have been nothing to him. That would have been nothing were it not for the mouth beneath his and the camera of desire that had immediately snapped.

It was in fact life that was breathing in front of Julien, the life of feelings, the possibility granted that life of being happy or unhappy; the risk also of having no further value of its own, only the value conferred on it by the eye of another: of Clarisse herself. This independent eye, a stranger to Julien and to his childhood, indifferent, ignorant of the secrets still lying between Julien and himself after many long years, still being amassed and carefully concealed, not

135

necessarily out of cowardice but often out of decency or even kindness—all those barriers, those veils, those accommodations which Julien had introduced between his life and his own view of it, masks and grimaces that had become instinctive, more real perhaps in their rejection of truth and more profound in their taste for lying than many other instincts rooted in childhood and regarded as natural. Already he balked at renouncing those masks, at tearing them away, even with the help of another. He balked at the thought of erasing, under pretext of sharing, of sincerity, every trace of that shameful and guilty cohabitation with himself. Unless—and this would be perhaps the worst that might happen and also the most desirable—the inadmissible liaison he had within himself were to remain unacknowledged. These cardboard masks would be kissed full on the mouth, this lifeless toupee would be stroked by warm hands; but there, he was convinced, within the shelter of his own make-believe, he would be bored, he would not love, he would be safe.

Already won over to this last hypothesis, so atrocious and so likely, Julien sighed with relief, almost regretting the happy moment when he might have burned all bridges, unburdened his heart and allowed someone to give meaning to his life; a tone, a pitch, a key. Then instantly Julien, thinking of himself as having missed out on love, and devastated by this inability of his to love, an infirmity almost glorious because acquired on the fields of battle; Julien, there in the dark, with eyes closed, offered up his face, both impatient and triumphant.

But the time it took Clarisse's face to approach him was time enough for Julien to regret the love he was missing. If he were to love, his future would be filled with people; streets, beaches, the sun, cities would once more become real and even desirable, since they were there to show one another, to share with each other. The earth he had seen as round became flat once more, open to view as the palm of a hand; there were concerts, museums re-opened, planes resumed their flights. And if he were to love, it would be as easy for him to share all these treasures as to forget them deliberately, to reject them in favour of a hotel room, a bed, a face. If he were to love, his past—that slightly old-fashioned but decent story that couldn't be told, which had died along with his mother, the only person who had cared right to the end to tell him about his own childhood, to lift it above the commonplace and make of it a series of unique events—his past would come back to life all on its own and come forward, impetuous and intransigent as the adolescent he would struggle to describe and re-create however inaccurate or duplicitous his memories.

But in the end Julien would never be more sincere than in his lies, since these distortions in trying to seduce Clarisse would reveal what was in his own eyes seductive. What he would depict through this false archetype of an adolescent was the adult he had become. For surely it was his dreams that he was bringing to light, his dreams and his regrets, the sole irrefutable means by which a man is revealed, landmarks far more reliable than reality, reality which like some dubious trophy always finishes up as facts on the pages of a calendar, facts to be dated, certified, recognised by the bureaucratic dotards of memory or moral judgment. But for Julien false tales and anecdotes were the means to recount his real life, a life of the senses, a life he could show had its own logic, one that was full, admirable and happy. Because for Julien not least among the forces of love was that which would make him present repeatedly to his loved one the image of a happy man. He wished to be fortunate, joyous, free, strong. To have been loved for his misfortunes would have seemed to him an insult to his manhood, since Julien enjoyed the duties just as much as the pleasures of love. It was while he was considering this generous and sentimental image of himself that Clarisse brushed his lips with a kiss.

Only when she pulled away did the earth lurch and everything became at once possible and diabolical: since Clarisse, already in flight, had been the first to speak, and as she ran towards the light, she said: 'We mustn't ever start that up again.'

The ground heaved slightly under the passengers' feet after just three days at sea. 'We'll have fun simply trying to stand upright by the time we get back home,' Simon Béjard observed. Edma Bautet-Lebreche, though always somewhat put off by the way he framed his remarks, nevertheless showed vague approbation of their content. After the futile and distant commentaries of her fashionable friends, such bluff common sense, expressed in crudely jovial terms, seemed very comforting to her. And even quite compassionate since Simon Béjard's rude jokes weren't the least bit mean. In short, to Edma Simon Béjard was not far from representing 'the people'—whom she did not know and from whom she had been separated as much if not more by an assiduously bourgeois childhood than by the luxury of her marriage. Moreover, in their extreme naiveté Simon Béjard's enthusiasm was contagious, and by moments even touching.

'This is really something!' he said in the horse-drawn carriage that was taking him, Charley and Edma to the

Piazzetta at a slow trot. Olga and Eric had said they preferred to go by taxi. 'Now this is a gorgeous spot! I'm going
to come and make a movie here, I really am!' he mumbled
with a resurgence of professional dedication even if with no
great conviction, since for once Simon was thinking not in
terms of usefulness but of pleasure.

'Isn't it beautiful?' said Edma, flattered, since she had
instantly appropriated Capri and all its charms. 'Pretty impressive, don't you think?' she added with that tic of the
worldly—and of some intellectuals—who tack a little restric-
tive adverb onto a flamboyant adjective. Thus Edma thought
Hitler 'rather dreadful' and Shakespeare 'quite brilliant'. In
any event her 'pretty impressive' seemed weak to Simon.

'I've never seen anything like it,' he said. 'The sea's like
a gorgeous whore!'

Edma flinched. But it was true, the sea was displaying
itself like a courtesan in all her finery—from midnight blue
to aquamarine, from flaming purples to shameless pinks,
from black to steel grey, languishing in these hues mixed
with self-indulgence, and in the no doubt solitary pleasures
of which the murky, shimmering surface gave no inkling.

'What do you think of the Piazzetta, Simon?'

'I can't see a thing,' he grumbled. For the well-lit Piazzetta was crammed with shorts, Kodaks and rucksacks,
and he could find neither Olga nor Eric.

'They must be at the Quisisana. The hotel bar is the only
quiet place. Let's go. Coming, Simon?'

But they were neither at the Quisisana nor at Number 2,
nor anywhere at all, Simon observed with growing irritability that gradually changed to disappointment and then to
grief. He had dreamed of seeing Capri with Olga, of mingling the dreams of his childhood with the reality of adult-
hood. He grew all the sadder as Edma and Charley, at first
optimistic and reassuring, began to sound more and more
sorry for him, speaking to him affectionately, laughing
louder and louder as his jokes became rarer if not lighter.

'They must have gone back on board,' said Edma as they
came out of their sixth nightclub, sitting down on a low wall

to rest her tired legs. 'I'm exhausted,' she said. 'We ought to get back too. They must be waiting for us.'

'Poor things! They're probably even furious,' Simon said bitterly. 'And we'll have to apologise! I'm whacked too,' he admitted, sitting down next to Edma.

'I'll get you something to drink from across the way,' Charley offered, though the consoling of someone else's pain did nothing for his own. Despite his indiscreet questions he had found no trace of Andreas. And yet he couldn't have gone unnoticed, not a beauty like him, and on the arm of la Doriacci. He would take advantage of his mission to question Pablo, the barman at Number 2 who always knew what was going on in Capri.

So Charley went off at his somewhat overly youthful dancing pace, though the set of his head did not correspond with that step; it showed no gaiety, and Edma knew why. Oh, how strange it was, this fiesta at Capri with these two broken hearts . . . For once she congratulated herself on her voluntary chastity. Well, if not voluntary, at any rate deliberate.

Eric paid the driver, and Olga and he plunged with no concerted plan into the crooked little streets of Capri. Eric remembered a beautiful spot that overlooked the sea just a step or two from the Quisisana. He paused for a moment at the hotel, conferred with the concierge, then returned to Olga looking disturbed. For all his being an inveterate cad, Eric still believed some little sentimental preamble was called for, that he couldn't decently drag a young actress off to bed without at least a bit of sweet talk. And the young actress expected no less: *It was so moving, Fernande, to see this man, so sure of himself and of his success with women, after all, to see him be so roundabout in confessing such a simple thing—his desire. It's because this man is part of that exquisite generation—a generation ultimately more manly than any other—which does not consider the body of a woman already won the instant it is found pleasing. We stood there on the terrace for ten minutes exchanging banalities before he could bring himself to say it. Can you believe? . . . I was moved to tears.*

In fact Olga, accustomed to more expeditious habits—

140

particularly in movie circles, where confirmed heterosexuals pounced on one another as rarities—had been afraid at first that Eric might be impotent. And when he said, 'I want you,' in that falsely casual tone, a tone in which she thought she detected, beneath the self-control, a vibration of desire, she said to herself a bit ironically, That's ten minutes wasted. An hour later, she would be entitled to feel the whole hour had been wasted—so expeditious had Eric proved to be, so brutal and ill-tempered, so little attentive to her own pleasure. If he had not been the publisher of *Forum*, she might even have dismissed him with a vulgar insult. But the aura of his background was such that she found his vigour admirable, his haste touching. Eric himself was dressed again in two minutes, pleased with his conquest easy though it had been, and already wondering how Clarisse could be apprised of it. But Olga stopped him at the door with a hand on his shoulder. He turned around in surprise.

'What is it?'

She fluttered her eyelashes, dropped her eyes and murmured, 'It was divine, Eric . . . really divine.'

'We must do it again,' he declared politely and without the slightest conviction.

They had made love in the dark, and he could not have said how she was put together. Olga had to insist before he would stop for a bottle of Chianti with her on the terrace of the hotel.

*A*ndreas had imagined himself dancing, indeed with abandon, perhaps the tango or the jerk, in some nightclub. Instead he found himself in a totally deserted cove where a warm and transparent sea lapped at the shore in the darkness. 'We're going swimming,' la Doriacci had said, and he was amazed to see her take off her shoes, her dress, and remove her combs. Her pudgy form passed indistinctly before his eyes, a white blur, as she went down to paddle about in the sea with happy cries. Not for an instant did he imagine what interior strength had been needed for this woman to expose herself, naked, even in the dark, to eyes she considered critical. Those eyes were so no longer. Had she weighed twice as much, had she perhaps even been ugly, Andreas would not have seen it. For three days he had been shot through with a feeling that closely resembled devotion and which he well knew would not help him prove his manhood. The greasepaint, the hang of her garments, the bearing of la Doriacci herself had filled him until now with a respectful terror, so when he saw her frolicking in the water with clumsy gestures, the marmoreal face covered with wet hair and the ringing voice reduced to a few high squeals occasioned by the cold, Andreas's terror gave way to his protective instincts. He undressed and ran to join la Doriacci in the sea, gathering her into his arms and bringing her back onto the beach—this time decisively, like the old trooper he had not managed to be for the last twenty-four hours.

Afterwards they lay there a long time on the beach, perfectly comfortable and content despite the unpleasant cold touch of the sand and the intermittent shivers that made them squeeze close together like schoolchildren.

'Did you do that on purpose?' he asked in a low voice.

'Do what on purpose?'

She turned towards him smiling. He could see the sparkle of her teeth and the mass of her shoulders and her head against the clear sky.

'Take out your combs on purpose,' he said.

She shook her head. 'I never do anything on purpose except when I sing,' she said. 'Apart from that I have never agreed to do anything whatsoever on purpose.'

'I have,' he said naively. 'You can't imagine how ashamed I've been.'

'You men are so stupid,' she declared, lighting a cigarette and putting it in his mouth. 'You have such notions about love . . . Do you even know what a good lover is, I mean, for us women?'

'No,' said Andreas, intrigued.

'A man who considers us a good mistress, that's all. Who is in the same mood as we are when we make love—sad if we're sad, happy if we're happy and not the opposite. All that business about technique is pure fiction,' she said with assurance. 'Who taught you what you know about women?'

'My mother and my aunt,' Andreas said.

She burst out laughing, but then listened to him with attention and, finally, a sort of maternal affection, while he told of his peculiar childhood. Still she refused, despite his entreaties, to tell him about her own. She likes people to unburden themselves but she won't do the same, thought

Andreas with a melancholy not deep enough to diminish his sense of well-being or his feeling of triumph.

$\mathcal{T}$hey ran into Olga and Eric as they reached the gangway. Dawn was not far off in the skies, nor drunkenness from the deck where Edma, Simon, and Charley were waiting.

The four of them moved towards the rocking chairs, la Doriacci and Andreas visibly pleased with each other—though she had released her hand from the young man's grasp—but with the innocent air born of pleasure, which was in curious contrast to the guilt of the two others. Eric's cold, stilted look could not offset the submissive and virginal rectitude veiling Olga's face—an attitude so deliberately angelic that it seemed a declaration bordering on insult. At least that's what Charley and Edma thought, and they hastily lowered their eyes as if Simon might have observed the certainty reflected there and been obliged to react. But Simon had drunk too much, and was too befuddled, and the declaration, however clear, seemed to him unwilled. It was something he would set to rights in private, though he was

145

not sure he had the courage to do so. Here and now, he felt guilty simply *knowing*. Olga sat down next to him with a false little smile, and Eric reluctantly sat down beside Edma, who didn't look at him. Charley, too, pretended not even to notice the handsome Viking beside him.

'What about one last drink?' said Charley to la Doriacci, who clearly hesitated. The tension gripping the little nocturnal group was almost palpable. But Andreas didn't give a damn; he dreamed only of reliving his amorous exploits. He pawed the ground, muttering that it was late. That decided la Doriacci. She sat down, stretched out her legs and in an imperious voice asked her cavalier for a lemonade. Edma and Charley breathed again: the presence of these two outsiders, less involved even than they, might keep the drama in check.

'We searched for you everywhere,' she said in a high voice, deliberately trying to sound frivolous for once, and hoping thereby to render banal the chase and fruitless search on Capri.

'Hey, now . . . where in the world were you?' Simon asked in a mockingly severe tone, rather simple-minded in fact. He was also trying to defuse the drama.

'Oh, just wandering around,' said Olga in an impersonal and colourless voice, her indifference pushed to such an extreme that Edma suddenly felt again a violent desire to slap the frightful little show-off.

Looking away, she caught the eye of la Doriacci and saw there the same desire, similarly stifled. She felt a sudden surge of affection for the diva: she at least showed self-control; when she wanted a young body she took it, without carrying on about it. And stretched out there, in her chair, looking contentedly sated, a pleasant smile on her face, she seemed, for all her fifty-five years, ten times younger and more naive than young Olga with her twenty-six.

'Julien Peyrat isn't here with you?' Eric said suddenly, in a tone of suspicion that seemed to Edma very unexpected. 'I didn't see him on Capri, so I thought he was your escort?' he imperiously asked Edma, who made no reply but went on staring straight before her. 'I thought he was your escort?'

he repeated, vehemently this time. Charley intervened, suddenly anxious.

'Why no,' he said. 'Edma had Simon and me to accompany her . . . Edma . . . Madame Bautet-Lebreche, that is,' he corrected himself hastily.

'Do call me Edma,' said the latter wearily. 'At least when Monsieur Bautet-Lebreche isn't here,' she added derisively.

She began to laugh. Charley whinnied after her, but no one else joined in.

'So Peyrat stayed on board,' muttered Eric.

'He must have been boring Kreuze,' Charley said obligingly.

'Ah well then! Chances are he wasn't bored,' said Edma.

And for the first time she gave Eric a sharp look, straight in the face—a jubilant look. On top of everything else, this imbecile was jealous of his wife! Now that she thought of it, there certainly was something going on between the charming Peyrat and the charming Clarisse. Though there was nothing obvious between them, still something showed . . . She was surprised not to have thought of it sooner. Eric met her gaze for a moment with something like hatred in his eyes; then he blinked and got up abruptly.

'I'll be back,' he said to nobody in particular.

And he strode away from the little circle. Soon they could see no more than the whitish spot of his sweater disappearing down the deck.

Simon Béjard sat with his head thrown back, as though floating between two shores. He was in fact floating between two vodkas and two inclinations. One, to get up, adopt an energetic stance and drag Olga off to the cabin—solution number one, as used by so-called macho directors in their movies. Two, to adopt an attitude of unconcern, propose a game of gin rummy (why not?) and talk of other things— solution number two, as used by so-called modern film directors. The solution in Simon's own personal, unsuccessful movie was to remain in the haven of his armchair, of Edma and Charley, of his not yet empty vodka bottle, and drink himself to oblivion through the small hours or even into the noonday sun. He did not want and was not

147

able to confront Olga alone in that narrow little room furnished with a porthole, that luxurious little cabin where he had felt so ill-at-ease from the start. For that would involve a scene; it would mean hearing himself say cruel things—things he sensed would be cruel—or else not asking questions, not asking anything, and thereby confronting a mute, deepening and unjust scorn which would, he knew, put him in the wrong. That beat everything, to have been deceived and to feel almost as though you had to apologise for it. Yet that was just where things stood, he realised with sudden terror. For the two other solutions, the 'normal' solutions—either to give the bitch a good beating, to exact excuses and promises from her; or simply to unload her or get off the ship himself at the next port without further ado—these solutions, the only 'proper' ones for a man, were both already out of the question. He couldn't bear the idea of this cruise without Olga, nor of the coming days without Olga's pony-tail, her slim, tanned body, her abrupt gestures, her studied voice, her irritability, and the childish face she revealed to him when she slept—the face that was ultimately the only thing he could really love about her and the only thing for which she was not really responsible. Simon Béjard felt as though, as they say in books, the deck was opening beneath his feet. Something akin to nausea clogged his throat and laid a cold sweat on his forehead—finally he admitted to himself that he was completely in love with this little bitch who did not love him. He closed his eyes and for a second his face wore a look of pained desperation, and he appeared much younger and more respectable than usual.

Edma alone caught this look, and was astonished by it. Instinctively she reached out a hand in the half-light and patted the arm of the chair next to his arm, close enough for him to feel it. Simon turned to her with the look of a drowning man, a red-faced, red-headed castaway, ridiculously crimson and miserable, and whatever was left of his heart attached itself once and for all to the elegant Edma Bautet-Lebreche.

Clarisse was asleep. Eric had come into the room silently,

his face set, gripped by a blind rage against he knew not what, a rage without the slightest connection with the evening's tedious though brief interlude with Olga. At the very least he should have enjoyed a sense of pride in this evening, but all he was left with was a hazy feeling that he had been deceived. But deceived by whom? He would have liked this sleeping woman to have been the one to deceive him—and to have discovered the flagrant proof as he entered the cabin: he would have liked to find her in the arms of that fellow Peyrat and had an excuse to strike him, insult him, make him pay for the wearying and vulgar three hours, for the promiscuity of his fling with such a girl on the make, for the vulgar crowd on the Piazzetta, the understanding smile of the hotel concierge with his flattering obsequiousness, the feel of a stranger's body, the little cries and phony little twitchings of the nitwit in his arms, to make him pay for the endless quantity of syrupy Chianti he had had to drink afterwards to celebrate it all. He would have liked to find her in the arms of Peyrat, and at the same time he could not have endured it. Eric stood next to the berth, by the sleeping body of Clarisse. He could only see her tawny hair on the pillow. He would never see more of her than that: that hair on the pillow, hiding a face he would never see again. She had slipped away from him. She had slipped away from him and he did not know why, nor how he could be so sure of it. He knew it even as he repressed the idea, rejecting it as fantasy, nonsense, a total impossibility. She was his wife—Clarisse, whom he had long since held at his mercy. That would not change for as long as he lived.

He turned abruptly on his heels and went out, slamming the door so that when he returned she would be awake and able to read on his face every trace of his amorous pleasure with Olga.

It seemed to him that he had spent only a minute beside Clarisse's bed; but when he went back up on deck, it was empty. He saw only Elledocq, girded up in his navy-blue uniform, fastening the chain at the gangway with a solemn air. The captain turned towards him with a satisfied expression.

'Everyone is back on board,' he said. 'We're leaving.'

He threw a murderous glance towards Capri and its infernos, towards that place of perdition, a glance that under other circumstances might well have made Eric smile.

rmand Bautet-Lebreche was still awake, alas, when Edma returned to their cabin. He never went to sleep before five o'clock in the morning and he woke up at nine, as fresh as could be for a young old man who wasn't quite so young any more. He cast a cold eye towards Edma; she looked rumpled and a bit drunk to Armand, who despised this condition in women generally but most particularly in his own wife. However, it was not so much his reproving look that drew Edma's attention; it was, of all things, his torso. Armand was wearing striped silk pyjamas, purchased at Charvet, and the somewhat oversize Russian collar made him look more than ever like a plucked bird. The sparse grey hairs nature had forgotten on his chest suddenly struck Edma as literally obscene, and she walked towards him without stopping to think. Even though he was lying down, which was to say untouchable under their regulations, she fastened the collar at his neck and patted his shoulder. Armand shot her an indignant look.

'Sorry,' she said between her teeth, not quite knowing

why she was excusing herself, but vaguely guilty nonetheless. 'You weren't asleep?' she continued.

'No. Do I look as if I'm asleep?' Stupid question, stupid answer, Armand thought crossly. He had no idea why Edma's gesture annoyed him so much. He was in a bad mood. That was all they needed, Edma thought as she sat down on her berth, her arms hanging down at her sides. It had been a dreadful evening.

'What a night!' she said in the direction of Armand, who had already gone back to the notepads and financial papers that were spread all over the bed and were gradually taking over the whole cabin. 'What a night . . .' she repeated more slowly and listlessly.

She couldn't bear the idea of getting undressed, particularly the idea of taking off her make-up. She was scared of looking old in that cruel mirror weighed down by mahogany. She had actually played a supporting role all night, and she could not help thinking about it. Of course she was still the backbone of her little groups, as people kept telling her, but she no longer fleshed them out. What's more, this evening she had even played the confidante, the lady of good works— the extra, no less. It had come to that! And as a matter of fact, compared with her usual role as firebrand or wicked teller of tales, the new roles suggested by her new kindness seemed exceedingly dull.

'Can you imagine . . .' she said in her clarion voice, provoking a sepulchral yelp from the lovely Fuschia on the other side of the partition. 'Can you imagine,' she repeated, much more quietly, 'that poor Simon, and poor Charley too, as a matter of fact . . .'

'Listen,' said Armand. 'Would you be kind enough, my sweet, to spare me the miserable depravities of your . . . well, of *our* shipmates. A whole day of them is already a little too much, don't you agree?' he added with a worried smile, for Edma sat very still, looking at him strangely.

What could he have said that was so terrible? After a moment's silence Edma got up and walked straight past him on her way to the bathroom. She was altogether too thin,

Armand noticed but without concern; for he had the same doctor as his wife and he knew her to be in excellent health.

'When it comes right down to it . . .' said Edma's voice from the bathroom '. . . except for your calculations and your accounts, when it comes down to it you're not interested in anyone, are you, Armand?'

'But of course I am, my dear, of course. I'm interested in you and in all my real friends, certainly.'

He got no response to this; he expected none. Stupid question, stupid answer, he thought again. Poor Edma. What an idea! Naturally he was interested in other people. Naturally!

But then, it was strange how sluggish Saxer & Co. had been the last few weeks . . . He buried himself again in his figures—they at least were logical. And in any event he would have understood nothing about the tears that hung in the corners of Edma's eyes, on either side of the crow's-feet, as if quite perplexed to find themselves there.

For nearly forty years now Armand had played the role of an old man, at first precociously, as a man who had never been young—a role that had pleased him early on because it had spared him from all the dashing about, all the frenetic activity, everything he abhorred. His role seemed merely to consist of paying restaurant or hotel bills left behind by merrymakers, a thankless task, but one that he performed without complaint, since the various means of spending money had always seemed to hold little interest for Armand, while the means of acquiring it were all-absorbing. So the role had continued for several aeons, to everyone's profit. But now it seemed that people were less tolerant of the signs of age in the already old than of the ageing of the perpetually young, who turned into waning revellers. They could display rolls of fat, general untidiness, a flushed complexion and ballooning waistline; still they evoked from the wife some tender comment such as, 'Ah, he's paying for his good years . . . he's really earned his wrinkles, that one!' For Armand, on the other hand, the addition of a single ounce or the slightest tremor was interpreted as a decline. 'Yes, he's ageing,' she would say, 'yet not for lack of care . . .'

And so, cruelly pursued all his life by people who bored him and whom he had to support, Armand now found himself scorned by those very people for having done so. It seemed that he evoked no joyful memory; except perhaps among a few children who loved sweets, nobody smiled at the mention of his name. Mention Gérard Lepalet or Henri Vetzel on the other hand, men who had burned the candle at both ends: brows would relax and a sort of grateful sympathy would ring in the ladies' voices. Armand wondered now whether the sexual exploits of those handsome dogs had been better than his own. They were the kind that slept with friends' wives while Armand slept with their secretaries. They made their wives miserable for a while, he made young women comfortable for a while. He wondered which set of ethics would win out. What most shocked Armand was when passion became involved in these worldly liaisons, when fooling around actually led to divorce between well-matched couples, when in short it became necessary to speak of love even among the well-brought-up. Naturally poor Edma was ageing and finding fewer lovers, but that was a classic situation; Armand Bautet-Lebreche had never admitted to himself that if Edma felt lonely enough to deceive him, it was because she was indeed lonely, and he was not the ultimate architect of her solitude.

Ten minutes later, everyone aboard the *Narcissus* was asleep.

*J*ulien Peyrat generally emerged from a sound sleep as though from a shipwreck, bewildered and frightened. But this time it was as though a vigorous young wave had just dropped him, naked, among these rumpled sheets, into the brilliant sunshine of his cabin—a sunshine that entered in waves through the porthole, that caressed his eyes while it opened them. And even before telling him where he was or who he was, it declared to him that he was happy. Happy . . . I'm happy, he repeated to himself with eyes closed, not yet aware of the reasons for this well-being, but already willing to surrender himself to it. And for the moment he refused again to open his eyes, as if this lovely uninvited happiness were a captive of his eyelids and eager to flee. He had plenty of time. 'The eyes of the dead must be closed gently, and so too must the eyes of the living be opened.' Where had that come from? Oh yes! It was a sentence by Cocteau he had discovered in a book twenty years earlier, a book he had found on an empty train. It seemed to Julien that he could still smell the grey odour of that train; it even seemed to him that he could see once again the flat photograph of the big snow-capped peak that looked down on him in that deserted compartment, and that he was seeing again that phrase from Cocteau, the black symbols on the white page. Today, beautifully reverberating passages he had supposed long-forgotten were rising unexpectedly in his memory. And Julien, who was not altogether sure of his current address, considered it little short of a miracle to find himself, unwittingly, a propertied man, for he was in possession of long tirades from Racine, seemingly peaceful in their unfurling music; in possession of sparklingly witty turns of phrase: of maxims involuntarily concise in content thanks to the deliberate concision of their forms; in possession of a thousand mingled poems. Among the densely crowded bric-à-brac of his acquiescent memory he had accumulated an inventory of immobile landscapes in all their banality, of martial music, of haunting popular tunes, of odours preserved from childhood, of frozen frames of life, like those in a movie. An ungovernable kaleidoscope unfolded beneath his eyelids. Julien, patient with his own memory, waited without stirring for the face of Clarisse, already recalled in his other senses, to be recalled to visual memory as well.

But there appeared first the faces of two other women. They were pale and distrustful, as if they had just learned of their recent disgrace. Then it was Andreas, who intervened for no reason, Andreas in a dishevelled state profiled against the sky. Then there was a yellow dog, lying stretched out by the harbour as the ship left Cannes. And finally there were two pianos, back to back and unrecognisable, whose origin Julien didn't bother to trace. He knew very well that among his recollections false images mingled with the true. He had long since stopped trying to place that river in China where he had never been, or the laughing old lady whom he had never met, or even the tranquil Nordic harbour. No matter how familiar and recurrent all three of them were, he did not recognise either the river or the woman and no, he had never set foot in that port though he knew its smell and could even describe it with precise adjectives. These memories, these flashes now mingling like stray dogs among his actual memories, the ones he had lived, must have once belonged to someone else, someone now dead. Ejected from their natural shell, thrown out of that object which now lay putrefying and disintegrating in the earth, these poor images had gone in search of a master, a memory, and a refuge. Not all of them, however. Some flew off scarcely glimpsed, no doubt towards another, more welcoming memory, and he did not see them again. More often, though, it seemed, they hung on desperately, returning for whole years at a time, trying to become a part of the real bona fide recollection. In vain. That port, unknown but burning to be recognised, would undoubtedly let go some day. It would set off again into the night to fling itself at some other enlightened consciousness, inhospitable as such must prove, since living; it would try in vain to slip in behind other eyelids. It would go off yet again to assail someone with its charm and nostalgia . . . unless Julien, good prince, should one day decide, in the kindness of his imagination, to arbitrarily assign that poor port to some old movie seen in childhood or to some schoolbook, and thereby persuade himself of the authenticity of the usurper.

Finally Clarisse's face appeared before him, smiling out of the darkness. All of a sudden it became extremely precise, and lingered before him for some time—long enough so that he could make out in detail her wide, clear eyes, frightened and voluptuous; the straight ridge of her nose and the cheekbone prominent in the light from the bar; the shape of the mouth, red beneath the paint, then pink, almost beige, after they had kissed. And suddenly Julien recalled exactly the feel of that mouth against his, so exactly that he started and opened his eyes. Clarisse's face was gone, pushed aside by the emergence of the cabin's mahogany, the white sheets, and the glint of brass in the light of the sun—a very lofty, very arrogant sun, whose rays passed unimpeded by the porthole left open the night before, now wearily banging in the morning breeze. The sun brought Julien back to the day, to his game and his cynicism. As if to compensate for the effects of a sentimentality he no longer recognised in

157

himself, Julien Peyrat opened his closet and took out the fake Marquet, which he proceeded to hang on the wall in place of the print of the schooner *Drake's Dream*, which till now had hung there. It was time to palm off his masterpiece on some sucker, to be a bit crafty—even if unconsciously he was already spending his take on a present for Clarisse.

After a few moments of contemplation he took it down again and put it back, carefully laid between two shirts and wrapped in newspaper.

Clarisse herself woke up horrified and ashamed, determined to forget everything that had happened the previous evening.

$\mathcal{T}$he early dawn off Capri showed a blue so pale that the sun's first, cautious rays seemed bright yellow; under such a sky Simon had no trouble pretending to be totally drunk in order to regain his cabin, and he counted on feigning a colossal migraine when he woke up. The first part of his plan went exceedingly well. He was put to bed by Charley, Edma and Olga, who actually tucked him in and wished him the sweetest of dreams. Later Olga did try hard to wake him up, but without success. Simon had been snoring so rudely, so resoundingly, that she had given up. But now, awakening at noon, he had the distinct feeling that the big confession that Olga had kept simmering since the excursion to shore was not to be avoided. And what a catastrophe that showdown was going to be!—a catastrophe for him, though he was the wronged party, the deceived one. For Olga would either remain standing and assume a virtuous air, hurt and indignant, denying any betrayal—which would allow him the peacock's cry of choleric dignity—or else sitting down, coffee cup in hand,

159

she would relate, in a monotone, all the details, all the charms of her adulterous evening. She would deliberately use very simple words, raw and natural words, rumblings interspersed with adolescent hesitations, the 'Uh . . . uh . . .' and 'We-ell!' and 'Oh! là là!' supposed to reflect her youth and its language, supposed to be the truth of the era—which had in fact become the common language of movie people, actors, journalists, even writers, all of them fairly mature. Simon wanted to avoid that: he did not wish to know officially what he already knew emotionally. This was not, as Olga presumed, a refusal based on vanity or manly sensibilities; it was quite simply so as not to suffer, not to have to imagine, place and see Olga in the arms of another man. But these reasons for refusing to undergo the confessions apparently so dear to Olga's heart would have to be kept from her. For if she knew that he loved her, she would trample on him with unadulterated bliss. Already as he lay there on the hard berth with its taut sheets, flat on his stomach with his face in the pillow as he used to do when he was twelve, Simon's suffering was extreme. His heart seemed to him to gorge with blood despite the perforations caused by certain images, certain desires. These again were associated with a woman, who at that time had been a little girl of his age with plaits. For twenty years now he had thought himself safely beyond that, so completely had he subordinated his love life to his material one. There was nothing left to lose, not even in a mad love affair, he had thought imprudently, neither vampy bitches, nor demanding women, neither the bus you wait for in the rain, nor shoes that are too small but have to be worn anyway. He had thought that his triumph at Cannes, his success had saved him from all that, along with the condescending glances of waiters at Fouquet's. But was he about to trade that servility for another kind which for the moment he could not envision as possibly being worse?

Everything had come to him because of his success. He had met Olga at Cannes because she was there as an actress making her name, and she had gone after him because she was ambitious. So her heart was fairly well protected, well

160

enough at any rate so that Simon's total lack of sentimentality did not seem cruel to her. He had chosen Olga because she fit his aesthetic criteria and because physically she was rungs above all her predecessors. After all, Olga may have been a chance encounter, but a chance encounter that was a necessity, one of the implacable necessities that passions produce. It was unfortunate for Simon that his first love should begin in pain, jealousy and deceit, or so he believed, forgetting that over the last twenty years he had made half a dozen offers of marriage, both to kind and dreadful partners. These women, he now clearly recalled, had all been touched by his proposal, and they had all retained a similar sort of affection for Simon. But Olga, Olga would laugh in his face, he knew that all too well; further, she would relate this madness to the high society of the Paris film world. He had to be lucid and logical: Olga did not love him. 'Not really, not yet,' cried a small, desperate voice from within the well-worn mechanism of Simon's mind—a small voice that refused to give up, that through all the set-backs, failures and material catastrophes of his venturesome life had assailed his ears with the same silly little phrase, 'Things will turn out all right.' And in fact things often had turned out right for him, almost despite himself. Life decides everything for us, Simon said to himself with eyes closed, not realising that it had been his own ambition, courage and enthusiasm that had made things come out right. This time, however, it was not Simon's courage, enthusiasm or determination that were needed, but Olga's.

She was not in her bed when Simon raised his head from the shelter of his pillow, and he felt a moment of hope. For once she must have awakened before him, gone to the dining-room for breakfast and let him sleep. That was really nice of her, especially when you knew how hard it was for Olga to get out of bed before breakfast. She did have spirit, that girl, and her instincts were fundamentally good, since they had led her to leave him in peace. He was warmed and comforted by that thought, which followed his first cruel reflections: for gazing at the heap of clothes in the armchair—the linen slacks, embroidered T-shirt, tiny bikini and

heavy Aztec belt—he imagined them being pawed by Eric's hands, Eric's hands which had tossed them aside before coming to rest on Olga's bare skin. At that idea Simon had again closed his eyes and slid back under the covers—just as Clarisse was doing in the neighbouring cabin. He was reawakened completely by the crash of a falling glass in the next room, followed by a fervent 'Shit!'

'Simon, are you asleep?' Olga called out.

He closed his eyes once more, but she was blaring out, 'Simon! Simon!' louder than ever as she came into the room and leaned over his bed.

'Simon, wake up. *Reveille-toi . . .*' And then she corrected herself, '*Reveillez-vous,*' because she thought it very elegant for lovers to use the formal *vous* with each other. The first example she had seen of that was in a B-film that traced the love affair of Lady Hamilton with Lord Nelson, and to please her, Simon was trying to do the same.

'I must talk to you,' she said more loudly still, all the while shaking him with a delicate hand (too delicate, clearly, to touch Simon's head or hair, or anything but his pyjamas).

These impressions, these intuitions so threatening to himself, slipped, like fish near the surface of water, into Simon's consciousness without lingering, immediately borne off again by a still powerful current of optimism.

'Tea,' he said in a voice full of misery. 'Tea, get me some tea . . . I'm thirsty, and I've got this headache . . . Damn migraine,' he said. 'Oh God . . .'

He dropped his head back on the pillow, a strong measure of terror in his scarcely exaggerated plaint. Now Olga was clearly getting ready for a complete confession. She must have been quite caught up in it. Perhaps she had already written it down during the night. Two or three times already, Simon had found scribbled in a notebook what seemed to be rough drafts of conversations to come, drafts whose outcome, as foreseen and desired by Olga, he had done little to disturb—drafts in which he had also found, somewhat simplified but otherwise almost verbatim, certain elaborate phrases which he had already heard spoken aloud. What he would do to escape Olga for the next seven days,

the only days in which the proximity of her offence made confession still possible! Later such a confession would have about it nothing truly abject, but would apply merely to some banal and vaguely embarrassing incident or else to a liaison deliberately entered upon and therefore more difficult to avow with appropriate lyricism. Meanwhile she was asking for a pot of tea over the telephone in a sugared, worldly voice, the new voice she was trying out on the ship's personnel, as Simon noted for a second time. She was overdoing it, but he preferred this demagogic zeal to its opposite, to the imperious or irritable detachment he had seen her use earlier, not even looking a waiter or a steward in the eye.

'You seem much better disposed towards the menials,' he said when she hung up. 'Or am I imagining it?'

'I have never been disagreeable with an employee,' said Olga. 'And what's more, I would like to point out, a certain tone of authority is what every good domestic recognises and appreciates.'

'Well, I find that strange in a woman of left-wing sensibilities,' said Simon without great interest. 'I find it strange that you should be patronising to "domestics", as you call them.'

He was feeling recklessly, daredevilishly heroic—but perhaps this new subject might spare him the confessional scene. Olga looked at him squarely with cold eyes. Then she smiled, slowly and thoughtfully, lifting her upper lip just slightly, as she did when she was vexed at someone and ready to hurt him deliberately, even if the affront had been involuntary.

'You don't understand because you weren't brought up with servants,' she said in that calm voice which he knew in Olga's case to be one of blind anger. 'It's odd, but it's not something you can learn—how to be at ease with domestics. It's too late, Simon . . .'

She smiled a little more and then went on: 'Well, to explain a bit . . . it's not the man, the human being, I'm snubbing, it's his job as a waiter, his uniform, his obsequious attitude. That's what makes me ashamed for him, because under that he is a man and a man who is no doubt my equal.

It's to the uniform alone that I address my sarcasm, don't you see? Not to the human being.'

'I see, yes,' said Simon. 'I understand, but perhaps he doesn't know all that. Well now, anyway, here's the tea,' he said cheerfully, as the steward came in bringing baskets of croissants and fruit that looked delicious. 'I'm starving,' said Simon joyfully.

'So am I. I didn't really eat any dinner last night. I wasn't hungry, I must admit.'

Olga spoke with a solemnity out of all proportion to her fast. The waiter who was serving them had drawn back the curtain from the porthole and was about to disappear when Simon, to his own horror, snapped his fingers at him and immediately blushed. 'Oh! sorry . . .' he said. 'Excuse me, it's quite unconscious,' and he made the same gesture, smiling.

Olga had turned away, in pain and disgust, but the young steward smiled back at Simon.

'When you have a moment could you bring me some grapefruit juice? Fresh juice if there is any.'

'It might take ten minutes,' said the steward. 'Just now everybody's ringing at the same time.'

'That's all right,' said Simon, turning towards Olga in ostensible surprise at her cross expression. 'What's the matter? Did you want some too? You can have mine.'

'No thank you. No, I can't talk to you in front of the steward. It's been a habit since childhood, a strict habit! My father would not allow us to reveal anything intimate to outsiders, even if they knew us.'

Simon felt his throat tighten in the grip of an anxious and ill-timed pity. Poor Olga, in her Chinese silk robe embroidered with the little flowers and crimson birds—poor little Olga in her floozy's wrapper talking like a bad pulp novel.

'Ten minutes is a good long time anyhow,' he said. 'What did you want to tell me? I hope you're not going to scold me about last night,' he went on hurriedly. 'I was so drunk that I don't remember a thing, not one blasted thing about the whole evening. Okay, I'm listening.'

But he knew that Olga would need some time for her big duet scene and that she would not brook the slightest interruption. Ten minutes . . . ten measly little minutes for her big role—no chance, it would be wasted. Shaving in the bathroom, Simon whistled like a magpie. He then made way for Olga, who took up a position in front of the mirror and, with the technique of a practised studio make-up artist, began to put on the face of a confessing woman. She left nothing to chance, reinforcing the blush of shame on her cheeks, lowering her eyelids, transforming herself into a woman of at least thirty, a guilty woman, all in the space of twenty minutes. She gave herself a last glance in the mirror before she went solemnly back into the room and realised that it was empty. The wronged man had flown.

The wronged man had, in departing, taken his sweater under his arm with his shoes in hand and was trying unsuccessfully to put them on in the passageway—unsuccessfully, because the ship was beginning to roll with a heavy swell. The abrupt motion of a more powerful wave propelled Simon Béjard head down, shoes still in hand, with hurried, tottering little steps, into the cabin of Edma and Armand Bautet-Lebreche, where his entry was received all eyes and ears, especially at the end, when his trajectory brought him up smartly against the bed where Edma lay astounded; Edma onto whom he toppled like some frenetic drunkard, while Armand looked on helplessly, Armand who himself had been pitched and then wedged by the same irresistible wave onto the luggage rack, which clamped shut in shock around his hips. Armand's amazement was brief for, with the same supple and preposterous motion the wave wrested Simon from Edma's bed with no less vigour than it had employed in depositing him there, and sent him staggering out backwards until he came to rest quite suddenly against the wall of the corridor. And at the same time the wave closed the door with equal force on the momentarily exposed marital intimacy of the Bautet-Lebreches. It must be an equinoctial wave, thought Simon in the midst of his confusion.

'That would be your paramour, of course?' Armand

Bautet-Lebreche enquired with a look of annoyance at his wife, the witty Edma Bautet-Lebreche, who for once in her life was speechless.

*A*fter trying on all the elements of his wardrobe without success—two jackets and two pairs of trousers that went together plus one grey-blue suit, Julien concluded that he looked awful in all of them. He had brought them in Cannes in a hurry, with no way of knowing that he would be falling in love on the trip. So Julien, at a complete loss, called for Charley—Charley Bollinger, the arbiter of elegance, at least aboard the *Narcissus*.

'How do I look, Charley?' he asked anxiously, to the great surprise of the purser whose romantic spirit was instantly awakened.

'Why, very . . . very nice,' he replied with warmth and curiosity, sails raised all at once and all antennae ready, ready for any script that offered him a part. He imagined himself playing gin rummy in the evening with Eric Lethuillier, stoically sitting there, not batting an eyelid despite the faint sound of oars and lapping of water as the lifeboat drew away into the night, bearing Clarisse Lethuillier and Julien Peyrat to their happiness.

167

'Very . . . very charming, very attractive, my dear chap!'

'Julien,' said the latter. 'No, what I meant was what you thought of me physically.'

At this Charley was momentarily silenced and then for a moment seized with extravagant hope: since Andreas wouldn't even look at him, since he was indeed unaware of his love, perhaps it would not be impossible to imagine a Charley consoled by Julien Peyrat. No, unthinkable. This Julien Peyrat was quite crazy, but also quite straight. All things considered it was a pity. He blushed a little as he answered.

'Do you mean in the eyes of a man or a woman?'

'A woman, of course,' said Julien innocently. The final wisp of hope vanished completely. 'Do you think a woman could fall for a fellow dressed like this—half casual, half formal? I look like someone's country cousin.'

'Well,' said Charley, 'it's true that you're very, very "mixed" as far as clothes are concerned. Really, quite a botch! But with your military build—military but attractive, of course . . . Let's have a little look at this wardrobe . . . yes, yes . . . put it all on for me, I want to see you in everything.'

Julien put on his three changes, grumbling at himself and his idiotic vanity. After the third change of clothes he came back in a bathrobe and looked at Charley, who had been impassive throughout the fashion show.

'Well then?'

'Well, it's the bathing suit that looks best on you! You're more natural, ha, ha, ha . . .' He had a sharp laugh, a laugh that grated like metal, and Julien suddenly wanted to turn him upside down like a toy. 'It's funny, Julien,' he went on. 'You can't be aware of it yourself, but your face changes every time you change clothes: you look a bit of a snob when you're in the grey suit, a bit of a cad in the polo shirt—a good sport and well brought up, of course. In corduroys and that appalling tweed jacket, on the other hand, you look calm, arrogant, very much the English aristocrat, all you need is a pipe and a gun dog. Is that unconscious?'

'Completely,' said Julien with annoyance. And he scarcely

thanked Charley before heading for the pool, hoping that a cold dip would jolt him out of his stupidity and adolescent reveries.

He did the crawl for three minutes, his maximum, but he was at the shallow end of the pool, with water up to mid-calf and shivering a bit, when Clarisse arrived. He felt piti-ful, covered as he was with goose-flesh, his feet in the water. She came towards him, also wading, and put out her hand in a polite greeting, eyes averted with an air of propriety—but since she too was up to her calves in the water Julien felt better, more of an equal. Reassured, he smiled at her furtively, for Clarisse, stripped of make-up for her swim, was unmistakably the same woman as the evening before.

'When can I see you?' he asked in a low voice, for the Bautet-Lebreches had just come to the poolside. They were deploying yards of towel, litres of sun tan oil, books, ciga-rettes, little pillows, reflecting screens, magazines, lemon-ade—a vast amount of clutter with which poor Armand was all the more unjustly burdened since he only enjoyed the sun from under a parasol or from the shelter of the bar. Edma waved at them with a little conspiratorial smile that completely terrified Clarisse.

'We mustn't see each other again,' she said very quickly. 'We mustn't, I assure you. We mustn't see each other again, Julien.'

As if he, Julien, could be near her now without kissing her! Or wake up without her image as close as the bedside table! As if he were about to leave her in the hands of that lout who made her suffer—as if he were really a good-for-nothing, a hopeless layabout. It was time to sell that Marquet so that he could take her away with him. He could very, very clearly imagine Clarisse at the racetrack, he could even imagine her with his racetrack pals. He could see her in all his old haunts. In fact, he couldn't imagine those places now without her.

'But Clarisse,' he said, with a gaiety that did not lend credence to his message. 'I love you.'

And as if realising the incongruity of his words and his voice, he caught hold of her wrist and held her firmly while with the other hand he stroked her hair in a paternal gesture. 'I can laugh when I say it,' he added softly. 'Because I'm happy . . . it makes me happy. It's crazy, I love you and that idea makes me happy. Aren't you?'

He was facing her with his cocker spaniel look and his hand was the same temperature, had the same touch and same texture as hers, and so she had a hard time answering no, that she didn't like the idea of loving someone. No, she didn't want to love him; or that no, loving someone made her unhappy.

'You've never been happy and in love both at once,' Julien said indignantly. 'Well, that's just it, you've got to have it happen to you.'

Before Clarisse could reply, Edma's voice rang out like a siren above their heads. 'How about a bit of dancing this evening while we're at Siracusa?' she said. 'A bit of dancing after the recital would limber us up. There really must be some delightful old records here on the ship.' She drew a deep breath. '*Charley*!' she yelled, rousing all swimmers and levelling all newspapers. '*Yoohoo, Charley*!' she repeated in a particularly piercing tone, and then explained to Julien and Clarisse, who were still transfixed, 'Charley is never very far away.'

And indeed, while the two barmen abruptly shaken from their naps looked to their bottles, Charley arrived on the run, out of breath, dancing his little tiptoe canter, elbows spread like a balance pole.

'What's the matter?' he said, slamming on the brakes at the slippery edge of the pool and coming to a stop by some miracle at Edma's feet.

'We would adore a little dancing tonight, Charley dear, to limber up our legs after the recital. Wouldn't we?' She looked towards Julien and Clarisse who mechanically nodded in agreement. 'Charley dear, where are the records and turntable?'

'I'll get them,' said Charley. 'What fun, a dance! We used to open the cruise with a ball, but in the last few years the average age has risen, so . . .'

'Yes, yes, but this year it has clearly gone down,' said

Edma with spirit. 'You can't deny it. Armand and I are among the eldest. So who could take offence? Aside from the ship's Abominable Snowman, of course. What do you think, children?' She appealed again to Clarisse and Julien, forgetting that she had already made use of their approbation.

'Why, it's a very good idea,' said Julien, delighted by the prospect of holding Clarisse in his arms for as much as five minutes, wherever possible.

'Clarisse, my dear,' said Edma, ruffling her magazine. 'Did you know that eighty per cent of women nowadays—you and me—prefer early-morning sex to the night-time variety? It's incredible what you can find in the papers . . .'

'Yes,' said Julien. 'But do you personally know anyone who has ever been polled? I don't. Not anywhere, ever.'

'Well, now that you mention it, that's true,' said Edma, disconcerted and showing it by scanning her neighbours anxiously but resolutely. 'Who are they, these people they poll? It sounds almost like some cha-cha-cha,' she added with a sing-song. 'Who are they, these people they poll?'

'Well if you ask me,' said Julien, 'they're poor people. They live in the caves at Fontainebleau, like troglodytes. They've been entombed in there so that they, unlike anyone else, will have time to read all the papers. They wear animal skins and carry clubs, and from time to time somebody asks their opinion: the men, whether they prefer European elections to universal suffrage, and the women, whether they know there's been an election in the first place.'

'Unless it's hereditary,' said Clarisse. 'A duty you're born with, to be polled, handed down from father to son, like a title!'

Edma and Clarisse burst out laughing.

She was standing in the shallow end of the pool, her elbows resting on the edge, and her chin on the palm of her hand as if she were in a drawing-room. She was beautiful, witty, and vulnerable, thought Julien in a great wave of tenderness, which must have shown on his face because Clarisse was disconcerted and blushed, though she did return his smile. This was the moment the ever waggish Simon

Béjard saw fit to arrive, appearing suddenly from behind the cabins at a run and diving into the pool, none too gracefully, right in front of Edma, who was more dampened than dazzled. A few drops even fell on the *Financial Times*, which Armand Bautet-Lebreche had to put down for the third time. Without a word, he got up and took refuge from Simon Béjard's aquatic ballet in the third row of deck chairs. Simon, quite unaware of this, appeared triumphantly at Clarisse's feet. It was then that he really saw her, saw her without make-up. He looked at her for a moment, incredulous, then at Julien, then again at Clarisse, all with the same bewildered expression. Opening his mouth to express his amazement, he was shaken by a fit of coughing, gasping, and hiccupping. Poor Simon had paid a high price for his dive, thought Julien as he pounded him on the back.

'Easy does it, easy does it,' admonished Simon as he straightened his sunburnt body, still thin despite the beginnings of a belly. 'Listen, Clarisse, you've got to stay like that, do hear me?' he said, impetuously hugging her. 'You've got to! I'll sign you on whenever you like, I really will. Lead role, every time! What do you say to that?'

'It's very flattering, but Olga . . .' said Clarisse with a smile.

'I can produce two films at the same time, can't I?' said Simon.

'And my family?' said Clarisse.

'Your husband's pretty much occupied with, uh . . . his newspaper, isn't he? So you've got a perfect right to go ahead and be a star. Right?'

'But I'm not the least bit equipped for it,' said Clarisse, laughing. 'I don't know how to act, I . . .'

'The theatre may be different, but in the movies you can learn in a minute. Listen, Clarisse, with your face I'm going to remake *The Eternal Return*! Eh? How about that, Julien? What do you say? But what's our Clarisse doing to herself with all that make-up? It's a crime!'

'Simon is right—it is a crime,' said Edma, coming close to the pool and leaning down towards Clarisse with an imaginary hand mirror. 'For anyone with such beautiful features, such beautiful eyes . . .'

'You see?' said Julien triumphantly. 'You see?'

He broke off, and there was a moment of silence which for once Simon Béjard did not underscore with some heavy-handed comment. Instead, he declared simply: 'I stick to what I said. It would be a stupendous career. Really! I mean . . . a beautiful actress, with class—that's exactly what's been lacking in French film! Take my word for it.'

'And Mademoiselle Lamoureux? Pardon me, r-o-u-x,' said Edma. 'Can it be you think she has no class?'

'Uhh, I was talking about women in their thirties,' said Simon, with a furtive look around him.

'But Mademoiselle Lamouroux, o-u-x, is no child, is she?' said the pitiless Edma. 'She must be very close to thirty herself . . .'

'Anyhow, she's much younger than I am, and much prettier,' Clarisse said sincerely. 'You can't compare the two of us.'

'Oh no, no . . .' said Julien in the same tender tone. 'No, we're not going to compare you to anyone at all.'

To escape being looked at by these three who she thought might only be professing to admire her, Clarisse gradually took refuge in the deep end of the pool, with nothing showing above the surface but her head and her anxious eyes.

'Come on, Simon,' said Julien, 'shall we race? A good swim while we're waiting for *The Eternal Return*, a couple of laps. I bet you I win . . .'

'Let's go,' said Simon offhandedly: all the more so since there was no sign at all of the very short shorts or impudent bosom of Mademoiselle Olga Lamouroux.

$\mathcal{H}$e had in fact not run the slightest risk that she might overhear him. The beautiful Olga had sent a message to Eric, who joined her a little later in the bow, where few people went because of the wind, which was not at all to Eric's liking. Their encounter had been too discreet for him to leave it at that. So he rested his elbows on the rail and heard Olga's customary prattle without listening to her infinitely subtle shadings of tone.

'You see, Eric, thanks to you I understood that I was debasing myself with Simon. He thought he could buy me with roles—bit parts, beautiful ones in fact. But thanks to you I realise that life is offering me a real role, a much more profound role, one greater than all the others and calling for the utmost sincerity. I'd like to know your thoughts on that, Eric. Since yesterday, I've been in a real quandary,' she said very slowly, her voice hitting F sharp, her mood B major.

Bored to distraction, Eric said coldly, 'I have no thoughts at all on the subject. I'm familiar with only one profession—

my own. And therein my role, as you call it, consists of telling the truth, come what may.'

'Do answer me, please, even if your answer is hard to take.' Olga was raving on beside him, her voice jumping a whole octave with the intensity of her interrogation. The word *squealing* could be read in Eric's eyes. 'Could you ever live with the knowledge that your ambition had put you on a false footing with your feelings?'

'Once again, the two go together for me,' he said with a show of patience. 'But it seems to me that I would be very angry with anyone who kept me from realising my ambitions, my goals.'

'Even if that person were urging you on?' Olga said, smiling off into space. 'And even if you were fond enough of that person to obey them in everything?'

These inanities were beginning seriously to exasperate him. In the first place, who was this person? Himself? Well in that case she was seriously mistaken, poor Olga. Béjard must have been too good to her; still must be.

'That would mean the person didn't really love you,' he said severely.

'Or too much?'

'It's the same thing,' said Eric, to cut things short.

He heard her draw a deep breath. After a moment she said in a low voice, with eyes downcast, 'The words you use are frighteningly cynical, Eric. Anyone who didn't know you would find you terrifying. Kiss me, Eric, so I can forgive you.'

She curled up against him and he looked with distaste at the golden, ravishing face, its peach-down skin and carefully defined mouth. He leaned towards her with a contraction of his whole body. He met her lips which opened and seized his, while a little moan rose from this body which meant so little to him. What in the world was he doing here? And without so much as a single witness.

'Come,' he said, pulling back. 'Come away. Someone is bound to see us.'

'Then kiss me once more,' she said, lifting an enraptured face toward his.

Incapable of another effort, Eric was about to refuse when he saw, behind Olga, wrapped in folds of multicoloured cashmere, unkempt and magnificent in the wind, la Doriacci herself, followed by her handsome Andreas. And so he gave Olga a long kiss much more passionate than the first, and found it altogether fitting that this time she clung to him with all of her ten arms and legs, caterwauling with enough ecstasy to scare off the seagulls.

He prolonged the kiss for another ten seconds to be sure of being seen, so that when he raised his head la Doriacci was staring at them fixedly from ten paces away. Her more discreet companion was looking off towards the open sea.

'Oh, pardon us,' Eric said to la Doriacci, gently pushing Olga away, who, following his glance, turned towards the newcomers, but with a look of defiance. Since the 'great big calf' incident she no longer looked la Doriacci directly in the eye. 'Do excuse us,' Eric said again. 'We thought we were alone.'

'I'm not one to be disturbed by it,' said la Doriacci. 'Don't apologise. At least not to me.'

'You mustn't think . . .' began Olga with what she thought was a brave hauteur, but la Doriacci cut her off.

'Concerning certain subjects I am frightfully myopic,' she said. 'And so is Andreas,' she added looking at the boy, who nodded, eyes downcast as if he were the guilty one. 'I did not see you, Mademoiselle Lamouroux, o-u-x,' she repeated, still looking at Eric.

'We have not seen you either,' Olga hissed with hostility.

'Well, I leave that entirely to your discretion,' said la Doriacci with her deep trooper's laugh. 'You wouldn't have a cigarette, Andreas?'

And she swept past, followed by her docile shadow.

'My God, Eric,' said Olga. 'She will tell everything! This is awful!'

She put on a despairing look, though she was thoroughly delighted—more so, no doubt than Eric, who appeared to be furious and continued to gaze at the retreating couple.

'No,' he said through his teeth. 'She will not say anything.' He had gone white with sudden repressed fury. 'La

Doriacci is the kind who says nothing. She is one of those who are proud of saying nothing, of doing nothing, who are arrogant about the things they don't do, don't say, etc. Tolerant and open-minded, don't you know? Proper, discreet—all the lost charm of the liberal bourgeoisie. They're the most dangerous. You might think they were on our side.'

'And if you defy them?' asked Olga.

'If you defy them, they remain tolerant—thank God,' Eric cut in, and for an instant a diabolic expression disfigured his handsome face.

It was at that moment, Fernande, that I knew the beast beneath the angel . . . the devil in the deity, the flaw . . . What shall I say? The precipice beneath the lake . . . Can you say a precipice beneath a lake? Well, after all, why not?

'Are you coming, then?' said Eric harshly.

'It's all my fault,' said Olga, once more lifting her face to his, this time quite overcome. For the last ten minutes she had been acting in close-up. 'It was I who begged that last kiss, though in the end it was you who gave it.'

'Yes . . . And so?' said Eric uneasily.

'You see, Eric . . .' Olga's voice achieved unsuspected depths for such a frail body. 'You see, I am quite willing to be insulted, to be scorned by the whole wide world for the sake of those kisses, Eric.'

She opened the eyes which she had closed in her fervour. She wore a brave smile, beautiful with emotion, that vanished as she saw Eric striding off down the deck.

'They must be terribly upset,' said Andreas. 'The poor things, they must be scared out of . . .'

'That's what you think!' said la Doriacci. 'They're scared of one thing alone, and just the opposite—that we might not talk about it. That Lethuillier thinks only about plaguing his wife, and the little hussy only of ways to make her poor nabob suffer.'

'You really believe that?' said Andreas with surprise.

For since they embarked he hadn't had time to reflect on anything other than la Doriacci. He saw all events on the

177

surface only. In his surprise he stopped walking, while she went on without seeming to notice. He had to run sheepishly to catch up with her. She paid absolutely no attention to him except in bed, and this humiliated Andreas almost as much as it hurt his feelings.

Behind his mistress's back Andreas tripped ostentatiously, then held his foot in one hand while with the other he hung onto a fire extinguisher, his face contorted with pain. La Doriacci did not seem to notice until he cried out to alert her—a genuine wolf howl, she thought as she turned back towards the hypersensitive little creature. He stood on one foot, swaying and holding onto the other leg, going 'Owww,' his beautiful face turned comic by the excess of melodramatic suffering. The wind blew his hair across his face, his golden hair that seemed to have been poured from a very light and priceless metal and then carved, lock by lock, around the clear outline of his head—a head that symbolised an unknown and dangerous race, the head of a child, either a little guttersnipe or a Georgian chorister. His body . . . He did have the body of a man of pleasure, that much was true. On that score the pious ladies of Nevers had clearly recognised the true charm of a young man for a mature woman of good taste: Andreas was born long of limb and had remained so. He had never acquired the musclebound shape of the touring prizefighters one inevitably saw around swimming pools. He was slim, thank God! And if that meant dieting, he did it in secret or at any rate was ashamed of it. That was it: la Doriacci recalled with mingled hilarity and exasperation a certain snowbound weekend in Oslo after doing *I Vespri Siciliani*. Her companion of one night, lacking competition at the hotel turned bunker, had remained with her throughout the rest of her stay: a handsome youth, very handsome, tanned and agile, even slim for a boy of nineteen, but insufferable for the complicated routines of abstinence that he wove into the fabric of his life; a regimented life, a life which—whatever security he might finally receive from a man or woman and perhaps brought about under the scarlet sign of debauch, orgy or ritual murder—would forever remain a life of asceticism and petty privations; a life

178

which, even if he killed himself driving a Bugatti off the George Washington Bridge, would not have kept him from toting up the calories in his leeks vinaigrette or asking the waiter for a sweetener without glucose. Shuddering at the memory of these farcical atrocities, la Doriacci began to laugh aloud.

'When I think of it!' she burst out. 'I really could have killed him! What a cretin . . . what a rat . . . My god, three whole days with that shrimp who smelled of powdered milk and poultices.'

'But who are you talking about?' Andreas asked. 'Powdered milk? Who do you mean? Why are you laughing?'

Since she went on laughing without giving him an answer, not nastily but not quite amiably, Andreas leaned a bit harder on his martyr's role, overdoing it. This annoyed her, even produced a hint of physical condescension, as if she had discovered in him a slightly sickening trace of femininity.

She turned back squarely to where he stood leaning on his post like a crane, and studied him with a remote new eye, the eye, thought Andreas, of an entomologist, which would have frightened him had she not—suddenly throwing back her scarves and letting loose arms, throat and hair along with all her warmth and vigorous affection—run towards him like a fat little girl wearing make-up by mistake; had she not thrown herself into his arms at the risk of falling, which certainly would have happened had Andreas really been injured the moment before.

Later, Andreas thought, it would surely be this image, the sensation of this precise moment that he would obstinately go back to, over and over again, like a worn-out record that occasionally sounds new, but always searing from the sheer force of memory. He would see himself there on the vast empty deck, with the white and grey of the deck and the sea, the ship's rail and the vacancy of the sky to the west where from time to time the sun disappeared. There would be this calm immensity slipping from coal-black to pearl-grey, slipping with delicate strokes from one nuance to another while a violent, barbarously mettlesome wind

179

made the ropes sing, lashed at their clothing and their hair in an extravagant, almost cinematographic way. It was an hour without light, without shadows. Andreas rested his face against la Doriacci's, nuzzled his cold nose and forehead against the warm bosom, with its perfume of amber and tuberose, and whose skin was covered in improbably fragile silks. It would always seem to Andreas that he had attained just then a sort of allegoric vision of his own life. Standing on a deck battered by the wind, terrified and benumbed as a man and societal creature but also overwhelmed as a tender and perverse child, fulfilled, clinging and buried in this refuge, in the ever-succouring and familiar warmth of women, the refuge of their demands and their tenderness—the one refuge still possible for him in this society given his particular training.

'You are a ninny,' said la Doriacci suddenly but with a gentleness that immediately comforted the ninny in question.

It took little to disorient Andreas or to give him pain, but it also took little to console him.

'Are you happy with me?' he asked gravely—so gravely that la Doriacci did not laugh directly to his face, though her first impulse was in fact to do so.

*T*he pool had returned to its normal calm after Simon Béjard, remembering professional obligations in the nick of time, hurried off, barefoot and barechested, towards the unfortunate lady in charge at the telecommunications bureau aboard the *Narcissus*.

So Armand Bautet-Lebreche regained his silence, Edma her *Vogue*, and Julien regained Clarisse, at least as a neighbour. For, still refusing to look at him, she had backed into the corner of the pool closest to Edma. Julien was thus obliged if not to keep quiet, then at least to whisper in a detached way, whereas in fact he was prey to a defenceless, almost tender anger and exasperated sadness—a feeling of impotence, of failure, that he could not bear, that he had never been able to bear. Until now Julien had always been able to change the object of his passion without changing its quality. He had loved only women whom he could make happy or who at any rate thought he could, and whom he therefore tried to gratify. He had invariably fled certain women before they could make him suffer. Occasionally this had been difficult, but he had always managed to do it in time. However, in this instance he knew that Clarisse would not persuade him to flee, since it was she who was really mistaken about the two of them, just as she was really mistaken about herself. It was the first time it had been obvious to him that the other person was mistaken.

'You can't say that,' he said, trying to grin towards Edma but feeling as if a hideous grimace were lifting his lip, a grimace about as natural as that of a horse being inspected by a horse trader.

'I just have to say this . . . promise me you'll forget everything.' Clarisse sounded breathless and supplicating; she was pleading for mercy, afraid of him. Julien couldn't understand why she didn't simply tell him to go to hell, why she didn't end the whole thing herself instead of urging him to do it.

'Then why don't you tell me to get packing?' he asked. 'Tell me I'm awful, that you can't stand me, anything you like. Why do you want me to be the one to give you up? Why do you want me to agree to be miserable? And to swear to you that I'll remain so? It's absurd!'

'It's because it has to be,' said Clarisse. She looked pale, even white, in the sunlight, she kept her eyes down, she smiled in a way so artificial that it was more revealing than a flood of tears—at least it appeared so to Edma, hidden away behind her dark glasses and her magazine, and watching the two of them with an involvement that was more than merely attentive. Ever since she had seen Clarisse's real face, her gaze and her smile, she had understood Julien's feelings. She understood them even if they caused her no rejoicing. Bah! She was past the age, but age did not do away with feelings. From a distance she gave Julien a tender and conspiratorial smile. Not until later would he understand it: for the moment it only made him look away with embarrassment.

'Clarisse!' said Julien. 'Tell me then that you don't love me at all, that you were dead drunk last night, that I don't attract you, and that you blame yourself for making the mistake. Tell me that yesterday you were temporarily out of your senses, period. Tell me that and I'll leave you in peace.'

She looked at him for a second, shook her head and Julien felt a bit ashamed. He had made ground with that manoeuvre; she could no longer take refuge behind the alibi of drunkenness, she could no longer use that miserable loophole, could no longer tell him she did not find him attractive.

'It's not that,' she said. 'But I'm not someone to love, I assure you. You would be unhappy too. Nobody cares about me and I don't care about anybody, and that's the way I want it to be.'

'It's not up to you to decide.' Julien turned to look at her squarely and began speaking very quickly, very softly. 'Look Clarisse, you can't go on living alone like this, with somebody who doesn't love you! You need someone, just like everyone else, someone who is your friend, your child, your mother, your lover and your husband, you need somebody who will respond to you . . . who thinks of you at the same instant you think of him. You need to love him and know that he would be in despair if you died . . . whatever can you have done that he should hold such a grudge against you?' he continued. 'Have you been so unfaithful to him, or made him suffer so much? What happened between you? What can it be that he holds against you? That you are rich?' he said suddenly and stopped dead, amazed by his own intuition. Then he began to laugh.

He looked at her with a look of triumph and pity, which made her turn away with a little sob of pain or exasperation. Julien took a step towards her. For an instant they looked at each other, standing there frozen with a nostalgia one evening old—for the hand, the breath, the skin of the other. Both of them were suddenly cut off from the blue-green swimming pool, from the silhouettes of Edma, Armand and the others, from the seagulls swooping above them; both were incapable of shielding themselves from the hunger that rebounded from one to the other, each time growing in strength. The hand hanging useless beside the hip yearned to reach out to the other body, to draw it in close; the hipbone needed to be pressed against the other's thigh, the

183

natural weight of one body needed to rest against the other; the thing straining in the throat needed to be sated; and both of them needed to be led to the far edge of all this, each to assuage the intolerable attraction between them. That their presence together become electric and irretrievable, that their blood thickened by ennui begin to flow like water, that they finally succumb to the same helpless abandon, red, fatal, concrete and lyric, accepted, desired, rejected, awaited, without any order.

She was a yard away from him, just as she had been the evening before while they stood near the bar up there on the deck, there where today it was so light and clear and cold. And she remembered his hand on her shoulder, and he her hand on the back of his neck. She lowered her eyes and Julien dived into the water and swam across the pool as if he were being attacked by sharks. A moment later Clarisse flattened herself up against the side of the pool, then let herself slip down into water so shallow that she found herself on her knees, forehead resting upon the pool's rim, inert. From her rocker Edma watched them not making love, and was dismayed.

'Were you thinking of having your lunch here in the water?'

Eric had crouched at the edge of the pool and was looking at Clarisse with an indulgent air. He had not spoken loudly, but noticed as he raised his head that everybody was watching them—Edma, Armand, Elledocq, la Doriacci, Andreas, all were looking at him and Clarisse with the same expression of careful indifference, a look he imagined to be already charged with compassion towards Clarisse. So the interlude with Olga had not passed unseen. For the moment he had to play the part of the good husband, his adultery must appear inevitable. He had to be pitied just as much as Clarisse. He caught up a towel and held it out to her with a protective air.

'Why are you depriving us of such a charming sight, Monsieur Lethuillier?' cried the piercing voice of Edma Bautet-Lebreche.

'No, no, I'm coming out,' said Clarisse, and as she

emerged from the water, he saw her as if for the first time in years. He saw her body half-naked though in a chaste bathing suit, and particularly he saw her face, completely denuded, cleansed of its usual greasepaint—a face as beautiful as it seemed to him indecent, and he blushed with rage and shame, an inexplicable shame.

'How could you?' he spluttered, his voice low, while he placed the towel about her shoulders and rubbed her energetically, even roughly.

She tottered, murmuring, 'Really Eric' in a tone of surprise. Then she asked, 'How could I what?'

He let go of her and drew back in pain, his ears burning and buzzing as the surrounding air became deafeningly shrill with seagulls, undoubtedly famished. 'How can you go swimming in this wind?' he asked between his teeth, trying with numb fingers to extract a cigarette from the pack, looking absorbed in his task but only too aware of the stupidity of his remark.

Clarisse, at any rate, had no way of understanding that he was reproaching her for nothing more nor less than revealing to others and to himself the face of a sensitive and desirable woman, a face no man there could resist looking at, with pleasure now and no longer with compassion.

Clarisse stood before him speechless and mortified. The others had stopped talking; they noted with evident surprise the violence of his gestures. Then Eric had an idea. Leaving Clarisse with a gesture of resignation that she found incomprehensible, he walked towards the bar, gave an order in a sharp voice, and came back to her, not without catching along the way the almost insolently attentive expression of Julien Peyrat.

'Here,' he said, bowing very low in front of Clarisse, dutifully, as if to demonstrate quite clearly that he did this in response to an order, and held out the double martini she had not requested.

'I didn't ask for anything,' she said, surprise in her low voice.

Surprised yes, but sufficiently tempted to reach out immediately for the glass and with the same motion lift it

185

hastily to her lips, fearing Eric would change his mind and repent this departure from the rules. Her haste, at any rate, was visible enough to shock the spectators, who returned to their conversations, as Eric, with a show of constraint in their direction, could plainly see.

When he turned back to Clarisse she had downed the contents of her glass, but she looked at him through its prism with calm and expressionless eyes, eyes which for once held his own for several seconds before releasing them. Draped in her towel, she headed for the cabins.

'You should forbid your wife to wear that hideous make-up,' said Edma Bautet-Lebreche as Eric joined their group, settling into the row of deck chairs.

'I've told her so a hundred times,' he said with a smile.

A smile designed to hide his embarrassment, thought Julien, who had dried himself and dressed in three minutes. He could not help noticing once again the influence of literature (of an inferior kind) in Eric's behaviour: as if he were re-enacting a puerile comic strip or playing the role of the solicitous husband in a remake. Until then Lethuillier's attitudes had seemed strangely academic and studied in their psychological banality. But now that he knew, or thought he knew, the motive behind them, Julien felt contaminated by their unpleasant and cruel aspect, their false good sense. And within himself he struggled against the outmoded idea, the simplistic notion of money as maleficent, as perpetually guilty, archetypical of the old families, hereditarily inexorable, the crude commonplace that had given birth to Eric's obsession—and which to some degree he himself had shared. 'Rich people are different from you and me,' Fitzgerald had said, and it was true. Julien himself had never been able to make close friends among the extremely wealthy people whom he had met and whom, over the past twenty years, he had occasionally duped to the point of robbery. But perhaps it was a refusal on his part to allow himself to feel guilty in advance that kept him on guard against his victims and prevented him from noting their charms or virtues.

At any rate Eric Lethuillier hadn't duped Clarisse on the financial level: the well-touted success of his newspaper permitted him to pay out large dividends to the Dureau family, even permitted him to maintain his wife in the luxury that she had always known. No, Julien thought, Eric had duped Clarisse not on that score, but on another, much more serious one. He had promised to love her, to make her happy. And he had held her in contempt and made her not only miserable but ashamed of herself. That was the outrage against her as a human, the outrage directed not against her goods but against her right to think well of herself; it was this that he had stripped away from her, leaving her in the desert, in the terrible misery of self-loathing.

Julien got up without even thinking. He had to be with Clarisse immediately—to take her in his arms, convince her that she could believe in herself again, that . . .

'Where are you going, my young friend?' inquired Edma.

'I'll be back,' said Julien, 'I'm going to see . . .'

' . . . whoever you like,' cut in Edma sharply, as Julien realised that he had almost pronounced the name of Clarisse and that Edma had sensed this.

He bowed low before her and, almost without breaking his stride, he kissed her hand, to the surprise of everyone. Then he was off down the deck with the perfect agility of a race-goer forever eager to arrive in time at the weighing-in, on the field, at the betting window, and always anxious to avoid other fans. Julien rushed down the companionway, passed two stewards carrying trays, leaped across the kneeling form of a sailor at work, overtook Armand Bautet-Lebreche who was absorbed in his own concerns and no doubt worn out from the sun and the chatter, darted around a startled Olga and without knocking entered Clarisse's cabin, where he took her in his arms. The door meanwhile had remained open enough so that Olga, who had doubled back and was standing outside, could hear them quite distinctly.

'My dearest,' said Julien. 'My poor darling . . .'

'You're insane,' said the voice of Clarisse, startled, fearful, but more tender than indignant, as Olga noted with interest.

Olga herself felt divided between the pleasure of indiscretion and the slight annoyance that one half of the victims of her idyll, the one on Eric's side, had removed herself from the game. Well then, Simon would just have to play for the two of them, she thought with logic. Clearly that could impair somewhat the drama of her impending recital, eliminate agonies for Eric, and so detract from the value of her conquest. On the other hand it would relieve her of the inevitable moral censure of Fernande, whose reproaches throughout the continued instalments of *The Extraordinary Adventures of Olga Lamouroux* had grown sharper and now even cast doubt on Olga's own sensitivity. Olga had come close to being classed among the growing band of sorry ladies who played the part of 'the other woman'; she suspected that she was on the verge of losing, in Fernande's eyes, the enviable status of *femme fatale* and acquiring the less dazzling one of disagreeable bitch—a role that was a little too common.

'My God, Clarisse,' said Julien, his voice recklessly clear. 'I love you. You are beautiful, Clarisse, you are intelligent, sensitive and sweet. Did you know that? You must know it, my dear, you're marvellous . . . Everybody on the boat thinks so, all the men have fallen for you. Even that ninny Andreas, when he gets his head off Doriacci's bosom long enough to see you, even he gets banjo eyes. Even Edma, cruel Edma of the sugarworks . . . even la Doriacci herself, who only cares about her sharps and flats, even she thinks you're exquisite.'

Clarisse's voice rose and fell, but Olga was not able to make out the words.

'Love yourself, Clarisse, because the world is yours! Do you understand? I don't want you to be sad any more.' Julien released her from his bosom and held her at arm's length so as to see the effect of what he had said.

And Clarisse, bewildered though vaguely warmed by Julien's words, Julien's body, and by the dry martini, but by no means convinced, did lift her head. And there, when she met the yellow-brown eyes of her cavalier, those carefree eyes with the devotion of a faithful gun-dog, she saw that they were misted over—as he too must have realised, for he pulled her back towards him with a groan of anger and a few unintelligibly murmured explanations against her soft, sweet-smelling hair, furious at himself, ready to excuse himself for this thing of no significance, or so in his masculine vanity he almost believed. He could easily have understood if at that moment Clarisse had begun to laugh, to tease him about his ridiculous sentimentality. It would have been only normal, justified by his ridiculous lapse.

'Julien,' murmured Clarisse. 'Oh Julien, dear Julien . . .'

Five or six times her lips formed the name against his neck before moving blindly to his face, sweeping it from chin to temple, inundating it with slow, avid kisses, a rain of them, an inexhaustibly tender downpour beneath which Julien felt his face open up, become a fertile and blessed land, a gentle and handsome face washed of everything, precious and perishable, a face forever cherished.

From the hallway, Olga could hear nothing, neither the echo of a word nor of any gesture, and she went away disappointed and vaguely jealous, without knowing exactly why.

*E*ric was drinking his coffee and smoking a cigar with Armand Bautet-Lebreche, who had taken refuge, as usual, behind an uncomfortable little table which until then he had considered inviolable. Besieged and routed, the Sugar Baron darted hostile looks at this handsome man, so obviously of his own class, who nonetheless had the gall to call himself a communist. There wasn't the slightest discrimination or finesse in Armand's political opinions, whatever the subtleties he allowed and himself invented in his financial affairs. He had adopted all the new methods of launching a business. Among the few industrialists of comparable age and power he was known as the most audacious; as they put it, he was one of those most open to his own times. But this did not help him recognise any distinctions in politics other than communists on one side and nice guys on the other.

Armand had recourse to similar over-simplifications in other domains, in all those in fact that had resisted the simplified circuits of his brain, a perfected portable

190

computer, provisionally installed—for sixty-two years now, and no doubt for fifteen or twenty more—beneath the cap of his cranium. For example the feminine gender: since his sixteenth year, it had been divided for him, as for Elledocq, into two groups, whores and ladies. And just as he refused to admit that a gentleman could also be a socialist or anyway left of centre, so too he refused to admit that a lady could also be in any way sensual.

He applied this classification universally, except, of course, to the women in his family, towards whom Armand felt a sacred obligation to behave as if blind, deaf and dumb. It would have been impossible, for instance, for Armand to have known nothing of the adulterous indiscretions of his wife, but it would have been still more impossible for him to make the slightest allusion to them, or for him to allow her to do so in his presence.

This total impunity had at first enchanted, then naturally annoyed, and finally mortified Edma. She had attributed it anxiously to one or another extravagant cause before settling on one alone, the only acceptable one—lack of time! Poor Armand had so magisterially arranged his schedule that it allowed time to be indifferent, and to be generally happy, if necessary; but to be jealous, and thus unahppy, it allowed no time at all. So far as Armand's classifications were concerned, he had very clearly placed Edma in the category of 'lady' when he met her: out of egoism, of pride in his method. An extraordinary demonstration to the contrary would have been required before he could contemplate re-opening the question. For Edma to be dropped from her place of honour to the ignominious one of ordinary women, she would have had to, at least, be found rolling about on the rug in Armand's office with one of his subordinates, in his presence, and all the while uttering obscenities or cries of ecstasy (something she systematically refrained from doing in any event).

This opacity and even stupidity on the part of Armand, this compartmentalising, could lead to the most unfortunate consequences; for, not content with confining himself to his primary judgments, Armand carried them to their ultimate

191

conclusion. He had dismissed honest men, humiliated charming women, and destroyed promising careers, simply because, unable to assign them at once to a superior rank, he had deliberately relegated them to an inferior one, or to total oblivion. The number of his victims, of his injustices, increased with age, and this in an obvious enough manner to frighten even Edma, though she was little inclined to occupy herself with her husband's relations and his employees, exhausted as she was trying to wrest from him even a semblance of sociability towards their mutual friends.

So Eric Lethuillier could do nothing but exasperate this man. To have adopted such an upper-class air while kowtowing to Moscow, particularly after his marriage with the Dureau Steelworks, amounted to treason against his class—or, if Lethuillier failed to qualify, then treason against Armand's class. At any rate, Eric was biting the hand that fed him; having launched *Forum* thanks to the bourgeoisie, it was utterly inappropriate that he now use it to abuse that class. Armand held this view despite the fact that he himself had, a thousand times over, used the arms or finances of an adversary deliberately to ruin them and then in midstream to buy back for a pittance the company whose arms would otherwise have cost him more dearly. But that was another matter entirely, that was business. He found it extremely indelicate for this cashmere communist to be travelling on the same ship—to be listening, be it with one ear only, to the same music, to be gazing for even one second at the same landscape; inhaling, willingly or not, the same mimosas as himself. Still Eric's encroachment upon all these domains should hardly have seemed important to our Sugar Baron; for he found nothing of interest in panoramas, pieces of music, perfumes or atmosphere, since none of them was purchasable. To Armand Bautet-Lebreche, esteem must follow estimates; he could value in a moral sense only what he already valued in a material sense.

On the other hand, a price could be assigned to everything aboard the *Narcissus*, his ticket as well as his comfort. And actual material things, in Armand's view, could not be shared with a communist, or at any rate ought to have remained too expensive either for his liking or his purse; the contrary was not normal. And Armand, so keen and crafty in business that he was famous on all five continents, could defend to the last that rudimentary reasoning (and yet so tiresomely repeated by honest people all over the world): the reasoning whereby one cannot have one's heart on the left and one's pocketbook on the right, that to pretend to do so constitutes an uncalled-for hypocrisy; the reasoning that it is more laudable to keep the pocketbook on the right and a hard heart to boot, that in the end having money is only embarrassing when you are bent on others having it too. And that ultimately is what separates those on the left from those on the right, and is the basis on which the latter have been accusing the former of bad faith since the first century AD.

But in any event, Eric Lethuillier's leftist leanings had gradually been corrupted: he no longer wanted poor people to have cars, he merely wanted rich people not to have them any more. Accordingly, the actual conditions of the poor were of little importance to him. This is what Julien had smelled out, what had begun to rise off the pages of *Forum*, what had gradually rendered it suspect.

Armand Bautet-Lebreche had been reluctant to speak to Eric about his paper, about his 'treason'. But by degrees, bored to death on this ship, without his staff, his three secretaries, his direct lines to New York and Singapore, his car telephone, dictaphones and private plane—all the sparkling panoply of efficiency which, more than efficiency itself, keeps a businessman happy, thanks to the proliferation and incessant progress of electronics—deprived in short of his black metal or grey steel toys with their sound-tracks, illuminated dials, buttons and singular powers, Armand had become so bored on the *Narcissus* that instead of remaining efficient, he was growing deliberately and visibly nasty. He crossed his legs, leaving one foot swinging in increasing agitation beneath the impeccable crease of his grey flannel trousers, a foot shod in soft leather moccasin purchased at the factory in Italy by one of his secretaries—for like all the immensely wealthy, Armand had a passion for the 'good deal' even in the most paltry matters.

Sitting facing him, Eric Lethuillier gave a contrary impression of calm and forbearance. Since Armand Bautet-Lebreche and his empire were what he most detested in all the world, or so he proclaimed loudly and often in his paper, he was experiencing even more than usual, in broaching a conversation with this hated man, a sense of his own profound tolerance and intelligence, all the greater because of the passions which had to be surmounted; a sense, too, of his own curiosity about the human race, a curiosity generous enough to include this autocratic little pygmy.

Eric's head was thrown back, his beautiful blond hair carefully combed, and he was holding between two fingers an expensive and savoury cigar, which from time to time he lifted casually to his lips with a weary and appraising air, as if he too, like Armand, had been born to it. He took pleasure in showing one of the most important members of the ruling class of his era that a rebel, born and raised in material want, a totally self-made man, could cut his meat and smoke his cigar with the same nonchalance as a capitalist from an old family. Thus Armand and Eric found themselves equally equipped on the same battleground. For it was in fact Eric's cigar, a Monte Cristo at forty-five francs a shot, that Armand held against him; the same cigar on which Eric was priding himself.

In this way the discussion, without seeming to, went straight to the heart of the matter.

'Do you prefer the number one, or the number two?' Eric asked, frowning slightly with that considered air, almost pious but arrogant, that smokers of Havanas generally adopt in speaking of them.

'The number one,' said Armand decisively. 'Never the other . . . the other is too coarse,' he added quietly, as though to make it clear to Eric that if he, Armand Bautet-Lebreche, proprietor of the largest refineries on the Pas-de-Calais, considered the number two too large, a cigar from plantations he could have bought in their entirety ten times over, then it would be indecent and ridiculous, even grotesque, for Eric Lethuillier, risen from the lower depths of the same fatherland, to declare it anything but choking.

Luckily Eric, unconscious of such hidden considerations, had always found number twos a bit strong. 'I quite agree with you,' he said distractedly.

An expression that said 'And a good thing too' gleamed in Armand Bautet-Lebreche's glasses before he responded. 'For that matter I find everything on this ship excessive— the caviar, the toilet water in all the lavatories—I find it all in very bad taste, don't you?'

'Yes,' admitted Eric with an indulgence entirely new to him, but which sprang from the context of tolerance where anything was possible, even a conversation with this capitalist symbolically smeared with the blood of the working class.

'Doesn't bother you that . . . but of course it would!' Armand said suddenly, opening hostilities at an absurd moment and completely reversing roles: capitalist was now judging socialist, the champion of justice turned to culprit.

They must each have felt the strangeness of the thing, because both stopped and chewed gently on their cigars and their perplexity.

'Anyway, I find all these people insufferable,' Bautet-Lebreche suddenly confessed in the whining voice of a sad little boy, and thereby succeeded in unsettling the publisher of *Forum*.

'Just who do you mean?' he asked.

'I mean . . . I mean anyone at all . . . Well, not my wife, of course,' Armand stammered, incoherently. 'I mean . . . well, I don't know . . . take that character, that moviemonger,' he wound up in a tone of disgust, as though he had said 'that rug merchant'.

This allusion to Simon, and the contempt he had evoked in both of them, saved the day. Instantly they found themselves allied against rug merchants, moviemongers, schemers and foreigners. Since this last was not yet clear in Eric's mind, he responded, 'I certainly agree with you.'

Eric's voice carried conviction, and Armand's worries and fury gave way to the camaraderie of class. Suddenly it was as if they had been schoolmates at Eton while Simon had spent his youth in some dive. Armand, reassured, temporarily renounced his bellicosity and sought antipathies he might share with 'his communist'.

'The little floozy he has with him is astonishingly vulgar,' he continued with feeling, ending with a disquieting dry laugh of the sort one might expect from a ruthless businessman in a B-movie.

Eric, who had winced at the word 'floozy', outmoded as it was, took comfort from the laugh, and went one better: 'Yes, a sort of intellectual starlet type . . . well, at least . . . with intellectual pretensions. One of the most aggravating little tramps I've ever met! Enough to make you pity that parvenu of a director. It won't take her long to ruin him. Poor Béjard!'

The two nodded in swift commiseration with the unfortunate Simon Béjard.

Neither of them heard Olga come up behind them, bringing them in her white hand a translucent black stone entrusted to her by a bartender. She had been about to ask these two keen minds what they thought; could it really be a meteorite, a vitrified star dropped by some miracle upon this liner from another planet, perhaps flung into space by a living being, alone, or supposing himself alone, in the universe . . . and so forth.

Olga, in short, had come up to them on tiptoe like a naive and enthusiastic adolescent, her hand extended in apparent ecstasy. She left on tiptoe as well, but with her fist clenched, like a mature and ferocious woman reeling with hatred and humiliation, a role which for once she had not the slightest difficulty playing. Out of sight, leaning against the ship's rail, Olga Lamouroux wept as she had not wept in a long while, at least not without witnesses. Presently she grew calmer and banished from her mind the lacerating little phrase that zigzagged in her brain from one corner to the other like a fly under glass—that little phrase of Eric's: 'Intellectual pretensions. One of the most aggravating little tramps . . .' It wasn't the 'tramp' that cut her to the quick— far from it—but the rest, and the fact that it had been said by Eric Lethuillier himself, publisher of *Forum*. Those words, quite apart from all sentimental considerations (which actually didn't even enter into it) plunged her into the despair of the humiliated, a state of despair that, judging by the writings of Stendhal, Dostoevsky, Proust and many others, can be the most painful. In fact Olga had never read Stendhal, Dostoevsky or Proust, nor the many others, whatever she might say. She had read only what was said about them, mostly in *Paris-Match* or *Jours de France* on the anniversary of their death or their birth; rarely in *Nouvelles Littéraires*. To those precious bits of information she had added a little personal touch furnished by Micheline, her intellectual friend; but in fact she had read nothing.

So it was without benefit of any literary reference that Olga Lamouroux—or more precisely Pauline Favrot, born in Salon-de-Provence of a mother who was both affectionate and a shopkeeper (the second preventing Olga from prizing the first)—that Olga wrung her hands to no avail for more than an hour, in an attempt to avoid delirium and the cries of wounded pride. Olga had absolutely no perspective on herself, only a false and stylised image; but she had managed to construct this triumphant version with a certain courage and against all the contrary evidence that life had dealt her. So, for all her vanity, this was perhaps the best thing about her—this courage, and thus the stubbornness, the naivety of a child dazzled by artificial lures, this rejection of a dull life, or of one she believed to be so. It was perhaps also her efforts, the sleepless nights spent acquiring even the semblance of a wider culture than that offered by the *lycée* at Salon, her confidence in life, in her own youth, her beauty and her luck—all this—that Eric had just blasted or thrown into unfavourable relief. And so this implacable decision, this desire for vengeance was as much a good quality as a failing. In a certain way the speed with which she put aside her suffering and began her search for weapons, for a means to make Eric pay, was altogether laudable. She was already putting together a deliberately misleading version for the benefit of her confidantes Micheline and Fernande: *I decided instantly that this would cost Eric Lethuillier dearly. He was*

*going to see what it meant to attack a young and vulnerable
woman—right in front of the future star Olga Lamouroux—even
if that woman were his own wife, the rich and young Clarisse
Dureau, of the great steelworks.*

While awaiting her revenge, Olga forced back her tears,
tasting them on her cheek, vaguely surprised by their lack
of salt. She did allow her shoulders to be shaken by sobbing,
more in abandon than in submission to her sorrow—a submission tinged with admiration, since after ten years of
faking them, she had thought herself incapable of real tears.
At that moment, however, real tears came thronging, spill-
ing past her lids while her shoulders hunched with uncon-
trolled spasms. This was someone she no longer knew,
crying in her place: a woman, or rather a child, in despair,
an Other. Amazed by the capacity for suffering shown by
this Other, Olga automatically began to heighten the cause
of the suffering. Gradually she began crying for the mediocrity of human beings, for the obduracy of men who should
have been different, men on whom the people, trusting and
generous, were relying to lift them out of the rut. She cried
for the naivety of the poor readers of *Forum*, forgetting it
was well-heeled, middle-class intellectuals, left-wing or
right-wing, who bought it so they could peer down upon the
people—the people apparently nobody but official dema-
gogues believed themselves to be part of or wanted to be
associated with; the people whose sole distinguishing feature, perhaps, was that they never used the word to describe
themselves.

Be that as it may, Julien had been taking a turn on the
deck, striding around, scaling the stairs four at a time with
the carefree spring of the love-struck—and when he stumbled on her and she caught hold of him, it was tears of
altruism she was shedding upon the tides, and which she
spilled against his jacket.

Why hadn't she gone for this one? she asked herself. Of
course he didn't appear in the least serious, of course he
didn't amount to very much, and of course till now he
hadn't been interested in the only interesting thing on board,
namely herself. But at least (Pauline Favrot whispered to

herself in her naive despair) he looks like a decent fellow! Of course he was in love with Clarisse, the beautiful Clarisse, the ex-grotesque Clarisse . . . and that unexpected rivalry didn't exactly suit her little plans, she thought to herself, realising as she did so that thanks to Julien her despair and future had shrunk to the level of 'little plans'. Perhaps it was the man's face that prompted this, with its thick eyebrows, white teeth, full lips beneath handsome brown eyes and a large crooked nose. His lashes were as long as a woman's, she noticed for the first time—unexpected in a fellow so masculine and so obviously delighted to be so . . . One could after all be jealous of this Julien Peyrat . . . and gorgeous Eric should really have thought of that from the start, she thought, reflecting on the scene she had overheard this very afternoon. For now that she no longer loved Eric—or rather now that she no longer told herself she loved him—he seemed much less tempting to her. Come to think of it, the escapade at Capri had been singularly unexciting on a certain plane—on that score no doubt Julien would have left her with better memories.

Olga was frigid, but she had traded this dreary adjective for a more seductive one: she called herself 'cold' so that no one could accuse her of it, and so might actually hope to change her. Eric jealous of Peyrat . . . Well, why not? Her tears, which Julien thought had dwindled, now resumed, this time at her command. Tears helped as part of any strategy with men like this, or so experience reminded her.

Julien's first impression of the tears had been disagreeable. On the ship he seemed destined, he thought gloomily, for the role of consoler, an unusual role for him. Immediately the thought struck him as blasphemous. After all, he knew Clarisse's tears were not to be compared with these, not for the motive and not for the eyes that shed them. And not, more prosaically, for the flow either. Olga was sniffling a lot as she cried, and Julien's sleeve glistened with rather alarming spots. He put a protective arm around Olga's shoulders and in an enveloping motion hugged her close for an instant. When he let go and she withdrew, he was delighted to see that they had disappeared. Satisfied, Julien turned his attention to the wronged one's speech.

'I overheard a conversation,' she said in a low voice, 'that shocked me . . . shocked me so much you can see what state it put me in! I suppose I'm just too ingenuous . . .'

She made a lost, bewildered little gesture that said all there was to be said about the consequences of her youthful naivety.

'And who in the world could have abused that candour of yours?' asked Julien without a trace of sarcasm, indeed with an air of gravity.

He was thinking of the report he would give Clarisse, of the laugh they would enjoy together, and realising with terror that already—already—nothing could happen to him that he didn't immediately dream of telling her. Was this what love meant for him, he wondered—the wish to tell one person everything and because of it to think that everything that happened to you was funny or fascinating? Along with being in love he was becoming cruel, he noted. For despite all her foolishness, young Olga could very well be miserable. For Eric Lethuillier's arrogance was certainly all it took to deeply wound two women.

'What happened?' he repeated, a sudden warmth in his voice, and for a moment Olga was close to telling him.

No, not actually Olga, but rather Pauline Favrot the eternal provincial, forever confiding and sentimental; thank God Olga Lamouroux kept watch over her!

It was Olga who replied, 'Nothing. Nothing in particular. It was just that Monsieur Bautet-Lebreche's ideas left me feeling hopeless. There should be limits to meanness, shouldn't there?' she asked in a flight of oratory.

'Yes, there should be,' Julien mumbled vaguely. Having made a sincere effort, he was now anxious to resume his windy promenade. 'If some time you should need me . . .' he concluded politely, hoping to make it clear that any such need was a thing of the future.

Olga smiled and gave a nod of gratitude as he rushed off. Watching him disappear behind a stack, she wondered why she had not been able to fall in love with a man like that, whom she could have made so happy (unaware that 'a man like that' was also wondering why he had never been able to fall in love with a girl like that). Quickly though, she returned to what really concerned her: how to punish Eric. Through his wife, of course, through beautiful Clarisse . . . That was the only chink she could find in his armour, though she had no concept of its importance nor did she know how it had come to be there.

*C*larisse, who was gradually coming back to life as she gave way to rash acts, feeling a joy that grew with her guilt, arrived at the bar before Eric with a distracted but sly look on her face. Having thrown on her clothes while Eric was whistling under the shower, she had slipped off without a sound and without closing the door. He would be exasperated by her flight and would turn up himself at any moment. But ten minutes, five minutes, even three minutes with Julien, the man who had made her like herself again—three minutes with Julien were well worth a scene. She had a thousand things to tell him, things that she had just rediscovered. And he, for his part, had a thousand answers and a thousand questions, all of which did not prevent them from sitting mute and motionless on their leather stools before they began to speak, both at once, and then stop, with identical excuses, as in the worst American comedies. They lost thirty seconds more as each at once offered and declined the chance to speak, until finally it was Julien who launched at full speed into an excited monologue.

'What are we going to do, Clarisse? You're not going to go off with that man again once we reach Cannes? You're not going to leave me? That's ridiculous . . . You know, it would be better to tell him right away! Do you want me to tell him? I'll tell him if you can't do it, my dearest,' he said intimately, with that tender look whose power she knew only too well.

Indeed Julien had the smile of a tender man, a genuinely kind man. It was the first time that Clarisse had been seduced by the simple virtue known as 'goodness'. This half-stranger, her lover, had given her, already, what Eric's glance had denied her: the assurance of being unconditionally accepted and loved, not judged by a superior being. Perhaps Eric simply didn't love her, perhaps he held it against her that she had done nothing that would permit him to divorce her. Maybe he would be delighted if Julien asked for her hand, however outrageous it seemed! But Clarisse knew it wasn't going to be simple; and the more Julien's glance, Julien's lust, persuaded her of her own beauty and her right to freedom and happiness, the more she realised how unfathomable was Eric's behaviour. She understood, without anger, that she had been confined by a negative vision of herself, by a glance not only intolerant but indeed aggressive. And what could it be that she had done to him, aside from being rich, as Julien suggested? But there she gave up her enquiry, stopping at the edge of anything to do with money as if before a putrid morass into which she would sink if she sought to follow Eric's footsteps. She knew, she was certain, that if Julien spoke to Eric, or if Eric learned from others about what was happening to them, the consequences would be terrifying for them both. However much Julien's glance reassured her, and assuaged her emotional famine, it also perturbed her when she imagined him up against Eric's subtle and icy manoeuvres.

'Don't say anything,' she said. 'I beg you, don't say anything now. Wait . . . wait till the end of the cruise. On this ship, with everyone together and everyone knowing, it would be awful, it would wear us out. I couldn't get away from Eric. I could only escape him on shore, and even there I'm not sure he wouldn't get me back by force . . .

'One way or another,' she continued with a gay smile and then a light laugh—the laugh bewildered him, that is until Edma Bautet-Lebreche's hand, reaching behind him to pick up a handful of nuts on the bar, informed him of its cause.

'My dear Clarisse,' said Edma, 'may I replace you at Monsieur Peyrat's side? Your husband, like some Othello, is almost upon us with his long strides. He would already be here, in fact, if Charley hadn't deflected him with some story about a telex.'

Leaving Clarisse to the right of Julien, Edma took the stool on his left and began talking to him with verve, thus making him turn his back on Clarisse, who in turn found herself facing la Doriacci and her conspiratorial smile.

'Do you realise, Monsieur Peyrat,' said Edma, with a smile that for once he found charming, 'do you realise that since the start of this cruise I've been bending over backwards to please you? I look at you, I wink at you, I address my remarks to you, I laugh with you, whatever . . . I make myself ridiculous and without the slightest reaction. I'm frightfully humiliated and frightfully sad, Monsieur Peyrat.'

Julien, his mind in a turmoil from Clarisse's last words, made a superhuman effort to understand what was being said to him, and once he had done so the effort only added to his embarrassment. He had registered the signals Edma mentioned and had thought it better, for her sake as well as his own, not to take any notice. That she should speak of it to him so openly terrified him; in fact he had always been terrified of the idea of humiliating anyone at all, particularly a woman.

'But,' he said, 'I didn't think . . . I didn't think you meant me . . . or anyway, that you thought . . .'

'Don't talk nonsense,' said Edma, still smiling. 'Don't talk nonsense and don't tell lies. It is true, I have paid you court, Monsieur Peyrat, but I did it, as it were, in the past. I simply wanted you to understand that if I had been on this ship with you twenty years ago—or even ten years ago for that matter—it's with you I would have chosen, if you were agreeable, to deceive Monsieur Bautet-Lebreche. It might seem questionable to you, but even in his milieu I've found some men charming enough for me to love. And I've retained an affection for the masculine species that's never been betrayed and won't ever be as there'll never be another opportunity. It was an altogether platonic admiration I was offering, an affection filled with regret but also happy memories, I assure you.'

Her voice was suddenly a bit sad. Julien, ashamed of his mental reservations and reticences, took Edma's hand and kissed it. Raising his eyes, he turned around and met the ironic, disdainful, almost openly insulting look of Eric Lethuillier, seated on the other side of Clarisse. While they glared at one another, Julien leaned towards Eric, brushing against Clarisse, who was staring straight in front of her.

'Were you speaking to me?' he said to Eric.

'Not on your life!' answered Eric Lethuillier, looking surprised, as though the possibility struck him as dishonourable.

'I thought you were,' said Julien in a toneless voice.

Between them was a sort of menacing void, as between two vicious dogs immobilised by hatred. Typically, Charley saved the situation by clapping his hands and calling out, '*Hello*, people!' in his slightly nasal voice.

Everyone turned towards him while the two men locked eyes in a moment's staring match. To make Julien turn towards Charley, Edma practically put her hands over his eyes and said 'Hush!' as if he were talking.

'Is everybody here?' cried Charley. 'Ah, we're missing Simon Béjard and Mademoiselle Lamouroux . . . and Monsieur Bautet-Lebreche too. Well, will somebody please tell them the new sailing orders? How would everybody like an extra stop before Carthage, tomorrow, at the Zembra Islands? A last swim of the season? We can anchor near a little island where there's deep water and wide beaches. I thought that would please everyone.'

The approving exclamations were fewer than the silences, the passengers aboard the *Narcissus* generally having no interest in baring their bodies. Only Andreas, intoxicated by the blue sea, and Julien (who had no great fondness for swimming, tennis, or any sport other than horse-racing, but was cheered by any escape at all from the ship as a chance to see Clarisse) applauded loudly. Eric merely nodded in assent. La Doriacci, Edma and Clarisse didn't stir—the first two for reasons of taste, Clarisse because from the moment Eric sat down next to her she had found herself afraid all over again: of a swim in the Mediterranean, a drink at the bar with Julien, of provoking knowing smiles from the other passengers. Clarisse was again afraid to love Julien, or anyone at all. She suffered a sudden migraine and took refuge in her cabin.

Everything there betrayed Eric's presence: his jackets, papers, letters, notebooks, shoes—and nothing reminded her of Julien, of his rumpled shirts and badly polished shoes for which she felt just then a yearning as intense as her desire for his body. She should go ashore at Syracuse, end the cruise there, and forget Julien. But though she might be able to carry out points one and two, she was not sure about the last. And she knew that she was not rejecting such an escape plan because of Eric's anger or reproaches about her inconstancy. She didn't leave the cabin either for dinner or for the concert, and spent a sleepless night caught between the two alternatives—to go ashore at Syracuse or to love Julien—opting for one or the other every hour. She fell asleep at seven in the morning, exhausted, but relieved at the thought that this exhaustion at least spared her from having to make the choice, and consequently from packing her bags.

*J*ulien had not been mistaken about Eric Lethuillier's hostility. In fact the latter hated him already, instinctively, with an even greater loathing than he felt towards Andreas or more particularly towards Simon. Eric of course had a few ideas about women that were altogether outmoded and crude considering the freedom for women proclaimed by *Forum*. Bad taste or good was perhaps not the question where the sexual preferences of a woman were concerned. He had come to find Clarisse sexually cold, almost frigid, though he had once known her to be quite otherwise. But it still did not seem possible that it was Simon Béjard to whom Olga had been alluding that very afternoon.

She had arranged for him to meet her in the first-class bar, where their arrival was rudely received, as if a difference of thirty thousand francs could create a sort of Harlem and transform the two of them into undesirable interlopers. But Olga seemed unconcerned about the other passengers. She had greeted him with such obvious demonstrations of passion that he was finally overjoyed to be hidden away here. With an indifference bordering on exasperation, he let her pull out all the stops and play her charms to the hilt. Then, smiling and as if by accident, she let slip the little phrase that was to ruin his day. It appeared at a point in Olga's monologue when she started suddenly worrying about Clarisse's feelings. She even claimed not to want to cause her any suffering (a bit late, it seemed to Eric). When she asked whether Clarisse was at all jealous of him and his amorous wanderings, he replied immediately, to dispose of the subject, that Clarisse and he had not loved each other for a very long time, that no doubt she, unlike himself, never had, because Clarisse was distant from others, indifferent almost to the point of schizophrenia, indifferent to him too. After a few words of enlightened consolation, Olga then said with a timid little laugh, 'Well, thank heavens, my dear Eric. I'm very relieved for you, and for her . . .'

'Why for me?' asked Eric automatically, prepared for her to bring up his own possible guilt.

But Olga refused all explanation with noble airs that only increased Eric's exasperated rancour. 'My dear Olga,' he said, after ten minutes' discussion on what right he might have to know what she knew. 'My dear Olga, I thought I'd made it clear by now that I am a candid person. You can't suppose that I would hide from you anything to do with Simon's being unfaithful; nor should you hide from me anything that concerns me even indirectly. If you think otherwise, it would be better if we went no further.'

Great tears rose instantly in Olga's eyes; her face contorted, torment showed in a thousand little flutterings of her eyelids; her lover grew less and less enthralled, until finally she told him: 'It was just that I saw her flirting a tiny bit just a while ago. I couldn't tell you who with because I don't remember. And even if I did, I still wouldn't tell you.'

'What do you mean, flirting?' Eric asked coolly, though suddenly pale under his tan (making Olga's little heart jump with joy: she had the weapon).

'Flirting . . . flirting . . . How do you define it yourself, Eric?'

'I don't define it,' he said drily, rejecting with a wave of his hand any definition of that futile activity. 'I never flirt. I make love with someone or I don't do it at all. Because I hate a tease.'

'That is one fault that you can't accuse me of,' said Olga with a simper, clutching at his arm. 'I really didn't resist you for long. Maybe not long enough . . .'

Eric had to restrain himself from striking her. He was ashamed to think that he had lain in the same bed with this shabby starlet, brimming with gossip and stupidity. In his anger, he even forgot what he wanted to know. Olga saw this and murmured, 'Well, let's say that they were kissing on the mouth. Passionately. I had to wait three minutes by my watch before I could go into my cabin, just beyond yours. By the time they separated, I was on the point of going back to the bar, it seemed the revels would go on for so long.'

'And who was it?' said Eric.

'I must point out,' said Olga without seeming to hear the question, 'I must point out, on the subject of teases, that I agree with you totally. And anyway I'm rather proud of having immediately said yes to you, Eric, my dear,' she added naively. 'But there is nothing that suggests to me that your wife is a tease, and it is very possible that she herself has put out the fire she kindled.'

'What do you mean?' asked Eric, with the same blank look, while he struggled fiercely to conceal his emotions (as Olga guessed, truly jubilant for the first time in twenty-four hours).

'I mean that Clarisse, like you, may have lovers, and that she behaves like an honest woman. At any rate, she won't stop at just lighting the fires with that one. If it hadn't been four in the afternoon, with the chance you might come back to the cabin, they would have both shut themselves in quite happily. I could see them trembling from where I stood, ten yards away.'

'But who?' repeated Eric loudly. The people around them turned to look.

'Come on, let's pay and get out,' Olga said quickly. 'I'll tell you once we're out of here.'

But by the time Eric had paid she had gone off without waiting for him, to take refuge in her cabin, and by cocktail hour she had still not emerged, so Eric didn't know which of three men had kissed his wife, and whose kisses she had returned. Andreas seemed preoccupied. Julien was a card-sharp, an adventurer, and thus incapable of that absolute in love that was Clarisse's only prerequisite. As for Simon, Olga could hardly have resisted telling him, had it been he. Perhaps, after all, it was Andreas. La Doriacci gave him perfect liberty. But he would have to have been a tireless lover, Eric told himself, scrutinising Julien to discover there perhaps the attraction Clarisse had seen. It was at that moment that Julien raised his eyes; they confronted one another like two rivals, and Eric knew the name of his enemy. Since sitting next to Clarisse he had felt himself boiling over with fury and something he refused to call despair. He retained enough self-restraint to spend the evening without giving way and saying too much. What humiliated him most of all was the idea of his foolish dallying, his clever psychological manoeuvring with Olga, while his wife arranged for her lover to come on board—unless he had only become her lover within the past three days. This possibility Eric could not and did not want to believe, since it would prove to him that Clarisse was still capable of the spontaneous outbursts of passion which he had once enjoyed, and whose reappearance on his wife's face he had gone to great lengths to prevent.

*D*espite this ominous start, dinner passed 'in good spirits', though the expression is perhaps a trifle over-cheery, if Edma's thoaty laugh and Eric's glare are taken into account.

At any rate, the dinner allowed Julien—who was already beginning to build castles in the air, which is to say his life already married to Clarisse ex-Lethuillier, become once more Clarisse Dureau, or rather, Clarisse ex-Dureau, wife of Peyrat: since from now on Julien would refuse a single centime, all the millions that belonged to her rich family, refuse any ambiguity that might cause Clarisse, his wife, to doubt his desperate love; and because of this refusal Julien set his mind again to wheeling and dealing—thanks in short to the tranquillity of dinner, Julien was able to entrust his Marquet to the care of Charley Bollinger, the ideal impresario for such a transaction; all the more so since Julien—having whispered in his ear the incredibly low price of the painting, the reasons for the price and the exceptionally complicated circumstances of its purchase, so complicated that by the time he had finished explaining them he himself was as baffled as poor Charley; Julien managed to convey his extreme fondness for the painting and yet, and also, the painful possibility that he might have to tear himself from it—since during dessert Julien had let himself be led by Charley, as if unwillingly, back to his cabin and there had taken out the painting, wrapped in newspaper and resting between two shirts, wedged in place by two pairs of socks (as only a great, a genuine painting can allow itself to be treated) and so irrevocably convinced Charley that one of the most beautiful Marquets in the world was actually on board the *Narcissus* and that any one of its passengers, had he a paltry two hundred and fifty thousand francs, might exchange them for this painting worth far far more, as was testified by half a dozen papers signed by great experts whose names were at once unknown and quite familiar to the ear. As he left Charley, Julien was altogether sure of the lightning propagation of his conviction among the rich and fortunate suckers assembled on board, all the more since he had practically made Charley swear not to say a word to anyone.

It was only at around two in the morning that Eric, awake in his berth, began to erect a plan of sabotage.

In the end it was not he who suffered most that night anyhow, in consequence of the revelations, but Simon Béjard, who had had no hand at all in any of it.

*E*ntering her cabin, her tears
long dried, Olga nevertheless hesitated for a moment. There
in his neat bed, his hair carefully combed, by now more
tanned than red, Simon Béjard was waiting in blue silk
pyjamas, an uncorked bottle of champagne between the
berths. He squinted at her with shrewd though naive eyes
beaming with pleasure, and for the first time she felt a sort
of gratitude towards him. He at least did not consider her
'a tramp with intellectual pretensions'. And for an instant
she almost told him everything about her humiliation, almost confided in him the tale of her wounds to be licked,
her pride to be avenged—or so implored her young twin
from the depths, Pauline Favrot. And no doubt if Pauline
had had her way, the relationship between Olga and Simon
could have become quite otherwise than it had been since
the beginning. But in the end, Olga won; humiliation was
less unbearable than the need for vengeance. She stiffened
her spine under the blow, turned to strike back, and perhaps
it was her better side that drove her to describe in fierce

detail, not the afternoon's insults but that evening on Capri, concealing nothing except the boredom and the absence of romance.

Simon was silent for a long time after this avalanche of horrors, unable to look at her while she hastily got undressed, with rough gestures, perhaps confusedly bothered by what she had just done and by the uselessness of her confidences. And actually Simon Béjard was less wounded by the fact she had slept with that prig Lethuillier, than by her having needlessly inflicted upon him a truth which she knew would be painful. It was not Olga's infidelity that he found most atrocious but her indifference towards him and his possible unhappiness—an indifference proven by her cruel account. And when, in order to break his silence since the end of her tale, she said, in a pious tone without turning around, 'I respect you too much to lie to you, Simon,' he could not resist rejoining 'But you don't love me enough to avoid hurting me.' His bitter, acerbic tone turned her from humble sinner into proud and sensitive Olga Lamouroux, born in Touraine to a good bourgeois family who, whatever their vices, kept their honour untarnished, it seemed.

'Perhaps you would rather have known nothing about it?' she asked. 'To be deceived and have people laugh behind your back? Or else hear about it from Charley the caretaker? In that case you would have shut your eyes to it, wouldn't you? Complacency is the in-thing with the film crowd right now, I believe . . .'

'I'd like to point out that you have been part of that crowd for eight years now,' said Simon in spite of himself, for he felt the last thing he wanted was a scene right then.

'Seven years,' corrected Olga. 'Seven years, I want you to know, that haven't diminished my horror for the *ménages à trois*. If that's what you like, go ahead without me.'

But Simon had reluctantly got out of bed, white with rage, and Olga drew back before the unrecognisable fury in his face.

'If we were three to a bed,' said Simon, 'it wouldn't be my fault, now would it? I'm not the one who's bringing in the third parties, am I? Don't think that . . .'

He was stammering with rage. Olga, cornered, broke away with cries that immediately calmed Simon, forever allergic to scandal. She threw her question back at him without deigning to answer his. 'You didn't give me an answer, Simon. Would you allow it, yes or no?'

'Certainly not,' he said. 'Either you stop this nonsense or I'll get off at Syracuse.' And at the moment he would have done just that, so humiliated was he at being made to suffer by this petty, lying female.

Olga understood this and suddenly saw herself alone at a Sicilian airport, suitcase in hand. Then pushing her imagination a notch further, she saw herself replaced by another young actress in Simon Béjard's next production. I must be mad, she told herself. Here I have two contracts with him that aren't even signed, and I play around with a boor and then go and tell him. Let's get hold of ourselves. Which she proceeded to do by melting into Simon's arms, watering him with her tears and shaking his shoulders with her sobs, all with enough realism so that Simon was only too happy to take her in his arms and console her, his heart heavy with the melodramatic lies she mumbled next to his cheek. But not for long, for soon he was listening to her lips and questioning her body with his own, though he drew from it no response beyond the same ecstatic cries, cries that told him nothing at all.

Later, while he lay stretched out on his back slowly smoking, his eyes on the porthole that breached the darkness, Olga moved in her sleep, her hand falling across Simon's hip with a little sound that he took for happiness and that made him lean blindly across the face of the docile child whom he wanted above all to love him. Then he tried to sleep, failed, turned on the light again, took up a book, closed it again, turned off the light. Nothing worked. Two hours later, he had to face the truth.

Lying on his berth, his knees crooked up and head bent down in the so-called foetal position, Simon Béjard, the most envied producer of the day in France and perhaps in all Europe, suffered the pangs of love. Instead of basking in his good fortune, here he was burrowed down in a berth rented for nine days at a small fortune, from Pottin Frères, a bed that was not and never would be his, a bed perhaps different from its precursors in luxury but not in solitude, which now bore down on him all the more heavily; a bed like all those he had slept in over thirty years, knowing as he left in the morning that he would never see them again. And Simon Béjard, whose only roof at the moment was in the Plaza on avenue Montaigne, felt suddenly desperately attracted by all that he had fled and scorned all his life: he wanted to live under a roof of his own, in a bed of his own, to be able to die there—on condition the bed and the life would be shared by Olga Lamouroux. All it had taken to reach this pass, after thirty years of poverty and solitude, was to have been given over abruptly to leisure, luxury and the lasting company of a woman. Three months had been long enough for him to fall in love with a starlet, to weep hot tears when she deceived him, instead of throwing her out and forgetting her in three days as he would have done before in Paris. Through all of these thoughts, he heard, like a deep accompaniment, the caressing, fleeting sound of the ship cleaving placid dark waters, and the sweet sound of free water, salt water, sea water; very different from the sound of a river, he noticed dreamily, his thoughts far from Olga. Suddenly he was back in his childhood, in that flat countryside, all bright green and yellow, where transparent rivers slipped by reflecting the heavens, where a child sat sweating in the sun, staring at the red cork at the end of a line; an intense and already awkward child. Why suddenly these memories in his head? He never recalled his childhood, had not done so for ages, or so at least he thought. His childhood, along with various scenarios too doleful or too dull, had been relegated to the stockroom archives from which they were supposed never to emerge again.

He got up in the dark, went to the bathroom and downed two glasses of water one after the other, with melodramatic gestures, then turned on the light and glanced sidelong at himself in the mirror. He contemplated the face there reproachfully—the lugubrious, rather ugly face, with its imprecise features and bulging blue eyes, the cadaverous pallor that persisted under the tan, the mouth whose sensuality had been appreciated now and again. But that had been twenty years earlier, when sensuality scarcely interested him, less than football and certainly less than movies. It was a face to which he would not have given more than a third-rate role in one of his productions—and what a role at that, the role of a man deceived by his wife, scorned by his boss, the role of a blunderer or boor. Out of what unconscious folly could this face expect to be loved by Olga? How could she even bear ever to have it rest against hers? How could she run her hands through his even sparser hair? Feel her slim, lithe body against his, bloated as it was by alcohol and hastily eaten sandwiches, a body whose muscles relaxed without ever having contracted, whose stomach grew heavy from too much driving? The fact that a Mercedes had replaced the old Simca changed nothing, though he had thought it would. He thought of the charming Julien, superb Andreas, handsome Eric. That dunghill, that cur, that handsome Eric.

Simon picked up a bottle of sleeping pills, swallowed one, rolled the rest about in his palm, tantalising himself by pretending to hesitate. But he knew very well he was incapable of that solution. And all in all he felt no shame about it. Quite the contrary.

*T*hey were to reach Carthage that evening, but at dawn it was raining. The *Narcissus* came out of the night into a steel-grey sky, hanging low over a sodden, oily sea of the same hue. It was as though the world ended there in that greyness, and the *Narcissus* would never emerge from it again. The passengers would be glum today, Charley thought as he surveyed the de-luxe-class passageways for the first time of the day, re-adjusting the tie he wore with the bronze blazer, ravishing though it might be, a let-down when he thought of the beige shantung suit he had foreseen the previous night. So he was astounded to hear la Doriacci's gigantic ringing laugh, a bit frayed by insomnia, which would surely have woken the passengers on this deck had it not been for the unintentional protection afforded by Hans-Helmut Kreuze and his enormous cabin. How could that unfortunate man sleep, Charley wondered as he slowed his pace. For that matter, did he in fact sleep? Perhaps he lived through long sleepless nights, and terror alone prevented him from complaining. Since the incident of the first day, Hans-Helmut, the maestro, had tiptoed around la Doriacci. As for Fuschia, the vet consulted at Porto-Vecchio must have understood his case, since, thanks to his pills, the dog had been sleeping continually for three days. A second burst of laughter stopped Charley completely, and he cast a furtive look about him. Elledocq had been at his command post for an hour, looking out across an unchanging course and avoiding non-existent obstacles; so Charley had time and the opportunity . . . he found himself bending his ear to the door of la Doriacci's apartment, ashamed and wriggling with pleasure at one and the same time.

'And then? And then? The old girl didn't want to pay the hotel bill? That's incredible . . .' la Doriacci was saying.

A resounding slap made Charley jump; he did not immediately realise what it was but hoped it was the diva's thigh rather than poor Andreas's cheek that had received it.

'That wasn't it exactly,' said Andreas's voice. A young voice. So young. Such a pity, Charley thought with feverish despair. 'She claimed that they'd given her a suite when she'd only asked for a room, and so on. The hotel-keeper said yes she had. She called me in as a witness. Everyone was there, the whole hotel, guests, employees . . . I was red as a beetroot.'

'My God! Where do you dig up these women?' said la Doriacci in a delighted ringing voice.

For years she had been hearing, in the arms of her young lovers, the names of the same rivals, those women of sixty or more who shared the supply of golden youths in Paris, New York and elsewhere. Even now the market was shrinking, hemmed in by the growing competition of homosexuals less tiring and usually more generous than the viscountesses and ladies still hot for prey. It had always been the Countess Pignoli, Mrs Galliver or Madame de Bras whose leftovers la Doriacci gathered in or to whom she bequeathed her own. And here was this very polite young man, without a doubt the most gorgeous she had seen in some time, the young man whose introduction into the market would cause a riot, here he was talking to her about Nevers as if it were Babylon, of the Paris-Saint-Etienne train as if it were a private jet, of

Madame Farigueux and Madame Bonson—respectively miller's wife and notary's widow—as if they were Barbara Hutton. And here he was, telling her of his adventures as a gigolo, not only without concealing the precise role he had played, but including anecdotes which often showed him up as ridiculous or a dupe. Really a strange young man, this Andreas from Nevers. La Doriacci admitted to herself that if she'd been thirty or even forty, she would have willingly kept him by her side a bit longer than usual (three months); which is actually what he was asking for, with an insistence that would have been odious in practically any young man of his type, but which seemed in him just a little childish. Also Andreas had unexpected reflexes for a professional: though he didn't conceal the fact of having lived by his body and his body alone for the past five years, he blushed when she handed a tip to the steward; which left her wondering how he survived on shore, where tips came a hundred times more frequently.

'Then what did you do?' she asked.

She reached out a hand to Andreas in his fine white cambric pyjamas, the like of which she had not seen since the 1950s. He was blond and dishevelled, he looked happy, he laughed with his mouth and eyes, he was charming. She ruffled his hair and straightened it again several times with unalloyed pleasure. She stopped when Andreas's eyes, forgetting to smile, became tenderly imploring, too tenderly, and she broke off abruptly with a brutal question.

'Why didn't she want to pay, your miller's wife? Because the service wasn't perfect—yours, I mean?'

He shook his head and his expression closed up, as it did each time she brought up such questions, however simple they were. 'She used me for a witness, and when I said I didn't remember, she said that it didn't surprise her, that Monsieur was above that sort of thing—Monsieur, that was me—that Monsieur was on a different level, etcetera, etcetera. Then the wife of the hotel-keeper began to laugh in a horrible way, and she said . . .' Andreas stopped dead with a look of concern.

'What did she say?' La Doriacci was laughing in

anticipation. 'What did she say? Tell me the whole thing, Andreas. They have a much better time in Nevers than in Acapulco, that's for sure. Why aren't there any light-opera companies in Moulins or Bourges?'

'There are, but you'd be paid three centimes,' said Andreas sadly. 'Then she said that Hugette—that's the miller's wife, Hugette—that she had nothing to complain about, she'd heard her squawking, that was the term she used, a good part of the night . . .'

He looked so embarrassed this time that la Doriacci giggled, and once she started it was difficult for her to stop. 'And you, what did you do?'

'I went to get the car,' Andreas said, 'and loaded the baggage. The hotel-keeper's wife asked me to pay the bill, but I didn't have a penny, and the hotel-keeper was asking *her* to pay, and the waiters in the restaurant were holding their sides. Oh, how I suffered. I really suffered. And you know the name of that motel? The Motel of Delights,' he concluded. 'The Delights of Bourbonnais . . . I left her at the first train station and went home to Nevers. Aunt Jeanne was awfully disappointed, but it was she who'd put me on the trail of the miller's wife in the first place . . .'

'*Mon Dieu* . . . *mon Dieu* . . . ' wept la Doriacci into the bedclothes, hugging the pillows to herself in transport. '*Mon Dieu*, enough of your stories . . . enough of your stupid stories and open the door. There's someone listening to us,' she concluded without changing her voice.

Charley practically fell into the room head first when Andreas—in all his candour and white cambric—opened the door. In her bed, bare-shouldered, face red from laughing and eyes sparkling with authority, though without anger or indulgence, la Doriacci stared at him.

'Monsieur Bollinger,' she said. 'Already up at this hour? Would you like to have breakfast with us? Unless this mess scares you off?'

And with her trim, still-smooth arm, she gestured at the room. A lovers' room, Charley noted sadly, with clothes, cigarettes and books, the glass of water and cushions scattered about in the inimitable disorder of pleasure. Stammering, he sat down on a corner of the bed, head down and hands on his knees like a communicant. With no further comment on his disreputable behaviour, la Doriacci ordered tea for three, also toast, jam and fruit juice. This breakfast clearly followed hard on late-night champagne, judging by the still-cool bottle and the not-so-cool face of the steward.

'It's my fault poor Emilio hasn't slept,' the diva told Charley. 'I commend him to your indulgence,' she added, pulling out of her bag a clutch of franc notes, which she placed shamelessly and without ostentation on the tray of the miserable Emilio, who turned pink all over again at the sight of them. 'Well then, Charley, to what do we owe the honour of this visit? Already new dramas today? Something's always happening on this ship, and none of it straightforward and simple.'

'What do you mean?' asked Charley, his curiosity fixing him a bit more squarely on the bed from which he had almost slipped off three times already, since shame had perched him precariously on its edge.

Andreas had come to sit down again on the bed, with his feet on the floor, a little to one side, with a discretion that to Charley's eyes was as useless as it was touching.

'Of course there's something going on,' said la Doriacci. 'One: your national treasure, Clarisse, has turned beautiful. Two: the handsome Julien is in love with her. Three: she returns the compliment, almost. Four: Olga and Monsieur Lethuillier, after their ill-starred tryst, are already bored with each other. Our carrot-headed producer and haughty Edma will soon begin a flirtation. As for Andreas . . .' she said, patting the nose of the boy as though he were a poodle, 'he's madly in love with me. Isn't that so, Andreas?' she added, cruelly.

'To you it seems presumptuous, doesn't it?' Andreas said to Charley. 'My feelings must seem false to you, or self-serving?'

The boy was obviously not enjoying this at all, and Charley once more wondered why he, Charley, always gave way to his curiosity since sooner or later he was punished for it every time. This time it had happened quickly, and he changed the subject in order to escape the punishment of this scene—which actually he could have retold with glee, but which pained him as it unfolded before his eyes.

'Do you know that we also have an artistic treasure on the boat?' he asked in a mysterious tone.

La Doriacci, already intrigued, pricked up her ears, while Andreas kept his eyes downcast.

'What is it?' she asked. 'But first of all, how do you know about it? I'm wary of your informants, my handsome Charley, wary of your sources. And yet, you do learn everything on this boat, even if we don't ever know how,' she said perfidiously.

But Charley was in no position to take her up on this, and continued. 'Two months ago Julien Peyrat bought in Paris, for a pittance, a view of Paris in the snow. It is signed Marquet, an admirable painter akin to the Impressionists. Some of his canvases are gorgeous.'

'I know, thank you, and I adore Marquet,' said la Doriacci.

'And he is ready to part with it for fifty thousand dollars,' said Charley slowly. He could not have looked more tragic if he had thrown a bomb on the counterpane. 'That is to say two hundred and fifty thousand francs! He's virtually giving it away!'

'I'll buy,' said la Doriacci, tapping her hand on the sheet, as if Charley were an auctioneer. 'No,' she corrected herself. 'I won't buy. Where would I put a Marquet? I'm always travelling. A painting must be seen, looked at constantly by adoring eyes, and this year I'm on the road the whole time. Do you know, Monsieur Bollinger, that when I leave this ship I immediately get on a plane for the USA, where I sing the following evening, at the Lincoln Center in New York, and that's where Monsieur would like me to take him.' Without looking, she stretched out a caressing hand towards Andreas, who drew back, so that she didn't touch him but ended up vaguely searching the air with her hand. She gave up with a bland look Charley had noticed before, as though she were talking to some poodle.

He got up unwillingly. He suffered for Andreas, which

surprised him, since it was obviously in his interest that la Doriacci give him back, or at least give him a chance to win the boy over. No doubt about it, he was too warm-hearted, he told himself, as he turned in the doorway and gave them a small, affected wave of farewell. A ferocious growl from the adjacent cabin made him hurry along the passageway, and he didn't stop until he came face to face with Elledocq, with his comforting huge beard.

After he had left the untidy room, la Doriacci stopped laughing. She was looking at Andreas and at his beautiful blond hair, cut too short at the nape.

'I don't like you to be sulky with me, not even in front of Charley,' she said.

'Why not in front of Charley?' asked Andreas, with a perfectly innocent and puzzled air that surprised la Doriacci once again. Such artful lying in a boy otherwise so open!

'Well, because it could only please him, for heaven's sake,' she said, smiling, so that he wouldn't take her for a fool.

'Why?'

That uncomprehending air suddenly exasperated la Doriacci. The lack of sleep was already getting to her nerves, she could feel it, but she couldn't deny herself these nights awake, the few moments when she had a little fun—and sometimes a lot; but her enjoyment did not at all depend on her partners, since it was in her own outbursts of wild laughter, her own clowning, well or ill-humoured, that she let herself go, in her own deliria, her plans for the future or her memories, all of them derisive, absurd and which appalled the poor young men more than amused them. Andreas had at least the advantage of laughing because she laughed, and of being able to make her laugh with his anecdotes, without, however, neglecting his duties as lover, which he carried out with a fervour impossible to find now among the young or old of today, who speak of sex only crudely, avidly and impolitely, and all in the name of freedom. It would not be right for Andreas, altogether frank about his means of gaining a living, to be a hypocrite about his habits.

'Because Charley is in love with you, in case you really

didn't know. And on this ship I am the obstacle between him and you. If we separate, he'll console you.'

'How?' said Andreas, turning very red. 'You think I'd let him console me?'

'And why not?' she said.

She began to laugh, but for once it was strangely unamusing to make Andreas lie as she had done with all the others, his predecessors, who were sometimes embarrassed by the question to the point of falsehood.

'In any event, don't give me any more sulky looks, all right? Not in front of anyone. Maybe I'll take you with me to New York, but not if you're moody.'

Andreas didn't answer. He closed his eyes and lay stretched out on the bed. She might have thought he was sleeping, except for the frown, and for the sad look around the mouth which betrayed a man awake and sorry to be so. La Doriacci hissed inwardly: it was time to bring things out into the open with this pseudosimpleton from Nevers, or she might be in for some real trouble . . . the memory, though it no longer shook her after all these years, though she never thought of it except when she chose to; it was the memory of a young stage manager in Rome, who committed suicide ten years ago, on her account, and the memory had never quite left her.

$\mathcal{U}$p on the bridge Captain Elledocq stared at the sea spread out before him, a sea flat as the palm of a hand, which did not prevent him from observing it with a mistrustful and aggressive eye. To Charley it seemed that Elledocq was on the verge of rubbing his hands together and saying, 'Now, my beauty, it's up to the two of us,' as if setting off in a ketch for the Roaring Forties. Elledocq's repressed, or at any rate untapped, heroism was the reason for his perpetually surly disposition and his solitary air, or so thought his understanding purser (though it did not seem to worry his lively wife, whom Charley had seen not quite two years before at Saint-Malo. They had no children: thank God, thought Charley, imagining a bearded troop of suckling babes). He looked up and called out, 'Captain! Hey-ho, Captain!' in a slightly hoarse voice.

The ship's master inclined a grave, imperious face towards Charley. He scrutinised him, noticing with dismay the brown velvet blazer, and grumbled, 'What? What's up?'

'Good morning, Captain,' said Charley, sprightly by

nature and still trying, despite long experience, to please his superior. 'Maestro Kreuze's dog is awake. I heard him growl as I went by, and that's not at all reassuring! Emilio, the first steward, has threatened to jump ship at Syracuse if the dog isn't tied up. And we've run out of sleeping pills for him.'

Elledocq, in the throes of his imaginary tempests and therefore intent on defying the Mediterranean, cast a scornful look at Charley and his domestic concerns.

'Boring as hell, this dog business . . . Heave it overboard . . . not my job . . . you settle it . . .'

'It's already happened,' objected Charley, displaying his shinbone. 'If that animal bites Madame Bautet-Lebreche, for instance, or the Sugar Baron, we'll have one law suit after another! Let me remind you, Captain, that you have sole responsibility for this ship and all that happens on board.' And to accentuate that responsibility, Charley clicked his heels, even managing to inject a certain grace into the military gesture.

'You? Scared?' Elledocq scoffed. 'Ha, ha, ha!'

He fell silent, and Charley turned to behold an awful sight. Propelled by quasi-mechanical legs and gathering speed, the dog in question was bearing down upon them. He seemed larger than life, thought Charley as his own legs delivered him with unprecedented speed to a hiding place behind a table, while in a mad frenzy the animal scaled the royal steps to the place where Elledocq sat enthroned.

Even as he called out in imperious impatience, 'Where's this pooch, Charley? Where is the blasted dog?' the response arrived.

Something caught him in the thick of the calf, cut through his stout naval uniform and woollen socks and, on reaching skin, dug in. The thundering roar was succeeded by a sharp whine of distress, which surprised the nearby helmsman into raising his eyes once again towards the innocent seagulls.

'Get the thing off me, damn it!' Elledocq commanded nobody in particular, trying to kick the unchained dog with his free leg. The kicks missed, and Elledocq toppled and fell on all fours before his executioner.

Charley, climbing the stairs at a snail's pace, raised his head to deck level, no further, and took in what was happening, his face showing the sympathy of one dog-bitten victim to another, but also the cowardice born of experience.

'Well? Can't you do something?' howled Elledocq with hatred as great as his despair. 'I'll have you sacked, put off at Cannes, Monsieur Bollinger!' he declared, regaining, along with his emotions, the practical use of subject, verb and object. 'Then at least,' he sobbed, 'call Monsieur Peyrat,' for Peyrat's courage towards the dog had been praised in his presence ten times over and in ten different though concurring versions.

While he continued to sob and yelp like a eunuch, Charley ran down the stairs, trying not to betray his satisfaction: Captain Elledocq terrorised by a bulldog! He couldn't stop laughing.

But Julien did not find it so funny. He had slept three hours at most and arrived on the scene of torture in his bathrobe, looking gaunt and bewildered. 'Why me?' he murmured sadly during the relatively long trek from his cabin to the bridge. 'Why does all this always land on me? I've already pulled you away from that dog, Charley, and with pleasure, but I don't feel like being quite so heroic on Elledocq's behalf. You understand . . .'

'He'll have my head if we don't get the brute off him instantly,' Charley rejoined. 'He's going to be humiliated, he'll be furious, it'll spoil the whole cruise . . . And anyway, what else has been landing on you, as you put it?'

'It's been like this from the start!' Julien said forcefully. 'First women in tears, then enraged dogs! I came on board for a rest, Monsieur Bollinger,' he said as they arrived at the doorway in time to see the lion felled by the rat, the two entangled on the deck. Julien lunged, caught the beast by the scruff of the neck and hindquarters but not quickly enough to avoid being cruelly bitten in turn. He finally heaved the animal out and shut the door, but his wrist and Elledocq's calf were streaming with blood—crimson in

Julien's case, almost purple in Elledocq's, noted Charley, who always liked to insert a bit of colour. While they traded handkerchiefs, the door resounded with clawing and barking: the dog deprived of his prey. Finally they saw Hans-Helmut Kreuze on deck. He had been awakened no doubt by the blood cry, and he was wearing a maroon-and-black wool bathrobe trimmed in garnet with beige frogs and loops. The whole thing was in ghastly taste, or so thought the three prisoners, for once in total agreement. Hans-Helmut retrieved the dog as best as he could, and the rest of them finished up in the sick-bay.

*S*o Julien found himself in the sickbay. And after an awful half-hour having his wrist sewn up, he fell asleep there, giving up any idea of going ashore or to the concert. And so it was there, towards evening, that he saw Clarisse come through the door. She had been preceded during the afternoon by Olga, Charley, Edma and Simon—the latter out of friendship, the two women so they could assert their femininity and natural compassion. As for Clarisse, Julien had resolved to turn her femininity to advantage, without seeking compassion, and despite the incomparable dreariness of the setting.

The sick-bay was one very large white room, even larger than the suites of the performer-kings; it was fully equipped for operations and contained, for any and all contingencies, two empty beds besides Julien's, and a trolley covered with medical equipment which he immediately begged Clarisse to push out of sight.

'Those are the scissors they used to torture me all morning,' he said.

230

'Are you in pain?' asked Clarisse. She was wearing bright colours below her newly pale face, which made her a negative of the woman who had come aboard five days earlier with gaudy face and a severe dark suit.

Once again Julien was struck by her beauty. Since she was lovely to behold, she would dress this way every day with him, in this conspicuous manner. Instead of fearing someone might look at her, from now on she would do everything to encourage it.

'That's a very, very pretty dress,' he said with conviction, and with an appreciatively proprietary look which annoyed Clarisse for a second and then amused her. 'Have you given any thought to yourself, to me . . . well, to us?' continued Julien, forgetting the sharp pain in his arm, so concerned was he for the fluctuations of his heart—now hammering against his ribs, now disappearing completely, as though he were near to fainting.

'What is there for me to think?' said Clarisse resignedly. 'That you have a weakness for me, Julien, is quite possible, though it seems strange to me. And though I have one for you,' she added with the openness that regularly disconcerted Julien, 'that doesn't change a thing. I've no reason to leave Eric, who has done nothing to me. And what pretext could I invent? His flirtation with that little actress? He knows very well I don't care. Or at any rate he should know.'

'Well then,' said Julien sitting up in bed. 'If fidelity isn't required in your "team" ,' he emphasised the word *team* derisively, 'then take me as lover—for a flirtation, as you put it. Some day I'll manage to legalise everything. Here we are alone—what prevents you, for instance, from kissing me, at this very moment?'

'Nothing,' said Clarisse in an odd, distracted tone.

Then, as if giving way to something in which her wishes and volition had no part, she bent down over Julien for a long kiss. And when she straightened up again, it was to go and turn the key in the lock. Then, having put out the light, she came back and undressed by his side in the dark.

An hour later he was at the bar with his bandaged hand and with Edma and la Doriacci, who tried to soothe his misfortune with a feminine compassion to which he submitted with masculine pleasure. Clarisse, next to him, said nothing.

'Still, it's a pity you didn't see Carthage!' said Edma Bautet-Lebreche. 'Well, anyhow you'll see Alicante.'

'I don't believe there could be any more beautiful city for me than Carthage,' Julien smiled, speaking in the slightly plaintive convalescent's tone he had adopted on seeing how his prestige increased with the bandages.

Clarisse, her head low and hair shining under the lamp, seemed to miss her mask, that hideous make-up which would at least have concealed her blush, which la Doriacci gazed at with an interest that managed to intensify it.

'*Va bene, va bene,*' she said with a smile.

Stretching out a plump little hand she patted those of the subdued Clarisse. The diva scared her, or at any rate made such a visible impression on her that Julien felt like pressing Clarisse to his heart for her naive and shameless admiration. Once again, for perhaps the tenth time that evening, he could scarcely restrain that desire. They had been mad to go to bed together, he thought. Feeling awkward and unhappy, he complained to Clarisse when he found himself at last alone with her after two hours of boredom and sweet memories.

'It used to be only my imagination operating when I imagined you and your body,' he murmured reproachfully, 'I was howling at the moon at night in my cabin. But now that my memory is mixed up in it, it's really awful!'

Clarisse, her face pale, looked at him without answering, her eyes moist and shining. Julien immediately reproached himself for his brutality.

'I'm sorry,' he said. 'I'm terribly sorry. But I miss you dreadfully. I'll be spending my time following you around the ship, seeing you and not being able to touch you. I'm bored without you, Clarisse. Two hours seems like two months.'

'For me too,' she said. 'But getting back to you won't be easy.'

$\mathcal{J}$ulien now regretted having allowed Charley Bollinger to arrange for the sale of his Marquet. He feared that with the purser's artful fussing, they wouldn't be any farther along by the time they reached Cannes. But at Cannes, Julien would have to hurry to the nearest bank to deposit the two hundred and fifty thousand from the painting. Half of it, unfortunately, would have to be paid over to his Texan partner, but the rest, thank God, was for himself, and would allow him to flee with Clarisse to bluer skies. But there would never be enough time, he thought, or enough ports of call for him to persuade Clarisse to follow him, a task as difficult as finding the means to do it.

Yet he knew from experience that the Marquet coup was bound to excite the passengers of the *Narcissus*. The wealthy had a lively but pointless passion for bargains. It simply enlarged their field of operation, since a mark-down on a pair of gloves in a high-street shop was just as interesting to them as a mark-down on sables in the rue de la Paix; the financial viability of the smaller shop concerned them no more than that of the furrier.

The acquisition of a painting was therefore one of the most absorbing possible transactions in their small gilded world, given the enormous differences to be realised, the sum to be saved by harrying a painter or being high-handed with a gallery. Of course it was stylish to take advantage of the ignorance or haste of a poor defenceless dealer, to pay him half-price for his canvas. And it was just as stylish to pay ten times the price for the same canvas at Sotheby's, for instance, the moment a shipowner or museum also wanted it. In either case, vanity or greed was satisfied; but only in the first case was it a good deal for these Midases. For if they had thought it over they would have realised that the deal could not be profitable since they would probably never resell the painting, not even at two or three times the purchase price—since they had no need to. They did not realise they were tying up their beautiful money in canvases which they did not like or understand. Thanks to thieves, they could mercifully leave their acquisitions forgotten in their vaults, from which they were removed only from time to time to be entrusted to some museum. Of course art aficionados, consulting the catalogue, would see written in small black letters 'Private Collection of Monsieur and Madame Bautet-Lebreche', though simply 'Private Collection' was also chic. And in looking at this painting which the owners themselves never looked at, the public would be admiring the collectors' artistic flair (although the collector might secretly have doubts about the painting), and not their business sense (which they certainly possessed).

This at least was the theory to which Julien adhered that morning, as he leaned on the railing and gazed at a grey-blue sea beyond which waited the port of Bejaia. Scattered haphazardly in highly cinematic disarray, one deck chair after the other, the passengers displayed languid faces, darkly circled eyes from some more or less pleasant form of insomnia. Simon Béjard's bloodshot gaze, Clarisse's drawn features and the sunken cheeks of Julien himself did not entirely evoke the serenity promised by the Frères Pottin.

Only Olga, a bit farther off, who was looking serious and pretending to read the posthumous memoirs of a politician (already known during his lifetime as a great bore) sported the healthy, pink cheeks of a young girl. Sitting beside her, Andreas, solemn and romantically handsome in his black sweater, looked more than ever the part of a child of the century—the nineteenth, of course. As for la Doriacci, with her head thrown back and occasionally emitting a raucous, unexpected groan which suggested the atrocious Fuschia more than the scales and runs of a coloratura, was smoking one cigarette after another, tossing each without ill intent or premeditation at the feet of Armand Bautet-Lebreche, who every time felt obliged to sit up in his deck chair, stretch out a foot and rub them out with his well-polished shoe. Some menace hovered over the vessel, in the midst of these civilised passengers. Yet the weather was fine, the air perfumed with that odour of sun-warmed raisins, white-hot earth, lukewarm coffee and salt that heralded Africa.

Even Edma, though she laughed at Julien's ideas and occasionally threw towards Clarisse the glance of an affectionate mother-in-law, felt the involuntary twitch in the little muscles of her neck and jaw, spasms she recognised as warnings of an impending seismic disturbance. From time to time she touched them, as if to control them with her fingers.

Armand Bautet-Lebreche, though his turn of mind was perfectly scientific, had been too much subjected to the reigning empiricism not to recall and fear the prospect announced by those quiverings in Edma's neck. It was undoubtedly this apprehension that made him extinguish the diva's long butts, one after the other, distractedly and with good grace. Lethuillier, as every other morning, carried on the dumb show of the polyglot journalist, sometimes raising his head from his Spanish, Italian, English or Bulgarian periodicals to cast a suspicious glance at the perfectly blue and perfectly flat sea, as if he expected to see rising, as in the report of the messenger, the horrible beast that was fatal to Hippolytus. Simon Béjard was playing a game of backgammon against himself to dissipate his melancholy, which seemed instead to bounce right back at him along with the monotonous and exasperating noise of the dice on the board. Charley's arrival gave new hope to the group, but he was listless and quickly settled into the prevailing gloom.

The gloom had reached such a pitch that seeing Elledocq and Kreuze bearing down on them from the other end of the ship, pounding the deck with a heavy tread, the passengers felt an instant of hope, even pleasure. Alas, the two men were no more successful than the others at enlivening the atmosphere, and the hope of better days skipped away towards some more joyous craft. Making a last effort, Charley called over the barman. But he could elicit orders for not much more than fruit juice and mineral water, and the tray that he brought back was so dispiriting that even Simon's double martini passed unnoticed. It was no longer one angel passing by in silence, but a whole cohort, a legion of them all with harps aquiver.

It was then that la Doriacci closed her bag with a snap so resounding it brought the most listless to immediate attention. La Doriacci removed her rhinestone-encrusted sunglasses, looked about her with flashing eyes and thin lips bitten without regard to pain by her own white teeth—that pearly whiteness only Doctor Thompson of Beverly Hills, California, could supply.

'This ship is certainly comfortable, that much is true,' she said in a firm voice, 'but the audience is appalling. Maestro Hans-Helmut Kreuze and I have been living for eight days surrounded by the deaf who, I'm afraid, are ignorant and pretentious as well. It may be Maestro Kreuze has been dubbed "the fat clod", but better to be a fat clod than one of the pitiful little morons milling about these decks.'

The silence that fell about her was total; you could hear the seagulls in flight.

'I am going ashore at Bejaia, Monsieur Bollinger,' she continued. 'Would you be kind enough to charter me a plane there, private or otherwise, to take me to New York? Well, to Cannes first.'

Struck dumb, Simon Béjard let his dice roll onto the deck with a clatter that sounded like an expletive.

'But really . . .' said Edma Bautet-Lebreche—courageously, for la Doriacci had given her a withering look at the first word. 'But why, my friend, why?'

'Why? Ha, ha, ha . . . Ha, ha, ha!' With more than sarcasm, la Doriacci repeated her scornful bark two or three times over, while she got to her feet and began to stuff into her satchel with methodical fury all the accumulated clutter on the table beside her—the lipstick, comb, cigarette-case, snuff-box, pill-box, compact, gold lighter, cards, fan, book, etc.; all these objects, after their breath of sea air, were returned to their customary prison. She turned towards Edma.

'Do you know, Madame, what we performed last night?' she burst out, closing her satchel so violently that the catch almost broke. 'Have you any idea what we performed yesterday?'

'Why . . . why of course,' said Edma in a feeble voice, a flicker of panic dawning in her generally assured demeanour. 'Of course . . . You played some Bach . . . well, I mean Maestro Kreuze played Bach and you sang some Schubert *Lieder*, didn't you? Didn't she?'' She turned towards the others, her eyes growing more and more anxious as each coward turned away. 'Didn't she, Armand?' she finally demanded of her spouse, hoping, if not for full confirmation, at least for a mute nod of acquiescence.

But for once Armand, his eyes panicky but unmoving behind his glasses, did not answer, did not even look at her.

'Well, then, I am going to tell you what we played! . . .'
La Doriacci went on, tucking her satchel under her arm and clutching it with her elbow as if she feared someone might take it. 'We did *Au clair de la lune*, Hans-Helmut Kreuze and I—he at the piano, with variations, and me singing in every language under the sun. *Al claro della luna*,' she began to sing very rapidly. 'And nobody turned a hair! Nobody noticed a thing! Am I right? If not, speak up!' she added, defying each of them with her eyes and voice as they all sank deeper into their chairs and looked at their feet. 'Only one poor lawyer from Clermont-Ferrand made some vague remark, and timidly at that.'

'But that's insane!' said Edma in a falsetto which so surprised her that she left off in mid-sentence.

'Yes, it really is insane!' said Olga, also heroic. 'It's unbelievable . . . Are you sure?' she asked stupidly, and la Doriacci's glare made her curl up inside her sweater and almost literally disappear.

A heavy silence blanketed the deck, a silence that infrequent rumblings failed to dispel and which seemed to be settling in for good when Elledocq, standing there, coughed twice to clear his voice, his face evincing the steadfast gravity of an ambassador plenipotentiary. Coming from him, that attitude, not to mention the simple clearing of his throat, aroused among them a sort of terror.

'I humbly beg your pardon,' he said—marking by the addition to his verb of the 'I', the 'your', and the 'humbly', the gravity of the occasion. 'I humbly beg your pardon, but the programme is fixed.'

'Pardon?' La Doriacci was unmistakably casting her eye about in search of some clammy creature, a snake or a steer, and found nothing to listen to. But that didn't deter Elledocq. He threw back his head, thereby revealing below his chin a beardless band of skin situated between his Adam's apple and his collar, a band of virgin skin which seemed to everyone almost obscene. He began to recite in his fine grave voice the chapters to his programme listings, ticking them off on thick fingers bent one by one to keep the tally.

'Portofino: *timbale* of sea-food, *osso buco*, ice-cream, Scarlatti, Verdi. Capri: Brandenburg soufflé, *tournedos* Rossini, pastry sculpture, Strauss, Schumann . . .' After citing the name of each composer, he pointed inquisitively towards the virtuoso in question. 'Carthage—grey caviar, *scallopine* . . .'

'Oh do be quiet, for God's sake!' cried Edma, beside herself. 'Do be quiet, Captain! Nobody needs to be quite so stupid, nor so . . . nor so . . .'

She was beating her wings, her eyelashes, her shoulders, her hands, she was batting the air and ready to batter the captain, when he placed a peremptory hand on her thin shoulder. Under its pressure she literally collapsed into her chair with a cry of rebellion. The men rose to their feet, Simon Béjard with the greatest fury and Armand Bautet-Lebreche with the least. But this did not for so much as a split second arrest the captain's worthy recollection.

'Carthage: caviar, *scallopine à l'Italienne*, *bombe glacée*, Bach, Schubert,' he concluded triumphantly.

Still indifferent to the furious glares of the men and wide-eyed stares of the women, he barged on. 'Attention to regulations obligatory. *Clair de lune* not entered on agenda for Carthage, should be Bach, Schubert, period,' he concluded. 'Failure to execute contract tantamount to . . .'

He stopped dead. For by one of those miracles that give one to wonder about God, Fuschia himself, though he had been confined to the hold with his wicker bed, rubber bones and thrice-daily pâtés, had escaped. Thanks to the general clamour he had crossed the deck without anyone's hearing his ominous panting, and negotiated a barrier of three or four pairs of legs negligently stretched out on the deck. Now after sweeping each of the terrorised passengers with the stare of his blind eyes, as if it were the Last Judgment, he inexplicably cantered off again towards the door of the bar, then disappeared. The wave of relief that overtook the unhappy passengers was unequal to their shame, of which la Doriacci, though much smaller on her feet than any of the four men, reminded them.

'If you are incapable of making love and listening to music at the same time, you do not embark on a musical cruise of this sort,' she said. 'Either the two of you board an ordinary and less expensive ship, or you embark alone and bring along sleeping pills! Anyone incapable of doing both, that is,' she said with an air of triumphant scorn.

And with majestic, outraged bearing, she went off after Fuschia. Andreas didn't even try to follow.

'*I*nsane! Insane decision! No good worrying. Blame blasted artists. Twenty-seven years cruising. Ten musical cruises. Never saw the like of it . . .'

Beside himself, Captain Elledocq zigzagged from one passenger to the other. 'You'd think he was an overheated locomotive,' said Julien to Clarisse. 'Letting off the steam of stupidity.'

'It's true, he does look like a train,' said Clarisse with a laugh as Elledocq suddenly ceased reassuring his flock and stood before Edma, who with a calculating eye had offered him her pack of cigarettes.

'Go on, go on, dear Captain, it's the only way to relax.'

And turning to Clarisse with a wink, she added, 'It's the captain's only vice, you know. He doesn't drink, he doesn't chase after women, he smokes, that's all . . . It's his only fault and it's sending him straight to his grave. I've been telling him the same thing for five years . . . I kill myself repeating it, but he's got to watch out.'

'My God, oh my God, oh my God! I haven't had a smoke

in three years!' bellowed Elledocq, crimson. 'Ask Charley, ask the maids, the head-waiters, the cooks on board . . . I don't smoke any more!'

'I never interrogate the personnel on the habits of my friends,' said Edma with a certain haughtiness. She turned her back on him to join the other group, which was animatedly talking music.

'Everyone is completely mad,' Olga was saying. 'It's quite incomprehensible . . .'

'Are you put out?' asked Edma.

'It's not for me to feel put out,' said Olga, amazed by her own rancour. 'After all, it's only the last few years that I've been able to take an interest in music . . .'

'To have a memory for music you mean? That's something else again,' replied Edma.

'But what do you mean?' Olga asked.

'Oh, simply that one can be eighty or a hundred and still not be able to hear music. I am not talking about *listening* to music, I am talking about *hearing* music.'

'It's more a case of deafness than madness,' interrupted Charley with too broad a smile. 'Now that I think of it, it really was *Au clair de la lune* she was singing in German yesterday.'

'I knew it reminded me of something,' said Simon ingenuously.

'*Au clair de la lune*, of course! You recognised it? You must have been really pleased . . .' said Eric Lethuillier abruptly. 'What a pity they didn't let you speak first.'

This savage outburst produced an appalled silence. Simon, his mouth agape, took quite some time before getting up uneasily and so hesitantly that Edma, disappointed but pitying, offered him a comforting, already lit cigarette, but in vain.

'Listen, you pathetic little pipsqueak, are you looking for trouble or something?' he said in a low voice, but audibly, Edma noticed, delighted at detecting a whiff of gunpowder.

All around the surprise was palpable. As at a tennis match, the music-lovers sat erect on the same folding deck chairs where they had been lounging half an hour earlier and began to follow the match with their heads, like metronomes—until Olga intervened.

'No, no . . . Don't fight! I couldn't bear it, that would be too stupid!' she cried, her voice already that of a young widow as she flung herself, arms crossed, between the two men—not a difficult stunt since they were glaring at one another six feet apart, poisoned by insults but lacking the minimum of conviction necessary for a scuffle.

They drew back, each defying the other with looks and grunting like dear Fuschia, but with only a fraction of his aggressiveness. Charley and Julien each put a hand on the shoulders of the two men, pretending to hold them back according to the rules of propriety. Despite its pitiful conclusion, the scene had nevertheless enlivened the atmosphere. Each of those present lolled back on a deck chair with a feeling of pride, excitement or regret.

*H*alf an hour later Andreas was the only person up and about, everyone else was stretched out somewhere. His forehead resting against the door of suite Number 102, la Doriacci's, he was waiting. From time to time he calmly knocked on the cold, hard wood, neither weakly nor aggressively, but as though he had just arrived that moment at the door and as though he were waiting for someone to open it with outspread arms . . . though a full hour had passed since it had been closed in his face. La Doriacci, who the whole time had not so much as answered his appeals, finally made an effort and cried out in her strong voice, 'My dear Andreas, I want to be alone!'

'But I want to be with you,' he declared through the door.

And standing there turned towards his voice, la Doriacci drew back as if he could see her through the wooden panel.

'But since it is my wish to be alone,' she cried, 'wouldn't you choose my wish over your own?'

The siren shrieked, doors slammed, and she felt as though

she were rehearsing an opera by Alban Berg with libretto by Henry Bordeaux.

'No,' he cried in his turn. 'No! Because my being there would be only a slight annoyance to you, and even that's not certain, whereas I . . . I'll be miserable without you. There's no comparison,' he concluded. 'I love you more than I can possibly annoy you, so!'

She laughed when he knocked again, she feigned anger. She would never speak to him again. She would pretend to be asleep and would even lie down and close her eyes as if he could see her. She realised he couldn't and picked up a book. She tried to read but from time to time heard those light knocks on the door which prevented her from becoming engrossed.

Then she heard a man's voice in the hall, a voice belonging to Eric Lethuillier. Pricking up her ears, la Doriacci was tempted for a moment to open the door and gather the country urchin into her arms, the boy who had so little pride, or rather so much that he scorned the ridicule and banter of others. She was standing up again when she heard Eric's deliberate voice from behind the door.

'How's it going, my friend? What have you been doing here in front of this door for the last two hours?'

To begin with, it's less than an hour, la Doriacci answered inwardly.

But Andreas didn't take offence. 'I'm waiting for la Doriacci,' he said calmly.

'You're waiting for her to open the door?' Eric repeated. 'But if it's the diva's door, then surely she must be out, for heaven's sake! Would you like me to ask Charley where she is?'

'No thanks, no,' said Andreas's calm voice, and la Doriacci sat down again, disappointed but pleased at the pride of her young lover. 'No, she's there,' Andreas repeated. 'She just doesn't want to let me in at the moment, that's all.'

There was a brief silence.

'Oh well then!' said Eric, after a moment's show of surprise. 'If you're taking it so well . . .'

His laugh was disagreeable. It sounded false to la Doriacci's practised ear, and she felt bad—why didn't she let the young fool in? She felt like complimenting him, and furthermore he was her lover. It would be so much simpler!

'All right, well then, good luck,' said Eric. 'And by the way, Andreas, are you going to New York or not? If so, watch out: in hotel corridors over there, people would have bumped into you a dozen times already. Can't loiter in the States; they don't look kindly on that sort of thing.'

I'll get even with that rat! la Doriacci said to herself, or more exactly, to her cross-looking reflection in the mirror, which scared her, and she calmed down right away. When someone provoked her to this level of anger, a sort of click went off in her head and she knew that a card had been entered in the file labelled ACCOUNTS RECEIVABLE. One day when the drawer was open it would pop up again all on its own—it was fated to, even if she herself forgot about it. Indeed, whenever she was angry with someone, no matter what the cause, la Doriacci knew in advance that person would come to regret it, and this pleased her. Meanwhile, what was Andreas going to do? She was pleased to see he was no coward—a fault that usually made her call off the whole affair, barring tremendous virility in a different sphere of activity.

'So, you're not going to answer?' Eric's voice continued on the other side of the door—an irritated voice, as if Andreas's silence had been accompanied by a dismissive gesture.

But that, as la Doriacci knew, was not his style. Andreas must have adopted a smiling, inattentive air. She tiptoed up to the door, cursing the poor field of vision offered by the fanlight which was too high. She could see nothing. She squinted sourly at the situation and swore in a low voice.

'And yet you're her knight in shining armour,' said Eric to Andreas. 'You should be able to go in. It's not much fun to be out here in the hall alone like some waif.'

'Yes it is.' Andreas's voice had softened and gone up a notch. 'Yes, this hallway is quite pleasant when you're alone.'

'Well then, I'll leave,' said Eric. 'Anyway, you're right to guard that door. La Doriacci's probably calling up your understudy this very minute.'

Andreas's voice went hoarse again, uttering an incomprehensible sound, then la Doriacci could hear nothing but the tearing of clothes, a kick against the door, something being dragged, two people breathing heavily. She tapped her foot impatiently and got a chair in an effort to see the fight better.

You can't see a thing, *per Dio*! But by the time she had climbed up onto the chair somebody was dragging himself away from her door, limping. One only . . . la Doriacci, who had been singing Verdi for three months, believed Andreas was dead.

'Andreas?' she whispered through the door.

'Yes.' The boy's voice was so close that she drew back.

She thought she could feel his warm breath on her shoulders, on her neck, that she could feel his forehead soaked by the sweat of the brawl, not at all the same thing as the sweat of love, which is salty and almost cold. She waited for him to ask her to open up. But he didn't, stupidly, just kept on breathing in deep gasps. She imagined that pretty mouth raised across white teeth, the beads of moisture on the upper lip; she could see again the small white scar left on Andreas's temple by a bicycle accident when he was twelve, just twelve years ago . . . reluctantly she called him first. 'Andreas . . .' she whispered. And suddenly she imagined that she could see herself the way a stranger would see her—half-naked under her peignoir, leaning against the door on the other side of which leaned an all too pretty young man who was bleeding, a young man who was not, after all, quite like the others, she thought resignedly while her other hand turned the key, and the door finally admitted Andreas. He collapsed against her shoulder, one eye already black and blue, his knuckles skinned and, moreover, bleeding onto her carpet—the young man whose shoulder and hair she kissed half unwillingly, who purred and played havoc with her room and her solitude, hoping one day to play havoc with her life.

For not quite six days Andreas had been feeling, time and again, like a dead weight, a stone in a witty, volatile, light comedy. Sometimes, on the other hand, he had the impression of being able to float above material things, of being the only one free to think like a romantic, able to judge these powerful, gilt-edged robots whose sole freedom was to make still more money out of what they already possessed. La Doriacci and Julien Peyrat alone escaped this classification. La Doriacci was by nature a free spirit and would be until her life's end—and the only places she was truly free were dark stages where, blinded by the spotlights, she sang before faceless people. Andreas dreamed of seeing her perform, he dreamed of being in a box, the only person in a dinner jacket, surrounded by men in uniform and women in low-cut dresses, hearing the people in the next box say, 'She's so charming . . . What talent, what a marvellous understanding of the text,' and so on, while he silently swelled with pride. Unless some annoying person next to them claimed not to understand what the others saw in her and spoke ill of her. But Andreas would not budge, for the curtain would be rising and la Doriacci would be making her entrance to bravos, bravos among which she would recognise those of Andreas, and then she would be singing. And during the intermission, a bit later, the fellow who had been so critical would turn to his friends with tears in his eyes and say 'How beautiful! What a marvellous face! What a superb body!' Andreas skipped over this last phrase rather hastily, a little guiltily, but why should he? And the other idiot would ask how he might meet la Doriacci, if it was possible to sleep with her, and so on, rambling on foolishly until his neighbour pointed out Andreas to him in a whisper, and the fool would blush deeply and bow low to Andreas, who would smile at him with all the forbearance of the happy.

That he would have been happy, with an unalloyed happiness, this he did not yet know. For, unwilling as she was to satisfy Andreas's fantasies, la Doriacci in fact suited his nature and, oddly, his age.

*B*eing a producer had at least taught Simon Béjard one thing—courage. He had learned how to lose all hope in a film at noon and still order a round at Fouquet's at one, showing a smiling face to the old owls perched there ready to laugh at another's misfortune, and reciting an anecdote that was, if not funny, then at least light-hearted. In short, Simon had learned to handle himself well in defeat, and this sort of behaviour had become rare enough in Paris for the three women on board to appreciate it. They were amused to think that it was thanks to his trade—usually so deplored, by reputation so vulgar—that in the eyes of Edma and la Doriacci, Simon Béjard had behaved like a gentleman. When Simon did not speak for more than three minutes, he couldn't last any longer, they became alarmed, taking it in turns to cajole him, making him laugh, each giving him to understand that she alone understood him, and Simon would feel vaguely comforted.

Clarisse was the only one who did not talk to him. Sometimes she gave him a fleeting smile, or poured him a lemonade or scotch, or did a crossword puzzle with him—crosswords so clearly in his view representing both their love lives, though his allusions always met with incomprehension and light-heartedness on her part. There was so little misery in her manner that she annoyed him; it particularly annoyed him to be outdone in stoicism by a woman.

After they reached Bejaia, he jumped on her, taking advantage of the fact that Olga and Eric had gone down to the quay to mail some letters. The sense of having little time in which to speak naturally impelled him to laborious phrases, dead pauses between silences. Finally after a few minutes, as he became more and more deeply embroiled, suddenly horrified by the thought she might not know what had happened and that it would mortify him to be her informant, Clarisse herself was obliged to bring up the subject, much against her will, in order to reassure him.

'No, dear Simon, my husband and I no longer love one another. It isn't the least bit important to me.'

'You're really lucky,' said Simon, sitting at her little table on deck—a table quite naturally graced by a bottle of scotch, though the bottle was less empty, and seemed to Clarisse less primordial, than usual. 'May I stay here?' he asked. 'I'm not too much in your way?'

'No, not at all . . .' began Clarisse, but her protests were interrupted by Simon's loud laugh.

'That would really be something, if we stopped talking to each other, you and I—if we only communicated by intermediary! We've got an odd point in common on this boat—the two big cuck . . .'

'Hush . . . Simon, hush,' said Clarisse. 'You're not seriously going to worry yourself about a ridiculous affair. It's just a thing of a day or two and will end there, for Olga and Eric alike. It wasn't anything, just a little physical attraction. If they hadn't told us we would never have known!'

'That's exactly it. That's what makes me sad about Olga,' said Simon looking down. 'It's that she didn't try to spare me. She told me everything without giving a damn whether it hurt me or not. For that matter your own charming husband told you too, didn't he?'

'Told me, no; not once! But' 'gave me to understand', yes—fifteen times over . . .'

'He's a handsome bastard, your husband, eh? Objectively speaking, little one.'

'I can't claim any right to objectivity,' said Clarisse. 'Eric's my husband, and after all there's a contract of mutual respect between us . . .'

Her voice was firm, and this exasperated Simon.

'But that's just my point, since he doesn't respect the contract . . .'

'I've always found it difficult to despise anyone,' began Clarisse but she was interrupted by Charley, who was literally prancing around in front of them, rolling his eyes mysteriously.

'I've got something to show you,' he said raising a finger to his lips. 'Something absolutely marvellous.'

He dragged them off to Julien's cabin, while Julien played deck tennis with Andreas, and showed them the Marquet with a thousand dithyrambic and boringly pedagogic comments. But neither one made a move to leave—Simon because he was looking at the painting and appreciating it with the new eyes given to him by Music, even looking at it with pleasure, Clarisse because she was looking at the mess around her, the blue T-shirt, the espadrilles, the crumbled newspapers, the stubbed-out cigarettes in the ashtray, the cufflinks on the floor, the total disorder of a college boy rather than a mature man, which seemed the very reflection of Julien and disturbed her excessively, she thought, but deliciously. For the first time she felt a protective impulse towards Julien rather than the other way around—and this, she realised, was because she knew better than he did how to fold shirts and straighten up a room. She felt a conspiratorial recognition for the three bottles of scotch stashed away in the bathroom, she admired the Marquet with Simon, honestly, since it was beautiful, but almost without seeing it, without being able to pronounce even the hint of an opinion, as Charley was asking her to do. She picked out only one thing in the painting: the woman rounding the street-corner. And through some corresponding turn of mind neither she nor Julien would ever know about perhaps, she felt a momentary jealousy. On leaving the cabin, Simon thought sadly that three days earlier he would have wanted to buy that painting for Olga, who didn't love him; he did not admit to himself that he also wondered whether such a present might not bring her back.

Up on deck they sat down again, with Edma. The afternoon was almost over. The conversation turned to Proust, and Edma dissected the dynamics of the cruise.

'It's odd,' she said, 'how everyone talks about general topics now. It's as though at the start we all wanted to know everything about each other, and everyone spoke about their private lives, and now that we know, we all want to forget the whole thing as soon as possible . . . We're all abristle, if you like, and we take refuge in the impersonal.'

'Perhaps the revelations turned out to be too explosive,' said Clarisse without malice, as if she played no part in these past indiscretions.

Simon ventured, 'Because you don't feel involved with all these crazy feelings? Pardon the expression, Clarisse, but if you're the Virgin Mary, then it seems to me your Joseph's neither friendly nor thoughtful.'

Clarisse burst into loud, delighted laughter. Simon was left complimented by her amusement but furious at not being able to share it. He simply let her laugh, though gradually he gave in to the contagion and joined in with his hoarse gasping, less chairman of the board than travelling salesman.

'Oh goodness,' said Clarisse wiping her eyes—this time without producing blackish streaks, thanks to the light make-up. 'Good gracious,' she said. 'What ideas, Simon! Joseph . . . Eric . . . there's so little . . .' And she was off again.

Laughing turned her pink and made her eyes glisten, made her look seven years younger, restored to her that delicious light-hearted youth which, in Clarisse's case, had spanned two generations and hence two concepts of love, since girls had gone from the age of forbidden love, of giggling with the boys at school, to the age of required love, of kisses in the dark with the same boys in cars. Girls kissed by lovers who had stolen toffees from them that very afternoon in a maths class.

'You remind me of my youth,' said Simon tenderly. 'That beats everything, actually. I'm twenty years older than you.'

'You're joking,' said Clarisse. 'I'm thirty-two.'

'And I'm almost fifty. You see?' Behind the interrogatory 'You see?' was not so much 'Right, I could be your father,' as 'Who would believe it?'

'You should have been in the same class as Julien,' he added. He gave Clarisse his pensive, limpid look (for his look could be as limpid as the situation was at first, as troubled as it became, or as calculating as it required).

'I don't quite follow you,' said Clarisse, who looked frankly troubled.

'It's that you belong to the same breed,' said Simon. He leaned back in his chair, head raised towards the skies, a thing he did readily when reflecting to himself. 'You're made for having fun.'

Clarisse looked so surprised that Charley cut in, 'He's right. It may not be obvious but it's true. Both of you are ready to go arm in arm with life. Neither of you knows or cares how others see you, so . . . If you ask me, Eric must be very strong-minded to succeed in giving you the idea . . . All the more so since it was so disastrous! Julien's the same way. He doesn't play the ladies' man, the gambler, the art expert, or the hell-raiser, but he's all of them.'

'But how are Olga and Eric, for instance, any different?'

'Well, because they try to seem what they aren't,' said Charley, elated at the interest provoked by the fruit of his meditations. 'The others only try to make people believe they're what they would like to be, and that's not so phoney—Edma wants to be as elegant as she actually is. You, Simon, wish to appear the perceptive producer you always wanted to be—that you've become too. Armand Bautet-Lebreche acts the chairman of the board he likes to be; Andreas the sentimental fool he's bound to remain; and even Elledocq plays the testy commander he also wants to be, however stupid the role. As for me, I play nice Charley, which I like to be. But when it comes to Eric and Olga, it's another matter. Olga wants to make us believe in her unselfishness, her artistic taste or distinction, which she would like to have but doesn't—begging your pardon, Simon! Eric wants to have us believe in his moral loftiness, his humanitarianism, his open-mindedness—qualities he lacks and which in his case he doesn't want. He just pretends to have them. The only cynical person on this boat is Eric Lethuillier. Your husband, dear lady'—and Charley came triumphantly to the end of his speech. Then, suddenly sitting up straight in his chair, he stared past Clarisse and Simon at something behind them. It was Eric, returning after only an hour from an expedition that was to have required three. He was approaching at a rapid pace with Olga in tow, breathless, her eyes gleaming, scarcely concealing her mysterious jubilation.

'But what has happened?' asked Simon, standing up, for Eric's expression—he was white with anger—could mean anything. Simon took a step towards Olga.

'Always so chivalrous,' noted Clarisse softly to Charley. 'He's a good person, Simon,' she said. 'He took Olga under his protection and there she'll stay no matter what she does.'

'What happened?' Simon repeated.

Eric looked him up and down. 'Ask Olga,' he said, and strode off towards the cabin.

Olga took her time sitting down, untying her raw-silk scarf and stretching out her legs. Then she picked up Simon's glass—allegedly lemonade but laced with gin—and drank down half of it at a gulp. Clarisse watched her with a sort of pitying sympathy which Charley noted. For though he had no great sensitivity when it came to women, he could not but admire the incredible improvement wrought in Clarisse from knowing herself loved, even if it were by a professional cheat. For Charley—whose job it was, after all, and indeed inclination—had cabled an old Australian friend, whose reply did not corroborate what Julien had told him.

Moreover, this same friend did know a certain Peyrat who was a big winner at card tables in Europe and America.

This was one of the principal reasons Charley had undertaken the sale of Julien's painting. He was not at all infatuated with his pictorial knowledge, and still less anxious to be of service to passengers whom he scorned for their snobbery as much as they scorned him (though less discreetly) for his sexual preferences. Charley had accepted the assignment only to have a little fun by indirectly conning one of the hardy music-lovers, so indifferent to anything beyond personal comfort. Furthermore he had felt kindly towards Julien ever since their tête-à-tête, and if certain pieces of information were to leak out about him, Charley would be able to intercept and deflect them. In the meantime this look of pity from Clarisse—a look that one would not expect from a woman who had been deceived even if she was miserably unhappy, not for her husband's mistress—this look of pity could only mean that Eric Lethuillier was no gift for one woman to give another, even involuntarily.

He came back to earth to hear Olga's shrewdly delayed explanation. 'Something absolutely incredible happened,' she said. 'It's absurd when you think of Bejaia, where it's located, the time of year . . . There's really nothing in that place to justify those photographers.'

'What photographers?' Simon asked smoothly. Olga's astonished look had aroused his lively distrust.

She went on without replying, 'I may well be an intellectual,' she said, laughing a bit too loud, as if her lack of delusions were so flagrant that the remark would surely evoke laughter. But nobody budged. 'I may well be an intellectual,' she repeated, laughing still harder, determined to drum up support, 'but I just couldn't believe they would send a photographer from Paris to take my picture in Bejaia on the arm of Monsieur Lethuillier. But then again, perhaps it was on his account. What do you think, Clarisse?' She turned directly towards Clarisse, who looked her in the eye for a moment and slowly smiled, as she had before. For a moment Simon and Charley both wondered why, until Olga dropped the next bombshell on the deck.

'Reporters from *Jours de France* and *Minute*,' Olga added, resting her hands on the arms of her wooden chair, and stroking them with delight as if they were the smoothest ivory.

Simon was speechless at first, frowning as though trying to solve a purely mathematical problem. Then he burst out laughing, a moment before Charley cracked up and split his sides laughing too (though he didn't wish to seem openly aware that any passenger had been made to look ridiculous or got their comeuppance). Edma's eyes sparkled. Olga tried hard to put on a surprised and ingenuous air, but the sweetness of her revenge was still too fresh for her not to gloat.

'But where did they find you?' asked Simon once he had calmed down. He was enthusiastic with admiration, overwhelmed with joy; his mistress had got even with the very man she had used to deceive him, and he rejoiced because Olga's spite showed that Eric didn't mean a thing to her any more, that she was his. As though it were the tale of their own reconciliation, a lyrical tale full of fine sentiments, he made her repeat it three times, the story of her perfidious little private vengeance, of which he was not the victim.

'Well, here's what happened,' said Olga. 'We got a little separated from the group, Eric and I, I guess he wanted to bring back some shoes for Clarisse . . . some sandals,' she said vaguely, looking more embarrassed than necessary at the weakness of her alibi. 'We were in a sort of souk, and there was a charming, deserted little square where I wanted to try on some shoes—ones I bought for myself. They're beautiful shoes, actually . . . you'll see, Clarisse . . . Unless Eric forget them in his fury,' she said, looking suddenly preoccupied. 'Oh, that was stupid. I should have thought of that.'

'Never mind, never mind, go on,' said Simon. 'Clarisse is about as concerned for her sandals as I am for my own slippers.'

'Well then, I was leaning over to slip them on, holding onto Eric's arm so I wouldn't fall; with one foot in midair, and then, pop-pop-pop—lots of flashbulbs, like at the opening night at the Opéra. I was scared . . . all of a sudden

255

these electric flashes after all that pure, pure light on the sea, the sky . . . it was horrible, like winter returning . . . it was quite terrifying. I don't know, I grabbed onto Eric but he . . . he's a lot quicker than me, a lot more intelligent of course—right away he understood what the photographers were after . . . but even so, he didn't know who they worked for! That would have killed him! So, while Eric was trying to loosen my grip on his arm'—she laughed at the mere idea of her own grip—'the guys skipped off. But I'd recognised them. And Eric was wild with rage. With good reason, too. I think when his pals see a picture of him draped around a starlet trying on shoes in some romantic little port, it's going to mean an odd spot of publicity. He's furious, absolutely, totally furious. You would have laughed if you'd seen him, Clarisse!' she continued, introducing a deliberate tone of complicity that seemed suddenly to awaken Clarisse, and to strip her of the remote and vaguely amused smile she had worn until then. Getting up, she said, clearly addressing Simon and Charley rather than Olga, 'Excuse me, I'm going to see what my husband is doing.'

Her departure seemed to Edma and to the two men, if not to Olga, a fine example of married decorum. But it was also clearly a relief to be just the four of them again. They cackled and gloated for more than an hour, during which Olga had the opportunity to give them a more fully annotated account. They toasted this with champagne. It was not until after the sixth glass that Olga Lamouroux admitted to her three companions that two days earlier she had sent a telegram to some journalist friends of hers—an admission that she might just as well have spared herself, since the surprise it produced was visibly slight.

*A*t Bejaia la Doriacci did not carry out her threat after all, but stayed on board the *Narcissus*. This is how it happened.

Hans-Helmut Kreuze, far from sharing the diva's anger, professed to be revolted by it, and after some reflection asked for a meeting with Captain Elledocq in his office. It was there that Elledocq kept his log which, inspected at random, revealed such items as:

- Bought 50 kg tomatoes.
- Repaired curtain-loops, main saloon.
- Interceded passenger dispute.
- Loaded 100 tons fuel.
- 40 kg spoiled *tournedos* dropped overboard
- Heating adjusted.
- Sighted dolphin school.

All but the last two entries could have been the daily fare

of an innkeeper. No matter; Elledocq found in it an Olympian majesty.

His cap, for once absent from his head, hung from a hook. Behind him on some shelves were a few books with such frightening titles as *How to Survive in a Sea of Ice, Rights of the Passenger to Refuse Amputation in Case of Accident, Transport of Cadavers from an International Port to a National Port, How to Prevent the Propagation of Typhus*. Naturally Pottin Frères had strictly banned all such ominous works from the ship's saloons or staterooms. They had also removed, from Elledocq's very walls, a cartoon poster that had a good dose of reality to it: it showed a miserable naked navy-blue passenger sticking out his purplish tongue while a robust sailor bullied him with a big smile, or so it appeared. This poster had been judged demoralising by the Pottin brothers, and so there remained to remind Captain Elledocq of the gravity of his task only the few books, forbidden by day but which he could consult at night in his library. And so when Kreuze appeared, it was plainly to indicate his authority and the gravity pertaining to his post that Elledocq gestured the maestro imperiously towards an armchair opposite his own without even raising his eyes from the papers lying on his desk, ads extolling the superiority of fishhook X over fishhook Y. Only the rap of a fist on his desk made him look up.

Hans-Helmut Kreuze had turned purple, for though he was sensitive to hierarchy, he thought Elledocq had got it wrong: the captain of an old tub sitting while a master such as Kreuze was standing! Elledocq got up automatically. They glared at one another, a stare shot with blood and cholesterol, that might have been the prelude to a heart attack, but which seemed merely comic since neither spoke.

'What did you want?' barked Elledocq, irritated by the banging of the fist.

'I wish to suggest to you a way out for the impasse with la Doriacci,' said Kreuze.

Faced by the uncomprehending, even slow-witted look of his counterpart, Kreuze spelled out his plan: 'I know two persons who can please the ear, two Swiss students from my school at Dortmund, who are vacationing at Bejaia. Two persons who can replace la Doriacci at a moment's notice, the moment she steps off this boat.'

'What will they sing?' said the captain, distraught, consulting his Book of Rules, the musical programme that had already been flouted by the diva.

'But these persons don't sing. It is flute and cello, and also violin by two persons. We will play trios, some Beethoven,' said Kreuze, excited by the idea of his vengeance against the diva. He imagined her that very night, replaced by him and his two unknowns. 'It will be exceptionally sensuous,' he said to Elledocq, who was leaning over his programme, his brow knit as if before a conundrum (and whose mistrust returned on hearing the word *sensuous*). 'Ouf . . . well, some chamber music,' said Kreuze, confirming Elledocq's fears even as the captain began to rejoice in the possibility of being delivered from the diva. However, she had been entrusted to him. Almost anything could happen to her in this forsaken country, and could it be that allowing her to leave would be tantamount to resignation and dishonour?

'Great inconvenience,' he said. 'Diva contract fee very high, I know. Pottin Frères furious, passengers furious. Passengers get nothing, no songs.'

'As if you get anything from hearing her sing *Au clair de la lune*, so what's the difference?' said Kreuze haughtily. '*Au clair de la lune* . . . ' he hummed with a shrug.

'What? What?' said Elledocq. 'What's the matter that tune? *Clair de lune* known all over, proof . . . Pretty music, pretty words, French song . . .'

'We will play it for you,' said Kreuze with his broad laugh. 'And so. I am delighted to have settled things for this boat, Captain.'

They shook hands and Elledocq, who was in the habit of crushing the bones of his acquaintances, noticed that Kreuze's hand resisted his effortlessly, and even drew a small groan from him. No doubt thanks to his finger exercises. Kreuze gone, the captain was alone with his programme notes. *Soup à la George Sand, Chicken Croquettes*

Prokofiev, and *Sherbet à la Rachmaninoff*, plus an unusual *foie gras* from the Lot and then la Doriacci was to sing from Act I of *Il Trovatore*—an entry which Elledocq struck from the programme, replacing it with the *Beethoven Trio played by Kreuze plus X and Y*.

Meanwhile la Doriacci was packing. La Doriacci was going to sing elsewhere for other philistines perhaps worse than these philistines, who were so rich and so uncultivated. But first she was going to give herself a week's vacation. Her reasons for going were so sound that she could forget the only real reason: la Doriacci was making a getaway from Andreas of Nevers.

At that very moment he was sitting on the foot of the bed, gazing at the bedclothes and closed face of his mistress who was engrossed in stuffing her long dresses into suitcases. At times Andreas rested a hand on the turned-down sheet, the way one might touch the sand of a beach that will be left behind, and undoubtedly never seen again, the way one might breathe in, by the light of a fleeting November sunset in the country, the despairing warm odour of the final vintage, a sweetness beyond recall.

Andreas was being abandoned, and he suffered without a word, without eliciting any sign that the diva noticed the despair that overwhelmed him.

As for Clarisse, she was trembling uncontrollably; for Eric had come out of the bathroom in his bathrobe, perfumed, impeccable, and saying quietly, 'You're looking beautiful this evening. What a lovely dress!' all of which was in fact an announcement of the impending enactment of conjugal rites that evening.

This duty Clarisse had carried out in body long after her spirit drifted away from Eric and before she had reached her present state of irritable indifference and even coldness towards the idea of making love. But now there was Julien, and she did not want to be unfaithful to Julien, she could not do it, even if their love-making had been awkward that first time. Because she knew that they would find themselves together again one day, and that Julien knew it too.

The idea of the coming night was already a torture to her. Her fear of Eric was still too great for her to refuse him the body he called cold, the face he called insipid. And indeed for several years now it had seemed that each time he came to her bed Eric was bestowing a gift, a gift of compassion and not desire.

Julien's love and professed desire, the way the men on board looked at her—all this had restored to Clarisse not just confidence in her charm, but the consciousness of her own body as her own property, with desires and denials until now deemed presumptuous but which had begun to seem to her perfectly licit. For years on end she had been able to yield to Eric her body, as unloved object, but she could not entrust to him the object that had become Julien's live and irreplaceable possession. By sleeping with Eric she would be betraying Julien, prostituting her body, denying herself. Julien was husband, lover, protector, she realised suddenly, thanks to the repulsion she felt for Eric and his blond beauty.

And so her face was white as she entered the bar in an evening dress, Eric at her side in his dinner jacket. For all her pallor, her entrance was striking, and Julien, who had had to borrow a bowtie from one of the barmen, who felt awkward, poorly dressed, and sad not to be alone with Clarisse, who for once was not pleased with the way he looked, at least was concerned about himself and his appearance, was astounded that this woman was his and loved him. She loved him: Julien Peyrat, cardsharp, forger, a shady character who, if recognised by any one of ten people in the world, might have to be locked up, who had never done a thing with his own two hands except lay them on women or cards or currency, and only to let them all go in the end. He was loved by this woman who was beautiful, loyal and intelligent, who had been so unhappy yet never become mean or cynical, this woman of character and quality.

And the conceit, the folly of wanting to take her wherever he might go, seemed to him so evident that he left the bar where everyone was gathered, and went to lean against the ship's rail, where the wind beat against his face and ruffled his hair, even undoing the knot of his tie and making him look like the shady mafioso or wino he would finally become. For a long while Julien faced that dark-blue sea, almost black against the lights of Bejaia, and despised himself. It had been a good deal longer than twenty years since he had thought at all about himself except to congratulate himself happily on his luck. He would have to cut the costs of this impossible adventure, have to sell or not sell the Marquet— it no longer mattered one way or the other. He would have to go ashore at Bejaia along with la Doriacci and forget the whole thing.

The captain was thinking—since Charley had gone off on some errand for the lovely Edma and was therefore unavailable to carry out the painful task. Elledocq had tried ten times to reach one of the Pottin brothers, but they were all off on vacation. Naturally they weren't waiting at their desks with pounding hearts for the Narcissus to return intact from its seventeenth cruise. Elledocq had been unable to reach anyone but the vice-president, a certain Magnard, whom he considered somewhat shifty without knowing why. When speaking of him he always shrugged in a way that, though he never thought about it, said all there was to say.

'Elledocq here,' he had yelled—for he always yelled over the phone. 'Elledocq from the Narcissus!'

'Yes, yes my good man,' Magnard's voice had replied. 'Everything all right? Having good weather?'

'No!' yelled Elledocq, exasperated. As if he would have put in a call to talk about the weather! Really, these bureaucrats!

'Well, here we're having marvellous weather,' Magnard continued. He must be bored stiff all alone at the office. 'That's really too bad for your passengers.'

'Nothing wrong there,' hollered Elledocq. 'Marvellous weather, but major snag: la Doriacci wants to quit! Prussian proposes two pals to replace. What say, Magnard?'

'What? What?' said Magnard, apparently appalled by the

news. 'What? But when? How did it happen? La Doriacci's still on board, isn't she?'

'Yes, but not for long.'

'What happened, Captain Elledocq?' Magnard was reminding him of his rank, a sign that the situation was graver than Elledocq had imagined, despite the welcome prospect of escaping the diva's hoots and trills. 'Captain Elledocq, you are responsible for that splendid woman. What happened?'

A heavy sigh shook Elledocq's barrel chest, then subsided. 'She sang *Clair de lune*,' he said in a lugubrious voice.

'Which *Clair de lune*? The sonata? But that's for piano. Which *lune* do you mean? The audience didn't like it? Or what?'

'*Clair de lune*, song,' said Elledocq, unimpressed by Magnard's musical pretensions. '*Clair de lune* that you sing— you know, at school.'

There was an incredulous silence.

'You don't really mean it, my good man,' Magnard went on. 'Now help me out, Elledocq, good man. Sing me this thing you're talking about so at least I can understand just a bit. Afterwards I'll telephone la Doriacci, but I do have to know what it's all about. Okay, go ahead, I'm listening.'

'But . . . but . . . I can't!' stammered Elledocq. 'Impossible. Anyway, I sing off-key! And I've got work . . .'

Magnard assumed his vice-president's voice. 'Sing!' he bellowed. 'Sing, Elledocq, that's an order!'

The captain stood in his cabin, phone in hand. Throwing glances of almost virginal anguish towards the open door, he began:

> *Au clair de la lu-ne*
> *Mon ami Pierrot . . .*

'Can't hear a thing!' Magnard yelled. 'Louder!'

With a little cough, Elledocq went on in a hoarse and pleading voice.

> *Prête-moi ta plu-me . . .*

263

He couldn't close the door without letting go of the phone, it was impossible . . . He wiped his forehead with his hand.

'I can't hear a thing!' Magnard was saying in a jovial voice. 'Louder!'

The captain took a deep breath and was off again in a voice that sounded to him true and harmonious. Suddenly he found a kind of pleasure in bellowing towards the window, in holding the receiver away from his chin just slightly:

> *Prête-moi ta plu-me*
> *Pour écrire un mot . . .*

He stopped dead at the sound of Edma's voice, ringing out behind him, and hung up dead on the vice-president of Pottin & Pottin Frères.

'Good gracious, what's going on in here? Do the Algerians slaughter pigs in autumn too? Gracious, Captain, my good friend, so it is you there? You haven't hurt yourself, I hope?' she continued. 'Did you hear those cries too? It's terrible . . . Charley? Where are you, Charley? No. Enough joking. Did you know that you have a very fine timbre, Captain?' said Edma Bautet-Lebreche. 'Doesn't he, Charley?' she added.

That cretin, thought Elledocq, coming back in that bloody blazer he likes to call wine-red but that's actually candypink.

For once Elledocq was exhausted. In a single day he had had to re-do the programme, menus and concerts, sing *Au clair de la lune* to the vice-president of the Compagnie Pottin, and now here he was with this 'fine timbre' business . . .

'One thing for sure, I'll end up bonkers . . .' he grumbled. Turning to Charley he added, 'I've had a terribly tiring day, old man . . .' He was forgetting to telegraph again, a definite sign of confusion in the little grey mass that made up his brain.

While Charley and Edma looked on, he shuffled towards the door with his back bent. But he turned around, suddenly livid. 'My God! The Prussian's Tweedle-Dees!'

'What Tweedle-Dees?' asked Charley, as he unconsciously

began to unload his packages on the captain's sacrosanct desk, while he, too tired to react, passed a weary eye over the blasphemous purchases, a gaze in which a befuddled memory wondered what was jarring about this spectacle of a T-shirt encrusted with rhinestones, a bargain-size bottle of body make-up remover, sandals with wedge heels—all of it on Captain Elledocq's blotter, inkwell and ship's logs. Charley and Elledocq looked at each other, Charley suddenly horrified, Elledocq vague. And it was more out of duty than because he wanted to that Elledocq swept it all onto the carpet, where of course a bag of curlers split open and spilled out the little pink and green gadgets which went rolling about gaily under Elledocq's dull gaze. He raised his eyes.

'Charley,' he said, 'go tell Göring to be back here in half an hour with his two little Swiss yodellers and their tin whistles and calabashes! We'll listen to them together with Madame Bautet-Lebreche. But let's not have any monkey business between them, for God's sake!' he added.

And he went out slamming the door, leaving his two spectators as surprised as they could be after forty or fifty years' experience of pretty wide-ranging psychological insight.

Overcoming her astonishment, Edma Bautet-Lebreche found her presence required at the audition to pass judgment on the two natives of Montreux that Kreuze had discovered. Much amused by Elledocq's solemn request, all the more so since ten minutes before she had heard him sing 'Ma chandelle est morte,' she went to join him, the two protegés and their patron in the main saloon. They were both fifty or close to it and hideous to behold, concluded Edma at first glance; with shorts too long and hairy legs terminating in woollen socks and sandals. Both promised to return with dinner jackets. Kreuze and Elledocq were already seated when Edma arrived, and though she wanted to slip in without causing a disturbance, Elledocq leaped up and with an iron hand guided her to a seat between himself and Kreuze. Even before hearing the first note, Edma leaned across to Elledocq.

'They're really quite ugly, don't you think, Captain?' she said.

'That's his buiness,' said Elledocq with a jab of the chin towards Kreuze and a sneer that Edma found quite inscrutable.

'Why?' she asked softly, as the two students, at an order from Kreuze, began to play. 'Why?' she repeated in a low voice.

'Ask him yourself,' Elledocq said.

So she listened as they played a Haydn trio, confidently, with impeccable technique. She congratulated the triumphant maestro gracefully, though she was surprised at the tone in which Elledocq congratulated him.

'You think the diva replaced?' he asked her as the two went off together, almost arm in arm towards the deck.

'You can't be serious!' she said. 'It's only on account of her that anyone is here. I admit that I could go without her this year if necessary, though she is divine. I have memories of other years on the *Narcissus*. But as for the others . . . you should speak to her, Captain. Or rather, tell her she has already been replaced, tell her she needn't worry or feel guilty. La Doriacci would leave willingly if it would cause a catastrophe, but not if her departure was simply an incident.'

'You think?' asked Elledocq, who over the years had acquired an instinctive if often perilous confidence in the psychological edicts of Edma Bautet-Lebreche.

'I don't think, I know so,' she said in an imperious tone. 'I know because I'm the same way—if I'm not going to be missed, I don't leave.'

Still Elledocq hesitated a bit; after today, he was hardly anxious to plunge back into a thorny argument with la Doriacci.

Edma took his arm kindly. 'Go on,' she said. 'Let's go. I'll come with you—it's safer that way. You can go and smoke a nice pipe afterwards,' she added a bit remorsefully, since Elledocq seemed so crestfallen, even though he didn't flinch.

But when they reached la Doriacci's cabin her tactics

turned out to be superfluous. There was no response, and since Elledocq had his pass key with him as always, they pushed open the door to find the room empty and all her baggage gone. They took just one step inside, made out in the dusk la Doriacci asleep, fully clothed, and the young man, half-naked, his fine golden torso tufted with short coppery hair, stretched across the bed, his head against the ankles of his mistress, his long legs sticking out from under the covers and reaching to the floor.

Elledocq blushed with modesty, and when Edma said, in a voice filled with respect, 'My, how beautiful!' he became strangely indignant. He let slip a quick laugh, but inwardly he regretted that he did not inspire the same respect in Edma. His scornful little laugh earned him an immediate request for a cigarette. He shook his head without getting angry, to Edma's disappointment.

'That makes three musicians and one coloratura for you,' she remarked vengefully, passing in front of him and leaving him there, unmoving. 'The Compagnie Pottin will be delighted with these added attractions. Now we'll find out how to play *Au clair de la lune* on flute and cello.'

$\mathcal{S}$hortly afterwards Andreas woke up drenched in a thin sweat, his heart pounding violently before he could even think why—la Doriacci was leaving him, had left him, he was lost. It was already dark in the cabin, and he imagined her on the platform of some station at that very moment, waiting for him. After a moment he gasped for breath, something tightened about his heart and made him slightly dizzy. He sprang out of bed towards the platform, out of that dark and well-loved bed, a forsaken bed, but as he sprang up, his arm brushed la Doriacci's well-rounded hip. For a moment he hesitated to admit she was there. For the first time in his life young Andreas hesitated in the face of a joy so quickly restored. He was afraid he would die of cardiac arrest; for the first time he was quite simply afraid of dying. And yet the moment she was gone what would he lose by dying? From the moment she left, his life would be empty and flat, and his death the same: empty and bored, and boring for Andreas of Nevers—but now, now he had la Doriacci and he tried to reach her with kisses through the sheets that she had pulled up over her head as a shelter, denying his lips the slightest surface of bare skin. And she was laughing and he was becoming annoyed, unable to touch her with his hands but grabbing a sheet between his teeth and shaking it like a small dog, pulling it off the bed while la Doriacci laughed all the harder and even began to bark in her beautiful, grave voice.

'What will I find behind that sheet,' she said. 'A pug or a Dobermann? Arf-arf?' she said in a deep voice. 'Or yip-yip? What are you tonight?'

'I don't feel like playing,' said Andreas, suddenly remembering the despairing young man he had been all day as he walked the interminable passageways of solitude, the pale and frenzied young man whose suffering he relived so acutely that he collapsed onto the shoulder of the woman who had inflicted it on him.

'Get a move on,' she said, with unconcern. 'I have to dress for the concert.'

And that is how he learned before everyone else that she was not going to leave.

This was the situation when Julien and Clarisse each individually absorbed the music played by the two Swiss Alpinists who, delivered of their woollen cocoons and lederhosen, played like inspired musicians, directed by Kreuze at the piano, prodigal in his sensitivity and tact.

Beethoven's Trio Number 6 for piano, cello and violin, after a loud but very rapid introduction, goes straight into a little phrase pronounced and described by the cello. A little phrase of seven notes that are taken away one by one and then returned again by the piano and violin. A little phrase that takes off arrogantly, as an affirmation of good fortune, a kind of daring, and gradually comes to obsess them, overwhelm them and drive them to despair, though they keep trying to forget it, though each flies to the rescue of the other when one seems to be giving in to its law and charm, though each occasionally runs ahead of the phrase or, to escape, ahead of the instrument playing it as though it were contagious; though the three anguishing instruments, continuously atremble at being linked by such a cruel little phrase, sometimes join together and noisily try to talk of other matters—like three men in love with the same woman who is either dead or has been carried off by a fourth and who would in any case have made all of them suffer just as cruelly. All these efforts come to naught. For hardly have they begun to sustain one another, to prove their vigour, gaiety and forgetfulness—a noisy forgetfulness—hardly have they tried to share that forgetfulness among themselves when one of them, as if inattentively and to the great despair of the other two, begins to hum the phrase again between his teeth, the forbidden phrase, and all see themselves bound to return to it through the weakness of the first. And all the time these efforts to talk of other matters; all the time these seven savage notes in all their grace and even their gentleness.

And Julien felt it was their story being told; Julien who didn't much care for music and whose knowledge of the subject stopped with Tchaikovsky or the overture to *Tannhäuser*, like Simon's—well, not quite, but almost. It was the story of himself and Clarisse, a story about to go wrong, as the music seemed to insist, as if the music were of memories never held, of defeat, of premonitory sorrow. And when the phrase came back for the tenth time, whispered by the violin to a silenced piano, which was both thrilled and weary to receive it, when the long notes came back to Julien, he had to turn his head away towards the sea under the mad burning pressure of long-forgotten tears beneath his eyelids. He had dreamed in his unreal and poetic way of a future with Clarisse, a life full of love and sentiment, in short his life as a lover; he had dreamed it in all its charms, and so seemed prey in advance to all its blows and lacerations: vulnerable in his very flesh, in that concrete reality that sorrow assumes in matters of love, making everything so precise, so abandoned, so earthbound and final.

Julien spent the rest of the concert with his head to one side, his face turned to the sea, as if he were totally insensitive to the music that was driving him to despair. And already as confidently discerning of her nature as he was doubtful of their future together, Julien knew that, sitting next to Eric but not looking at him, Clarisse too had linked the theme with their meeting and their separation.

After an unbearable andante, the fourth movement of the trio gathers up the pieces for an allegro that is false gaiety— a sort of social parody not unlike the one which followed the concert, after interminable applause, that is. The two new artists were congratulated with a warmth all the greater since they were new on board and seemed sent to the rescue of space-capsule *Narcissus* by good old planet Earth. This was so true that people not only shook their hands but clapped them on the shoulder, taking them by the arm as though to ascertain their reality and therefore deduce the existence of dry land. Julien and Clarisse, without even looking at one another, had remained in their seats a few minutes after everyone rose in commotion, not hearing it. Only then had they really looked at each other, unaware that Eric and Edma were watching them, or rather not even considering it, since by now Eric had become more irritant than obstacle. They did not see him blanch and take three steps towards Julien while he moved towards Clarisse.

Julien was about to sit down next to her at the very moment the sailors, having pushed back the piano, switched off the stage lights. He stumbled a bit in the gloom as he took his place beside her. At first they could see no more of one another than the whites of their eyes, wide with panic. 'Clarisse,' said Julien in a low voice, leaning towards her. 'Julien,' she replied, laying her hand on his and interlacing her fingers with his; the way children do, he thought quickly, when it's night and they're scared and running along a sunken narrow path. But Clarisse was a child to him no longer, she was a woman he desired, a woman he already loved so much he suffered that he couldn't kiss her on the spot, suffered acutely and yet not just with physical desire.

'What are we going to do'? said Clarisse in a voice that was toneless and low, a seductive voice that made Julien blink.

'We're going to leave,' he said, forcing himself to sound confident, but still lowering his eyes before she did and ready to hear no and all the arguments to go with it that would fall from Clarisse's mouth like an awful downpour of hateful rain; he was not ready to hear the thunderbolt that dropped at his feet as she replied, 'Of course we'll leave together, but what about tonight . . . what am I going to do tonight?'

Then Clarisse stopped short, for Julien had understood and drawn back, seeking a darker obscurity, a greater distance from the image that passed before his eyes, of Eric lying on Clarisse. Not for an instant did he think to ask 'Why tonight?' 'Why now?' 'Why is this time different from others?' 'How did she know what Eric wanted or demanded?' He knew only too well that Clarisse would never do anything to hurt him, that she wasn't burdening him with one of these painful truths delivered casually by one's closest friend or dearest relative. Clarisse had taken him once and for all under the protection of her love, and Julien's first reflex was to mutter between his teeth but loudly enough so she could hear, 'I'll kill him, I'll kill him! That's the only thing to do!' He sought out Eric with his eyes, found him and looked at him as if he was a total stranger, never seen before but who had to be struck down. Clarisse's hand on his arm pulled him back from the movement of hatred, and he turned on her a face both distracted and vaguely bitter. He caught his breath, flung a last look at Eric, who was now sitting farther off; they were like two dogs glaring at each other after they had threatened to fight and been forcibly separated.

'Calm down,' said Clarisse tenderly.

'I spend my whole life calming down,' he said.

And yet Julien was telling himself over and over 'Calm yourself, calm yourself,' in the slightly annoyed tone he used when gambling, with women, or in front of a painting. 'Calm yourself, calm yourself,' in a tone at once detached and firm, as if to a runaway horse. 'Calm yourself . . . That's not the right card. This woman doesn't love you. That painting is a fake.' And suddenly he envied all others, the ninety-nine per cent who always seemed to be exhorting themselves in the opposite direction—towards danger, desire or confusion, like horses either too relaxed or deprived of feed. But his exhortation wasn't working. He realised that what revolted him even more than the idea of handing over Clarisse to another was the idea that this other was Eric—a man who did not love her and who would in any case try to hurt her. Julien was surprised to realise he almost wished she could feel a little love for this man who wanted her—for her sake though it would be to his own loss. And this was the first time Julien chose to suffer himself rather than have another suffer.

'Oh, how I love you . . .' he said ingenuously.

Immediately he felt reassured by the gravity of his love, by the hopeless tenderness she inspired in him, as if this love's virtues assured him of reciprocity and continuity. Poor fool that he was . . . but someone new appeared inside him who refused to share what as lover he had always shared before. In the past it had always been enough to be the favourite; he had found the wish to be the one-and-only a barbarous idea, particularly in a latecomer. For a moment he yearned for that other Julien, telling himself, 'Well, all right, she's not going to die from it. Obviously it's got to happen sometimes, as with any other couple. And since he's so repulsive to her . . .' It was the last part that gave him pause. He imagined Clarisse trembling, afraid, enduring Eric's weight, his coarse gestures, heavy breathing. He scarcely heard Clarisse beside him in the dark, repeating, 'What are we going to do? What are we going to do?' in the same childlike voice. And suddenly Julien had an idea.

'Look at me,' he said gently, in a low voice.

A voice so low that she turned to him, surprised, and he leaned towards her and immediately kissed her on the mouth. At first she was terrified, then suddenly yielded to him, to the languor, sweetness and transitory nature of a furtive kiss before a hundred incredulous, then astounded people.

Edma with her eagle eye saw them first, and stared. This had definitely been a day full of surprises, even for a woman of the world. Hurrying up to Eric she literally mesmerised him, blurting out at random 'What's your readership, my

273

friend? Two hundred thousand, I believe?' 'Do you get more readers in winter or summer?' 'Surely that cannot be?' and other total nonsense. She realised she was blathering but her mind kept wandering, as she saw out of the corner of her eye, without wanting to, the two shadows caught up in the same madness, intertwined against the night-blue sky. She went so far as to reproach the dumbfounded Eric for not running a knitting column in his oh-so-serious *Forum*, when the bulging eyes of the steward, holding a bottle immobilised over their glasses without pouring a drop or even registering Eric's frown, finally made Eric turn towards the engrossing spectacle. And Edma, though not generally lacking in gall, dared not look while he watched them.

*I*t took only a minute for la Doriacci, who was getting ready with her customary phlegm to climb onto the platform, to see all, understand all and react quickly, with the same admirable sang-froid as Edma. The sang-froid of the old warrior that is granted by experience alone and for which youth, no matter what the young may think, can offer no substitutes. With one look she had called together the musicians, with two strides reached her place, and with a nod of her chin she electrified Kreuze. And so it was to the first scene of Act III of Verdi's *Ballo*, though she was in fact a bit unnerved and began in the middle to the complete dismay of the poor trembling cellist behind her—that Eric made his rush towards the couple. Succeeding events were therefore accompanied by the fine, perfectly calm voice of la Doriacci. Someone had forgotten to hold up the mike but she did very well without it, indeed never missed it. And actually, though a sturdy voice was needed to overcome the noise around her, she had no need to fear the pizzicati or pitfalls lurking in the aria since no one was especially interested in that particular libretto. At any rate it was to '*Morrò, ma queste viscere,/Consolino i suoi baci,*' inauspiciously translated as 'I die, but your kisses will console my cadaver'—a coincidence that struck no one but herself since the Aristotelian unities were entirely abandoned in this new spectacle—that Eric sprang into action. It was to the next verse that he crossed in front of the podium, his white face almost alight with anger. And it was to '*Dell'ore mie fugaci*' ('The fleeting hours of my life') that he threw himself upon Julien.

A brawl ensued, further confused by the arrival of the first-class passengers, who had been alerted only by la Doriacci's voice and not in time for the start, and who therefore supposed themselves forgotten; they arrived sulkily looking for their seats, only to find themselves facing emptied rows while two men with tousled hair were fighting furiously, not like civilised Parisians but like cowboys—with hard kicks that sometimes found their mark. First class, already isolated from de luxe by one deck, thirty thousand francs, and a wealth of undiluted scorn on either side, now saw itself further isolated by these two fanatics—perhaps an even more insurmountable obstacle. Andreas and Simon tried to hold back the combatants but only received, respectively, a kick and an uppercut, and that promptly put an end to their pacifying. In short *it was a bestial butchery*, as Olga put it to Fernande, *a flagrant but symbolic confrontation*, Micheline version. 'A barrack-room brawl,' said Edma, and 'a regrettable incident,' as Elledocq was obliged to report to Pottin Frères. Finally the two were separated, thanks to a few stewards rounded up by Charley, who was actually overcome by terror and delight at the sight of two males grappling and doing bodily harm to one another. Each had been asking himself by what ill luck he had chanced upon an adversary who was also versed in French boxing. They were both in sorry shape. If only I'd known, thought Eric, secretly massaging his groin, bruised at the start by a kick from Julien. If only I'd known, recited Julien to himself, as he rubbed his ribs.

Finally Eric, who was suffering visibly, was carried off to

spend the night in the sick-bay. But Clarisse did not go and commiserate with him as she had with Julien; or as any decent woman should have, thought Edma Bautet-Lebreche, who with hair still on end from the excitement and looking distinctly raffish steered her by the shoulder away from her own cabin and directly to Julien's. He arrived right on her heels, having suborned the nurse and thus assured his adversary a restorative sleep.

Clarisse sat on the far edge of the bed, eyes downcast, hand on her knees—the very image of disarray, Julien thought as he closed the door behind him.

'I'm going to call you Clarisse-in-Disarray,' he said. 'Like the village.'

'You mean there is such a place?'

'No,' said Julien as he threw himself into the armchair farthest from his bed, looking relaxed. 'No, there's no such place, but there could be, don't you think?'

He felt as though he were facing a slightly nervous criminal or a wild animal, too highly strung and too scared—a creature that might do him harm without even meaning to. He looked at her coldly, and then at the bed with such obvious tenderness that Clarisse suddenly began to laugh.

'You look just like the cat in the fable, that stole the chestnuts, do you remember? I mean, there really is such a fable, isn't there? But what is that on your neck? You're bleeding? You're bleeding!'

Julien glanced in the mirror with unconcerned distaste, like a real he-man, and saw a trickle of blood oozing from behind his ear. He touched the cut with the same expression of disdain. Except that the disdain turned to gratitude when he saw Clarisse leave her refuge and come towards him with eyes full of apprehension and compassion, when he saw her take his head between her hands with a rush of reassuring words, as if it were he who were in need of physical reassurance. He had been wounded, and so she had him within reach, at her mercy. Julien became again the child who might be cared for, who might in any event be touched. As one gesture gave way to another, it was an adult Clarisse now found in her arms, but one who was tender and gentle,

277

an adult who wanted not only pleasure, but also the best for her.

In the dead of night, Clarisse had broken ten years of solitude. She now felt desire for someone, and for this someone to love her as he loved her, someone she now felt herself ready to love as well.

'It's odd,' she said a bit later, 'I thought you were a gangster, the first time I saw you. And then I thought you were an American.'

'But not both at the same time, I hope?' said Julien.

'No, separately,' said Clarisse. 'What role do you like best?'

'I'd like to be an English bobby,' said Julien, looking away—for he dreaded the moment when, knowing the truth about him, she would interpret his guardedness, his extreme discretion as odious and deliberate lying.

Would she realise then that in some way those lies were the truth? As long as she didn't forget, then, that all of it, all the well-laid plans had been worked out for love of her, and in the single hope that once they were together night and day, confiding in one another all of their cares, Clarisse Lethuillier would feel so happy with him that she wouldn't be able to leave him, thief or no thief.

'You look worried,' she said softly. 'Is it the famous sadness after the embrace?' she added abruptly.

Julien looked at her a moment, astounded by the suggestion he did not think her bold enough to make.

'That's a stupid question,' he said with a smile.

And leaning towards one another, simply cheek to cheek, they had the satisfied, tender, slightly fanatic look of lovers who have been awake with pleasure on their first night together and not with regret.

'I have to go back,' she said. 'Eric will be waking up. Now what will happen next? What are we going to do?'

'Which we?' Julien asked, with a look of imploring surprise.

'You and me, of course. Eric will be on our trail. It's going to be awful . . . I'll have to go ashore at Alicante, and meet you again in Paris. I just won't be able to wait all that time for you,' she added right away. 'You might be run over by a bus or go the wrong way and end up in Sydney. Too many things are possible for me to let you go off on your own.'

'I haven't the slightest intention of letting you get away,' said Julien.

He was sitting up in bed among the crumpled sheets, hair tousled, looking far more like an adolescent than a man of forty, Clarisse noticed with delight.

'At any rate,' he said, lying down again, 'after last night, quite contrary to what you think, Eric is going to be totally reassured. And for the rest of the trip, too. He believes, not without reason, that when lovers are serious they're careful. And generally that's true. Believe me, the fact I kissed you on the mouth in front of a hundred people is going to make us seem a hundred miles apart. I kissed you by force and that's a cheap trick, I had to use violence—and so you are mad at me, you don't like me, you're innocent. See?'

'Yes, I see.' Clarisse blinked and then turned onto her stomach, closing her eyes and tucking her head under Julien's arm. 'No,' she said. 'I don't see. I don't see a single thing . . . I absolutely don't want to see another thing, ever. I want to stay here in the dark for the rest of my life.'

A while later she fell asleep. But Julien, who lay awake just as he had the first times he made love to a woman he liked, watched her for a long time while she slept. The small of her back was lovely, her breasts beautiful, she had slender joints, smooth skin. He tried to do a horse trader's summary, but couldn't. Beyond a doubt this woman had a beautiful body, but for the first time in his life he felt that even if it had been repulsive, still her voice, her eyes and her hands would have been enough to make him love her just as much. An hour later she woke of her own accord, much to Julien's relief, for he felt incapable of telling her she must go back to her cabin. When she had gone, Julien fell back among the sheets, searching for her odour, her perfume. He found them and fell asleep exhausted, as confused and sensual images, close-ups of her shoulder, her hip, unrolled before his eyes. But this time they belonged to the person he knew so well . . . Now they were his own memories that Julien saw unfolding beneath his eyelids.

*A*ıst a steel-grey sea and sky the *Narcissus* emerged from the depths, giving off clouds of steam, her bow slicing like a knife through that silken and softly yielding sea, with the delightfully alarming sound of something tearing slowly apart. It was six o'clock in the morning, and Julien climbed furtively to the top deck. He liked to go out at that hour wherever he happened to find himself, in strange city or country lane; for an hour he would stroll like a drowsy and somewhat unruly dog. His body still asleep but already free from the shackles of dream, he would paw at the edge of boulevards or fields still to be crossed. In an hour he would take that body back home to bed, even if unwillingly, because it needed sleep—sleep to prevent his hands from trembling as he dealt the cards. That body whose instincts, it seemed since Clarisse, he had passively slaked with dozens of women never really desired. This was perhaps Julien's principal strength, so little armed was he against the idea of life as a battle: this capacity to remain always the same, to think himself the first in error, to pay no heed to the Julien of the day before, to admit he could be wrong about everything. Men, and women too liked him for this. His friends spoke among themselves of his sincerity, perhaps so as not to speak of his pride. Even so, Julien did not invest his pride with all the little bitter-sweet signs of workaday vanity. And so he ran the course, arm in arm with his social personality, his bluffing and his lyrical reveries without ever thinking to question one of the three when things went badly. As Edma Bautet-Lebreche said later in recapitulating the events of the cruise, 'Julien Peyrat wasn't conceited, but then he never stood back from himself either; he had no conception of himself at all.' And she added wisely: 'In this era intoxicated by hand-me-down Freud, inevitably a warped version, he was probably the only person who saw morality only in relation to what he did rather than in the light of the motives that inspired it.'

On that particular morning Julien, awake and unable to stay in that teeming bed, found himself on the top deck facing an immense grey-blue postcard of the Mediterranean at dawn in September. He was tired, happy, and his hands trembled a little, which annoyed and also moved him. The moment he was loved by a woman or fortune smiled on him, Julien was pulled out of his generally benevolent indifference towards himself and others; he would find his body pleasing, solid and gallant, all good qualities as well as trump cards in the conquest of women; trump cards, however, that Julien did not protect. He had inherited, luckily, a sense of pro-portion, what his mother called his 'sense of balance', a quality he clung to even when staggering out of the most unsavoury gambling halls of Paris.

He crooked his fingers in towards his palm, and closed his thumb over them; it was a slightly posed gesture, he realised when he saw the astonished reaction of Edma Bautet-Lebreche, who was standing there in a lilac robe, her hair uncombed, holding in one hand the coffee-pot she had just pinched from the kitchens. Curiously enough, her cash-mere silk robe was tied with a sort of heavy belt from which hung a strange key or which at any rate seemed even more bizarre to Julien than the fact she was on this deck at this hour—a coincidence that, however unexpected, did not elicit the slightest explanation from her.

'It's a forest ranger's belt,' said Edma in reply to Julien's mute question. 'But don't you ask me what it was used for, or I'll give you as awful an answer as the one I gave poor Kreuze.'

'What did you tell him?' asked Julien. 'I'm all ears,' he added truthfully.

For he enjoyed Edma Bautet-Lebreche's vivid chronicles of shipboard gossip, first for their humour, and then for a sort of moral rectitude, for their reaffirmation of bourgeois values. Like many of her contemporaries, Edma sometimes scorned and trampled upon these values, only to proclaim them firmly on other occasions. No doubt the values were indispensable, as she claimed; perhaps so as to avoid being taken too much by surprise in old age, wondered Julien, or maybe to show today's rough and desperate young people, as she chose to think of them, what it was to live a peaceful life of gentle comforts.

Edma had put down her coffee-pot, and the two of them sat down in a couple of wicker chairs. She looked at Julien out of the corner of her eye, from behind her cigarette; a very thirties pose, observed Julien nostalgically. Almost from birth he had dreamed of a world guided by gentle and beautiful women, tender or mythic women, at any rate women who would protect him, women who had much more common sense than men, or more than he at least. In such a world men would remain at the feet of women, at their service, which meant for him the foot of the bed and service in love. Of course it was understood that services might be postponed if necessary, in the event of victories at Longchamp or when breaking the bank at Divonne.

'What were we saying?' Edma asked in her loudest voice. She never asked a question in the plural except to answer it in the singular. 'Ah yes! my belt. Well, I told Kreuze that it was for hooking up pianos. Pretty feeble, agreed . . . Worse than feeble, I grant you.'

'Don't grant me a thing,' said Julien. 'I like slightly heavy-handed answers like that . . . they're a breath of fresh air. It takes you back to an age when it was easier to amuse . . .'

'The jokes of a feeble-minded child,' replied Edma, 'that's what I'd see in your mirror. No, you see, this belt, it seems, was meant to hold the little hatchet that forest rangers used to cut their kindling for heating and cooking . . . Why do you look so dubious, Monsieur Peyrat? If you please?'

'Just that the hatchet would have to be terribly long for your forest ranger to lean over without wounding himself in the hip or knocking himself in the . . . in the . . .'

'In the crotch,' Edma concluded helpfully. 'Yes, that's possible. At any rate I never lug around a hatchet on social occasions. Though one might at that; in fact, perhaps one should, often . . .'

'But don't you practise a sport like that at a distance? I seem to remember . . . you wouldn't want to throw the hatchet till after leaving the wigwam would you? Or is it before?'

'Ah, but I must disabuse you. I've seen some splendid hatchet-work!' said Edma, elated by a combative memory that gave her eyes an expression both savage and sarcastic. 'I remember one day, at the home of that old madwoman de Thoune. You're surely not unaware who she is, Madame de Thoune? The most beautiful collection of Poliakoffs and de Chiricos in the world, she and the Thounes of New York.'

'Ah yes, I know exactly who you mean,' said Julien between his teeth. 'And so?'

'And so old de Thoune had been thrown over by a handsome Swede, one Jarven Yuks . . . who divided his time between her and young Darfeuil . . . Come to think of it, you too must have seen Jarven in New York? He was head auctioneer at Sotheby's. Tall and blond, the Viking type . . . a bit like our Lethuillier. Good. So then, the poor boy wasn't asked to dinner one evening in September when both his women were, and all quite by chance. Madame de Thoune, then, and la Darfeuil, who at the time you would have said was my age at least,' she said with a satisfied look. (Though no sooner had she said it than she wondered whether it was quite the right thing to say. She had worried very little about her age all her life, but referred to in that way it became rather menacing.)

'So there she is at the table with de Thoune who talks, talks, talks, it's frightful how she talks. An avalanche of words for the tiniest little square inch of conversation. How can I put it, dear Julien? If she talked to you about horses or going for broke you would develop an allergy for horses and casinos, you would give up the game altogether! And become a marriageable man!'

'But,' said Julien, caught between laughter and terror at the word *marriage*, now that he was thinking of it (and for a moment his heart's madness overwhelmed him), 'but what an odd idea!'

'Are you all right?' said Edma. 'You look a bit shaken all of a sudden. Oh but of course, it's the word *marriage*. You haven't ever been through that.'

'Am I that transparent?' said Julien, rather put out but laughing anyway.

'Absolutely, to a woman like me. Absolutely transparent. But not to the others, rest assured. They're all asking themselves what you really do. But not one is asking what you really are down deep.'

'And that's a good thing,' said Julien. 'I don't really see how what I do or how I act could be of interest to anyone at all . . .'

He had assumed a humble air as he spoke, which evoked a whinny of incredulous joy from Edma.

'We were saying, I believe, that I was transparent,' Julien insisted in a flat tone.

'You think I'm altogether in my dotage, don't you?' said Edma. She had delivered this in a carefree tone, too high, which made her quack and then cough in the same falsetto, while she turned her face away. 'Well Julien, are you going to answer? What do you think of this talk we're having? Isn't it heart-rending?'

'I do find the beginning odd, yes,' Julien said, 'but not the way you interrupted it.' He smiled. 'In your life you must have interrupted a lot of things that way, on the spur of the moment. For instance, I haven't heard the end of the story about Madame de Tanc . . .'

'De Thoune,' corrected Edma automatically. 'That's true, you haven't. Well then'—she took up again her offhand manner and was already cross at herself for having momentarily lost it. 'Well then. Madame de Thoune meets a young woman at dinner, a dinner at which they were brought together by chance, but not introduced—again by chance— and so neither knew that the other was 'the other' with whom she was sharing her handsome Jarven. Well, they both began to talk about men and about love, about male cowardice, etcetera, and for once la Thoune, the tiresome magpie, let someone else have their share of air-time. They were so much in agreement on the subject of this repulsive lover, a lover they were both talking about without the slightest notion that it was in fact the same one, that that very night they both upped and decided to break off with him. Both of them. And the next morning that's what they did. And when, long afterward, they learned who was who, they could only burst out laughing in relief. And that's how poor Gérard found himself alone. His name was Gérard by the way, not Jarven nor Yuk,' she concluded absent-mindedly.

'He's dead?' asked Julien, looking sad.

'Why, not at all. Why did you think he was dead? He's in very good health.'

'So his name isn't Gérard any more?' Julien insisted.

'But of course, naturally. Why did you think?'

'Oh, just because,' Julien said, and, seeing that he had got off to a bad start, gave up. 'Would you like some hot coffee? Your pot must have gone cold. And we could have it in the bar? It's chilly out here.'

'What I would truly like is for you to show me your Marquet,' said Edma, sitting up in her chair before getting to her feet—quite gracefully, she felt sure—and taking Julien's arm.

'I'm afraid it's not entirely up to your standards,' said Julien, halting in front of her, still smiling.

Suddenly he felt queasy. Here he was again walking a

minefield. He loved a woman who probably would not care to see her lover exposed, who would feel no tenderness for illicit profits or con games. The menace that had been in the air since the trip began, though discreetly and without alarming him unduly, had now finally been articulated by Edma. It was beginning to take on a sharper tone, introducing inevitable discord into the balance struck between happy, frivolous Julien and Julien in love—a fragile balance, no matter what he might think—and setting his own life at variance with that of Clarisse. The discord could well sound particularly shrill and odious to her ears.

'This Marquet is not completely authenticated,' he went on with a bow to Edma. 'I'm afraid it might mar your drawing-room, which looked so splendid in the *Geographical Review*.'

'Well, well . . . is that magazine here? How amusing,' Edma chirped, taking the magazine that he held out to her. In fact, she had personally dropped off a few copies on the ship's reading tables. There were indeed several highly detailed photographs, taken at flattering angles, of the Bautet-Lebreches' sumptuous Paris apartment. 'That's not so,' she went on coldly. 'A Marquet, my dear Julien, whether signed or not, is exactly what my apartment lacks.'

'Oh but it is signed,' said Julien. 'It's just that I really couldn't swear to you the signature's genuine.'

She realised that he was putting to her a clear-cut choice: either become an accessory, or denounce him. She opted at once for the first, not for an instant worrying on account of her bourgeois morality. Julien pleased her too much for the tiniest cog of that complex apparatus to come into operation.

'At any rate,' she said, 'as long as my dear Armand is persuaded—by whatever I tell him—then what does it matter? In any event if you manage to sell it,' she threw out as she moved towards the companionway a little pink in the cheeks from this final effort, 'well, the painting is perfectly genuine. I find you very pessimistic.'

And Julien, who had seen the painting finished and fervently signed by a friend as gifted as he was unprincipled, found this last a worthy thought. No, he definitely could

287

not sell this Marquet to Edma. It would be worse than a swindle, it would be asking for charity. The thought rooted him to the spot, and as she turned back Edma must have understood, for she too stood transfixed for a moment. Then, gently and with a shrug, she said, 'Let's go see it anyway.'

*E*ric had come back from the sick-bay in very good humour—an untimely good humour, Clarisse thought; after last night it made him look ridiculous and hence contemptible. Eric was quite sincere, however: after such an evening of scandal, the possibility of adultery seemed to him non-existent. He had not after all been deceived, not there, ten yards from where he slept—the possibility was so vulgar and odious to his pride that he rejected it immediately as inconceivable. Clearly, the kiss stolen from Clarisse in front of the whole crowd had not been willingly given. Poor Clarisse, thought Eric. First she had had to push him away and then call for help (for so he remembered it). Poor Clarisse was definitely not about to be spirited off. There had been a time, it was true, when she would have found a way to prevent a man from approaching her, or known how to resist him without drawing attention. She had been a clever and scornful woman, a great lady and a bit of a vamp. She had snubbed Eric for a long time, exasperated and finally excited him. That the previous

289

evening's virtue was the fruit of masochistic timidity and not emotional fidelity pleased him less. But in the end it amused him to realise that it was she, Clarisse, who was giving the gossip-mongers on board ship something to talk about. It was even comic.

'Clarisse, virgin and martyr,' he said, gazing at her image in the mirror while she sat on her berth, staring out to sea, her hands trembling, her face smooth and drawn. She was beautiful just now . . . Beautiful more and more often, he thought. 'Have you seen my fellow gladiator this morning?'

'No,' said Clarisse without turning. 'I've seen nobody this morning.'

She spoke distractedly, her mind elsewhere, which was something Eric couldn't stand in anyone, least of all in Clarisse.

'I'm not disturbing you, am I, Clarisse?' he asked. 'Are your thoughts totally engrossing? Or else too intimate to share with me?' Eric smiled openly at the thought of how unlikely either possibility must seem to anyone, including Clarisse; particularly the idea that Clarisse should be engrossed in her thoughts.

'Yes, yes,' she said. 'Of course . . .'

She wasn't listening, she hadn't even heard him, and he got up so abruptly that she gave a little cry of fright and turned pale. For a moment each looked the other straight in the eye. Clarisse, surprised, saw again the colour of his irises, a colour so familiar to her and yet just now so foreign, those pale eyes synonymous with iciness, with severity. He was searching her out once again, reproaching her for something, she could feel it. And, with her eyes still riveted on him, she studied every feature of his face, this handsome and repellent face. The instant this description came to mind she blushed violently, blushed that the impression could be strong enough to come to mind unbidden and in such crude terms. She tried to repeat to herself, handsome and repellent, handsome, I find him handsome. Repellent too. There it is. It's as though there were something vicious, abject and arrogant in that closed jaw, as if clenched on some palpable horror, on some terrible words . . . That handsome witty mouth so scornful at rest, a mouth so precisely drawn that you couldn't for one moment imagine it on the little boy Eric must once have been.

'Well, then, no answer? Do you realise you're becoming very rude?'

Eric's scathing voice jarred her for a moment, and once more she looked up at his mouth with its gleaming teeth, straightened by the Dureau family dentist, the best dentist in Europe and America (whose exorbitant fees had for once failed to unleash Eric's democratic outrage. Actually, though Eric naturally reproached them for their extravagance where his own interests were not concerned, in matters of great importance to him—his health, his pleasures, his investments—Eric was quite willing to take advantage of the services the Dureaus could call on.)

Clarisse made a polite effort towards the exasperated stranger who was almost screaming at her, 'What are you thinking about?'

'I was thinking about you as a little boy. Your mother must be sad that she never sees you. Perhaps you should . . .'

She stopped. What's got into me? she thought, before realising that it was her entirely unconscious inclination towards generosity that made her talk like this, her wish to not abandon him to solitude. But at the same time she knew that nobody liked Eric enough not to laugh if she should abandon him. He would be wild with rage, of course, before he became sad.

'I'm going to have breakfast up on deck,' said Eric, exasperated. And he disappeared.

Once left alone, Clarisse breathed deeply. She saw herself in the mirror with her hair dishevelled, looking innocent, and couldn't help smiling at the woman Julien Peyrat loved, the woman he found beautiful, of whose touch, warmth and sensuality he never tired—his woman, given over entirely to him. She raised a hand to her cheek, turned her head towards the odour, the perfume of her fingers not yet free of the night. She got to her feet and went towards the door, the deck, towards Julien. For she knew he too always had breakfast up on deck.

He was sitting at one of the tables in the dining-room bright with sunshine and china, seemingly unaware of the seated figures behind him, of Eric, Armand Bautet-Lebreche and Simon Béjard—all of whom glanced at Clarisse with mingled surprise and reproach, for at that hour this dining-room—like the drawing-room in good English families—was generally the preserve of the men. But Clarisse didn't see them: she was watching Julien try to spread butter that was too hard across a slice of bread. His disgruntled look and furrowed brow, his thin tanned face, his funny large nose and straight neck, so virile in a cotton shirt, his large hands, so clumsy to the eye and yet so skilful, everything concentrated on this action . . .

Clarisse closed her eyes on a precise memory. She loved Julien's body at that moment more than she had ever loved any other. She loved his hollow cheeks, blue with a growth of beard, the ridge of his nose, his wide full lips, his eyes that were so mobile with their strange mahogany colour, his hair—a bit too long like his eyelashes—in thick disorderly locks that lay across his head, this head with its hard bones and the gentle movements of a young colt. She would have liked to take him in her arms, cover him with kisses. Suddenly he was part of her blood, her species, her world, her friends. He was her double, her exact counterpart. Surely he had the same memories and the same childhood. She took a step towards Julien's table. He looked up, saw her and stood up, his eyes awash with pleasure, smiling half-unconsciously at the violence of his desire.

'Madame,' he said in a hoarse voice, 'I beg your pardon for not having forcibly detained you this morning. I love you and I desire you,' he continued, with an affectation of repentance in his face intended for the distant witnesses.

'I too desire you and love you,' she said with head held high—haughty from a distance but mad with love in close-up.

'I'll wait for you all day in my room,' he said, still whispering.

He bowed as she left to join Eric, whose expression, as she reached him, bespoke a scornful indulgence.

'Well, then? Your suitor begged your pardon? He was drunk or something?'

'Listen, you wouldn't have to be drunk to pay court to your wife, my friend,' said Simon Béjard from his table.

'But not kiss her in front of me, surely?'

Eric's voice was curt, but it didn't seem to bother Simon in the least.

'Well, there I have to agree with you,' he said. 'To kiss a woman right in front of her husband is in very bad taste. Behind his back would be better form.'

Eric paused. He was clearly in a poor position to preach morality to this vulgar film-maker whose mistress bore the name Olga.

'Yes, of course. Yes, of course,' he said. And he turned back to Clarisse without too much aggressiveness. 'So, the handsome dog made his excuses?'

'Yes,' she said.

'To you. That's a good start. We should be grateful for small favours. He didn't offer any apologies to be relayed to me while he was at it?'

'Oh! Why yes, of course . . .' said Clarisse.

She smiled at him from the depths of her eyes, and in those depths was the self-revealing look of love. For a moment Eric was struck dumb. Then he saw her turn the same look towards Simon Béjard and Armand Bautet-Lebreche, who were also amazed, as if thunderstruck. But their astonishment was as nothing compared to Eric's. He was speechless; he felt touched in some corner of his mind by a memory he could not place: Clarisse smiling in the sun and turning towards him with that same look. Clarisse surrounded by leaves, flowers, trees, the wind. Perhaps it was on the terrace of a restaurant? Or at her house in Versailles? No, he could not place the instant nor say what it was about that look, what it meant, reappearing now in Clarisse's eyes. Was it simply his own heart, his youthful memory of Clarisse in love with him? Clarisse at twenty-five, her eyes washed with tenderness as she looked at him, surrounded by a whole jungle of blue buds, like so many promises. Good God! What was he doing? What was this grotesque stuff? Yes,

Clarisse had believed she loved him. Yes, he had been witty enough to make her believe it. Yes, she had treated herself to a young husband with left-wing views, and him to a newspaper with the same tendencies, fervently hoping to bring them both over to her side, to her people, stifled by their luxury and comfort. Yes, she had pretended to take an interest in *Forum*, pretended to join him in deceiving her reactionary uncles, but she had not succeeded. *Forum* was alive and their love had died. He no longer held her by anything but fear, he knew that now; that she had been able to turn upon him that look of love inspired by another, was the best proof, the most unmistakable, that all was over between them, that she didn't love him in the slightest. And it was just fine like that. He had made her suffer enough, poor Clarisse. Except . . . Except . . .

He sprang up, made it just in time. He was confused and surprised, as he bent over the teak-trimmed toilet, not to be spitting up pieces of lung, and tatters of heart along with the fried eggs and toast; blood swallowed in error along with the smile on Clarisse's lips.

When he returned to the dining room it was empty, and the cheerful voices of his wife and the bogus producer were moving away down the deck. He stood still, listening to the fading voices. It was Olga who brought him out of his torpor.

'You're all pale, poor dear,' she said, dabbing at his temple with a handkerchief and looking concerned. 'You've had some accident?'

With great effort he turned to her.

'In a way,' he said. 'I ate a bad egg. When I think of the price of eggs on this ship,' he burst out suddenly, 'it's the limit! Find me the head-waiter,' he bellowed at a stupefied Olga as he stormed towards the kitchens.

Well, that was really nothing like a man of the left, thought Olga, while he insulted the cook and the cook's assistants in a way that would have undoubtedly seemed excessive even to Clarisse's uncles. Olga watched him mistreating the dismayed personnel with a scornful joy which she concealed by nodding her head approvingly when he called on her as witness.

'Let's go,' she said when it was over. 'It's not the fault of those poor people that you paid so much for this trip . . .'

'I don't like it when people don't give a damn about me,' said Eric. 'I don't like it in the least. That's all.'

He was white with rage and nausea, he felt emptied, clammy and outraged. He even questioned the merits of his own outburst. Oh, but in the end what did socialism mean on this luxury cruiser? The snobby flunkies merely had to do their job properly. That's what they were paid for, just like the office boys who did errands at *Forum*, just like he himself was paid to run the paper and . . . Only Clarisse was paid to do nothing.

'I really am sorry, you know, Eric dear,' Olga said once she was seated in the sad little bar off the staircase between de luxe and first class.

This supposedly conciliatory location had in effect made of the bar a no-man's-land where no one dared appear—de luxe passengers out of disdain for first class, first-class passengers disdaining disdain. There was an old bartender left over from the 1890s. He mixed undrinkable cocktails which he either drank all alone or with a tippler from the lower deck whose wife hadn't yet thought to trace him that far. So he got drunk, and already placed by fate between two classes, two floors, two ports and two centuries, he now found himself half cut, between two drinks. He gestured a hazy but enthusiastic welcome to the two newcomers, and despite Eric's total indifference and Olga's reservations (she worried already about her liver), he decided to have them try one of his house specials. Olga watched out of the corner of her eye with growing disbelief as he tossed cognac, kirsch, gin, green mint, some candied fruits and a dash of angostura into his shaker. She decided they had to be fake bottles and, quite mistakenly reassured, turned back to Eric who was questioning her with a weary voice.

'You really are sorry for what?'

'Sorry to have been so well informed about your wife.'

'It doesn't matter in the least . . .'

'But really, that Peyrat is such a boor! I was ashamed for you . . . ah! Eric, when I saw you go after that brute, I was really scared . . . and not without reason, unfortunately.'

'How do you mean, "not without reason"? He got his comeuppance didn't he?'

Eric was furious, and furious at being furious—furious to have wanted not to lose such a ridiculous brawl . . . As if there had been a winner and loser! He was bursting with anger, unwillingly but also wilfully, since it seemed to him that any pretext whatever for violent emotion might relieve a less violent but much worse feeling, might spare him the recurring thought of that look of Clarisse's, so full of promise for another, so oblivious of him. I will inevitably miss her, as any executioner misses his victim, he tried to tell himself, to delude himself, so recently struck down by that misdirected smile; all the while taking in from time to time across the clink of glassware, the sad phrases of Olga and the cheerful ones of the bartender; all the while still hearing with indifferent ear Clarisse's 'Why yes, of course,' but feeling it now as a heavy blow. He, Eric Lethuillier. Ah, she would see! She would find out who this man was whom she thought she loved. She would learn a few things, and he wouldn't be the only one to tell her. He had sent a telex the night before; the answer should be in already.

'Come along,' he said to Olga, interrupting a pertinent dissertation on the versatility and unraised consciousness of the women of the world—a theory that had already attracted total adherence from the bartender who was obviously ready to back it up with his own personal experience.

But leaving behind a royal tip (which was not his usual habit) and half their drinks, Eric dragged Olga to the wireless room. Indeed the telex was there, and it exceeded all his hopes, or rather all his expectations.

Once again he had done it. For Eric had been the man behind the scenes, directing his sleuths, in an investigation of the society Squad (gambling division). And not by chance either, for it wasn't at the gambling tables that Eric Lethuillier had risked all and won: it had been no easy venture launching and keeping alive *The Forum of the People*, no easy venture to sustain it through the seventies and into the eighties when the very notion of a free press was as laughable as the idea of a workable democracy. To achieve his aims, he had needed not just Clarisse's fortune but stubbornness, ambition, and skilful double-dealing, in short all the makings of a good publisher, to which he added one exceptional instinct of his own, a nose for people's weaknesses. At first encounter Eric Lethuillier could sniff out a person's perversity, cowardice, cupidity, alcoholism or vice, without fail, just as he would always shut his eyes to their strong points, however evident. This flair might have made him a marvellous police chief, and had promptly led him to Julien's weakness: gambling. The telex that had just arrived from the prefecture once more confirmed his cynical hunch. It told him of files at the Quai des Orfèvres on a certain Peyrat, Julien: single, neither alcoholic nor drug addict, no deviant habits despite an erratic career, several times suspected, though without proof, of cheating at gambling, and of fraud and art forgery (a complaint on that, from Montreal two years earlier). The tag 'Not dangerous' concluded the police report. Eric could discern in these bleak lines, in the very style of the detective who had drawn it up, something like a weakness for good old Julien Peyrat, such a splendid fellow . . .

'Yes, and so mediocre,' he intoned savagely to himself, unintentionally loud enough for Olga to hear. Once again she was sitting opposite him in the main bar. He said it so savagely in fact that she felt a vague feeling of pity or dread for Julien Peyrat.

While she waited placidly for Eric to finish reading, she, Olga Lamouroux, on whom the hopes of French cinema were pinned, ignoring the crass behaviour of the man facing her, was fingering in her pocket another envelope, one addressed to her. It came from *Echos de la ville*, the scandal sheet where her old boyfriend worked, the rag with all the best gossip on the habits and idiosyncrasies of the hairy and hoary of Paris society. Finally Eric looked up, appeared to take note of her presence and, folding his papers, put them in his pocket without a word of excuse.

'You're not having anything to drink!' he said, less as a question than an affirmation. 'Very good, then I'll see you later.'

He got up and would have disappeared without further display of sentiment if Edma's sudden appearance at the doorway had not made him lean down with a suddenly winning expression, towards Olga's face, impassive and smiling with hatred.

Olga watched him leave before opening her blue envelope from which she drew, slowly and with a kind of acid pleasure, the report her friend had sent her. 'Eric Lethuillier, scholarship boy, lower-middle-class family, mother a widow, postmistress at Meyllat. Invalided out of service with nervous disorder, graduate Ecole Nationale de l'Administration, husband Clarisse Dureau. No man, woman or particular vice, except the Ecole.' She twisted and turned the note in her hands, at once disappointed and intrigued. It had to be the first time that the *Echos* couldn't turn up some little horror story in a person's life. She searched her memory for something that didn't quite fit the picture, but was unable to locate it.

*J*ulien had to go back with Simon
Béjard to see his Marquet again, and Clarisse followed
them.

'What a beauty, really! Why didn't you hang it up earlier,
as soon as we left Cannes? It makes ideal company, doesn't
it?' she said as they stood in front of the partition where the
Marquet had permanently replaced the usual brigantine.

She stopped, blushing, and Simon, with his habitual
heavy-handed tactlessness, succeeded in heightening her
colour.

'Well now, Clarisse! Maybe it has been there since the
beginning? How could you know after all?'

He broke into a sardonic laugh that made Clarisse cast a
pleading glance towards Julien.

'Now look here, my friend,' began Julien in a tone of
ringing seriousness. 'Now look here, my friend . . .' he
repeated with an idiotic solemnity that merely increased
Simon's merriment.

'Now look here, what? I haven't said anything . . . except

that Madame Lethuillier couldn't have seen the painting. That's all.'

He leaned towards the supposed Marquet, squinting, his heels together, which made him stick out awkwardly fore and aft.

'But tell me . . . tell me . . .' he murmured. 'You know, it's very handsome, this Marquet. Do you realise it's a very good deal, a Marquet of that period for fifty thousand dollars . . . Bravo, Monsieur Peyrat! Lugging that around between two shirts, a toothbrush and dinner jacket; that's got to be a lot more chic than lugging around ten poplin suits like me. You were afraid the view wouldn't satisfy your artistic appetite, my friend?'

'It just fell into my hands on the last day,' said Julien distractedly. And anxiously.

The list of his possible buyers was narrowing still further. No, he couldn't do it to Simon. As for Edma, it was hopeless. That left only a lawyer, a certain Madame Bromberger, an American, the diva or Kreuze—who obviously kept a tight hold on his purse strings. Nevertheless it had to be sold, his lovely fake, if only so he could take Clarisse off to some comfortable place for ten days—after which either material comfort would never again mean anything to him or it would serve no purpose.

'What do you think of it, Clarisse?' asked Simon in a shrill voice.

Clarisse smiled at Julien before answering, 'Not bad at all.'

He leaned towards her and asked 'Well?' in a low voice while Simon, curling his fingers like binoculars and peering through them, examined the painting now from close up, now from a distance, in imitation of a connoisseur. He nodded with conviction, as if approving his own thoughts, which remained secret, and with the resigned and slightly weary smile of a devotee whose aestheticism has been satisfied, he turned back to Julien.

'Ah, yes,' he said. 'It's the right period, and not expensive for that period. I can tell it's no dud, that—no gouache.'

Julien's expression must have seemed irresistible to

Clarisse, because she turned on her heel and without further explanation went into the bathroom, closing the door behind her. Alone together, the two men abandoned the painting while Simon let his eyes wander from Julien to the bathroom door, from the bathroom door to the bed and from the bed back to Julien with the same expression of admiring approbation as before, but with a salacious glimmer. Julien remained marmoreal in the face of this masculine complicity, but marble had never intimidated Simon Béjard.

'My compliments, old man,' he whispered loud enough to carry through three partitions. 'My compliments . . . Clarisse, wow . . . especially with the paint removed . . . a real catch, my friend, like the Marquet. So there you are with two fine prizes, Monsieur Julien Peyrat, and neither one a fake, right?'

Julien, who any other time might have roughed him up, reluctantly acquiesced with the assertion 'no fakes', and immediately reproached himself for doing so.

'How are things with Olga?' he said quickly, and immediately regretted it as he saw the vivacity drain from Simon's face, now brick red.

'It's going just fine,' he said between his teeth. Then springing back again he said, 'I can't take Clarisse from you, alas, old man, but I'm taking the painting. That at least is a safe investment. If I hit a losing streak—and in the movies, you know, that can happen—it'll give me something in the kitty. And drinks at Fouquet's, well, they're not giving them away . . . What's the matter, old man? What's on your mind?'

'I'd like to wait for the certificate from the Australian gallery,' Julien stammered, hating his own weakness. 'I'm sure it's genuine, but we've still got to see papers . . . I'll have them by the time we get to Cannes at the latest. But you'll have first offer, I swear,' he concluded, suddenly hurrying Simon Béjard towards the door.

Simon protested, said something about cocktails, and then, suddenly remembering Julien's guilty love, became tangled in excuses and tore off with affected haste more embarrassing than his hanging about had been. Once he was gone, Julien leaned against the door and shot the bolt. He couldn't hear a sound in the bathroom. Clarisse hadn't even turned on the light in her refuge, and he hesitated at the door to this mysterious darkness. Only the whiteness of Clarisse's body gave off a dim glow, and he moved towards it, his hands held out in a gesture that was at once supplicating and self-protective.

*S*imon Béjard, foolishly moved, it seemed to him, by the lovers, went back to his cabin in a sentimental mood. There he found Olga coiled on the bed, in one of those graceful positions she liked to assume, gazing at the ceiling. One of her hands—actually a bit plump and red—lay on her heart, the other trailed off the bed onto the carpet. Simon bounded across the cabin, bent to lift the solitary hand and kissed it with the suppleness of a page—or so he thought as he straightened up, his face reddened by the effort.

'You're going to split the seams of your Bermudas,' said Olga coldly. 'I'm warning you.'

'You made me buy two dozen of them,' Simon reminded her sourly.

And he lay down too, hands behind his head, firmly resolved to keep silent. But after three minutes he gave up, incapable of rancour, incapable of resisting his urge, the most persistent in a long time, to share his plans with this particular young lady who wasn't in the least bit interested, this young lady whom he could call his own without laughing or making anybody else laugh either.

'You know, I've been thinking about that role of yours,' he said, knowing that this subject at least would draw something out of her besides grunts or weary sighs.

'Oh yes?' she answered, her voice bright, hand off the carpet and tucked quickly under her chin. She trained her eyes upon him with an expression of avid interest, though he knew it was only a spin-off from the label PRODUCER twinkling above his head since the Cannes festival.

He suddenly felt like saying 'I give up' or 'It's not working'—something that would finally draw floods of tears from this heartless young girl, who never stammered like Clarisse Lethuillier—yet Clarisse was older—never blushed, never put a foot wrong, never glanced at strange men with loving eyes that belonged to another, who in her career feared nothing but defeat and wanted nothing but success. The career of a lark, an empty-headed bird, a career of echo, of pretension and affectations where the falsest attitude was ultimately the best, the one she would cling to without knowing why, that would furnish her legend and her motto, behind which she could nourish and enrich herself, lose hope and grow old in despair and solitude perhaps but in the intoxicating knowledge, ever rarer with the passing days, of being known to the multifold unknown. Like many in her profession, she endowed this multifold and abstract unknown with likes or dislikes, fidelities and excesses that—were the suppositions true—would have made it, the public, an infirm monster, bloodthirsty and simpleminded. The public was her god as it was others', a barbarous god whom they worshipped as do primitive savages of Africa, a god whose caprices she venerated, whose disgraces she hated, a god-public made up of individuals who were to be scorned when they asked for autographs, but adored when they crouched in the dark, invisible and all-powerful, determined to applaud.

Poor Olga would never love anyone, man, woman nor child, with the gloomy ardour, an ardour at times not far from grandeur, that she felt for that herd of unknowns. And he, Simon, was merely an intermediary between her and that thousand-headed lover, a go-between to be hated like a blundering messenger when he brought back a negative response, rewarded with a show of adoration when he brought home her lover's bravos. And indeed Olga would be right to hate or love him, depending, since failure or success would finally depend solely on him, Simon Béjard. It would depend on the choice he made for her. He had heard her say with equal conviction, 'I would rather make films with so-and-so because he has talent and doesn't go for the bucks and because that's real cinema,' or 'I'd rather make films with such-and-such because he makes what the public likes and in the long run the public's the only thing that counts.' Olga's belief in her two contrary theories was unshakeable, while she dreamed of one thing only: of signing her name in the little white space that Simon's finger would indicate on that paper filled with mysterious signs, that was a Contract to producers, Life to actors young and old. To the end of her days Simon would remain in her eyes the man with his finger on that first contract. The man who would remain more important to her than her first lover or first love.

'Well?' said Olga, 'what were you thinking?'

Her voice had a nuance of doubt, as if 'to think' were a slightly pretentious verb with respect to Simon. He sensed this, wondered if he should be irked, then shrugged and began to laugh aloud. He was thinking of Clarisse and Julien, of how he had left them in that large cabin aired by a sea breeze coming through the open porthole—of how he had left Julien standing there with a smile of incredulity, made younger by that expression of disbelief, his face turned towards the darkened bathroom where that charming, frightened woman was waiting for him, the woman he must have dreamed of all his life without knowing it, a woman the likes of which he would never see again. He thought about what had drawn Julien to Clarisse and what had brought them together, he thought about them there in the darkness, the strangeness of the draughty bathroom just like his. He imagined them colliding in the darkness with the

305

awkwardness of overwhelming desire, and pictured the cabin itself a few feet away, open to the sun, a blue metallic sea slapping at the porthole, reflections from the polished wood, the snows of the Marquet evaporating in the unexpected sunlight. And already a camera followed Simon in his reverie, crossing the cabin in a long, tranquil dolly shot, while in the background the music was both gentle and unhurried. The camera stopped before the slightly open door of the bathroom, then passed a darkened zone and froze upon Clarisse's uplifted face, hair wet on her forehead, eyes closed and mouth half open uttering incoherent words . . .

'But what are you thinking about?' said Olga. 'You have a certain kind of look . . . were you thinking about a part for me, or what?'

'No,' said Simon distractedly. 'No, not for you . . .'

He spent twenty minutes repairing the damage caused by that little phrase. But it wasn't important. He now knew that he would not use Olga to shoot that scene. Not Olga, nor alas, Clarisse. But surely, sooner or later, he would find a woman who would fit the image.

*F*or the first time since embarking at Cannes Charley found himself alone with Andreas. He had studied the ways of pederasty with knowledgeable masters whose sole definitive motto—tried and tested, so they said—was that you never knew. This obstinate fixity of desire, this blind belief that it took very little for any individual of either sex to forget for an hour that normality enjoined one from loving someone of one's own gender, had been Bible and consolation for our unhappy purser. Now that he had Andreas alone and within reach, leaning against the railing, his beautiful hair blown about by the wind, his face softened by happiness or by the assurance just regained that happiness was possible, Charley gazed upon him with the exquisite despair brought on by inaccessibility, even refuted inaccessibility. It was just not possible, he thought as he ticked off Andreas's features that were aesthetically and sexually satisfying to men of his persuasion: tanned neck, vulnerable eyes, youthful mouth, slim but muscled torso, fine hands, a polished image carefully cultivated for

the treasure it was. Logically, all this should inevitably bring
Andreas to his bed. No boy of twenty-five ever had nails so
well manicured, hair so well cut, cufflinks and lighter and
pen so well matched, tie knotted so offhandedly to one side,
nor such a severe yet placid way of looking at himself in the
mirror, taking for granted all the admiring looks that beauty
drew—from both sexes—with a calm assurance that was
wholly feminine. Charley saw Andreas as narcissistic, knew
that narcissism led to homosexuality. He did not understand
how Andreas could be at the feet of the diva and not Charley
at his.

'It's ridiculous, we never see each other,' he said with a
forced smile, for suddenly having Andreas alone and perhaps
accessible made the situation as disquieting as it was delicious. 'And you can't say it's my fault,' he added, smirking
in spite of himself in an exaggerated way, which elicited a
look of pure surprise from the beautiful impassive face before him.

'Why would it be either your fault or mine,' said Andreas
with a laugh. 'And what sort of fault anyway?'

'That I don't yet know,' said Charley with a little pearly
laugh.

For whatever his tact and finesse in everyday life, however
understanding and even intuitive as purser and jester for the
rich and blasé, Charley became silliness itself—clumsy and
inept—when he permitted himself to follow his inclinations
and turn effeminate to please. He was charming in a blazer,
insufferable in a jellaba. He seemed as natural when faking
masculinity as he seemed outrageous when following his
natural bent. In short, when Charley took up position in the
hard, unceasing and painful wars of sodomy, he seemed to
be making fun of it, to be subjecting it to derision. This
paradox, so often a burden to him, also saved him on many
other occasions from having his face punched in, since no
one could believe that an adult could lisp and flap his wrists
that way except in mockery. So Andreas and he looked at
each other for a moment like china dogs, Charley telling
himself with beating heart, 'This time he's read me,' and

Andreas asking himself what had come over this nice guy and wondering whom he was apparently trying to ape.

'I don't get it . . .' he said, smiling. 'I'm sorry, I don't get it.'

'You don't get what, my friend?' said Charley, batting his eyelashes. 'You don't, or don't want to?'

And he came a step closer, a strained smile on his lips, his heart in his throat, holding out that smile like a white flag that he could quickly raise if things went wrong. It was the face of a martyr he offered Andreas's astonished eyes, obsequious, falsely cheerful, panicky, forced, tense and almost trembling from forehead to jaw in anticipation of the blow that might fall. Andreas drew back a step and Charley, exhausted, relieved at his temporary defeat, almost gave up the campaign. He had to summon all his self-discipline to carry on, but this time with a face grave and sad with reproach and sorrow, a substitute for the earlier conspiratorial one bright with daring and possibility. Oddly, the sadness reassured Andreas who, though he could not seem to share the bizarre gaiety, was ready to share sorrow, since it was more accessible.

'Do you realise you're making me suffer terribly,' Charley moaned, coming to lean on the rail near Andreas and gazing towards the calm sea with desperate eyes sweeping from right to left and left to right, as if following a performing shark.

'Me? I made you suffer?' Andreas said. 'But when? How?'

'Why, the only thing you seem to notice is our dream creature, our national diva. You seem to forget all your old friends on the ship. Come on, don't tell me,' he continued, while his fair beloved (whom he would soon consider moronic with all this marking time) looked at him wide-eyed. 'Don't tell me a young man like you can't keep up more than one amour at a time. You don't have the body to be faithful, my pretty. How unfair to others who love you just as much . . .'

Andreas's eyes, light blue eyes as naive as the eyes of certain soldiers in lockets from the First World War, fixed on a point just above Charley's shoulder, and beneath a furrowed brow Charley thought he could see clicking away behind open blinds a rickety slide projector: one by one, it showed Andreas the faces of all on board who might love him 'just as much'. Charley could see Clarisse going by, Edma and Olga; he could see the machine stop, run backwards—Olga, Edma, Clarisse—more slowly; he saw it zip forward a last time before coming to a dead stop, with the sound of clanging metal and catastrophe, on himself, Charley Bollinger—indeed the one who 'loved him just as much'. Andreas's face froze, a sort of spasm rose to his throat and he murmured, 'Oh no, please!' in a pleading voice that would have made Charley laugh until he cried, coming as it was from this strapping fellow, except that he was already close to tears of another sort. He caught them in time, and with an incoherent groan turned and rushed towards his cabin and towards the only reliable man he had ever known: Captain Elledocq.

With a grieved and guilty look, Andreas watched him go. Then, as though suddenly waking up, he ran off to report the whole thing to his mistress.

According to programme the *Narcissus* was to stop at Alicante before docking at Palma—Alicante, where passengers were to drink sherry while listening to De Falla played by Kreuze and the great aria from *Carmen* sung by la Doriacci, that is providing she gave up *Au clair de la lune*. Spanish climes promised an excess of passion. But a sudden sirocco, sovereign ruler over heart and most of all body—confined nearly all our heroes to their berths. Clutching their sheets in the grip of seasickness, they renounced all emotion, or felt only feeble glimmers. The elements triumphed over almost everyone in de luxe except for Armand Bautet-Lebreche, who passed the day proving his good fortune by distractedly pacing the inclined passageways of the *Narcissus*. Nonetheless he loathed being physically alone though since childhood he had been both dedicated and resigned to being inwardly so.

So at the day's end the *Narcissus* took refuge behind the

island of Ibiza for an interminably leaden evening having missed one of its favourite ports of call.

*A*t Palma the *Narcissus* was hardly docked before passengers started dashing down the gangway. They went into raptures about the fresh air on this baking hot island, as if the *Narcissus* were a sealed cargo ship, or the entire de luxe class had been thrown into the hold in Cannes. In truth a cooling sea breeze swept every cranny of the *Narcissus*, but something unmistakably spoiled was in the air, a menacing stagnation seemed to hang over the deck, and except for la Doriacci and Kreuze, who still ate with gusto, everyone had sent his lunch plate back to the kitchen untasted.

In some way the die was cast. Everyone felt it, whether or not they were directly involved, and it lent a sinister reverberation to every word. Even Edma Bautet-Lebreche, experienced though she was in situations of this sort, accustomed to reducing important events to trifling incidents, even beautiful Edma was finding it hard to manipulate her little world. Every one of the players had become too nervous, even Julien Peyrat, whose tense, frowning face had lost all sign of his habitual nonchalance. By some quirk of fate the only one to thrive apparently on the general tension was Clarisse Lethuillier. She was wearing make-up again, but now skilfully applied. Her cheeks were less hollow, her eyes clearer and more animated; her spectacular beauty spoke for itself. Everyone's eyes were on her, from Captain Elledocq to the boiler-room crew. They watched her pass by on the invisible arm of her intemperate love. Happiness had gained the upper hand over her confusion, so much so that by moments it affected even Olga. And now Clarisse drank too much only in the evening, and ordered her own drinks.

At Palma Olga bought copies of all the French newspapers right under Eric Lethuillier's nose, though they made no secret of going ashore arm in arm—to general indifference since all shipboard eyes and ears had obviously turned to Julien and Clarisse, whose romance had taken precedence over the affairs of Olga and la Doriacci. This did not fail to annoy Olga. Though she could congratulate herself on the affront given Eric, she would still have liked the whispers and idle chatter to remain focused on herself rather than poor Clarisse. She kept on calling her 'poor Clarisse' so that she could continue to pity her and avoid having to envy her.

Olga was the first back on board, the newspapers clutched under her arm with perhaps excessive care. She was closely followed by Eric Lethuillier, who looked very pleased with himself, and later by Julien Peyrat, who had spent the afternoon on the phone. Finally, by eight in the evening everyone had gathered at the bar up on deck, and everyone was smiling as if that walk on dry land had restored their good humour. Only Andreas was giving everyone black looks, but that was because the diva wasn't there, because she had been gone all afternoon and had not yet come back, with only two hours left before her concert. This had been noted by Captain Elledocq, noisily draining tankard after tankard of beer under the reproving eye of the bartender, who was used to serving him in his cabin, where all his noisy inhalations were less disturbing.

In his defence it must be said that Captain Elledocq had

been greatly affected by the brawl of two days before. Contrary to what one might think, given his corpulence, build and dictatorial airs, Captain Elledocq was not a bellicose man. He was not one of those quick-fisted sea dogs out of Jack London who strike one another down like oak trees after twenty bottles of beer and a hundred uppercuts. Quite the contrary. Captain Elledocq had taken part in only two brawls in his long if uneventful career, and those in self-defence: in fact, when he was vilified as an idiot, cuckold and coward, he had taken on his detractor because otherwise his crew would have been upset. And both times he had been literally torn to pieces by smaller men, once by an Irish quartermaster, then by a Chinese cook. In double time and three movements, they had sent him, his cap and authority flying across the piano and bar stools of that particular den of iniquity.

The rapidity and violence of the 'Julien–Eric' brawl had filled Elledocq with boundless admiration for both passengers, whom till then he had regarded with scorn. Yet for all his admiration, Elledocq dreaded the consequences of the brawl. His panic grew with the sojourn in the infirmary of one and the spreading rumour about the good fortune of the other. He could picture himself welcoming on to a blood-stained deck the four brothers Pottin, the Cannes police commissioner, and maybe even the Minister of the Interior, to whom he would tearfully admit his failure to maintain order according to ship regulations.

So the captain had worn a worried look all morning and afternoon, until finally Charley noticed it and for once gave good counsel. Elledocq, with an olive branch between his teeth, like a dove, would have to go and see the combatants and extract from them a promise to keep the peace.

The captain began with Julien, since everyone on board was talking about his Marquet and it gave him a good pretext for the visit.

'Nice job . . . pretty . . .' mumbled Elledocq by way of commentary as he found himself in Julien's cabin in front of the snowy scene.

'You like it?' Julien Peyrat asked, looking askance but smiling amiably.

Again Elledocq mumbled, 'Nice job . . . nice job,' this time with a degree of earnestness. He was reluctant to begin. A sort of manly modesty inhibited him from exacting from the grown man who faced him, a man no more than fifteen years younger than himself, a promise not to strike a chap of his own age—it was as if the two were school chums and he the head prefect. So Elledocq carefully blew his nose and, after inspecting his handkerchief, folded it up again and put it in his pocket, to Julien's great relief.

'You and that *Forum* fellow . . .' began Elledocq. 'Turning nasty, eh? Bang, bang?' The captain smacked his palm vigorously with his fist to illustrate the observation.

'Yes,' said Julien intrigued. 'Yes, it's true. I'm terribly sorry, Captain.'

'You'll have another go soon?' enquired Elledocq in a roguish tone.

Julien began to laugh. 'I haven't made any plans,' he said, 'I can't promise you anything . . . You enjoyed it that much? A real brawl, eh, not bad?' His eyes were shining and he looked suddenly quite pleased with himself.

Elledocq wondered if he wouldn't have done better to avoid the subject since it so obviously delighted Julien.

'Brawling forbidden on this vessel,' he continued severely. 'Next time, you and him, under arrest.'

'Under arrest!' Julien burst out laughing. 'At the price we're paying? Captain, you're not going to lock up people who've spent ninety-eight thousand francs to cruise around for ten days in the open air? If so, lock up Kreuze, and his piano with him! And his scores for good measure! We'll ask for our money back! Though it might not be so bad after all, the music, in chains and all that.'

The captain had to withdraw without obtaining any further assurance from this scatterbrain. But he was much more successful with the other little pipsqueak, who, to Elledocq's great surprise, completely agreed with him. Eric Lethuillier showed himself more than ready to make peace, to seal the promise with a handshake, man to man. Without a moment's pause over the look of helpless amazement and even fear on the face of Clarisse, who witnessed their interview, Elledocq went back and told Julien, who also seemed surprised but had no choice but to follow him to the peacemaking cabin and go through with it. Whereupon Elledocq left, quite pleased with himself. As he finished describing the negotiations to Charley and Edma in the middle of their gossip session, he was astonished by his failure to arouse their well-warranted curiosity or enthusiasm. In truth, this peace left in its wake considerable fears and doubts.

*A*long with fresh fruit, flowers, food supplies and mail, the plague had crept aboard the *Narcissus*. In the form of newspapers. One newspaper in particular, the one Olga was hiding in her bag and which had also found its way into the stack of daily papers put out by Pottin Frères. It was, of course, Armand, the least interested party, who happened to pick up the paper and kept it for a long time mixed up with his financial reports. He did not understand at the time, or later for that matter, why little Olga kept following him around, with a smirk on her face, asking for investment advice. Finally he opened it. He managed an 'Oh-ho' and 'ah-ha' when he saw the fateful photo, and after a furtive glance at young Olga from behind his spectacles, he loosened his checked tie with his finger, and said, 'You look very good in this photo, you're very photogenic, really.'

'Yes,' Olga shrugged. 'Monsieur Lethuillier isn't bad either,' she added in the same offhand manner; then, 'May I?' she said, grabbing the paper and running off with it.

She went into her cabin, bolted the door behind her and sat down on her bed, breathing hard. It was as though she held a bomb between her hands. She hesitated now, torn between an irresistible desire to see Eric's face when he saw it, and a fear of what the handsome rat might do when confronted with the article, the text and the picture, whose caption she kept repeating to herself—a first reading had engraved it in her memory. Unable to decide, she went in search of advice. But in effect this already was a decision, for instead of going to consult Edma, whose social instinct as a *femme du monde* was to avoid all scandal and who would thus advise silence, she went in search of la Doriacci, who showed a predilection for drama.

To Olga's disappointment, this particular squabble failed to stir the diva's warrior instincts. Her eyes lit up at the start like headlights, but then immediately dimmed and seemed likely to remain so.

'You mustn't do that,' she said to Olga, taking the folded paper and brandishing it rather like a club, thought Olga, impressed. 'You mustn't. Already the whole thing's difficult. She's frightened and he's a nasty customer. It wouldn't help to annoy him, don't you see?' La Doriacci's expression changed, as for an instant she became the Italian housewife, honest and compassionate. 'You know, they really do love each other.'

'Who's they?' asked Olga with annoyance as she took back the paper. 'Ah yes, Julien and Clarisse. I know. Yes, I know,' she added with an ironic little smile, which abruptly put the diva into a rage.

'You know! You know what! What do you mean you know? You're not capable of knowing. You can play at being in love if need be, that's all. And even then, only just . . . You don't know the first thing about giving, you poor little thing, or about great feelings. You think you're already a star, and all your life you'll think it means something, that's all. And so I'll keep that paper!' She snatched it from the hands of Olga, who stood there indignantly, her mouth gaping.

'But . . . but . . .' she stammered, her face turning red. 'But . . .'

'But nothing!' said la Doriacci, closing the door on her and brushing her hands together as if to say a good thing done.

She would have been less satisfied had she known about the other fifteen copies Olga still had in her cabin.

'ome, come, little one. You're not going to hide from me what I already know, are you? Then what is it?'

Edma addressed Olga with an air of mild exasperation, like a teacher who might overlook a student's late arrival for class but would not allow them to forget the date of the battle of Lepanto. She stared at the ambitious starlet with a resigned smile, a smile so resigned that Olga weakened and gave way. The question was, Why was there not a single French newspaper left in all Palma, and why had Olga brought back a barrowload and hidden them God only knew where?

'You guessed?' Olga said weakly, in a last vain effort to escape from 'Agatha-Christie-Bautet-Lebreche'.

'Oh no! It's not that I *guessed* a single thing, pftt! No. I *understood*, and that's not the same. I didn't see what happened, but I saw the *cause* of what happened—a fake smile, a lack of attention, one too many low tricks, and suddenly a woman can't stand a man any more . . .'

Of course it was Clarisse that Edma meant, but her words applied perfectly to Olga, who, never once imagining that someone might be speaking of anyone else, took it to be herself and marvelled at Edma's lucidity. Basically, Edma was not the hard-hearted person she appeared to be, since in fact her ultra-sensitivity, her ultra-snobbery made her almost human, almost a real woman at times, Olga concluded. Proust would have had a fine old time on board (if her reading of the two pages in her school *Anthology of Great French Writers* was correct).

Edma's friendship suddenly seemed of prime importance to Olga Lamouroux, 'o-u-x' and not 'e-u-x' (this deliberate rudeness having now become an amusing aberration). Olga could very easily see herself taken up by the Bautet-Lebreches, this rich society couple. She saw herself the guest of honour at parties on the avenue Foch where ultra-rich austere sexagenarians were dazzled by her youth, her audacity, her breeding, the way she had restored a touch of class to French film (and film society). Thanks to Olga, these all-powerful industrialists would recall that Louis XIV had entertained Racine at his table, and la Champmesle. (Was that right, la Champmesle? She must check.)

Thanks to Olga, they would forget the bosoms and buttocks of the sluts without style who had been touted as stars for over a decade. But in the meantime, before she arrived at the avenue Foch and entrusted her casually styled mink to the old butler who already adored her, and before she could ask nicely after his rheumatism, Olga, still aboard the *Narcisuss*, showed her great new friend, her second mother, the envelope hidden in her purse. She sat down next to her in a dimly lit corner and bent over the pages of her boyfriend's weekly. The photo was perfectly clear. You could see Eric Lethuillier, who looked carried away by passion, clutching to his side the surprised and slightly fearful Olga Lamouroux. Of course that day Eric had seized Olga by the waist with the instinctive authority of a man who sees a woman about to fall, and no doubt it was also the fear of falling that gave Olga her look of annoyance. But the photo didn't suggest an accidental physical fall, as Edma remarked between her teeth with a little whistle of appreciation mingled with alarm.

'Well, my fine young friend, now I understand your fears. Lethuillier's going to hit the roof!'

'Don't worry about me,' said Olga bravely, still clinging to the role of adoptive daughter. 'He won't see it until Cannes, and I'll be far away.'

'But I wasn't worrying about you!' replied Edma, who found the idea quite fanciful. 'It's Clarisse I'm worried about. A man of that sort always makes somebody else pay for any unpleasantness he may suffer, even if they have nothing to do with it. My God, what a photo!'

'And did you read the article?' Olga asked with a sigh of pleasure.

Edma went back to the paper:

"Could this be the handsome Eric Lethuillier? Could the publisher of *Forum*, that austere journal, be trying to forget politics and humanitarian cares? So it would seem. The latest cause he has embraced is none other than our number one starlet, the beautiful Olga Lamouroux, who seems somewhat less enthusiastic—perhaps because she is thinking of her producer Simon Béjard (who does not appear in our photo), whose *Fire and Smoke* is still a runaway success in Paris. Well, perhaps the discovery of capitalism's charms will make Monsieur Lethuillier more indulgent towards bourgeois luxury (though he might well have learned that already from his wife Clarisse Lethuillier, née Dureau, of the Dureau Steelworks (also missing from our photo)."

'That's quite a good start,' said Edma with a nervous laugh.

'There's more,' Olga laughed, though a little uneasily. 'Listen:

' "Why is Eric Lethuillier, the Friend of the People, spending his vacation aboard the *Narcissus*, on a music cruise that costs a cute ninety thousand francs? Is it to expose his cruise companions, or to learn to understand them? Our readers will know what to make of it." '

'That's truly vile!' said Edma. 'Good heavens . . .' She retrieved the paper from Olga's hands. 'What's that about ninety thousand francs? Why, that's completely mad! Wait till I get hold of my secretary!'

'You didn't know that?' said poor Olga, completely outclassed, not realising that snobbery among the rich meant finding everything too expensive.

'What do you think Eric will do?' she said, her heels clattering along the dark deck behind Edma, whose pace had accelerated with her indignation.

'I don't know, but it's going to make quite a scene! Tell me, is he very much in love with you? No, of course not,' she went on, since Olga was silent. 'He's in love with nobody but himself. And you, my dear? Is it very troublesome for you, all this, all this gossip?'

'For me and Simon, yes,' said Olga in an earnest tone that abruptly revived Edma's antipathy.

'Oh no! Don't try to tell me that you've got the slightest concern for poor Simon! That would be too much! You know, he's a very, very sweet man, that Simon. He's so alive, he has such a sensitive side to him, it's quite surprising . . . *very* surprising,' she went on pensively, like an ethnologist confronted by an unclassifiable race.

'Simon is a dear fellow, poor thing, but . . .' Olga was about to say, but checked herself. 'He's a character,' she said.

'What do you mean by that, my friend, eh? Let's just sit down here for a moment,' said Edma, ducking into the ladies' lounge and sinking, as if exhausted, onto a stool in front of the mirror.

'I mean he's marvellous as a friend, but he's a problem as a boyfriend,' said Olga with an embarrassed laugh that she herself found charming but which caused Edma to grit her teeth. 'Simon was so scared I wouldn't like him for himself that he practically hid from me the fact he was a producer! Would you believe that? It was only at Cannes that I heard he was both a producer and winner of the Grand Prix. A year ago he was practically unknown. And I must say not many were betting on Simon Béjard,' said Olga, with a little laugh of pride in acknowledgment of her unselfishness and finesse.

Unfortunately, she didn't realise Simon had already told Edma about the night the awards were given, how four starlets had thrown themselves at him, one of them Olga Lamouroux, o-u-x, herself. Bravo, a thousand times bravo! Edma jeered inwardly.

'Except that now he's sure of me,' continued Olga, immersed in idyllic reveries, 'sure of me and of my fidelity— on a certain level . . . Because, you see,' she went on brightly, while Edma, stifling her anger, was tossing her head and grinding her teeth as if having reverted to an animal state, 'I'm talking about real fidelity, the kind that lasts . . . not the kind that's upset by a little fling after work, a mad impulse, an evening's explosion of passion—the kind of thing that just happens to us young people . . . us women!' she corrected herself just in time, or so she thought.

But not quite soon enough. Edma had heard what she said and noted the unintended insult. She began jerking her head furiously against her hairbrush, which remained almost stationary. This was what first struck la Doriacci as she entered the oasis of the lounge. Her eyes blazed furiously, but still observantly. She stopped in front of Edma's performance and watched her, perplexed at first, then amused, and finally breaking into a low, resonant laugh that was altogether irresistible.

'What's wrong with you?' said Edma (vaguely put out at being the cause of such merriment but ready to join in). Her head came to an abrupt halt.

'It's this,' said la Doriacci, imitating her in the mirror. 'You were moving your head but not the brush—you know, like the Belgians and the matchbox? When they want to find out whether there's anything in it, they shake their heads and not the box!' She gasped, then collapsed into laughter, into her cascading, uncontrollable paroxysms that were as infectious for Edma as they were annoying to Olga, who couldn't forget the 'young calf' episode.

'We worried about you,' she said in a slightly nettled tone to la Doriacci, who had sat down and was powdering her nose with an immense, bright pink puff.

It was odd how all of her accessories were outsized, Edma thought in passing. In Paris they would come up with a theory for that one, however far-fetched or Freudian.

Olga, anxious now, persisted, 'But what could anyone do for a whole afternoon in Palma?'

'It's a very pretty place,' la Doriacci said with a twinkle in her eyes. 'There are some charming spots, and there are always old friends to look up, depending how you feel. Nothing happened aboard our phantom ship while I was gone?'

'Andreas almost wore holes through the deck with his pacing about, but that's all, I think,' said Edma.

'How funny, here we are, the three As—Doria, Edma, Olga . . .' said Olga Lamouroux in a fluty voice. 'We all have the same endings,' she said again to the vacant stares of the other two.

'Just so long as it's not the same family, it's not serious,' said Edma Bautet-Lebreche decisively.

Then, finished with what was actually a very poor job of putting on some make-up, she rose, adding in a slightly exasperated tone, 'My dear Olga, do be good and keep that paper to yourself, won't you? We'll talk about it later . . . that and your psychological problems.'

Left alone together, the diva and Olga avoided each other's eyes until they met, distrustfully and unintentionally, by way of the mirror. La Doriacci had on her autographing look, Olga her pinching little smile.

'How is Monsieur Lethuillier?' said la Doriacci in an amiable if scornful tone as she curled her black lashes around a brush caked with mascara, with a cold and lofty air.

'You would have to ask Clarisse Lethuillier,' Olga said distantly. She would gladly have fled had the thought of the diva's critical eye on her back not filled her with horror (though which of the two should have really been feeling pangs of remorse?). So she decided instead to polish her toenails with the bottle that, thank God, never left her side.

La Doriacci snapped shut her vast satchel. 'If I were to ask the beautiful Clarisse anything, it would be for news of the handsome Julien. You are very ill-informed, my child. On this ship the couples are not always legal.'

Her irony was only too obvious, and Olga, pale with rage, spattered a few scarlet drops onto her new jeans. She desperately searched for a suitable answer, but despite all appeals her frantic brain rang hollow.

'You ought to dye your hair,' concluded la Doriacci as she strode to the door with her regal gait. 'You would have a stronger personality in Venetian red. That bleached-blonde look is just a bit washed out.'

And she was gone, leaving Olga in a rage bordering on tears. She went up to get a breath of air, fuming, and on the deck took what comfort she could from the sight of Andreas ravaged by grief. Hesitating at first, Olga finally alerted Julien Peyrat.

'You're taking exercise in this weather? What a good idea . . .'

Julien fell into step with Andreas, whose pallor did in fact worry him though Andreas tried to turn away. What he saw by leaning over was a face rejuvenated but also undone by sorrow, the face of a young man ready for God-knows-what. How could this fine fellow allow himself to get into such a state over a sixty-year-old woman who had had a hundred lovers before him, and who would certainly have others? Things were completely topsy-turvy. And despite the affection he instinctively felt for la Doriacci, Julien was furious with her. This gigolo didn't have the calculating coldness of a real gigolo and she had no call to make him pay so cruelly. The justification Clarisse saw only worried him; coming from her, it was almost a betrayal.

'You don't realise what it means,' Clarisse had said. 'To decide to love someone of one's own age is traumatic enough. La Doriacci is sixty, and to allow herself a soft spot for someone like Andreas could absolutely ruin the rest of her life. Even if she does love him, what would happen in a year's time, in five? Tell me that?'

'What will happen, what will happen!' Julien, who instinctively preached the temporary, said dismissively.

He had not been able to say a thing about himself to Clarisse. It was not so much the fear of losing her that kept him from speaking up as the fear that she might be hurt and disappointed all over again, and her confidence in men destroyed. It was both irksome and enchanting to find himself more concerned about Clarisse than about himself. This was an attitude he had long thought affected only by masochists or the sentimental, people absorbed in their own misery and whom he instinctively detested for what he took to be their lack of character. To love another for your own good seemed normal to him, but to care more about the other person's good than your own seemed pure fantasy, almost unhealthy. Nonetheless, the thing that horrified him most was to imagine his tender and beautiful Clarisse driving off with Eric as soon as they had gone ashore, Clarisse forever resigned to loneliness and hating him, Julien, for making her think she might escape. He imagined Clarisse in a modern glasshouse leaning her forehead against window-panes streaming with rain and boredom, while behind her, in a luxurious and desolately beige setting, Eric Lethuillier and his cohorts waited mockingly for her to have a drink. Waiting for her to drink too much. Julien sometimes writhed in pain on his bed at this naive image, though the refined iciness of it detracted from the naiveté. There was, in the furtive kisses Julian gave her when chance permitted, a compassion and sweet anger that delighted Clarisse. In unguarded moments she gazed at the wide, full lips of her lover with a tenderness and gratitude that was almost independent of her love. That warm fresh mouth seemed to possess an inexhaustibly gentle breath, alone capable of restoring to her the thousands of kisses she had been deprived of, stolen from her over the years.

She liked Julien's slim and muscular body, his neat, childish body with nooks of soft and virile skin, nooks covered with a stiff down lighter than his hair. She loved the child in Julien, the way his eyes lit up when someone spoke of gambling, horses or painting. She cherished this child, dreamed in those moments of giving him horses and canvases, his toys. And she loved the man when he looked at her, his eyes turning deep and murky, unhappy at having to restrain himself, when his jaws clamped shut on words of love. She loved his deep voice, that too held in check, it seemed to her. That masculine, clear voice concealed from others' eyes a sensitive and cheery Julien. She loved him for thinking himself strong in order to protect her, and capable of being it if the need arose. She loved him for wanting to decide everything, share everything with her except the one decision which he alone had to take and to keep to. She loved his way of leaving her in the dark about his fears for his freedom, his reticence about becoming deeply involved. She loved the fact that he had never asked whether they were right or wrong, whether they should think it over, whether she was sure, whether she wanted time to decide.

In short, Julien had never let her think it was up to her to choose, and in denying her the choice had spared her the role of responsibility that she feared so much, taking it on himself though it had never been his way to do so, nor in his nature. But for the rest, he already shared everything with her; already Clarisse had to tell him the night before what he should wear the next day—what shirt, what tie, what sweater went with which—and that he should drink his tea before his first cigarette of the morning. She had entered his life in one week more than she had Eric's in ten years. She knew she was already needed there and, miraculously, the idea revived her more than it horrified her.

*A*t the very moment she reached the deck Julien and Andreas were striding towards her, and she saw Julien raise his eyes and smile as he caught sight of her, and he began to run. She quickened her pace too so she could see all the sooner her reflection in his eyes, the image of happiness.

'Andreas is unhappy,' he said, pushing the boy towards Clarisse and looking at her with an expression of relief, as though she could do something about it.

Julien clearly believed her to be all-powerful, responsible for everyone else's happiness as well as for his. He was beginning to retrieve the lost and injured for her with the application of a good hunting dog. She smiled at him, aware that Andreas was only the first of a long line. For the rest of their life together Julien would be bringing her, from his ramblings at the casinos or at Longchamp, a series of winos, neurotics or ruffians that he would drop off triumphantly so that she might bind their wounds or solve their problems. Resigned to it, she took Andreas's arm and went off with

him for a turn around the deck while Julien, lazy and pleased
with himself, leaned on the rail and watched them disappear,
looking satisfied that a duty had been accomplished. What
could he have said to combat the grief of this little boy who
was too grown up and too beautiful?

'Julien told me I should behave like a man,' Andreas said
in answer to the question she had not asked. 'But I don't
really know what it means to "behave like a man".'

'Julien doesn't either,' said Clarisse with a smile. 'And
neither do I for that matter! It's just an expression . . . But
what you should do is behave like a man who would please
la Doriacci. That's all, isn't it?'

'Exactly,' said Andreas. This clarification seemed indispensable to him. 'How am I supposed to know what kind
of a man? Where did she go today?' he asked suddenly in
a low voice, as if ashamed on her behalf. 'She seems to have
a lover in every port!'

'Or a friend,' said Clarisse calmly.

'I hadn't thought of that,' Andreas stammered, as if thunderstruck by this simple notion.

'Of course not,' said Clarisse. 'Men never stop to think
that the women they desire might not be desired by everyone
else. It doesn't occur to them that we could possibly arouse
interest or affection and not lust! It's rather upsetting for
us, don't you think?'

She was surprised, in fact astonished, to hear herself
making a speech, to hear herself comforting someone when
three days before she had been the embodiment of anguish.

'But why does she hurt me since I love her?' he was
saying.

Clarisse mused over just how gorgeous or innocent the
man must be not to seem ridiculous saying such things.

'Because if la Doriacci loved you, she would suffer too
much,' she said. 'After a while, anyhow. It's a sign of how
much she thinks of you that she's so cruel to you. It's
because she could love you. And she's scared of that, with
good reason.'

'Scared of what? I'd follow her everywhere, all my life!'

cried Andreas, stopping short. 'It isn't only physical what I feel for her, you know?' He was whispering. 'I love her character, her courage, her humour, her cynicism . . . Even if she doesn't want to sleep with me any more, I'll wait until she does. After all,' he concluded with disarming sincerity, 'that isn't the main thing, is it, getting into bed?'

'Of course not,' she said with conviction, feeling somewhat disconcerted nevertheless. For, ever since Cannes and despite Julien's intuitive feelings, she had regarded Andreas all along as a coldly professional gigolo.

Once again Julien's optimism had proved right. And here I am, she thought with a nervous laugh, trying to console a gorgeous young man of twenty-five about the supposed infidelity of a woman close to sixty. Clearly anything was possible, at any age. This comforted her. Clarisse was now in her thirties: 'that thankless age' which followed the charms of youth and preceded those of maturity—so said Eric; 'that auspicious age' which followed the pretensions of youth and preceded those of maturity—so said Julien. It just depends on how you look at it, she reflected.

'If she leaves for New York without me,' the lover soliloquised, 'I will kill myself.' He said it in a voice so devoid of inflection that Clarisse was suddenly anxious. 'This time I'd be too much alone, do you understand?' he finished quite pleasantly.

'But why alone? You must have friends or family somewhere, don't you?' Now her voice was anxious. Clarisse in love, Clarisse responsive to others, was worried about this sad young man.

He replied in self-excusing tones without raising his eyes, 'The last of my aunts died a year ago. I have nobody left, not at Nevers nor anywhere else. And if the diva doesn't take me with her, I couldn't even follow her. The cruise cost me my last penny. Even if I sold my clothes and tennis rackets I couldn't go to New York,' he said, sounding quite desperate.

'Listen,' said Clarisse, 'if she doesn't take you to New York, I'll pay for the trip. Here, I'll give you a cheque right now. And if you don't use it, you can tear it up.'

She had stopped at a table and was rummaging in her bag to find a chequebook that was worn but intact after six months. This meant that she had not wanted anything for those six months, nor had anyone come asking. Clarisse wondered which of these two realisations was the more shameful, the sadder.

'But I can't do that,' said Andreas, looking pale and shocked. 'I can't accept money from a woman I've never . . . that I don't know.'

'Well, it'll just mean a change in your regulations,' said Clarisse, pulling a pen out of her bag and beginning to fill out the cheque. 'But how much?'

She didn't know the price of anything any more. Eric paid all the bills and bought everything himself, except her wardrobe, and she hadn't changed that for two years. Now, the minute she got back she was going to dash to all the designers, cover herself in blue fox, because that's what Julien said he adored. Of course she had no more idea of the price of blue fox than of a ticket to New York. She wrote out 5,000 in figures, then added a 1 before the 5, on the offchance.

'Here,' she said imperiously to Andreas who took the cheque, turned it over, and looked at the amount without the slightest false modesty. He whistled between his teeth.

'Oo la la!' His eyes shone with happiness. 'But that's a lot of money! It's less than three thousand now from Paris to New York. But how will I ever pay you back?'

'There's no rush,' said Clarisse, delighted with his delight. 'The Dureau works are doing very well, you know.'

Andreas hugged her to him and kissed her, first as he would a child, then for the woman in her. Clarisse, astonished at first, realised how la Doriacci and those other ladies back in the provinces had developed a weakness for this young man. The two of them were both red-cheeked when they separated and laughed at each other's expressions of surprise. That, too, I have rediscovered, thought Clarisse exultantly, the attractions of men. And to put an end to Andreas's apologies, she kissed him back, lightly, just on the corner of the mouth.

*O*lga felt a little less hatred for Eric Lethuillier since she knew that he had been made to look ridiculous, and she was carrying the proof of it in her handbag. She even rediscovered a certain physical charm in him, despite his meanness and bad behaviour. She had wanted to believe the theory put forward by the newspaper; she had even begun to phrase a similar account to herself: *What a time I had trying to shake him off! How small the ship could seem with that guy who wouldn't let me out of his sight!* And she almost succeeded, for Olga, like many of her generation, had reached the point of believing the papers and television more than her own senses. In other words she almost believed that it was Eric Lethuillier who had assiduously pursued her, that it was her refusal to yield to him a second time that had provoked the terrible things he said to Armand Bautet-Lebreche. Vigorously she rallied her spirits with that vainglorious version, but then her memory—that wild beast, not yet domesticated—unexpectedly played back Eric's voice for her, the voice that said 'one of the most aggravating little tramps—with intellectual pretensions', and immediately she was overwhelmed by the same shame, the same hatred, as three days before. She turned towards the publisher of *Forum*. He was looking at her with that handsome son-of-a-bitch face, she thought suddenly, and a burst of rage lit up her face, making her almost desirable to Eric, who was patiently repeating his question.

'Yes, I'm willing to buy the painting,' she replied. 'But with whose money? Yours, of course. Only Julien Peyrat is no fool. He'll find it a little peculiar that I suddenly have two hundred and fifty thousand francs, and very peculiar that I'm putting it all into a painting.'

'Tell him you're buying it for me then,' Eric said curtly. 'Where's the harm in that? At any rate, he has to sell it.'

'How do you know that?'

The girl was beginning to exasperate him. Eric adopted a patient tone. 'Because, my little one, it is obvious.'

Olga looked squarely at him, her eyelids fluttering, her voice ingenuous. 'I don't think he is a man with his back against the wall. He looks very happy with what he has. He doesn't seem to want anything but . . .'

She stopped with calculated embarrassment. Eric's response was a cold look, and Olga was afraid she had gone too far.

'Oh, I'm sorry, Eric . . . you must realise I didn't mean to say that . . . Oh God, I'm thoughtless, it's awful.'

'You just take care of the painting,' said Eric without inflection, not even a note of interrogation.

Olga nodded, her handkerchief pressed to her blundering mouth. She had seen Eric blench because Julien was happy. She had seen him catch his breath, and she felt gleeful as he went off at his rapid pace, this time perhaps a bit too measured.

The bar was smoky with a gauzy blue smoke that made it look like a movie set, and most of the passengers sat or stood near the piano listening to Simon Béjard play the theme of the *Narcissus*—actually a Bohemian folk tune, he claimed. Only Armand clung to his own little table of refuge, while

Clarisse and Julien leaned up against the bar, apparently heedless of this supplementary recital. The two were laughing with the relaxed and carefree air of people who have been in love only a short time, when Eric appeared in the doorway.

His face was impassive as he called to Clarisse in a low but peremptory voice; for five crushing seconds an acutely embarrassed silence reigned in the bar. It was broken by Edma who, accustomed to such burlesque tensions, slapped Simon's hand onto the keyboard as she would have done to a child balking at his scales. The resulting *plunk* set conversation going again. Only Julien, who along with Clarisse had uneasily pushed away from the bar, looked anything but light-hearted. La Doriacci appeared on the scene at just that moment and, realising exactly what was going on upon seeing Julien's expression, made an effort to remedy the situation.

'You're not going to let me drink by myself, Monsieur Lethuillier?' she said. 'I was just about to consult you about my programme for this evening—you and your friends, of course. Mahler's *Lieder* . . . How do you feel about them?'

'We have complete confidence in your choice,' said Eric with exaggerated courtesy. 'Would you excuse us for a moment, please.' And he pushed Clarisse ahead of him. La Doriacci turned to Julien and, lifting her hands palms upwards in a gesture of powerlessness, uttered a '*Ma che!*' that was expressive if not discreet.

'You look pale,' said Andreas to Julien, tapping his arm protectively. He had switched roles. 'Have a drink, old fellow,' he said, pouring him another straight whisky, which Julien drank down without even looking at him.

'If he touches her,' he mumbled in a choked voice. 'If he even touches her, I'll . . . I'll . . .'

'Come on, come on! You'll do nothing, Julien. Nothing at all. You're crazy . . .'

Edma now crossed the bar under full steam and sat down at their table, looking both maternal and reasonable.

'Lethuillier is far too much of a snob, too tame really. He's not about to beat his wife as if this were some Zola

335

novel. He's too conscious of his origins, it would appear, and he must realise that only the aristocracy can strike their wives without its being thought vulgar. And I don't mean aristocrats who bought their titles from Bonaparte! Anyway, that poor boy's got no sense of where people draw the line these days. He should have realised it's all the same now, housekeeper or postmistress. Well, of course housekeeper does sound more exotic, but then postmistress has a touch of Queneau, a certain literary charm . . .'

'What are you talking about?' said Andreas. 'Whatever, it's a very sound theory, very sound,' he said, nodding at Edma, who gave him the quick glance and artificial smile reserved for clumsy flatterers. The young man's face, however, belied such curt dismissal. He was incredibly ingenuous, this sentimental, renegade gigolo, thought Edma.

'I assure you, Julien, you shouldn't get worked up. At any rate, dinner will be served in ten minutes.'

'And if Lethuillier doesn't bring his wife to the table, I'll go and get her myself,' said Simon Béjard.

He was almost putting the spurs to his pinto when Charley joined them. He, too, looked depressed. The only ones besides a few apathetic old-timers who sat apart, still clinging to their own little table as though it were a life raft, were Olga Lamouroux and Kreuze. Kreuze, the learned sage far removed from 'all that', was telling the story of his inspired and studious childhood.

'I wonder how that poor Lethuillier could have made himself so unanimously loathed . . . well, almost unanimously,' said Edma with a sidelong glance towards Olga and an affectionate squeeze of Simon's hand. She said it with a laugh, but he turned his head away.

'Ten centimes for your thoughts, Monsieur Peyrat,' she continued unperturbed. 'No, make it an olive,' she said, filching from Julien's glass the black olive that she had been coveting ever since she sat down. 'How is it that Clarisse, who's so beautiful, so rich, so . . . sensitive . . .' (Edma Bautet-Lebreche never spoke of a woman's intelligence unless the woman was positively repellent). 'How could Clarisse have married that Savonarola?' Her voice dropped in uncertainty at the end, uncertainty over both Savonarola's career and where the *o* went in his name. He was some fanatic or other, of that she was almost sure.

'Poor little Clarisse,' said la Doriacci with a smile, though a little put out that Edma had been first to filch the olive she too had been coveting. 'But in the last two days she's become ravishing! It's always unhappiness that spoils people's looks,' she said tapping Andreas on the chin; he looked away. 'My, but the men on this ship are dreary,' she went on haughtily. 'Andreas, Charley, Simon, Eric . . . It's not the very best of cruises for the men, it seems! Now, on the other hand, it's exquisite for us women,' she said, throwing back her head and displaying her beautiful throat with a crystalline, ingenuous laugh that clashed hideously with what had caused it.

For a moment the entire table sat staring. La Doriacci glanced about her with a look of defiance, gaiety and anger that clearly betrayed a soul untrammelled by the judgment of others. Nobody moved a muscle except Julien who, despite his sadness, could not refrain from giving this exemplar of freedom an admiring smile.

'What is it you want to say to me?' asked Clarisse, who had been sitting on her bed while the minutes dragged by.

Eric was pacing up and down in front of her, changing his clothes, without a word. He was whistling, always a bad sign. Clarisse, however, watched him without antipathy. He had saved her from five or ten troubled minutes in the time spent sitting face to face with the person one loves without knowing him well, that confused, emotional, urgent time; avid, perpetually insatiable time. Whereas now, in the quiet of the cabin, Clarisse could simply remind herself that she loved Julien, that he loved her; she could let her arteries, lungs and heart expand while thinking of him. She had forgotten Eric and almost jumped when he sat down in front of her in his shirtsleeves, apparently intent on doing up his cufflinks. He had sat on the foot of the bed, and Clarisse instinctively pulled her knees up to her chin for fear he might touch her, even her foot. Instantly recognising what she had done, she blushed and looked fearfully at Eric. But he had seen nothing.

'I'm going to ask you something,' he said. Having completed his task, he put his hands behind his head and leaned back against the wall in an offhand manner. 'In fact, I'm going to ask you to answer yes or no to some rather blunt questions.'

'Then it's no,' said Clarisse instinctively. She saw him turn pale with fury, unaccustomed as he was to having her interrupt the playing-out of his little scenes.

'What do you mean no? You don't want to answer?'

'That's right,' said Clarisse calmly. 'I don't want to answer blunt questions. There's no reason at all for you to speak to me bluntly.'

There was a silence, and Eric's voice was emotionless when he began again.

'Well, I'm going to be blunt anyway. This whole ship seems to think you're sleeping with Julien Peyrat. May I know whether it's true. Unthinkable and impossible as it seems to me, I shall need to have an answer if anyone speaks to me about it. Otherwise I'll be made to look ridiculous or a liar.'

He had thrown out his words in a sarcastic and slightly disgusted tone, but suddenly realised that she might in fact answer his question, and the answer might be appallingly frank—and in the affirmative. Suddenly he would have given anything not to have said anything, not to have imprudently broached the subject. What madness had he committed? What aberration had seized him? He had to calm down. No, it was simply not so. Clarisse had not done that, not here on this ship, not confined, as he was too, to this limited space, where he could have discovered her and killed her . . . Why killed her? Eric told himself he would have had no choice, he would have been forced to become a killer had he entered a cabin by chance and found Julien and Clarisse there, naked and intertwined.

'Well then, will you answer me or not? My dear Clarisse, I'm quite willing to let you think it over during dinner. I'll wait till after the concert for your answer, but my patience ends there. Agreed?'

He had spoken very quickly so that she would not in fact have a chance to answer him. He could not quite figure out why he was putting off the ceremony for two or three hours, could not quite make himself understand that it was a respite he was allowing himself rather than her.

Clarisse said in a very weary voice, 'As you please,' and sounded less relieved and more sorry than he.

*T*o start with, dinner was awful for Julien. As on the first day, he was sitting next to Clarisse. And without looking at her directly he saw again the hand and lock of hair that had physically excited him that first evening. That hand, that face were now his, the permanent objects of his desire, and he wanted them to love and defend against Eric Lethuillier, against that legalised predator with the cold eye. The hand, the face that he was not sure of keeping, or keeping from harm. He hated Eric now. He had never known the miasmas and suffocations of hatred, but now he felt infected by it, made gangrenous in some subterranean part of himself that he did not like.

He was rather scornful of this new Julien so full of hatred, so much the jealously fearful keeper of the treasure, watching Clarisse in fact as closely as Eric did. When he stretched out his foot to touch Clarisse under the table, it was against his better self, and he was sure she too would disapprove of this vulgar token of understanding. She would stiffen her leg and give him a glance—not of contempt, for she had never known it—but at least of hurt. And then what would he do? He could neither withdraw his leg nor pursue Clarisse further. He moved towards her all the same. It was the first time in his life Julien was doing something against his better judgment, something that was not in the interests of his eventual happiness and prospects of success, the first time he was acting against his own code and his own desires. He stiffened in anticipation of Clarisse's surprise.

He was already looking in her direction with a stubborn and uncomprehending expression, when their knees touched and he felt Clarisse's foot slide beneath his and her leg press eagerly against his own. She turned to him with a troubled smile on her face—an expression of gratitude that immobilised Julien, caught at his heart and left him speechless: in the throes of an intense tenderness, to be sure, but also its prisoner forever, he realised in one of those sudden moments of lucidity that so often accompany so-called blind joy. So we play footsie with the ladies, and we blush, said a cruel little voice out of nowhere, a small voice that then relented, having allowed itself this undermining observation only as a matter of conscience.

*T*he stop at Palma, where they were now berthed in a violet haze, called for a Shostakovitch concerto in which Hans-Helmut was to play the piano while the two boy scouts provided accompaniment. La Doriacci was to sing Mahler, which meant she would sing something else. It was the next-to-last performance; the last would take place the following day at Cannes, where they were to arrive at the end of the day. Abruptly the cruise was coming to an end, and suddenly everyone was aware of it. It was with a feeling of regret that passengers of both classes took their usual seats and adopted their usual poses.

Hans-Helmut looked more solemn than ever as he sat down at the piano, as if even his pachydermic hide were porous enough to register the change in the atmosphere. As he placed his hand on the keyboard, Julien and Clarisse were sitting across from each other, on opposite sides of the floodlit arena, as they had on the first day. Simon and Olga, as on the first day too, were sitting behind the Lethuilliers. Andreas's seat was set apart, the seat closest to the microphone, of course, where la Doriacci would soon stand. The Bautet-Lebreches were sitting on the end of the first row, so that Edma had a good view of Kreuze's hands on the keyboard and the violinists' playing.

It was no more than a week since the supporting players had embarked, but it already seemed to them a small eternity. There was a sense of having to take leave of one another in twenty-four hours after having got to know one another so slightly and so fortuitously, the sudden certainty of really knowing nothing about companions they had thought so thoroughly dissected—suddenly this seemed silly and presumptuous. Once again they found themselves face to face with strangers. Chance became omnipotent once again; a sort of retrospective timidity seized them all, from the most apathetic to the most percipient, and made their glances furtive, surprised, and curious. This was their last attempt at understanding, their last display of curiosity; they knew now, as they did not at embarkation, that their curiosity would never be satisfied. There was a piquancy to everything. A sort of melancholy aura of missed occasions, and the cheerfulness of regret, hovered about the heads of the most tedious and disagreeable.

The first notes that Hans-Helmut Kreuze wrenched from his piano gave further weight to this melancholy. After two minutes, there was not one whose eyes had not been lowered at least once over some secret, inner thing, something which the music suddenly revealed and which had to be hidden at all costs from the eyes of others.

The wild romanticism of the landscape, its grandiose aspect, was the very opposite of this concerto in which Kreuze, sustained by the two instrumentalists, struck again and again in persistent reprise the four or five deliciously inevitable notes. It was an evocation of childhood, rain on summer lawns, cities emptied in August, a photo rediscovered in a drawer of love letters one had laughed at in one's youth. What the piano was saying was all half-tones, nuances, in-between seasons, in the imperfect tense at any rate; and it was said with tranquillity, like a confession or a happy reminiscence softened by sadness and the irretrievable.

Each one was submerged in a personal past, but with a greater or lesser sense of joy, for it wasn't the good old times as people usually tended to think of their past, its image subtly changed over the years to reflect the way they now saw themselves. For instance, Julien's memories of uncomplicated happiness or innocence were not recollections of an evening's gambling, or a woman's body, nor even more spectacularly a painting discovered in a museum during his adolescence. He saw a rainy beach on the Basque coast, one summer when he was nineteen, a grey beach edged with foam almost as grey, where in his sweater caked with sand, with his bitten fingernails, he had experienced the sensation of being no more than the temporary inhabitant of his body that was so alive, so perishable, and suddenly, for no precise reason, he was overwhelmed with an intoxicating joy.

And it was not the Cannes Festival and the bravos of the audience, not the spotlights trained on him, not the flashbulbs, not even the little boy wandering from dawn to dusk through one dirty theatre after another, that Simon Béjard remembered. Rather it was a slightly overweight woman named Simone, older than he, who loved him madly, she said, and asked nothing more than that he be himself. Simone, who kissed him on the station platform as he left for Paris, a woman whom already, from the vantage point of his eighteen years and the steps of the railway car, he found a little provincial, and of whom he was a little ashamed.

The music was gently devastating. It threw each of them back into a state of frailty, to the need for affection (though not without the countervening tide of bitterness, inevitable fruit of the cycle of defeat and hunger that is the human lot). When Kreuze stopped and got up from the piano with his deep, abrupt bow—it left him flushed, as the blood went to his head—he had to wait several seconds before receiving the usual acclaim. And even then the applause was feeble, uncertain, and almost grudging, though interminable. La Doriacci, who should have come on almost immediately, did not in fact enter the circle of light for another hour; and oddly enough, a good half-hour had passed before anyone protested, or anyone grew impatient.

Three times during that unforeseen intermission Charley went to tap on la Doriacci's door. Three times he had to restrain himself from his habit of putting his ear to the door. What he heard was not strictly speaking raised voices, but rather a kind of psalm recited evenly by the unmistakably youthful voice of Andreas. It was Andreas talking without passion and, as it were, without punctuation, an Andreas whose intonation, curiously enough, failed to convey the sense of what he was saying. Each time, Charley waited three minutes after his brisk 'You're on,' but through it all he heard la Doriacci's voice only once, and then briefly, in a voice exceptionally low even for her, it seemed to him. He had gone off shaking his head, perturbed about Andreas in spite of himself. He upbraided himself for worrying over a liaison whose inevitably sad outcome was the only one that he in fact might welcome. 'I'm too kind,' he mumbled dejectedly, and then laughed at himself with scorn—without reason this time, for Charley Bollinger was actually a good-hearted man, and would have been even further crushed had he heard clearly what those faint voices were saying.

'What you need is a mother,' la Doriacci had said at the start of her long-deferred speech. 'You need a mother and I'm past the age for playing mother. It's too close to the truth. Only little girls up to but not including the age of twenty-five can play mother to men of all ages. I can't any more. I can't allow my emotions to get the upper hand or adapt my behaviour to a situation over which I have no control. You can't go mooning about the inevitable, particularly when the inevitable is unpleasant. Do you understand what I'm saying? I should be looking for a protector, my dear Andreas. I'm fifty-two, and I am going to look for a father—perhaps because I never had one, or because later I had too many, I don't know which, and I don't care. I don't think you're any more up to being a father than the other gentlemen I've been seeing for the last ten years. Not

345

having a father, I always fell back on gigolos, on playthings. But there again, you're not up to it, my sweet. You're too sentimental to be a plaything. I can't wind up your machinery with a pair of cufflinks, nor your morale either. And I don't have anything else to offer you, nothing but cufflinks. You want a woman, and all I can offer is a trousseau.'

She said the whole thing without pause in an agreeable and elegant tone, then took refuge in a long silence which Andreas's voice scarcely disturbed.

'It makes no difference to me what you can and can't do,' said Andreas without expression. 'That's none of my business, and none of yours either, in the long run. The question is do you love me, not can you love me? It's not a choice I'm asking you to make. What I'm asking is that you let yourself go completely. What difference does it make if you're happy against your better judgment, as long as you're happy?'

'I wouldn't care, but alas I can't do it,' la Doriacci told him once more. She looked splendid tonight: in a low-cut black dress that made her appear slimmer and set off the dazzling whiteness of her shoulders, giving her a sort of unreality in contrast with the weight of her presence. 'I've reached an age when one cannot let oneself go any-which-way because any-which-way has no voice for me any more. Our feelings bend immediately to what we want, and that's it. That's what old age is, Andreas, don't you see—to love only what you can love, and desire only what you can have. It's called wisdom. And I confess I agree that it's altogether disgusting, but that's the way it is. I'm in possession of my senses, and therefore cynical. You're in possession of yours and therefore eager. You can afford to treat youself to grand passions, even unhappy ones, because you have the time afterwards to treat yourself to others, equally delicious. But not I. Let's say I love you: you will leave me—or I you. But I would never have the time to love someone else after you, and I don't want to die with a bad taste in my mouth. My last love was crazy about me, and it was I who left him ten years ago.'

Andreas listened dumbfounded to these painful

assertions, dumbfounded with admiration and, strangely, gratitude, for it was the first time she had talked to him at such length and about matters so important and so interwoven. At other times, she had limited herself to moments of thinking aloud, brief comments on the leaps and continual shifts in her rambling but witty train of thought. This time she was making an effort and it must be to let him know that she didn't love him, that she couldn't love him.

'But if you can't love me,' he concluded with force and ingenuity, 'then don't love me! After all, I could keep on hoping, and I wouldn't leave you. You won't have to fawn on me, I won't be a threat. Treat me as a shabby gigolo if you like, it's all the same to me, I'm not proud. I don't give a damn about being respectable if it keeps me from seeing you. Incidentally, I've got some money now and I'm going to follow you to New York.' He looked smug all of a sudden, smug and scared.

'For me to live with you without loving you? The idea's a perfectly good one. But you're too modest, my dear Andreas. The danger would still be there.'

'You mean you might end up loving me?' said Andreas, his face glowing with all the signs of pride and surprise.

La Doriacci remained pensive for a moment, almost troubled, it seemed, by that face.

'Yes, I certainly could. So I am going to give you a very good address in Paris, dear Andreas, to avoid that drama, because that is what it would be for me. The Countess Maria della Marea has been living in Paris for two years. She is charming, richer and younger than I, and she's crazy about blond, blue-eyed men like you. She has just thrown out a Swedish lover who became a tiny bit too interested . . . well anyway, who showed it too much. She's full of life, she's got all sorts of friends in Paris, your career is made . . . Don't put on that pained shocked expression, please. You're the one who told me about your upbringing and ambitions.'

It was then that she saw Andreas, his face obdurate and almost ugly from rage, a face unused to such rage and lacking folds and nooks to accommodate it, now creased here and there as if at random, mouth tightened, and clashing with the clean line of his jaw—in a word, disfigured. As he left the room still wearing this new face, la Doriacci caught herself hoping it would not be the last, the one she would remember him by. She was cross with herself, she confessed to her reflection that she could see from across the room. But when she drew close to the mirror she became a good deal less so, for here the mirror flung back at her a thousand little lines, a thousand shadows and a few pockets: the definitive and total confirmation of what she had been saying.

*S*urprised at first, the passengers had grown tight-lipped, and from tight-lipped exasperated, and from exasperated finally enraged. All without apparent effect on la Doriacci's closed door, bolted as it was on her emotional problems, or rather those of Andreas. And despite the warmth he felt towards the young man, Charley was not sorry to see him depart the baleful cabin, leaving the door ajar, his face first disfigured by rage, then head down and dazed by sorrow.

Charley let him pass and went to knock more discreetly than he would have liked. After all, this was the fifth time he had come back to confront the door without success. He had continued to tap lightly despite all exhortations from the bridge. For he knew very well just what would happen: la Doriacci would make a mannered entrance, throwing a few radiant and grateful smiles to the passengers for their patience. She would sing without any fuss, and he, Charley, would be disgraced for having the temerity to disturb the beauty sleep of the marvellous Doriacci. So he waited in the doorway, waited a good long time in fact. Finally, la Doriacci appeared on the threshold. Her face betraying anger, even fury, she swept past him without a word or a look, certainly without an excuse, and marched towards the stage as if to war. It was only as she was making her entrance that, without once stopping or turning but simply tossing her head back as if in a tango step, she flung a remark at him: 'You really expect me to sing in front of these cretins?' and made her entrance without waiting for a reply.

By that time the audience had reached a worrisome state of exasperation. They were muttering. Olga, looking very offended, had already persuaded a few impatient customers to follow her example of applauding ironically, though Simon refused to join in. He would get back at her later, she thought, yawning ostentatiously and looking at her watch for the umpteenth time. She had reassumed her attentiveness on spotting the arrival of what she thought of as the advance guard: Andreas, the laggard's official marshal. Paler than before, almost livid, Andreas collapsed into a chair near the Lethuilliers—or rather, near Clarisse. Olga saw her turn and lean towards him anxiously, say something and take his hand between her own.

'I had thought,' said Olga to Simon, 'that it was Julien who had won the heart of your friend Clarisse.'

'But it is Julien,' said Simon, following her glance. 'Ah,' he said. 'Andreas simply needs to be consoled, that's all. I must say I find Clarisse very comforting to a man.'

'Not to all of them,' said Olga with a quick laugh that raised a timid protest from Simon.

'What do you mean by that?'

'Well, her husband doesn't seem to be looking for consolation. Not from her at any rate.'

There was a silence, which Simon broke uneasily in an almost inaudible voice.

'I don't know what pleasure you get from being so awful, so hateful with me. What do you have against me except your own nastiness?'

'You use me,' she said in a hard voice. 'You only think

about your own pleasure and you don't give a damn about my career. Admit it.'

'But you know, don't you,' said Simon, who unwillingly let himself be drawn into a conversation knowing that in the end he would, as always, be the one to lose, 'that I'm going to give you the leading role in my next production?'

'Only because you hope to keep me that way, making me go from one part to the next, selfishly trying to replace my private life with my professional life. That's all.'

'Are you blaming me for not giving you a part or for giving you too many? It's awfully contradictory.'

'Yes,' she said with a scornful calm. 'Yes, it is contradictory, and I don't care. Does that bother you?'

He should have stood up and gone away, never to see her again. But he sat riveted to his chair. He looked at Olga's hand, at her fragile wrist so soft to the touch, so childishly thin. And he couldn't do it, couldn't leave any more. He was at the mercy of this upstart starlet who could sometimes be so tender and so naive, who badly needed his protection, no matter what she said.

'You're right,' he said. 'It's not important, but I would like . . .'

'Hush!' said Olga, 'Hush!' La Doriacci's coming on. And she doesn't seem to be in a good mood,' she added softly, instinctively ducking her head down between her shoulders.

And just as she spoke, la Doriacci came on stage. She moved into the light with lowered brow, face marked by greasepaint and anger, the corners of her mouth pulled down, teeth clenched. At the sight of such fury there was a stunned and anxious silence, a silence in which the spectators could not tell whether the anger might not be directed at them. They trembled in their rattan chairs. Even Edma Bautet-Lebreche, who had opened her mouth, slowly shut it again. Clarisse unconsciously squeezed Andreas's hands. He seemed to have stopped breathing, and his very stillness made her anxious. He was looking at la Doriacci with those round glistening eyes of night-roaming rabbits caught in the glance of headlights.

But the person most affected by her appearance was

Hans-Helmut Kreuze. All the time he had sat at the piano, his dignity as a star offended by having to wait for anyone at all. When the diva appeared he rose like a martyr, believing he would feel the weight of general admiration and compassion on his shoulders. But the attention of the crowd were turned elsewhere, to the furious, half-clad madwoman. Hans-Helmut tapped her on the arm with his score to remind her of her obligations, though she appeared not to notice. She caught up the microphone with a brusque circular motion, the gesture of a music-hall artiste. Her gleaming black eyes swept over the crowd before fixing on him.

'*Il Trovatore*,' she said in a cold, hoarse voice.

'But . . .' whispered Hans-Helmut, tapping his score against his music stand, 'but tonight we do the *Kindertotenlieder*.'

'Act Four, Scene One,' she declared without hearing or listening. 'Begin.'

There was so imperative a note in her brevity that instead of protesting further Kreuze sat down again and attacked the first bars of Scene One. A timid cough behind him reminded him of the existence of his two fifty-year-old students. In one motion he turned towards them where they waited, instruments in hand, like forks, a pose that exasperated him. '*Il Trovatore*, Act Four, Scene One!' he barked without really looking at them. Hastily they joined in.

The first bars had scarcely died away when la Doriacci's voice rose like a cry, and Hans-Helmut suddenly realised with delight that he was about to hear beautiful music. He forgot everything. He forgot that he detested this woman. Instead, he threw himself into her service, her aid, her support. He bent himself entirely to her impulse, her caprice, her direction. He was no longer anything but the most servile, discreet and enthusiastic of her admirers. And la Doriacci, immediately feeling this, called to him with her voice, made him pass before her, appealed to the cello, wafted compliments to the violin, rushed ahead of them once again, drew back, played with them in total confidence. She forgot about their knee socks, their bald heads and silliness; they forgot her whims, her rages, her dissolute ways. And for ten minutes the four of them loved one another and were happy together, in a way they had never been with anyone else in their whole lives before.

Clarisse felt Andreas's hand go tense between hers. She, too, tightened her grip when the diva sang too well, when tears and the wish to make love seemed to rise in her throat. But for Andreas, it was as though each detail of this musical beauty were hurting him anew. All this beauty he was clearly about to lose. What he felt must have been excruciating, for Clarisse herself found she yearned for la Doriacci, wanted to touch her, to hold her close, to lay her head against that superbly swelling throat, to rest against that heart and shoulder, to hear the inception, rising and bursting forth of that prodigious voice, all with the same voluptuous awe she felt when a man reached his pleasure.

At last la Doriacci launched into the penultimate note, stretching her voice to hold it there, vibrant and powerful, brandishing it above her audience like a threat or savage outcry. Interminably. So interminably that Edma Bautet-Lebreche unconsciously rose from her chair, as though lifted by the extravagant perfection of that cry; that Hans-Helmut turned from the piano to look at her squarely through his spectacles; that the two simpletons sat with bows in the air, numb with fright; that the ship seemed immobilised in the water, its engines and passengers struck dead. The note hung there not for half a minute but an hour, a lifetime, to be abruptly cut off as la Doriacci uttered in a harsh voice the final note, exhausted by having to wait its turn so long. The ship got under way again, and the passengers exploded into frenetic applause. On their feet, they yelled 'Bravo! Bravo! Bravo!', their faces full of unearned pride and excessive gratitude, or so it seemed to Captain Elledocq, who, in the face of all this noise, couldn't help but cast an anxious eye towards the sea. The very notion that someone on another craft somewhere might see his hysterical passengers gathered in a pack around a piano, cheering in the middle of the night, was enough to shame him in advance. Thank God there wasn't the smallest fishing boat in the vicinity. Elledocq mopped his brow, applauding in turn this caterwauling female who was unmannerly to boot—since she went off without even bowing to these fanatics, these poor masochists who had after all waited an entire hour for her, and who now pounded their hands together hard enough to crack the joints. Well, they had paid for it, Elledocq acknowledged, then wondered what his cap was doing on the ground and what he himself was doing, applauding like this.

*C*larisse had tears in her eyes, Eric noticed with amusement when la Doriacci had gone. He was feeling better, much more sure of himself. He could no longer understand his own grotesque panic before dinner, his fear of what Clarisse might answer. Obviously she would answer, and answer with nothing! She would deny everything, flounder about, and in so doing would tell him the truth. For nothing had happened, he now saw clearly. Clarisse was incapable of doing anything, for good or ill. She was afraid of her own shadow, afraid of herself and disdainful of her body, beautiful though it was, he had to admit. The very idea of this body that was so despised, this face so disfigured, because of an inferiority complex . . . Well, there was a comic aspect to it all . . . How could Clarisse deceive him?—poor Clarisse, who didn't love herself enough to let anyone watch while she put on lipstick; poor Clarisse whom he always made love to in the dark so as to encourage her modesty; whom he always moved away from afterwards as if embarrassed. (In fact he always moved away from women after that ridiculous, but inevitable pantomime that must bore to death half the human race—the men anyway—though they never ever dare say so.) It was quite understandable. These weak creatures who flirted with intelligence and spent their lives behind a shield of fragile organs, sick nerves, abject sentimentality, mawkish to a degree and tenacious as an octopus, these spineless creatures who now claimed the right to vote, to drive, even to conduct the affairs of state, who claimed to engage in sports (and there they paid dearly—they disqualified themselves from lovemaking); these feeble chirping things who, in the circles in which he moved, were either alcoholic and neurotic like Clarisse, or else intolerable gossips like Edma, or else operatic ogresses like la Doriacci—all of them exasperated him and always had. And in the end it was that miserable Olga who seemed the least burdensome because she at least had the decency to be humble.

Olga was humble, but Clarisse was not humble. She was proud, though her pride was not alas in her wealth. She was proud of what she was hiding from him, what he had been unable to bring out into the open and so crush—some feeling, or faculty, some ethical principle or hallucination, at any rate something she had kept out of his reach and which he could not force her to destroy since he did not even know its name or nature. The certainty of this muffled yet determined resistance hidden somewhere in the hidden territory of her personality had at first amused him, the struggle was at once so open yet undeclared. But it had begun to annoy him when he realised he was incapable of unmasking it. In the end it had ceased to matter, for he regarded Clarisse as sufficiently vanquished on too many other fronts. Until this cruise he had even imagined that her resistance had been abandoned somewhere, like a worn-out banner. Now Clarisse had not only demonstrated that the flag was still there, but even raised it as if to remind him what colour it was.

This was where he intended to begin, but he was prevented by the music that suddenly blared from the loudspeakers. It was a popular tune—'As Time Goes By'—from a movie everyone had seen in the Forties.

'Good heavens,' said Edma. 'Good heavens . . . does anybody remember?'

And she looked around for someone able to share the memory with her. But she wasn't among her own crowd, and if she questioned Armand, the only companion of those days, about the date, he would be reminded of the merger of one of his own factories with God knows what else. Actually, she couldn't really reproach Armand for not remembering in detail the face and body of Harry Mendel, her lover at the time; they used to amuse themselves doing scenes from the movie, imitating the gestures and intonation of the two actors they idolised. Her eye fell almost by chance on Julien Peyrat, sitting silent in a corner. Love did not appear to be turning out well for him. But then, by whatever mischance, it never had been a boon to the men she had known.

'Doesn't this song remind you of anything, my dear Julien—it's so exquisite, so melancholy?' There was a quaver on the last word, a narrowing of the eyelids upon a remote and secret pain which Julien, given his own state just then, found more touching than laughable.

Edma realised this and pressed her advantage. What were he and Clarisse going to do, the two of them—he the seductive idiot, and she the poor charming rich woman? Even Edma had no idea for once. She simply knew that in Clarisse's place she would have taken off with Julien Peyrat at the first invitation. But women of her generation were still womanly women, thank God; they didn't consider themselves the equals of men, they considered themselves shrewder. And if they ever voted, they voted for the most physically attractive candidate and didn't involve themselves in political discussion.

'Yes it does,' said Julien. 'What on earth was the name of that marvellous movie? Of course, it was *Casablanca*!'

'You cried too, I hope? But of course you'll say no. Men are ashamed to admit they're sensitive. They're even proud of showing they're not. Such a misguided instinct.'

'So what would you like us to boast about?' Julien asked

in a tense voice she would not have recognised. 'About being able to suffer? Do you like men who complain?'

'I like men who like to please, my poor Julien,' said Edma. 'And to me you're willing enough to please not to pull that long face. Do you know why I had them put on that record? You who are so sensitive, do you know why?'

'No,' said Julien, smiling in spite of himself at Edma's perpetual gush of charm and compliments.

'Well, then, I bought it so that I could be in your arms without making you panic. Isn't that delicious? Doesn't it show heart-rending humility?'

She laughed as she said this, levelling her brilliant, bird-like eyes upon him. And despite her wrinkles, the skin of her whole face glowed with youthful desire and coquetry.

'I don't believe you,' said Julien, taking her into his arms. 'But you'll dance with me anyway.'

With a triumphant whinny, tapping her heel on the floor, Edma flung herself to the right while Julien also took a step to the right; both apologised and sailed to the left, bumping into each other again, forehead against forehead. They stopped, looked at each other, and burst out laughing, holding their heads.

'Now, I'm leading,' Julien said gently.

And Edma, docile, eyes closed, followed his more careful movements round the floor.

The look on Eric's face might have killed in anyone else all enthusiasm for indulging in such a grotesque form of entertainment, but he was carried off towards the dance floor by Olga. He resisted with barely civil refusals that she overcame with a terse: 'No dance, no deal on the painting.' Meanwhile, Clarisse gave Simon Béjard what she meant to be the approximation of a wink, though he responded with an apologetic smile, a confused and unhappy little smile that was momentarily painful. Charley dragged her off to the tum-te-tums of the music.

'It's not that you danced badly,' said Edma, extricating herself. Like many men who don't know how to dance, Julien had held her close to his shoulder and chest, thereby

358

cutting off her view of the dance floor, as if that temporary blindness might persuade her to believe in his talents as a dancer. 'You don't dance. You simply walk a woman around! Only the woman's face to face and not on your arm. It's like taking a walk in harness, don't you think? I am restoring your liberty.'

'My liberty, well . . . uh . . . as a matter of fact, it's Clarisse, you see? If she isn't there, I feel strangled . . . by her absence.'

'It's that bad?'

Edma wavered between pride at having him confide in her, and faint resentment at not being the object of his fevered melancholy. Freeing herself from Julien's arm, she caught Charley by the shoulder, stopping him dead in full whirl.

'My dear Charley,' she said, 'you who are an expert dancer, deliver me from this great lanky fellow and his childishness! You'll have to pardon me, Clarisse, but my feet are mincemeat.'

And she collapsed against Charley, leaving Clarisse and Julien face to face. She didn't want to turn back—anything but that—and see them slowly come together and begin to dance, not without a noticeable stiffness, that excessive indifference so revealing of lovers happy in love. Julien and Clarisse moved cautiously as if embracing a porcelain partner, but gazing into one another's eyes. Olga, languishing against Eric with a suggestive sensuality, couldn't resist pointing this out to him.

'Don't be so listless, Eric dear. Try to look attentive when you hold me. Look at how Julien takes to heart whatever he does with your wife. It's a good thing you're not jealous.'

'Did you ask him about the painting?' said Eric after a moment of silence in which he avoided looking at the spectacle just mentioned.

'I haven't spoken to Julien yet. But I thought I'd do it tomorrow at the swimming pool. We'll be alone, and I won't blush so much. Telling him I want to give that painting to Simon! It's going to be hard to make him buy that, I can assure you.'

'You are an actress, aren't you. If I'm not mistaken?'

'Yes, but I'm not sure whether Julien knows that,' she said with a vague attempt to be funny.

But he said no more and squeezed her more tightly against him, since as he turned he had glimpsed Julien and Clarisse in profile.

She was dancing close to Julien and felt as though she were leaning against a high-voltage wire. The same short circuit was going to run through them both very soon. Once again, anything might happen—happy, unhappy, or simply different. Life was anything but monotonous, and what was left to live out, what a week earlier had seemed interminable, now seemed dreadfully short. For now it was to be shared with a man who wanted her. She had to show Julien every landscape, every painting, have him hear all the music, tell him all the stories tucked away in the attics and cellars of her memory, stories of her childhood, her education, her loves, her solitude. And it seemed to her that she would never have time to tell him everything about that life, uneventful as it had been, as desperately uneventful as she had considered it up till now and which, thanks to Julien's way of looking at her, his desire to understand her, to take her and remember her, had suddenly become a life full of anecdotes, and odd, sad tales to tell, simply because she wanted to tell them to someone else. This man who trembled as he touched her with anticipated pleasure that also left him a trifle ashamed, this man had not only given her back the present and promised a future, he had also given her back a past that was dazzling and vital, of which she no longer needed to be ashamed. She hugged him impulsively, and with a sort of sob against her ear he murmured, 'No, please don't,' before backing off, and she laughed out loud at his sheepish look.

Time was going by. Edma and Charley were now doing the *paso doble*. Even Captain Elledocq, encouraged by Edma's entreaties, seemed on the verge of doing a few flat-footed steps on the dance floor, and couples were coming together and separating again at random, as when they first boarded the ship.

Olga had disappeared for ten minutes, but now her voice suddenly rang out just as the music stopped.

'I would like to know,' she said in a blaring voice, 'who has been rummaging in my closet! In my personal belongings!'

There was an appalled silence. Comments of 'What?' 'Why do you say that?' 'She's mad,' rose from all sides, while the dancers looked at one another in disbelief.

'Everyone went off for a minute some time or other, my dear Olga,' said Edma, once again taking charge. 'Except for me. When I dance, I dance till daybreak. What are you telling us? Has something of yours been taken? Some money? Jewels? It seems very unlikely to me. Don't you agree, Captain? Come on, Olga! What has been taken from you, Olga dear? It's not worth making a scene over a pack of cigarettes . . .'

'Nothing was taken,' said Olga, white with a rage that made her ugly, as Edma again noticed. 'But someone wanted to take something, and went so far as to rummage amongst my things. It's intolerable. I won't put up with such an outrage.'

Her voice was rising, working towards a yelp. Edma, annoyed, pushed her down into an armchair and offered her a cognac, as if she had narrowly escaped some sort of disaster.

'But what were they looking for?' she said with a small twinkle of humour. 'Do you have the least notion what anyone might have been looking for amongst your things?'

'Yes,' said Olga, her eyes on the ground. 'And who that person was too,' she added, raising her head and looking at Simon.

He was wearing his grumpy, sullen look. He shrugged and looked away.

'But,' Edma hesitated, 'then isn't it a private matter? If you think it's Simon, little one, then you might well spare us these domestic scenes. Has Simon gone back on his contract? Did you find it in shreds in the lavatory? Are you not going to be the heroine of his next movie any more?'

'This person was looking for sordid evidence to incriminate me,' said Olga in a piercing voice which to everyone's surprise sent Armand Bautet-Lebreche into fits of laughter.

It began as a little cry that startled the gathering, then continued with diminutive whinnies, like his wife's but in miniature, and touching in their modesty.

Seemingly unaware of this ill-timed diversion, Olga went on. 'This person is of course too cowardly to own up, but I would like him to do so in public. Everyone really ought to know just how distinguished and elegant this person actually is. It would give me great pleasure, it really would.'

'Evidence of what?' shrieked Edma Bautet-Lebreche, suddenly exasperated by the vagueness of this accusation as much as by the idiot laughter of her husband, which seemed to have infected Charley as well.

'Evidence of my infidelity!' cried Olga. 'That's what this person was looking for, and incidentally did not find. I must have arrived too soon before the person could put everything back in order. And I consider that repulsive . . . really repulsive!' she repeated, yelling again—which made the spasms produced by the Sugar Baron rise another octave.

Clarisse, leaning on the table where Olga was holding forth like justice enthroned, had been watching Simon since the beginning of the altercation, and suddenly she found him thinner, older, distraught and convulsive in his movements. She sensed his exposed nerves, she saw him as she herself had been, coming on board eight days before—she who was going to go ashore in triumph, the way he, Simon, had arrived, loving someone and believing himself loved by that person. It seemed to Clarisse that she had robbed Simon of that blessed assurance, that she owed him some compensation for that terrible loss. She could see just how far Olga would go to humiliate him, but she did not see the reasons for the cruelty of this affront. Something in her pushed her forward, something she had had since childhood, for lame dogs, for old ladies on park benches, for sad, humiliated children in general, and she heard herself pronounce, almost to her own surprise, the only phrase that could deflect punishment from Simon.

'I did it,' she said in a low, soft voice that had the effect of a bomb going off.

'You?' said Olga.

She got up with dishevelled hair, looking like a Medusa, thought Clarisse, recoiling as if Olga were about to strike her.

'Yes, me,' she said very quickly. 'I was jealous. I was looking for a letter from Eric.'

In the ensuing turmoil, Clarisse slipped between the witnesses to the scandal, pausing on her way by to squeeze the hand of Julien, who beamed at her, and slipped off to her cabin. There she collapsed onto her bunk and closed her eyes with a strange sense of triumph. She tried two or three times to imitate Armand Bautet-Lebreche's absurd laugh, and after these hopeless-sounding attempts, she slept like a log until Eric arrived.

Clarisse's departure was followed by a general hubbub.

'What could she have been doing in my room?' Olga was saying with the pained fury of seeing her just cause dismissed, in front of her friends, by a tactical ruse.

Edma responded to her trembling voice in a wordly tone, somewhat dry, somewhat ironic, a tone which suddenly seemed to Julien the peak of amenity and tactful elegance.

'I'm not going to let anyone make a fool of me!' cried Olga. 'What would Clarisse be doing in my room? She doesn't love Eric any more, it's Julien Peyrat she wants, him, not that handsome rat Lethuillier. And I can very well understand her, and I wish lots of luck to Monsieur Peyrat, and I . . .'

'Olga!'

There was nothing nonchalant now in Edma's voice. It was a voice of command, the voice of a woman who for years on end had given orders with unwavering egoism to various groups of servants without ever offering one of them an opportunity to answer back. It was the voice of a woman who, in the course of her day, used the imperative ten times more often than any other mood. She gave orders to her maid, cook, butler, chauffeur, taxi driver, to the saleswoman and the model in the dress shop, and then went home, where she continued to command obedience. The interrogative and indicative were rare, the exclamation point sufficed for almost any question. Beyond this, there were only a few scattered future tenses or the past imperfect for talk of travel or lovers. The present, it seemed, was recommended only for illness or functional difficulties.

'Would you like to tell us what it is you want, Olga dear? Should we all blame Simon for an indiscretion he didn't commit? Should we accuse Clarisse Lethuillier of lying? There's nothing pleasant about that kind of declaration for any of us, as you can well imagine. So what is it you're trying to say? That Simon is a liar and Clarisse a masochist? You ought to go to bed.'

'This is ridiculous, all of it. Ridiculous and in very bad taste!'

Eric's exclamation went unheard. It seemed, after all, as though neither the existence nor the presence of the one initially responsible for this whole farce was much desired. And Eric was well aware of this. That the whole chain of events had been launched by him, for him—whether to hold on to him or keep him away—he knew he was the object of a contest and he felt as if he were its most insignificant pawn. He threw a furious glance towards Simon who, pale rather than flushed, seemed riveted to his chair, his arms hanging useless, while Julien plied him with drink as though he had just been injured.

'It wasn't Clarisse,' said Simon, giving his glass back to Julien—as he would to a barman, thought Eric, or to a trainer, thought Julien.

He felt an immense pity for Simon Béjard, who had gone off happily on his first cruise as a rich man, happy about his success at Cannes, about his charming mistress, about his future. Simon Béjard who would leave the ship on Sunday at Cannes wounded, several thousands poorer and without a single remaining ray of trust in the feelings of young girls. Simon, who was still trying, despite his sorrow, to reassure him, Julien, about Clarisse's 'jealousy'. Julien felt a burst of affection for Simon such as he didn't remember feeling for a man since his school days. Julien had pals everywhere, but no real friends; his pals were drawn either from among drifters whose conceit and cowardice exasperated him, or they were respectable types to whom he couldn't possibly have explained the details of his livelihood. Simon Béjard would be a good friend. Clarisse already liked him very much.

'I know perfectly well she was never in there, I haven't taken my eyes off her,' he said, smiling at Simon.

'But why do you think she did that?' Simon suddenly looked bewildered.

'Why? Or do you mean to say for whom? For you, I think. You were heading straight for catastrophe.'

'She made herself ridiculous for me? Do you realise what that means?' Simon said in a trembling voice. 'Now there's a real woman. She's teaching me a thing or two!'

'Oh yes? And what's that?' said Julien, handing him a second glass, again like medicine. Simon took it and swallowed it in one gulp as if it were undrinkable.

'I mean she taught me that being ridiculous doesn't mean a damn thing.'

And he looked at Julien with misty eyes. This frightened Julien. It was enough that he could not bear to see women cry, since he would hold them close so as not to see them and anyway he liked that, drawing them in and consoling them with his hand and voice, as he would a horse. But a man in tears had exactly the opposite effect on him, it made him vicariously ashamed, made him turn away. So he was stunned when he turned back, after the silence that apparently served as an answer to Simon, to find him in his rocker looking tanned and smiling again without visible effort, his eyes the same blue as before.

'I don't know what more to say, my friend, because I can't bring myself to believe it. But it's all over, I'm rid of Olga,' he said, giving Julien's arm an affectionate tap.

'It really is all over?'

'Yes.'

The two men looked at each other and began to laugh as Simon's smile elicited one from Julien too.

'No kidding?' said Julien. 'No kidding? You're finished with it, just like that?'

'I think so, at any rate. It's like one less thorn in the side, you know? Has that ever happened to you?' he asked amiably, with an expression of relief in his voice that was perhaps not entirely unpremeditated, but too good to pass up.

It seemed to him that Olga had gone too far, much too far, and that she might have won this round had it not been for Clarisse's quickness.

'In trying to save my honour, Clarisse reminded me that I had an honour to save,' he said. 'Do you understand, old man? After all, I'm not going to allow myself to be crucified by a starlet, for God's sake!'

'You're right, by God!' Julien said. 'You're sure it's not just pride that's cutting you off from love so fast?'

'You will see tomorrow.'

*C*larisse was leaning back on her pillow in a very becoming sea-green nightgown, and she was reading, or rather re-reading, *The Brothers Karamazov*, by the light on the bedside table. Her eyes shone with a sort of Russian fervour that she did not have to affect, the Dureaus being half-Russian on the maternal side. Eric closed the door, bolted it and leaned back against it with an enigmatic smile, or what he intended as such, though to his wife it appeared simply to have been lifted from a bad American movie. Since Julien, Clarisse had changed; she was excessively critical of Eric, excessively indulgent towards Julien and even the other passengers. She could not help seeing the posing and the ulterior motives in Eric. She reproached herself a little for this severity which she regarded as suspect, since it had begun the same day as her feelings for Julien, and she would need it if her feelings towards Julien were to prosper.

'Well?' he said, hands in his pockets, elegant and blond.

'Well, what?' she asked, laying down the open book in front of her, as if to make it clear that she was busy.

Again Eric flinched. He hated having people read in front of him. For a moment he struggled with a furious desire to tear the book from her hands and hurl it through the porthole in anger. He barely managed to control himself.

'Well, are you pleased with your little performance? Does it amuse you to encourage poor Olga with such suspicions? Don't you see the absurdity of that ransacking expedition? And why do you have to drag me into your grotesque scenes. I'd like you to shed a little light on all this, my dear Clarisse.'

'I don't understand you,' she said, this time closing her book and putting it within reach on her bunk—ready to be opened the minute this tiresome person left her in peace, thought Eric once more. 'I don't understand you. All this is quite flattering to you, isn't it? That I should go so far as to track down my unhappiness in my rival's chest of drawers—isn't that just one more laurel wreath for your brow . . .'

'Cheap successes bring no pleasure,' said Eric, and an expression of disgust and severity passed over his beautiful features, making them ugly. She suddenly remembered the countless times that same expression had completely humiliated her, when she had not tried to resist since it was out of the question to doubt the intelligence, sensitivity and absolute rightness of Eric Lethuillier. Calm down . . . Calm down . . . she said to herself.

'Anyway, that's entirely secondary. Tell me the truth, why did you do it?'

'Why, for him,' said Clarisse, shaking her head as if at the absurdity of the question. 'For Simon Béjard . . . that little bitch was about to tear him to shreds.'

To hear the word *bitch* on Clarisse's lips upset Eric still more. For years, by tacit accord, all pejoratives had been reserved for his own use.

'You still interest yourself that much in the affairs of others?' he asked spitefully, then, realising his error, bit his tongue, but too late.

'When one of the others is my husband, yes. For the sake

of appearances. You know very well that I have no interest in stories about others. I'm hardly interested in my own,' she said sadly, closing the lids over her blue eyes.

'Have you at least . . .'

He hesitated for a moment. He felt as though he were doing something stupid, as though he were taking a risk whose outcome he could not imagine. It was pride and pride alone that made him finish the sentence. 'Have you at least enough interest to find out Julien's real story, my dear Clarisse? Remember, you still owe me that answer. And don't ask to which question; that would hardly be kind.'

He looked at her sternly. She raised her eyes and dropped them instantly upon meeting his glance.

'Does it really matter to you?' she asked in a hesitant voice.

'Why yes, it does matter to me. It is in fact the only thing that matters to me,' he said, almost smiling.

Although he did not admit it to himself, Eric hoped with that smile to hold Clarisse with an aura of propriety, to make her take responsibility for any change in their relationship. What Eric unconsciously meant was: 'You see, I'm smiling . . . I am being accommodating. Why not go on this way without creating any difficulties for ourselves?' and so on. Though it was in effect an accommodating smile, a smile of peace, the smile was so unfamiliar to Clarisse that she attributed it to the usual causes: scorn, condescension, incredulity. So with an angry movement she sat up, gave Eric a severely warning look as if to put him on his guard, and spat out in a cold voice, 'You asked me whether I was Julien Peyrat's mistress, is that right? Well yes, I have been for several days now.'

It was only after she had spoken that she heard her own heart beating, violently, in double time, as if it feared a reaction from Eric, as if her heart were warning her, but too late. She saw Eric by the door turning white, saw the hatred in his eyes, the hatred and also relief, that feeling of relief she knew so well, the same one he had every time he caught her in the wrong, every time he had humiliated her with his reproaches. Then the colour returned to Eric's cheeks. He took three steps towards her and caught her by the wrists. With one knee on the bed, he tightened his grip until it hurt. He spoke to her a bare six inches from her face, in a breathless staccato that she scarcely understood because of her fright. At the same time she found herself looking at a blemish on Eric's face, where usually none was visible, a blackhead that could only be explained by the lack of a magnifying mirror on the ship. I must have some alcohol, she thought absurdly. It's really not pretty there, right under his nose. He should do something about it. What is he saying?

'You're lying! That seems to be one thing you know how to do, lie! You want to get on my nerves, to wreck this cruise for me? You are an abject egoist. Everyone knows it. You behave like a savage with your friends and your family. Under the pretext of fun, you have no regard for anyone, my dear Clarisse. That's your weakness: you don't like people! You don't love your own mother. You never went to see her . . . not even your own mother!' he was saying with rage when she interrupted.

'At any rate,' she said calmly, 'it's not important.'

'So . . .' he said, 'none of this is important? Your purported frolics with that forger, that seedy pimp . . . that's not important, none of it?'

But his anger had strangely subsided, and when she answered in an expressionless voice, 'Well, perhaps,' he went into the bathroom as if he had not heard the reply and as if it truly was no longer important.

*O*lga had gone to bed well before Simon, who stayed at the bar that night to get drunk—without succeeding—and who, when he returned to the cabin, would find himself subjected to one of the two new expressions that had been perfected by his gentle mistress: either one of indignation, indeed shock, should she arrive after him and find him already bedded down in the cabin, or an expression of distant politeness should he come in after her. The two expressions were intended to help Simon become aware of his insignificance and the disdain this inevitably merited. But what about this hangdog look her dear producer had lately adopted? Without anyone knowing why? Olga had so little conception of the possibility that someone besides herself might have feelings, that making Simon suffer was not so much deliberate as simply natural. Unfortunately her nature lacked mercy. She looked upon this man, this gift of destiny, first as her producer and only then as her lover. Surely she was giving him proof of everything he wanted, she thought, by yielding to his demands every night. Even when she held back it was half out of honesty; he must know that in the end the whole thing was a bore to women. For it to be otherwise he would need to have a different build. Of course Simon's nature was already known in film circles, but that was the way it always was: men like Simon were obsessed with sex, while men like Eric, or like Andreas come to think of it, were half frigid. Unless of course they became actors and gave into the narcissism of their calling; then their appetite for women became excessive.

For the time being, Olga treated Simon to her glance of non-recognition, and indeed had no difficulty sustaining it, since Simon's actions thoroughly astonished her. He sat on his own bunk with both hands occupied, one taking off a shoe, the other lighting a cigarette. And when she spoke she got the impression, for the first time since the beginning of the cruise, that she was disturbing him.

'Where did you go after Edma's hysterical outburst?' she asked.

He frowned without answering, a sign that she was indeed disturbing him. It was in fact the first time in a long while that Simon had not seemed completely subject to Olga's whims. For the first time his hands were busy, as were his eyes and his thoughts, with something other than an anxiously pleading contemplation of her. Olga sensed this at once, thanks to her perpetually operating high-fidelity radar system, a system that made her instantly aware of all moods in the vicinity and showed up the lights at every intersection—without, unfortunately, indicating whether they were red or green. Here, for instance, she thought they were green, and she ploughed on towards a collision which her radar, had it been intelligent, might have spared her. But it was only instinctive, not truly sensitive, and the light went on and off without telling her a thing.

'You're not answering?'

Simon looked at her, and she was surprised by the blue of his eyes. It was a long time since she had noticed how very blue they were. It was also a long time since she had noticed even that he had a way of looking at things.

'What is all this?' he said with a sigh. 'I didn't notice Edma Bautet-Lebreche being hysterical.'

'Oh really? Perhaps you didn't hear her shouting?'

'I certainly heard you shouting,' said Simon in the same voice.

'Me? Me shouting?' said Olga. 'Me?'

She shook her head with a look of astounded innocence, a role for which she was not very well suited, as Simon's glance informed her. For the first time in days, she was worried. It was not only the colour of his eyes she had not remembered, it was the acuity of his glance.

'What do you mean? That I lied?'

'No,' said Simon, in that same slow voice, which annoyed Olga and began to frighten her. 'No, you didn't lie, you told the truth, but in front of twenty other people.'

'So?'

'So that is twenty too many,' he said, getting up and slowly taking off his jacket, tired, old, but also weary of her, Olga Lamouroux, second-class starlet who would have nothing to do on her return if Simon Béjard changed his mind. Olga Lamouroux who called Simon 'my sweet' in a tender, childlike voice, and who began, too late, to sulk in the dark while waiting in vain for him to console her for her own perversity. At her first attempt to change bunks Simon Béjard got up, put his sweater and trousers back on in a vague way, and went out.

In the mirror of the deserted bar he saw through his glass a red-haired and slightly pasty-faced man, but one who would brook no joking, with a stare so cold that you would notice neither his hair nor his paunch. Well, he said to himself, that's the end of great music and grand passion for Simon Béjard. He said it with bitterness, averting his eyes from that reflection, from what he was going to become.

*M*uttering to himself all the while, Armand stepped into the bathtub—an enormous one, ridiculous for a ship, he thought—clutched the security handle with his right hand, and progressively immersed his thin white body, a body so lacking in muscle that without his clothes he looked like a naked odalisque. Propped up in the bath, Armand wiggled his toes smartly, splashing and making joyful little noises. He even managed, incredibly, to snap his toes like fingers—a feat he had been working on for years, though up till then without really giving it a thought. Edma would think him a dim-witted child if she caught him at it.

Abruptly, he had drawn up his knees to his chin and was soaping himself vigorously, like a boy at boarding school under the watchful eye of the prefect, when he heard the door of his cabin open rapidly. A perfume which he could not immediately place wafted as far as the bathtub, sensuous and musky as a fox, a blue fox of course.

But didn't I bolt it? he thought absently but with regret,

resigned to getting out, tearing himself away from the pleasure of the warm water and the sight of his feet all the way down there, and then realised that the answer had preceded his question. He couldn't hear a word out there. Edma was doubtless alone, and moreover she was whistling, in fact whistling a bawdy song it seemed to Armand, who couldn't have heard more than three of them in his lifetime: as soldier, as cousin of a young hospital intern, and before then at boarding school. She hadn't called out to him, though his suit was hanging on the hook by the porthole, and she couldn't have missed seeing it. Meanwhile he was beginning to get cold in the lukewarm water, so he hugged his knees between his arms and hunched down at the bottom of the tub, his chin resting between his knees.

'Edma?' he bleated sadly, not quite knowing why. When she didn't answer he called out, 'Edma!' in a sharper voice, as authoritative as he could make it.

'Here . . . here . . . coming,' said a powerful voice which wasn't Edma's at all, he suddenly realised, but la Doriacci's, a fact evidenced by her appearance in the doorway.

She wore a rumpled evening dress, her thick make-up was smudged, her black hair was falling into her eyes, and she looked cheerful and lively as though enjoying some lewd remark. In short, la Doriacci. And he the Sugar Baron, Armand Bautet-Lebreche, stark naked, without his glasses, without his dignity or even a towel to cover himself. They stared at one another for an instant like a pair of china dogs, and Armand heard himself pleading, 'Get out, please . . .' in a hoarse and unrecognisable voice which seemed suddenly to rouse la Doriacci.

'Good gracious,' she said. 'But what are you doing here?'

'It's my own room . . .' began Armand, raising his chin the way he did in executive meetings, but with his voice still squeaking.

'But of course it's your room . . . you see, I was supposed to meet Edma here, or rather in the sitting room, to be precise. And I was there, what's more,' she added gaily before going to sit coolly on the edge of the bathtub, next to and above Armand who clamped both hands across a not very imposing manhood.

'But you must go away . . . You're not going to stay here,' he said.

He turned upon la Doriacci a beseeching face suffused with such intense fervour it made him look like one of the diva's thousands of fans, as she saw them at the foot of the backstage staircase in opera houses around the world, fans on the look-out for an autograph, and turning to her—to her notoriety, her legend, her art, her false eyelashes—that same hungering, idolatrous face. The illusion was so powerful that, seized by a generous impulse, la Doriacci bent over the bath and caught hold of Armand by his soapy neck, violently pressed his clean mouth to hers and then pushed him back as if the poor wretch had put himself forward even an inch. And leaving him so much off balance that he slid to the bottom of the tub looking for his security handle, she departed in triumph.

It was with a profound sense of relief, a sense of having barely escaped with his life, that Armand, for once unmindful of his sugar, settled into the narrow berth in his cabin and began to set out on the bedside table the ten items indispensable for that other crossing—the crossing into sleep. He laid out sleeping pills, tranquillisers, kidney pills, anti-nicotine pills and so on. There were also, in anticipation of morning, medications to produce the reverse effect: waking-up pills, energy pills, alertness pills and so on. All of this was drawn up on the cramped surface in military array, the way Napoleon drew up his Old Guard in Austria. The process took almost half an hour every evening. And in fact, his maniacal systematising was all to the good given those nine days of deadly boredom. Though of course Armand Bautet-Lebreche felt not the slighest impulse to rebel against this total boredom caused by inactivity, nor to get used to it either. Perhaps he was bored, he thought, because he was boring. Or perhaps it was the others. At any rate, there was nothing wrong with being bored; it was less serious than an unexpected decline in the market or an embargo on sugar. Moreover, Armand had been bored to death all his life by his parents, his friends, his in-laws, and indeed by his wife, though to be honest he would have to say that, thanks to Edma, his life over the last forty years had been a great deal less boring. For one of the wifely species Edma had always been 'a pain but not a bore', in the words of an author whose name he couldn't remember.

But what was she up to now? Frequently, he had to admit, and not without surprise, that although he never gave a thought to her during the day in Paris, the moment they went on a vacation his wife, Edma, was always on his mind. She took care of everything, saw to it that there were no problems with tickets, baggage or bills. She took him by the arm and brought him along. Wherever they went she saw to it that his hair was neat, he was well fed, well supplied with a variety of financial journals and stock-market reports. As a result Armand had marvellous vacations, though when Edma disappeared for more than five minutes he felt utterly lost, even desperate. When, three hours later, Edma returned from an expedition in the desert on a camel, or escapades to pleasure ports, in the arms of a young man, she would always find Armand awake, sitting up in bed, watching her come in with such happiness, such pleasure and such relief that she sometimes wondered if they hadn't basically always been madly in love with each other, or at any rate he with her.

This would make a very good subject for a movie, it had occurred to her, and she had suggested it to Simon Béjard. A man and woman live together on good terms for years. Little by little, one detail after another indicates to the woman that her husband adores her. Convinced of this at last, she leaves him just in time—before he can declare his love—with the help of a childhood friend of her husband's who has remained quite normal.

Simon had started laughing while she told him her idea, though she had not revealed its origins. And she was still laughing about it, at the expression she would see on Armand's face if she should say to him, 'Armand, I love you,' just like that, point blank, after he had had his tea . . . he would fall out of bed, poor dear man. Sometimes for a minute or two Edma would dwell affectionately on the fate of this cautious little worker ant by the name of Armand Bautet-Lebreche, her husband—sometimes for even longer—until she remembered that he had ruined more than one of his own friends, that he trampled on the weak, that on his lips the word *heart* meant the core of a factory or machine. Two or three times, she had seen him behave like a slave trader, and her bourgeois education, fully and deeply inculcated, had taught her once and for all the ethical differences between the bourgeois and the very rich—differences F. Scott Fitzgerald could never have stressed too much. After all these years, these memories still gave her chills up her spine.

There was a knock at the door. Given his attachment to normality, Armand was incapable of supposing that at this late hour it could be anyone but the steward. Having regained his tone of command, it pleased him to call out suddenly, twice as loud as usual, an irritable 'Come in.' It was as if with the air he drew in and released he was also expelling the memory of la Doriacci, of her mouth with its smell of roses or carnations (Armand really couldn't tell which was which when it came to flowers), the memory of the embarrassment that had poleaxed him almost to the point of drowning him. But when he saw the door still ajar and heard no eager voice answering his 'Steward?', he thought he was lost for a second time—la Doriacci had only gone to put on her night-clothes, some arachnidan outfit. Since, as he gathered from certain conversations, young men bored her with their insipidity, she clearly had designs on him, Armand, perhaps because of his age, but mostly for his fortune. Despite her own millions, la Doriacci must have her eye on the Lebreche fortune (Bautet was his mother's maiden name; the family had given in to her wish to tack it onto his father's out of generosity, since the Bautet holdings were scarcely a third that of the Lebreches).

Well, Doriacci or no Doriacci, Armand muttered feverishly to himself, the sugar fortune amassed by my parents, grandparents and great-grandparents will not change hands!

This he would explain immediately to la Doriacci, perhaps frightening her . . . in his innocence, Armand assumed a grimace which he thought would provoke anxiety, but proved instead to be merely comic, for Eric Lethuillier, now standing in the doorway, burst into laughter.

Now what was this one doing here? Armand Bautet-Lebreche blinked from the depths of his bed and muttered desperately, 'Get out! Get out!' just as Pope Alexander must have said to the little Borgias who were watching him die. 'Get out!' he repeated feebly, rolling his head from left to right—just like the sick and dying in American movies, he thought abruptly, and blushed at the probable opinion of this man behind his pensive, reasonable look. He sat up in bed with a start, coughed to clear his throat and, holding out a small but virile hand that did not go with the pyjamas, said, 'How are you? Excuse me, I was dreaming.'

'You were dreaming that I'd gone,' said Eric with the handsome, chilly smile that had earned him a degree of respect from Armand, as of one predator for another. 'And I'll fulfil your dream very quickly. But first I have a favour to ask of you, sir. Let me explain: my wife, Clarisse, will be thirty-three tomorrow, or rather the day after tomorrow, when we arrive at Cannes. I would like to give her our friend Peyrat's Marquet, which she has been dreaming of having, but I'm afraid our stupid row might have antagonised him so as to prevent him from selling it to me. Could you make the purchase for me? Here is a cheque to repay you.'

'But . . . but . . .' stammered Armand, 'Peyrat will be furious.'

'No.' Eric smiled somewhat conspiratorially, leaving Armand vaguely disturbed. 'No, if the painting goes to Clarisse he can't decently object. And once the painting is sold, that will be the end of it. What's more, I believe our friend will be quite pleased to have the painting sold.'

There was an intonation in that 'quite pleased' that instantly put Armand the money man onto the scent, waking him from the slight anaesthetisation of the cruise.

'What do you mean by "pleased"? Are you sure the painting is genuine? Who authenticated it? Two hundred and fifty thousand francs is two hundred and fifty thousand francs,' he said, not altogether sincerely. For despite his avarice, the number of zeros on a cheque meant nothing to him any more, nothing at any rate that gave pleasure, since it was not even a large enough sum to work effectively on the stock market.

'Peyrat has all the certificates, and he's the one who guarantees them,' said Eric offhandedly. 'And after all, you know, if Clarisse likes the painting, it's because it's beautiful and not for any snobbish reason. My wife is anything but a snob, as you've been able to see for yourself,' he added, tilting his head slightly with the same conspiratorial smile, which this time really repelled Armand.

'All right, then,' he said, more drily than he would have wished. 'I'll find him at the pool first thing tomorrow morning and give him a cheque.'

'Here's mine,' said Eric, taking a step towards him and holding out a piece of light-blue paper, the idyllic pastel used by French banks. Since Armand did not extend his hand to take it, Eric stood undecided for a moment, looking uneasy. Finally he asked, 'What shall I do with it?' in a hostile tone, to which Armand Bautet-Lebreche replied in the same way, 'Put it anywhere you like,' as if the piece of paper were ugly to behold.

The two men looked at one another, and for once Armand was attentive. Eric gave one of his flashing smiles, bowed graciously and said 'Thank you' in the beautiful warm voice that had exasperated Armand on television, as he now remembered.

Then Eric was gone.

Armand Bautet-Lebreche settled back in his bed once again, turned off the light and lay quietly in the dark for three minutes. Then, feverishly turning on the light, he got up and swallowed two more sleeping pills which would suffice, should the need arise, to withstand la Doriacci's voluptuous enterprise.

*I*t would take the *Narcissus* eighteen hours to get from Palma to Cannes, a journey across the open sea and without stops. They were due to arrive at dinnertime, before the farewells. The weather was gorgeous. The pale sun was tinged with red and the air was cooler, strained, it seemed, but with a different tension from the one that prevailed on board. It was instead a tingling, slightly chilly vitality they felt that glorious day, walking the deck of the ship that was bringing them back to winter and the city. If you took a poll you would find more passengers terrified by winter's approach than anticipating it, Charley thought. Among those for whom Paris sounded a note of promise, there were probably no more than three: Clarisse and Julien, to whom Paris represented ten thousand tranquil, secluded rooms; and Edma, who would enjoy regaling Parisian society with details of the trip. She was returning full of love for the elite circle that awaited her, a crowd in which she was fond of no particular individuals, but whose general quickness, acrimony and snobbishness strangely but surely warmed her heart.

Perhaps snobbishness was really one of the saner passions once you were too old for any other, Charley philosophised as he looked at Edma, who was throwing breadcrumbs to the dolphins just as she had to the seagulls, and with the same motions that she might very likely use at home to serve caviar on toast, or *pâté de foie gras*. Charley had been horrified by her at first, but over the past four years he had slowly become attached to her—particularly this year, when she had been perfectly charming and had not sent her breakfast back to the kitchen more than four times, nor threatened even once to get off 'at the next stop'. Progress, indeed. But was it perhaps due to the other distractions this year aboard the *Narcissus*, Charley wondered, which had hardly left Edma time to pause over her toast or the press of her shirts. She was obviously gleeful and as she tossed her bread into the air, laughing her loud socialite's laugh, she looked like an overgrown schoolgirl. She did indeed seem to be right in the middle of that awkward age, Charley said to himself. He suspected she would never escape it, no more than Andreas would his childhood, Julien his adolescence or Armand Bautet-Lebreche his dotage.

'But what's the matter with them, Charley? Don't these birds eat bread?'

Charley ran to join elegant Edma. Madame was dressed in a vivid blue jacket and pleated toast-coloured linen skirt belted over a silk blue-and-white-print polo shirt with a cloche hat to match the blue of the jacket. She looked like a fashion model. She was elegance itself, he told her, bending over her gloved hand, and he began to inform her of the habits of cetaceans. But she cut him short. 'Today's our last day, Charley. This year I'm really sad.'

'We agreed yesterday not to talk about it before Cannes,' he said with a smile.

But his heart was bleeding, and he would have liked to confess as much to Edma. For at Cannes, Andreas would vanish from his life, from the diva's and the others'. Andreas was not of their world; not their circle, their city, their little group. Andreas, like a prince strayed from his kingdom of Nevers into the midst of ignorant plebeians, would very soon return there to lead a pleasant and hard-working existence on the arm of a woman who would be jealous of him his whole life long. At least, this is what Charley saw lying in wait for him, and what he could not resist sharing with Edma.

'Ah . . . you see him tucked away at Nantes or Nevers all middle class and cosy? It's odd, but I don't,' said Edma squinting past Charley towards the horizon, as if she saw Andreas's future written there. She tapped her lip with a finger and seemed to have difficulty formulating her own view.

'What do you see instead?' asked Charley.

'Well, I see him getting off to a bad start,' she said musingly. 'Or rather I see him never starting off at all . . . not even leaving the ship. I find it hard to imagine just what he's going to do now, on shore with no money and no family. Really, my friend, God knows up to now I've never been sorry to discover that a handsome man preferred women. But in this case I think I'd rather know he was in your arms and not simply torn from the diva's.'

'Me too,' said Charley with an attempt at a smile.

But there was a tightening in his throat, and it frightened him that Edma also had fears about Andreas—Edma who was never frightened for anyone at all, unless it was whether he or she might not be invited to a ball she was attending.

'Clarisse is also worried,' he said in a low voice.

Edma looked at him, saw his face, and patted his hand as if touched. 'The cruise must have been hard on you too, my friend.'

'I was just trying to count the winners,' he said. 'Let's see . . .'

'Oh, what a good idea.'

Edma rested her elbows on the rail beside him. In an instant their eyes were shining with excitement at the idea of all the wicked or idiotic things they had to tell one another about their travelling companions. They warmed to it with such glee that for two hours they entirely forgot about Andreas and his fate.

'Come with me,' la Doriacci said to Simon Béjard, whom she found, this morning, to be remarkably cheerful once again, and almost elegant in his jeans and oversize sweater. It was easy to see that Olga had not overseen his attire this morning; and that she hadn't had time since dawn to clobber the poor fellow with a disagreeable phrase or two, phrases that he would have spent the rest of the day trying to shake off. He would of course have succeeded, though not without a visible effort that was painful to behold.

The night before, la Doriacci had even considered suborning the doughty Simon into taking the principal role in her plan, rather than that of a witness, as things now stood. But it would have been too complicated, and above all it would not have appeared credible to Andreas. So she scudded along to the bar and sat down quietly behind the counter, where she rested her elbows and began to refurbish her beauty without stinting on the lipstick or mascara. There were circles under her eyes, which gave her an unexpected fragile aspect—almost desirable, thought Simon, forgetting for an instant his preference for fresh young things.

'You mean to entice me to drink with you at this hour?' he said, sitting down next to her.

'Absolutely,' said la Doriacci. 'Gilbert, we'll have two martinis, please,' she said, with a dazzling smile and a rather broad wink to the blond bartender, who felt a thrill of pleasure. The message of the wink was confirmed when he set the glass down in front of her, and she rested her be-ringed hand for a second on his and addressed him as 'my angel'.

'I wanted to ask you something, Monsieur Béjard, apart from getting you horribly drunk before the sun is quite risen. Why don't you put my protégé into the movies? He has the build for it, wouldn't you say?'

'Well, I have thought about it . . .' said Simon, rubbing his hands together with a cunning expression. 'I've thought about it, you know. And as soon as we get to Paris, I intend to have him do a screen test. There's a shortage in France of young leading men of his class, men that don't look like hairdressers or hysterical gangsters. I entirely agree with you . . . I entirely share your view,' he reiterated without paying attention to what he was saying. This made la Doriacci laugh.

'What view?' she said, swallowing her cocktail in one—devilishly strong though it was, thought Simon. 'What view do you believe I hold?'

'Well . . .' said Simon, his face suddenly red. 'Uh, well, I meant that he would *also* be very good for the movies.'

'Why *also*?' she repeated, looking serious.

'For the movies also.'

'But what is this *also*?'

'Damn it, I'm only getting in deeper . . .' said Simon. 'Well, my dear Doria, don't torment me. I'm telling you I'll do anything you like for the boy.'

'Are you sure?' she said, dropping her ironic tone. 'Can I count on you, Monsieur Béjard? Or are you saying that just to make up for your gaffe?'

'I mean it seriously,' said Simon. 'I'll take care of him and his upkeep.'

'And his morale as well?' she asked. 'I think the boy is still young enough to suffer the pangs of love. Promise me you won't laugh at him for that? Remember how painful it is to be unhappily in love.'

'That doesn't take much effort,' said Simon with a smile. 'I can well remember.' He raised his eyes to meet that smouldering look and saw it come tenderly to rest on himself, and was moved. 'You know . . .' he began.

But she vigorously clapped her hand over his mouth, so that he bit his tongue and came back to his senses.

'Yes, I know,' she said. 'I thought of it too, you can be sure.'

'So what's the objection?' said Simon lightly.

'Stop it,' said la Doriacci nervously. 'I did think of you, I did indeed, to convince Andreas of my infidelity, or you might say my perversity in the love department. And then I thought it wouldn't work: he would never believe it.'

'Because of me or because of you?' asked Simon.

'Me of course. I like them young, very young. You must know that. You do read the papers?'

'I read them, but I don't believe a thing I read except when it suits my purposes,' he told her.

'Well, for once they were right. No, I think Gilbert would be more believable.'

'And how do you think you can make Andreas believe it? And why?'

'Your questions are in the wrong order,' she said sternly. 'I want him to believe it so that he won't be dreaming about me for weeks, or convincing himself that I'm waiting for him in New York. And I want him to believe it to put his mind at ease, and mine too. But for once, perhaps, more for him than for me. As for how I hope to make him believe it—my friend, there is only one way to prove adultery. It has to be done in front of him. That's why I would be grateful to you, should you agree on the necessity of this vaudeville act, to send Andreas to me at around three on some silly pretext. I'll be in my cabin, but I will not be alone.'

'But . . .' said Simon uncomfortably. 'I wouldn't want it to be by way of me.'

'Think it over.' La Doriacci looked suddenly weary. 'And have another martini, or two or three, to my health. I won't have the time, alas, to drink with you. I have things to do here,' she concluded, tapping her ring against the chrome of the bar.

And Simon with a bow and a few mumbled words turned on his heels, leaving la Doriacci to her tête-à-tête with the fair-haired Gilbert.

Through the bar door Simon could see Edma dressed smartly in blue and white throwing something over the railing with a sower's sweeping gesture, an unlikely one for her. Simon was intrigued; after all seagulls didn't fly that low. But a sailor put an end to his perplexity by telling him about the dolphins that were accompanying the ship. Ordinarily Simon would have hurried to the rail, would have instantly thought up a movie in which the dolphins played one part and Olga another. But now that he had carried off his big coup, he could no longer allow himself such amateurism. He had no further excuse for losing, since he had already won. But as the producer in him reawoke nonetheless, he reflected with a certain satisfaction that the rows and weariness with Olga meant that when he got back he could use Melchior, sweet little Melchior, in his next film. She was stunning and didn't try to talk about Einstein or Wagner. She charmed French males of every age, and women also warmed to her—feelings Olga had admittedly never aroused in either sex. And if he dropped Olga, he could use Constantin, whom he had given up so as not to displease Olga, who hated him. That way he could be sure of a brilliant cast for the box office, one that would even go over in New York.

Not for an instant did he wonder how he would break it to Olga; he had loved her too much these last few days, been too cruelly hurt, to retain the slightest forbearance in breaking off with her. It was not that he was being deliberately vengeful, but his heart, worn out by the repercussions, could no longer imagine a sorrow beyond itself, a sorrow other than its own.

Out on deck, he lit up a cigarette. Then he stood in the sun, his hands in the pockets of his old trousers, with a feeling of autonomy and well-being that he had not felt in what seemed like a century. The ship was definitely charming, and he had to recognise that Olga, without knowing it, had chosen well. He really liked Edma. He would miss her like a classmate, like the pal he hadn't been able to have these last few years. She was feeding the dolphins over there, or trying to, with the absurdly sweeping gestures, the piercing and authoritative voice that he now found disarming. Coming up beside her, he put an arm affectionately around her shoulders, and after a momentary start, Edma Bautet-Lebreche seemed to like it. She actually leaned against his shoulder, laughing, showing him the dolphins as if they were her personal property.

'I'm going to miss you,' he said in a husky voice. 'I'm going to be bored without you, I think, beautiful Edma . . . and in Paris we'll never be able to see each other again. There must be a great barley-sugar Wall of China surrounding your place in Paris, isn't there?'

'Why no, not at all!' said Edma, squirming, still a bit surprised at the change in Simon's personality, from role of victim, hence asexual, to that of lone male hunter—naturally more becoming, she thought, looking at his placid blue eyes, his comfortable stance and that slightly red skin beneath hair which, though carrot-red, was still thick and healthy. 'No, of course not,' she repeated. 'And of course we'll see each other this winter. It's you who will be run ragged, Simon, with your movie, and what with the probable provocations of Mademoiselle Lamouroux, o-u-x, to boot.'

'I do not believe that in the end I will be able to use the services of Mademoiselle Lamouroux, o-u-x,' said Simon in a calm voice that forbade any teasing. 'At any rate I live by myself in Paris and elsewhere.'

'Oh, I see . . . so this has been your vacation, here on the ship,' she said with a laugh—as if the word *vacation* were ridiculous, and in fact it was, given the emotional torment of these last ten days.

Simon lowered his head at the painful memory of Olga on her bunk telling him in detail about her evening on Capri. He shook himself and smelled Edma's perfume, a sophisticated and delicious perfume which he realised he would also miss. It was as though that perfume had soothed the whole trip, so generously had Edma used it, propelling herself all over the ship untiringly, from the hold to the upper deck, trailing these emanations in her wake like a banner. Simon tightened his arm around her. Edma, surprised, looked up at him, and to her amazement, this vulgar producer who had never heard of Darius Milhaud kissed her briefly but enthusiastically on the mouth.

'But what are you doing? You're out of your mind . . .' she heard herself groan like a young girl.

The two of them stood there for a second dazed, looking at each other, before they both burst out laughing, then started off arm in arm, keeping step and still laughing, on the classic turn around the deck. Yes, thought Edma, lengthening her stride—yes, she would see him in secret . . . Yes, there would be a liaison, platonic or not, no matter. He had said he was going to miss her, and she was going to miss him, this little man whom she had found so unprepossessing and vulgar, and whom she now found so charming, and who needed her, as he was telling her at this very moment in a bantering but tender way.

'Perhaps I could manage to learn proper manners if you gave me lessons every week in Paris . . . don't you think so? It would please me very . . . very much, if you had time to give me instruction . . .'

And Edma, her eyes shining with idiotic joy, nodded in vigorous agreement.

So it was in a good mood that Simon returned to his cabin around eleven in the morning, expecting to find it empty as usual, with Olga gone off to play deck-tennis or backgammon with Eric Lethuillier. He was more disappointed than surprised to find her curled up on the bed, in a bathrobe that was too short, legs tucked up under her, a book in hand and her eye make-up on.

Well, well, at last she's thinking about the film, observed the cynic who had been calling the shots and doing the thinking for Simon since the night before. It would be in his best interest not to tell her anything until after Cannes. A series of scenes in this cabin would be intolerable. And when Olga gave him a smile that seemed slightly anxious, Simon forced himself to return it with one full of charm. This new, obviously forced friendliness threw Olga into a panic. Since nine o'clock, when she had awakened alone beside a bed that had not even been turned back, she had been frantically running through the latest events, pained to admit her numerous outbursts of language and gesture might have been too much for him. What on earth could have driven her to it? For once, instead of launching into a lyrical account of her romantic fancies for the benefit of her faithful comrades, Olga kept her words to herself.

It was indeed a question of Fernande and Micheline, or more precisely of what a boring account it would be if her day consisted of nothing else but her reports to them; besides which, the account in question might lack zest if it turned out to be about a starlet out of work. She had to get Simon back—thank God, she felt altogether capable of doing it. All at once what she had considered Simon's repugnant demands were welcome, since it was through them that she might find herself again close to him, and might regain her power. As for the servile kindness she had so deplored in him, she was glad today to know it was there, since it would, she thought, prevent him from throwing her out like an old suitcase. So when he came in, she discreetly raised her bathrobe to her thigh in a quick gesture that he caught in the mirror as he turned around. It prompted a crude rejoinder, which he suppressed only with difficulty.

'Where on earth have you been?' she said. 'I was scared when I woke up . . . I could see myself lost on this ship, all alone with these strangers, out there with people who basically annoy me . . . ah, my old friend, next time we'll go off alone, won't we—just the two of us? We'll rent a little boat with just the man who runs it. We'll stop off at any old bistro whenever we feel like it, with none of this classical music and no panoramas. Just some little bistro, the kind you like . . .'

'That's a very good idea,' said Simon in a measured tone, as he looked for something to change into quickly. 'But personally you know, I've enjoyed this cruise one hell of a lot.'

'Really? You're not bored with all these snobs?'

'I think they're charming,' said Simon, his head now halfway into a clean shirt. 'Very pleasant, in fact.'

'I must say, you're very indulgent . . . no, believe me, to an outsider, Simon, you're so genuine compared with those smirking puppets . . . I can assure you, there's no comparison . . . In fact, from that point of view, it's quite fun to watch!' she added with a quick laugh of amusement, but with lugubrious overtones.

It was only by chance that the laugh rang false. Otherwise she could have gone on. But it so obviously grated that she broke off and Simon energetically buried himself in his shirt, each of them aware that the discrepancy between the laugh and the words that had preceded it could not honestly pass unnoticed, both knowing that the laugh had just shattered what frail chance remained of their walking down the gang-plank of the *Narcissus* as good friends, or at any rate with a pretence of being as they were when they first came aboard.

Olga slowly drew down the robe over her legs since her instinct told her that a useful argument was no longer to be found there, and Simon let his shirt hang down over his trousers, knowing that escape inside it was no longer possible. They both sat on their bunks, eyes on the floor, not daring to look at each other. And when Simon proposed in a mournful voice, 'Well, what about a drink?' Olga nodded in agreement, she who for the sake of her complexion and lucidity never touched alcohol before eight in the evening.

*T*he alarm on his bedside clock was surprisingly quiet, and besides it stopped, out of breath, the moment he opened his eyes. It must have been ringing for some time, thought Armand Bautet-Lebreche, surprised not to have heard it sooner and vaguely wondering why, until the steward placed the breakfast tray across his knees with the complaint that he had knocked three times without any answer. At least this is what Armand gathered from the incomprehensible whispering that reached him. For he had gone deaf.

Once again a slight cold and general vexation had conspired to strike him with deafness. It happened to him every five years or so. He blew his nose energetically, tilted his head right and left without managing to unclog his ears, which seemed as traumatised as he was by the unrecountable events of the previous evening. He might have believed it was all a bad dream if Lethuillier's cheque on the bedside table were not proof to the contrary. Edma was sound asleep or else had already gone out, which he was about to ascertain when he remembered that she had spoken with elation the night before of her desire to spend the whole day in the sun. The last sunshine of the year, she had said plaintively, as though in November she wouldn't be joining the pederasts in Florida or the Bahamas, as she did every year.

He dressed with little methodical gestures, shaved with an electric razor and, having looked through the porthole to make sure that the ship was still moving—his suspicions aroused by the total silence of the engines—he started out on his morning promenade around the deck without once acknowledging the various 'good mornings' addressed to him. On completing his circuit above the soundless sea, he went back to pick up his chequebook and then turned up to knock on Julien Peyrat's door. He actually knocked several times, forgetting that Julien could hear him. Julien opened the door and said something totally incomprehensible but which seemed to be words of welcome, to which Armand answered with a quick nod.

'What a nice surprise!' said Julien Peyrat. 'You must be the only person who hasn't paid a visit to my cabin to see my masterpiece. Is it belated curiosity that brings you?'

'No, no, not at all . . . in fact, I don't feel like playing tennis this morning,' said Armand Bautet-Lebreche at random. 'But we'll be able to play this afternoon,' he went on with a benevolent air.

Julien appeared anxious, even disappointed. Perhaps Lethuillier was right, perhaps this Peyrat, forger or not, wanted to sell the painting to a dupe. Eric Lethuillier seemed too well informed to play that role . . . Armand shrugged.

'I believe you're selling that painting?' he said, pointing to the thing hanging on the wall of his cabin. 'How much? I'd like to buy it,' he concluded drily.

'Your wife knows about this?' said Julien, looking perplexed and less pleased than Eric Lethuillier had led him to expect.

After all, Armand thought, if the painting is genuine, it's worth a good bit more than two hundred and fifty thousand francs.

'I'm persuaded it's worth twice what you're asking,' he

said by way of reply. 'But since you're selling it, why not to me? Eh?' he added with a little satisfied laugh.

'Does your wife agree?'

Julien was bellowing now. He was red-faced and dishevelled, not at all a gentleman, thought Armand, pulling away from the white teeth so close to his ear.

'What?' he said out of politeness, with a gesture of helplessness towards his ear, causing Julien to yell one last time, 'Your wife! Your wife!' before he finally gave up trying to be honest.

After all, Armand didn't look as though he cared much either way, and he certainly would never have to sell the picture in order to live, whatever happened. So, swearing a little, Julien went to his suitcase for the forged certificates—all but the last one, which actually went with another Marquet, a real one that Julien cherished. He put them into the hands of Armand, who stuffed them into his pocket without so much as a glance—a surprising lack of concern in this wealthy man, thought Julien. Edma must have staged a scene to make him buy it, out of kindness towards Julien, and Armand was simply in a hurry to be done with the whole affair.

'How much?' he asked in his even voice, his glasses glinting in the sunlight.

And the set of his jaw as he filled out the cheque made Julien shiver. With his weapon in hand, his chequebook, Armand Bautet-Lebreche looked ferocious and brutal, even dangerous, an image he did not convey on vacation, when the only danger he represented was stultifying boredom.

'Two hundred and fifty thousand francs!' he yelled once or twice, and the dog he had thought dead or muzzled, though it was two cabins off, began to howl with him.

Julien wrote down the figure and showed it to Armand, who with brief thanks headed off down the passageway, painting under arm. The whole thing had been so quick and unexpected that Julien had not had time to make his farewells to the carriage, the woman, the snow. Perhaps it was better that way, he thought, a tear in one eye while the other gleamed with pleasure—for, thanks to the blue slip of paper left by **Armand**, he would be able, starting tomorrow, to take Clarisse away for days in the sun and nights in his arms. They would go to the Var, or Tahiti, or Sweden, Lapland, anywhere at all, anything she wanted. Now he could give her that. Money didn't bring happiness, it was true, but it did bring freedom.

Armand, with the same hurried little steps he still could not hear, crossed the padded companionway, knocked at Lethuillier's door, and went in without waiting for the 'Come in' that would not reach him. He watched Eric say something, several things in fact while his handsome face lit up with pleasure. And without paying attention to the play of his lips and his agitated hands, Armand laid the painting on Clarisse's empty bunk and went out again without having said nor heard a single word. He went back to his room, where the quality of silence seemed superior. The *Financial Times* had arrived in the mailbox. He settled down on his bed, completely dressed, and opened it at the page where he was expecting to find a gripping article about discount rates on Dutch petroleum stock. After all, he reflected, Clarisse had nothing to complain of in her husband, and Edma didn't know what she was talking about. There wasn't the slightest discord between the Lethuilliers.

Julien was burning with impatience to find Clarisse and tell her the news. But on the other hand, he ought not to look too carried away. He had swaggered and shown off before Clarisse for long enough already; now he could be open about his triumph, and speak of it as something other than a bagatelle. And so he adopted an air of detachment as he lit a cigarette with his bakelite lighter—which spoiled the whole effect, it occurred to him, and he had a sudden desire to laugh.

'You know, I think I've finally arranged our trip back . . .'

'The trip back' was the way they had chosen to refer to their escapade, a trip that would undoubtedly take them back across the Mediterranean towards the October sun in some far-away place, as if the cruise had been only a re-hearsal—as if, he thought, this ship, these blond bartenders, these sophisticates and rich people, as if all this divine music, all these phosphorescent notes tossed from the deck at night onto the sea where they seemed to float for an instant before disappearing, as if these odours and seascapes, these stolen kisses, this fear of losing what they had not yet won, as if the entire trip had been conceived and executed for Julien as a setting made-to-order for their meeting. Julien loathed Richard Strauss, but he was unable to stop humming the five notes of the *Burlesque*, five notes that were triumphant and tender—just the way he felt now, at least while Clarisse was looking at him. You're insane, he berated himself feverishly. You're insane to have got involved in all this! When you haven't a franc left you'll undoubtedly go and cheat somebody, leaving Clarisse alone to wait for you, in a palace bedroom or a country inn, depending how your luck's been going. She could never bear that, even if he were happy with her and showed it. For he knew instinc-tively that Clarisse dreamed not so much of being happy herself as of making someone else happy and having that person unequivocally tell her so all the time.

'How did you do it?' asked Clarisse, sitting beside him on a deck chair drenched in sunshine—whose canvas, a raw red before summer, had been faded by spray, sun and wet bathing-suits to a watery rose, somewhat kitsch and out of place in the open air. 'How did you manage it?' she said again. 'Julien, tell me everything. I love to have you tell me stories about your work, with that long-suffering look some of your memories inspire . . . It's a sad look, as though you've just been saved by a miracle: Julien, after working madly for eighteen months, now ten years later . . .' And she began to laugh, in spite of herself, at the indignant look on her lover's face. 'Seriously,' she continued vivaciously and with a shrug, as if tossing her own teasing remarks onto the scrap heap of nonsense, 'seriously, do you often get those sudden windfalls?'

Julien threw out his chest—or tried to, since it was dif-ficult to do so, he noted with annoyance, sitting in a deck chair. 'I don't see why it should come as a surprise, or seem suspicious,' he growled.

'But it doesn't,' said Clarisse, again suddenly serious.

What if Julien were offended, what if he were to hold it against her and not take her in his arms any more with words of love? She looked at his taut and angry face, she saw her hope of a happy life with him rapidly diminishing. And her face revealed such desolation, such confusion, that Julien instinctively drew her to him and covered her hair with innumerable kisses, almost brutal with self-reproach.

'And so what about the painting?' she said presently, when the fear of his no longer loving her ceased to hold her by the throat. 'What are you going to do with it?' She lifted her face and began earnestly kissing him on the temple, at the corner of his mouth, on the rough skin of his cheek, the angle of his jaw she had seen clenched a moment before. Now and then she pulled away from that side of his face, her eyes still closed, and with a soft, cautiously caressing movement of the head drew her hair past Julien's chin, hiding the sun and then letting it through again, with her fleece as blonde and silken as a window shade, and anchored herself on the other side of his face under the right cheek, neglected up till then.

'You're killing me,' said Julien in a hoarse, almost menacing voice, as with a pleading gesture he freed himself from her arms.

Armand Bautet-Lebreche, who had not of course heard them, swerved on seeing them absorbed in one another under the clear sky, making a lovely picture. With firm step he entered the golden aura surrounding them and, throwing out a passing glance apparently not in the least surprised at having seen them in one another's arms, called out 'Thank you very much! I'm in no danger. I have my hat,' before disappearing down the crew companionway.

'You're sure you haven't sold the painting?' Clarisse asked when they had caught their breath from their puzzled laughter over Armand's behaviour. 'You're sure you still have it?'

'But I've already told you . . .' Julien began. 'I told you I sold it, I really did,' he added with a laughing, sheepish, triumphant face, a face so perfectly masculine and perfectly childish that instead of hearing him, she simply said 'Liar!' and looked him up and down, both serious and overcome with pleasure.

'Kiss me some more . . .' Julien demanded in a plaintive voice, his back against the rail, his eyes half closed against the sun, entirely blissful with well-being and above all with relief, a relief whose source he did not know, but one which made of that morning a milestone in his emotional history— one of those moments in which the sun, Clarisse's hand on his neck, the sunlight's red spots through his lids, the slight tremor of his body, exhausted by a whole day of unfulfilled pleasure but trembling still from the requited pleasures of the day before, in which all this was engraved forever in his memory. Julien foresaw and took note: this was a moment he would remember all his life, one of those rare instances when the mortal loves and accepts the idea of death as the conclusion of a life suddenly become sublime. For a moment he found his own fate and that of humanity not merely acceptable, but much to be desired. He blinked, contented as a cat, and looked up to see Clarisse's eyes resting on his face and eyes with a tenderness that was almost intolerable. It was a devoted look, pale blue, a flashing and fluid look that reflected his whole being and dreamed only of reflecting him over and over, till the end of the longest cruise.

*A*round midafternoon the coast of France appeared in the distance, and it brought a crowd to the rail that had not gathered to see the statues, temples or historic sites throughout the voyage. Though apparently similar to the Spanish or Italian coast, at this distance anyway, the sight was greeted by an admiring and meditative silence, at least from the more chauvinistic French passengers.

For Clarisse and Julien the coast was the place where they might not only love one another, but where they might kiss without hiding in corners, unsatisfied desire having evidently reduced their most essential aspirations to that puerile a level. Edma looked forward to her lady friends at the Ritz and her cocktail parties; Armand to his calculations; the diva and Hans-Helmut to the stage, the orchestra, the applause; Eric to his efficient staff; Simon Béjard to his work and the respect of his peers at Fouquet's; Olga to her public; Andreas, to no one knew what. As for Charley, he would look up 'the fellows' and tell them about Andreas, perhaps carrying matters a bit further than reality had permitted. And Elledocq? The captain would rejoin Madame Elledocq, whom he had twice alerted already concerning his return. For on the rare occasions he had failed to do so, he had had the misfortune of discovering the mailman or the baker in the matrimonial bed (both of them were solid, pleasure-bent sorts). This had quickly made him realise that his one true love was the sea.

'We're to dine within view of Cannes this evening, I believe. Isn't that so? As melancholy as one could wish . . .' said Edma Bautet-Lebreche. 'Departure time is still open, either tonight after the concert, or tomorrow during the day . . . What do you plan to do, Julien?'

'I don't know.' He shrugged. 'It will all depend on . . . on the weather,' he added after glancing towards Clarisse, who was still sitting in her chair with her head thrown back and her neck showing, her eyes half-closed, her mouth beautiful and suddenly sad.

And the idea that it was he, Julien, who was loved and desired, who day and night was going to possess all of that, he the owner, sentimentally speaking, of that tawny hair, those cheekbones, those large grey-blue eyes that rested on him with an expression of love. He couldn't make himself believe it. It was too much luck, too much pleasure, too much happiness, too much artlessness all round.

The look he gave Clarisse reawoke a nostalgia in Edma. Who was there who had looked at her that way over these last few years? And how long had it been since she no longer aroused such a look, the marvelling, jealous look of love? Surely not recently. Ah yes . . . Edma blushed, suddenly remembering that it had been the look in Simon's eyes that reminded her of Julien. What madness, she said to herself, but she was smiling. What madness . . . Me and that flamboyant producer, a redhead besides. But still she had needed Julien's glance to realise what had been contained in the other. Suddenly Edma softly called out in the direction of the *Financial Times* open beside her, 'Armand, are we getting old?' It took two or three desperate calls to bring about the fall of the paper and Armand's pince-nez, ungrateful object that might well have dropped in boredom, boredom and the monotony of being given over to figures and still more figures.

'What are you going to do with all that money?' she asked with a new irony. She went on before Armand could reply. 'It's ridiculous . . . what will you do with all those dollars when we're dead?'

Armand Bautet-Lebreche, nearly recovered from his temporary deafness, considered her with distrust and indignation. It really wasn't Edma's style to lack deference towards money, to make fun of it: because of the straitened circumstances of her childhood, she had long kept an instinctive and admiring respect for it in all its manifestations. Anyway Armand did not much care for sarcasm on the subject.

'Would you repeat the first question?' he asked drily. 'The second seems rather uninteresting.'

'The first question?' said Edma, as though distracted, laughing at her husband's dignified air. 'Ah! Yes, yes. I was asking whether we were still young.'

'Certainly not,' said Armand calmly. 'Certainly not. And I congratulate myself on it when I see the thievish little whippersnappers and incompetents who are supposed to take over from us as heads of business and government. They won't go far, I tell myself.'

'Answer my question,' she said, her voice now weary. 'Are we old, you and I? Have we aged since that rainy day at Saint-Honoré-d'Eylau when we were wed for better or for worse?'

Armand cast a suddenly alert glance at her, coughed, and his question seemed to just slip out of its own accord: 'Do you regret it?'

'Me?' Edma burst out laughing. 'Me? Why no, Armand, my Armie, my Lebreche. Me regret the delicious life you've given me? I'd have to be mad or neurotic not to have developed a taste for it. No, it's been charming, altogether charming, I assure you. What could I have lacked with you there?'

'I often wasn't.' Armand, his eyes lowered, again gave his little cough.

'But exactly! It's the mode of life I found appealing,' said Edma without the slightest hypocrisy. 'It's always frantic cohabitation that makes households so fragile. By seeing each other very little, or not very much, you can stay married for years: the proof . . .'

'You don't feel lonely from time to time?' said Armand in a voice almost anxious, plunging Edma into a state of anguish.

Armand must be gravely ill to be showing interest in anything besides himself, she reflected without animosity. She leaned towards him. 'Do you feel well, Armand? You haven't been out in the sun too long? Or drunk too much of that excellent port? I'll have to ask Charley where it comes from. It's not only very good, it's a very heady port too . . . But what was it you were asking me, my dear? I can't remember.'

'Nor I,' said Armand Bautet-Lebreche, raising his standard once more to eye level and telling himself that he had just had a narrow escape.

Hans-Helmut Kreuze stood in the middle of his cabin dressed in ceremonial tails instead of his usual dinner jacket. He gazed at himself in the mirror with mingled satisfaction and doubt. He still couldn't understand why la Doriacci hadn't fallen into his arms, hadn't assured him of an even better cruise. For in the end, aside from the captain's pique against poor Fuchsia, the trip had been delightful. But never, never again would he do another concert with la Doriacci. He had bitterly complained about her to his students, had told them man to man about his fornication in Berlin. They had appeared as scandalised as he at la Doriacci's behaviour. They had even suggested—respectfully suggested, for that was the only kind of suggestion Hans-Helmut understood—that perhaps he should reveal her odious character to the managers of concert halls in Europe and America. Certainly that way he could blow some smoke into the blue sky of la Doriacci's career; but he feared that if by chance she got wind of it and where it came from, she herself might not hesitate to reveal the whole story behind the night's debauch, even the motive for his bitterness.

This evening he was to play Fauré, she was to sing Brahms and Bellini, but God only knew what she might choose instead. Yes, he recognised feebly, yes, he would gladly have stepped again into la Doriacci's bed. Of course, Hans-Helmut's experience had been quite limited, and his most patient mistress had been his wife. But in the dark recesses of his mind he seemed to see the white flash of a shoulder passing in the night, the red and white of her laugh, the natural whiteness of gleaming young teeth, black irises below black hair, and in particular a hoarse voice saying things in Italian that were scandalously immodest and untranslatable, if not incomprehensible. Though it shamed him to think of it, some bad angel or provocateur had left him with the intimate and secret conviction, scarcely admissible to himself, that among all these grey days and nights, in all these grey years of work, of recitals, of triumphs, amidst all this grey that now hung over even the wildest applause—only that one night thirty years before in Berlin had been in colour, though it took place in the dark of a hotel room.

'Never let yourselves fall into the clutches of sensual gratification or debauchery,' he pronounced, turning towards the two elderly students as they stood in his sitting room. The recommendations of the good maestro seemed quite superfluous: in their shorts, socks and sandals, they seemed to have fallen from a planet where such temptations were forbidden. So be it, said Kreuze to himself. There will always be some pure hearts to produce good music.

La Doriacci, in the midst of a scene of amazing disorder which she kept trampling underfoot, watched two exhausted stewards closing her suitcases. Both of them had managed several times not to look in the least surprised while packing a man's socks, a man's underpants, collars and bow-tie, even secretly congratulating themselves on their proverbial discretion, but then la Doriacci ripped each of these masculine articles from their hands and laid them aside on her bed, saying with the most natural indignation and not the slightest shame, 'Leave that out, for heaven's sake, you can see it doesn't belong to me!'—as though appalled that they should wish to plunder the rather unexciting wardrobe of her young lover, even if it were for her. So she sent for Andreas, returned his belongings without appearing to notice the young man's total indifference to the restitution. He was pale, not having cultivated his suntan during the cruise, and quite obviously miserable. La Doriacci was filled with tenderness and pity for him. But not love. And that, alas, was what he needed.

'My sweet,' she said in his general direction, stepping over dresses, fans, scores, and finally leading him through the door into her bedroom, which was just as cluttered. But here she could shut the door on the two stewards. 'My sweet, you mustn't look like that, for heaven's sake . . . You are handsome, very handsome. You are intelligent, you are sensitive, but this—all this will pass. You are good and, I tell you, you are going to have a triumphant career. Sincerely, dear heart,' she added with a bit more verve—for he stood immobile, his arms at his sides, hardly looking at her, his face inscrutable and expressionless, as if he were overcome with boredom. 'My sweet,' she went on again. 'I assure you that if I could have loved anyone in the last ten years, it would have been you. I'll send you postcards from all over, and when I come to Paris we'll have lunch together and all afternoon we'll deceive your mistress in a hotel room. And that's always delightful in Paris, particularly if no one knows . . . You don't believe me?' she asked in a slightly annoyed tone, very slightly annoyed, and he started almost fearfully.

'Yes, yes, I believe you,' he said precipitately and rather heatedly, almost too heatedly. Then he mumbled useless apologies while she kissed him on the mouth and hugged him to her in an irrepressible movement of tenderness before pushing him towards the door and putting him out, with no apparent protest on his part.

I hope I haven't been too hard on him, she said to herself with vague remorse.

When Charley came to ask her if she had seen Andreas getting off the boat with the first to leave on the big outboard sent from Cannes, she appeared incapable of answering. She was almost certain that Andreas could not have endured one last evening on board and had hurried ashore to get on with his career. The fact he had temporarily left his baggage behind showed that he had left the *Narcissus* on impulse. Another impulse would surely bring him back on board in the morning. Actually she preferred it that way, because singing in front of him had become a torture, or at least an embarrassment; all the words of love in Italian (which, thank God, he was unlikely to have understood), all those words she addressed at the whim of the score to tragic lovers, seemed to her just so many presents that she had not given him, and which might drive him to despair the instant he heard them.

She opened her diary at random and whistled between her teeth in a most suggestive manner, completely out of character for the diva of divas. In three days she would be in New York, in ten Los Angeles, in fifteen Rome, and in twenty-five Sydney (indubitably not the home base of the charming Julien Peyrat). Ah, New York! Who was it waiting for her in New York? Ah yes, young Roy . . . he must already be seething with impatience, assembling a flock of anticipatory lies that would allow him to slip away from Dick, his protector, so rich, so old and so boring. The face of Roy—remote, canny and usually cold, though it occasionally dissolved into laughter—suddenly appeared before her, and she began to laugh too, and in confident anticipation.

*W*ithout the slightest feeling of desire Simon Béjard was watching Olga's rump—if the term could apply to a body so slim—as she leaned over his suitcase. She was packing it first, before hers, in a fit of servility that would have pleased him more if it had been less tardy. He watched the little mouth, closed across capped teeth, and listened as it uttered pompous little platitudes, laboured banter, or obscene pathos. He wondered at the absurd man who had usurped his place these past several weeks to the point of persuading him that he loved any of this: the pretensions, the egotism, the hardness, the high-falutin' nonsense she exuded through every pore. He bent over backwards at times to give her a friendly answer, or simply to answer her at all. Ah, how he had desired young girls in the first flower of womanhood! How he had dreamed of being father, lover, brother and guide to this intellectual goose, half frigid and wholly artificial! Well, that was one thing he needn't worry about any more. When he got home he would go and see Margot, Margot who was his own age, who had a rump and generous breasts and a generous laugh. Margot who found him brilliant and was more intelligent than many other supposedly refined women.

Simon was lucky to have seen Olga outside their limited circle of movie people, who were so lacklustre that sometimes she seemed better than they and perhaps was. He had had the good fortune to compare her with two women who were truly refined in feeling and expression, or at any rate manners—Clarisse and Edma, the one unsurpassably elegant in her heart, the other in dress and social graces. La Doriacci herself was in a different class from poor Olga. Simon wondered again what Eric had seen in Olga: perhaps nothing more than the chance to make his wife suffer? Simon, with his natural sense of gallantry, found this an insufficient motive.

For Simon, this was his first and no doubt last cruise, at least for several years. Still he would miss Edma, he said to himself with a pang, and much to his surprise. He could have been happy with Edma if she were not so chic and if he weren't so certain to humiliate her in the presence of her cronies from the avenue Foch every time she had to introduce him. Perhaps he would venture to see her in secret anyway, quietly, just the two of them. That way they could giggle together, make fun of the same things, leap from one subject to another, holding their sides, as they had done for ten days. The two of them laughed at exactly the same things, though their education and lives had been completely different. That juvenile merriment, Simon now knew, was a better trump card for any union between man and woman than all the erotic-sentimental-psychological understandings the papers were filled with.

Moved by a sudden impulse, forgetting Olga still buried in his suitcase, Simon lifted the phone, asked for the Bautet-Lebreche cabin, and of course got Edma. He had never spoken to her on the telephone, and that high-pitched voice at first made a bad impression on him.

'Edma . . .' he said. 'It's me. I wanted . . .' he hesitated.

'Yes, speaking. This is Edma,' she said at the top of her

lungs. 'Yes, this is she . . . What is it? What can I do for you?'

Her voice faded, she was silent, and the two of them were left hanging on opposite ends of the wire, a bit breathless, vaguely uneasy.

'You were saying?' Edma's voice now came slowly, as though she were whispering.

'I was wondering . . . I was wondering whether perhaps we could see each other after Tuesday . . . if you have time,' said Simon, also in a whisper.

His forehead was covered with sweat, without his knowing why. There was a silence during which he almost hung up.

'Why yes, of course,' Edma's voice said finally, as if from the great beyond. 'Yes, of course. I even put my phone number in your letter box just a while ago . . .'

'No . . .' said Simon. 'No . . .'

And he burst into his resounding laugh which brought Olga out of his suitcase, incensed but powerless. Edma laughing in response was almost enough to make her rip the receiver out of Simon's hand.

'No,' he said. 'No . . . That's really funny . . .' And added, 'That's a hoot! I could have got in touch with you even without this call . . .'

'It is a hoot,' Edma agreed, using the word for the first time in her life. 'There we were, doing this big bashful act!'

And they hung up at the same time, hilarious and triumphant.

*A*ndreas lay stretched out on the deserted deck at the far end of the ship, where the laundry was hung out to dry and where, consequently, he couldn't be seen from the passenger area. No one, apart from a miserable Arab cook, had seen him pass by, and he, poor soul, looked as if he had seen a Martian. It was strange, come to think of it: all these individuals on the ship who didn't know each other, would never know each other, but who, if the ship happened to encounter a stray mine, would die all at once and for the same reason.

Andreas lay on bare wood—to hell with his white flannel trousers—flat on his back, his face to the sun, his head resting on a coil of rope. He smoked one cigarette after another, the taste increasingly bitter to his parched throat, while the smoke seemed paler and paler against a blue and sweet-smelling sky. His mind had become a great vacuum. Or more precisely, his mental activity had been reduced to a tune he had discovered in the bar the night before, a record by Fats Waller. The notes seemed to spring from the piano, tumbling off its smooth white keys, just as they were extracted painfully from the lowest depths of the clarinet. Quite a happy tune. A tune that he didn't know, that he had never heard before but whose every note he nonetheless recognised; a tune that could not have come either from his childhood without record player, nor his adolescence devoted to rock and roll, nor from military service, nor his crazy mistresses after his career began. These fifty- or sixty-year-olds of his dreamt only of the jerk, of flinging themselves about in front of him with untidy hair, arms raised high, exposing powdered armpits under the the lamé. He thought of his several 'patronesses'; saw them filing past in disordered ranks, and asked himself, without bitterness or remorse, how he had managed to tolerate each of them at table or in bed.

In fact at the time he hadn't known what it meant to share a bed. In that domain he had never shared anything at all; he had given, had produced gestures and offered his splendid body to persons who had used it to obtain a pleasure he did not share and whose blossoming and cresting he watched with a total objectivity that was at times tainted slightly with embarrassment. Or conversely, when he was the one who had achieved his object, abandoning the other to her personal fantasies, he had never had any feeling at all of sharing. On the contrary, many a time in the course of these liaisons—which, when he was twenty, should have suggested sharing and closeness—Andreas had felt just the opposite: that making love put him forever at a distance from his lover.

At any rate the faces he was trying to dismiss would come back to him, they or others like them, at Nevers or wherever. At Nevers first, since he had no more money and would practically have to wait at the station café for the sale of the three lots of land that had been acquired over three generations by the men of the family. They were men who had died at their work without having known the pleasures of the city, and it was they whom Andreas was now surprised to find himself envying. They had laboured, and perhaps died in the midst of that labour, but at least they had died with people around them, mourned and cherished. And perhaps work had seemed endurable to them since it made a living for their wives and children. As for him, he knew that from his own career he would reap only jewels, man's jewellery he would never part with, which he could not even give away because of his initials engraved on them in gold . . . He was going back to the provinces where he would move from drawing room to drawing room, from bed to bed with women lacking in allure or spirit, women idle like himself, who would have neither the resounding laugh nor bad manners and foul language, nor soft skin and laughing eyes, nor of course the voice of la Doriacci. Ah no, he really didn't feel like going back to Nevers and driving past that empty house he knew so well, whose hold on his memory neither palace nor motel room had yet been able to dislodge. Now there would be other recollections added to those tender blue pastels of childhood, memories whose colours were more raw and violent, but whose perfume was rooted in happiness.

Reluctantly, compelled by suffering and a sense of rebellion, Andreas raised his head and shook himself. He tried to escape his cruel enemies by sitting up, but slid down again, arms crossed over his chest, giving in to the combined assault of imagination and memory. 'But I'm all alone, God help me . . .' he groaned indistinctly to himself, and to the sun out there, which was tanning his already golden skin, the skin that was to assure him a livelihood and defined his existence.

A seagull wheeled in the sky like a vulture or bird of prey. It was not flying, but dropped, on open wings, in one fell swoop, from sky to sea. It climbed straight back up into the sky without having seen or found a thing. Andreas followed this allegory of his own life with sympathy and a feeling of camaraderie. In a few days he would have to plunge once again for fish more solid and rapacious than those of the sea . . .

'What am I going to do?' he said abruptly out loud, half sitting up with his elbows propped behind him on the coil of rope. 'Just what am I going to do?' He was going to return the cheque to Clarisse, since la Doriacci didn't want him to follow her, and following her regardless would lead to nothing.

Not only was she determined not to love him; worse still, she did not love him. Perhaps he should go to Paris; but it came to the same thing—what would he do for money? There he would have to allow himself to be introduced to la Doriacci's friend and be added to the stable of those women. But he didn't have the courage for that. Or more precisely he was afraid that if he ran into la Doriacci a year later with one of these de luxe patrons on his arm, one she herself had proposed, he would die of shame and regret. Clearly he had nothing left but Nevers, where his adventures had already given all his miserable relatives a good laugh. And this time, with his three aunts gone, the laughter would not be mixed with any tenderness; since the owners of the word *tenderness* had died without revealing to him where the treasure was buried, the inexhaustible treasure of tenderness with which they had surrounded him all his life—without so much as warning him that they were taking it away with them, that he would have to get along without it. And without even foreseeing that he would be attacked and eaten alive by his relatives (like a wild animal that has been domesticated) the first time he ventured out alone.

Those were the two routes open to Andreas (other than the Foreign Legion, but he detested violence): the mockery of Nevers or the bitterness of Paris. Leaning on the coiled rope under the blue sky of morning, he heard the engines of the *Narcissus* implacably pursuing their course towards a land where he was no longer awaited by anyone. When he had thoroughly mulled over this last piece of intelligence, he lit one more cigarette, got up, and went to the bulwarks, where an iron door, situated lower down, allowed him to lean out a bit farther over the water, into which he tossed his cigarette.

The stub floated casually on the blue billows; then, caught up by a long eddy, it disappeared from Andreas's view on its way towards the bottom, where the water went black. Perhaps, he thought absurdly, it had been this same wave that he had watched just the other day with la Doriacci, the other day when he had been happy, so happy, without knowing it. She had been close to him, she had laughed as she caressed his wrist, her warm fingers slipped under the cuff of his jacket, murmuring erotic Italian words, obscene ones even, she had told him with a laugh. He should have been light, witty, impetuous, seductive. Perhaps he could have kept her if . . . If what? He had tried to be all those things. He had been as light-hearted, as witty and seductive as he could be . . . and it hadn't been enough. It would never be enough. He could have been anything he might wish in his life, by insisting, by applying himself, by forcing himself—anything but light-hearted. And she had known it, for his deficiencies had provoked neither anger nor scorn, but indifference. And that same sea, in its abstracted gentleness, seemed to exemplify, to symbolise what awaited him. Along its shores men must have complained all through the centuries; how bored it must have been. It stood for that world outside himself, for everything else. It was beautiful, cold, indifferent.

And his solitude, in the past and still to come—the uselessness of his life, his lack of direction, or resistance, or realism, his desperate and puerile need to be loved, all of that seemed suddenly too difficult, too much of a burden. All this made him lift his right leg over the gate and hoist himself over it. For an instant he held a precarious balance—time enough for the sun to touch his neck and for his skin to take pleasure in it, time enough for him to experience a sense of waste at throwing overboard this smoothly running mechanism, this luxurious body—and he let himself fall.

The *Narcissus* was taller, much taller than he had supposed, and much faster. Something cold, something thin, lashed at him, wrapped itself around his chest and encircled his neck. Something like a rope which, for a fraction of a second, he thought he would just be able to catch hold of. And Andreas died believing he had been saved.

*D*elighted for once with Clarisse's absence, Eric made two or three telephone calls to Cannes to verify that his dragnets were in place. In a few hours the card cheat, thief, suborner would be behind bars.

But it was high time . . . Eric held in check the impulse to insult and kick the contemptible thief, this knave of hearts, this old roué, he thought, overlooking their similar age and worries over his own appearance. Eric had always been proud of his physique. He carefully concealed but inwardly cultivated the idea that his male beauty, an almost superfluous beauty, should evoke in others, particularly women, a sort of gratitude—gratitude towards a man who was not only just, profound, reliable and humane, but who also made these virtues, so often associated with an undistinguished physique, appear seductive.

In all candour it was not only Clarisse's money for which he now reproached her, but her beauty—the air of youth, defiance, and also vulnerability she had possessed when they met and of which by now he would have liked to see no more than a trace. Indeed, he had thought there was no more than a trace left under the barbarous make-up. But now he had seen her in the light of day on the deck of the ship, in the sun, by lamplight, without make-up; and above all he had seen her radiant with desire for another man.

He had sometimes thought, with forced contempt, that she would end up an aged little girl. But occasionally, after he had imposed his lovemaking upon her and she lay curled up in the foetal position so dear to psychiatrists, sleeping with her back towards him, he had been surprised to find himself looking at her with eager deference, at the fragile and indomitable nape of the neck. And at times he had even allowed himself to succumb to a desolate and long-forgotten melody almost like a requiem—the memory of what Clarisse's body had been to his at the beginning.

Of course the memory of all the things he no longer was to her, as he tacked vulgar names onto them, rang false to him too. But it was likely that by morning her happy face would melt away, giving way to something quite different. He imagined Clarisse's face when she learned about her handsome lover's character and past. Already he could see her face grow paler still, see her incredulous eyes, her shame, the desire to flee that little by little would close over her visage. He would have to be careful, afterwards, not to say 'I told you so!' too often. That would only reduce the awful blow to a mere irritant, and spoil his triumph.

Yet, it was time now for morning to come. He was leaving the field to Clarisse, loosening the reins so that she would suspect nothing, so she would think him indifferent to her whimsical behaviour, so they would arrive together, the two of them, disarmed by their unawareness and their star-crossed love, before the Cannes chief of police. Again and again he ran over the scene in his mind: wife guilty, husband upheld by the powers of justice, miscreant foiled and thrown into the dungeon.

Meanwhile he had taken the Marquet out from under his berth and placed it on Clarisse's pillow with a three-word note: 'Happy Birthday. Eric.' He knew this would rob the painting of most of its charm. But what was Clarisse doing right this minute? Where on the ship was she, talking bash-fully to her lover before passers-by who would observe, without her knowing it, the bated breath, the tension, the insupportably drawn-out-desire? Somewhere on the ship, on the deck, laughing with abandon at her lover's silly jokes, which she found so droll, laughing, laughing as she had never laughed with him. In fact, it was Eric himself who, from the very start, had introduced a strained solemnity in their relationship. That, for him, was the tone of passion, and it excluded laughter. Actually he didn't like to laugh himself, just as he despised wild laughter in anyone else. Nevertheless, he would have liked to present her the paint-ing in the presence of Julien Peyrat; but that was impossible. And in any event he would have to wait until the last motorboat for Cannes had disappeared into the gathering night, leaving Julien on board, unable to avoid the trap.

'What are we going to do?' Clarisse was saying. She was in fact sitting in the bar, trying to avoid gazing at Julien too long or too closely.

From time to time, if she made a great effort and held her breath, she managed, for a moment or two, to see him not as her lover, but simply as a man sitting opposite her, with chestnut brown hair and brown eyes. For a few seconds she managed to forget the warm feel and perfume of that hair and wry mouth, and speak to him soberly. But then her glance became uneasy, her words slower and she turned her head, unable to bear the delicious pain, hunger and need for him.

Julien was reduced to the same brief expedients and forced distractions, even briefer for him, for the instant he glimpsed her she was his, avid, obsessed, impatient, and he would say to himself, 'I'm going to kiss her right there, I'm going to do this to her . . . I'm going to stroke her right there, take her in my arms and hug her just like this,' spinning vol-uptuous, burning images in his mind which the nearness of this woman, even dressed, rendered cruel and indecent.

'What am I going to do?' she asked, turning her glass round in her long fingers. 'What do you want me to do?'

'Oh simple . . .' said Julien with the self-confident air he wielded against himself—'You'll simply pack your bags to-morrow morning, tell him you want to go off again, alone, on another cruise . . . no . . . well, that you want to go on another cruise without him. And you get into the car where I'll be waiting.'

'Right before his very eyes?' Clarisse was pale with apprehension.

'Yes indeed, right before his steely blue eyes, exactly!' said Julien with forced gaiety. 'He's not about to throw himself at you and drag you into his car by force, for heaven's sake. He won't even try.'

'I'm not sure,' said Clarisse. 'He's capable of anything.'

'He'll take you off over my dead body!' said Julien, swaggering like a stevedore. 'But if you're too scared of him, I can be there when you tell him. I can even break it to him myself. I've already told you that.'

'Oh, that would be wonderful!' said Clarisse in a daze, before admitting to herself that things just weren't done that way.

She was indeed in a turmoil, but Julien was prey to other problems. It had seemed best in the end to rent a car at the dock and take Clarisse to his place. But even if he telephoned from Cannes, would the house be warm enough for them to sleep there that night? Of course, there were hotels, but they shouldn't begin their life together as wanderers. On the contrary, Clarisse should cast off all moorings and seek a sheltered port as soon as possible, even some fishermen's cove, some stable place that would be and would remain their own. That meant Julien's cabin in the Causses, the only thing that really belonged to him after twenty years of poker, casino and racetrack, and in fact was a family inheritance. Clarisse, who was watching him out of the corner of her eye for reassurance, would have been astonished to know that her seducer was mentally searching in a distant closet for the following night's pillows and bedcovers.

Dinner began very well, in spite of everything. On this last evening Captain Elledocq, looking as grave and important as if he were preparing to abandon ship, cast benevolent looks about him, or what he intended as such, for they never failed to terrorise the young barmen and waiters. But he had hardly sat down on the big table with his guests when he was called away to the telephone.

'Well! Now who is going to lead the conversation?' Edma asked in her piping voice, making everyone laugh. 'Will it be you, Monsieur Lethuillier? You ought to write this up for *Forum*. This anthropological phenomenon. Just think about it for a moment. Here we've been, thirty of us, thirty human beings on board this ship, entirely regimented and kept in line for nine days by order of an orang-utan in officer's clothes. A beast who hasn't understood a single thing we've said to him and who's talked to us in gutturals. Though actually he's no fool . . . for instance, he understood very well that the bell meant "eat", "food", and was the first to head straight for the dining room . . . isn't that curious?' she asked, to the laughter of her neighbours and la Doriacci, whose laugh alone would have drawn a whole room in its wake.

'What a pity we didn't think of it sooner,' said Julien, wiping his eyes. 'King Kong, we could have called him King Kong.'

'He wouldn't have minded one way or another,' said Simon. 'The truth is he wanted us to tremble in his presence, his dream was that the men at least should stand to attention when speaking to him.'

'Hush,' said Edma. 'Here he is. But without Charley. Now where the deuce can Charley be?' she enquired, noting his, and Andreas's, vacant chair.

'He could not have gone fooling around in those perverted night spots in Cannes, not tonight,' Elledocq was muttering to himself. 'Unless he did it on purpose to annoy me.'

Charley would indeed stay away the whole evening, to the great dismay of his ladies. And not without cause; for he now sat in his cabin, on the edge of his bed, his head over the enamel washbasin and hands gripping the hot and cold taps, vomiting and crying both at once over what he had seen on the chief cook's bunk, near a crew dormitory. It was a beige-and-blue cashmere sweater, the same blue as its owner's eyes, still showing the rip where the mechanic's fishing line had snagged it, a tear edged with a tenacious brown trace of blood that all the water of the Mediterranean would not be able to wash away.

Of course he would have to keep quiet until the passengers were long gone. Nothing untoward should spoil the final artistic pleasures of this music cruise. Charley cried all through that night, sincerely, for memories at once false and tender, for the hopes Andreas had left him, for all his love, love that might have prevented the fatal gesture. He cried for what was no more than a biased account of a solitary drama. In a few years, he already knew, this account would be replaced by another, a story of burning passion and despair, of Charley who, forsaking this passion, caused the death of the only man he ever loved.

Dawn found him in the same spot, his face swollen and aged by ten years. And it was out of true kindness of heart that he restrained himself, on at least ten occasions that night, from going to cry on la Doriacci's shoulder.

And that was how Charley Bollinger missed a farewell dinner aboard the *Narcissus* for the first and last time. He even missed the strains of 'Happy Birthday', triumphantly announced an hour later by the dimming of the lights, and played by Hans-Helmut Kreuze himself. The chef in his white toque emerged from the entrails of the ship after nine days of anonymity, carrying at arm's length the full proof of his talents, an enormous cake with 'Happy Birthday, Clarisse' written on it in spun sugar. Everyone turned with excited smiles towards Clarisse, who looked petrified. She raised her hand to her mouth.

'Good grief,' she said. 'My birthday . . . I forgot.'

Beside her Julien, surprised and delighted as he was by all festivities, smiled at her a little mockingly, quite pleased at being able to make her forget her own birthday.

'You really didn't remember?' said Eric, his smile devoid of all warmth though it spread from ear to ear.

'Dear Clarisse, how did you manage to forget your birthday?' Edma sang out. 'I, alas, never fail to remember mine, and I say to myself' 'Another . . . and another . . . and another.' But it's true, you wouldn't yet suffer from such sombre reflections.'

'What do you mean "and another"?' said Simon Béjard jovially. 'Here we have the youngest of women, and she's complaining!'

He had been taking things a bit too far for Edma's liking since their tryst over the phone. He looked at her out of the corner of his eye, or straight in the face, smiled endlessly at her, winked—in short, gave himself over to the pantomime of a happy lover. Even in the absence of her husband, this would have been outrageous and, moreover, in bad taste. Edma was simultaneously annoyed, amused, and flattered to see the surprise of the others at this preposterous connivance. What an odd character, what an odd character, she repeated to herself, her reserve mingled with pleasure, and either smiled or made eyes at him according to whim, changing her mind every two or three minutes.

'But my dear Edma,' Simon was saying just then under cover of the fuss over the cake, 'Edma, dear friend, of course you don't take any notice of the passing years. You are and always will be eternally young, you know that. The waistline of a young girl! A wasp's waist even . . . I swear, from behind you'd pass for a fifteen-year-old,' he added, less felicitously.

But Edma had turned away in time not to hear him, and Simon carefully wiped his mouth three times over, as he did whenever he made a gaffe and realised it. Edma went on with a benevolent smile in his direction. 'But how many candles? How many?' she called out in the high voice that had once so annoyed her red-haired wooer and now quite touched him. 'Well then, Clarisse, will you own up? How many?'

'It isn't done to tell,' said Eric. 'Even a young girl doesn't tell.'

'No, but you can in the case of old ladies,' said Edma with bravura, and a sacrificial expression passed over her

421

face like a cloud across the blue sky. 'Take me for example, the old lady of these parts. I'll tell you right off: I'm fifty-seven.'

Armand Bautet-Lebreche rolled his eyes heavenward, and after a vague calculation mentally added five years to this confession. A slight pause followed—hardly a polite one, thought Edma, wounded. But already her squire picked up the gauntlet with his customary elegance.

'So what? Fifty-seven, fifty-eight, fifty-nine, sixty, what difference can it make as long as you're as free and easy as you were at twenty. I don't see what else there is to say!'

'You could tell him to be quiet,' Julien suggested gravely.

'Now there's a good piece of advice,' said Edma with a dignified air, which her smile belied.

'What's that?' Simon was off again. 'What did I say wrong? It's true—sixty really is a splendid age for a woman nowadays . . .'

As far as gaffes are concerned, thought Julien, Béjard seems to have switched his tempo once again. During the cruise he had seemed to have temporarily misplaced his six-shooter, firing one at a time. Tonight the old Simon was back, and all in all it was a good sign. Julien glanced at young Olga, who now seemed to have lost her youth. Dissatisfaction and fear had aged her by a good ten years. Olga in an exotic silk dress with plunging neckline that made her look too tanned, too much a fresh-air girl for a dress that sophisticated. She was drinking in Simon's every word, laughing loudly when he asked for the bread and persistently removing crumbs from his jacket with maternal or voluptuous gestures, crumbs that were invisible to anyone but herself. She's simpering, thought Julien. That was exactly the word, simpering.

But why in the world had Clarisse concealed her birthday from him? Had she really forgotten it? And he had nothing to give her. He bent towards her to complain, but her perplexity told him that she had in fact forgotten. And as if she had read his thoughts, she turned to him and said simply, 'Yes, yes, yes . . . it was because of you,' smiling at his mute insistence.

'You know this is very disconcerting,' said Edma while the cake was being placed in front of Clarisse and a knife to cut it was handed to her. 'They didn't even let us in on it. I have nothing for Clarisse except clothes that wouldn't suit her and jewellery she wouldn't want. I'm really cross,' she said to Eric, who bowed in contrition.

'Nor I, nor I, nor I . . .' The others around the table all showed signs of regret.

Elledocq himself emitted a groan, as if he already imagined himself on the main deck, surrounded by the whole crew at attention, presenting the good-conduct medal of the *Narcissus*, the Compagnie Pottin's birthday-present offering, 'To Madame Eric Lethuillier'.

'Don't worry,' said Eric with a laugh. 'I knew each of you would want to please Clarisse. So I bought her a present for all of us, from me and from all of you.'

And he got up with an air of mystery, went to the cloakroom, and returned with a rectangular package wrapped in brown paper. Even before he placed it on a chair at the end of the table everyone recognised it. Some as the Marquet, others as the fake Marquet. After an instant of surprise everyone broke out in bravos, compliments for this generosity, this absolution offered by a kind and understanding husband, however adulterous himself. Only Julien and Clarisse exchanged glances, Clarisse in fright, Julien in consternation.

'What do you think of it?' Eric was saying as he looked him straight in the eye. 'I should have bought it from you directly, Monsieur Peyrat—or may I call you Julien? Now then, Julien, I should have bought it from you directly, but I was afraid you might still have bad memories of our boxing match and refuse to sell it to me.'

'I'm the one who officially bought it,' said Armand Bautet-Lebreche, quite excited and all in all quite pleased to have played some part in this orchestra in which for nine days he had played nothing more than a succinct triangle.

'You?' asked Edma, frowning.

'Well, yes,' said Armand, delighted and proud of the little ruse, he who, all day long at his office, hatched plots a thousand times more complicated and more pernicious. 'Not bad, eh?' he said with a smile. 'It's a hoot, don't you think?' he added, as though tossing a pebble onto the table cloth; this 'hoot' actually landed with rather a dull thud.

'Hoot, hoot . . . what is this hoot business?' grumbled Edma, though he had picked up the expression from her.

'Well, Clarisse?' said Eric. 'Isn't it a beauty? You look bothered . . .'

'It's the surprise,' she said bravely. 'And a lovely surprise at that. I adore the painting.'

'Well then, enjoy it,' said Eric with an icy smile. 'I'll hang it in your bedroom, and you'll be able to see it all night long. That will be at least something,' he mumbled inaudibly.

Excusing himself, he got up from the table and went back towards the companionway, leaving the passengers speechless for an instant until the ebullient Edma, apparently blushing, found herself being asked to dance by Simon and then literally carried away. She began to waltz with him, gradually drawing the others onto the dance floor. Clarisse hid against Julien's shoulder.

'What do you think of it all?' she said finally. 'I find this present very strange.'

'Why?' said Julien in a tone that was cold and suddenly almost annoyed. 'Why? Aren't you used to having presents on your birthday? Would it have been better if I had given it to you myself, would that have been more natural than having it come from Eric?'

'You're crazy,' said Clarisse, quickly rubbing the top of her head against Julien's chin. 'You're crazy. I would have been furious. We need that money for our trip back, don't we? No, what worries me is that it's a present for me alone coming from Eric. Eric has never given me anything but things meant for the two of us—trips for us both, cars he drives himself, things for the house he uses too. But just now I think he really did say "your painting". God knows all through my childhood I was showered with presents just for me. But for ten years I've only had "communal presents", as Eric calls them. "The only honourable kind," he

424

says. You're going to find me awfully selfish, because I adore having presents just for me.'

'You can tell me all your secrets,' said Julien with spirit. 'And I'll love every last thing and give you beautiful presents just for you.' And he hugged her to him tenderly, with a tenderness born of distress, though Clarisse did not imagine any such thing.

Simon bowed low before them with a spectacular gesture, as if sweeping the ground with the plumes of his hat, and drew away the 'gracious lady' as he called her, for a particularly old-fashioned tango. Julien, now left alone where Clarisse had just been, seemed the very picture of confusion. So Edma told herself, passing in front of him in the arms of an elderly American, a flat-footed robot whom she docilely allowed to propel her about the room.

Despite the absence of the best dancers, Andreas and Charley, whose prospects so promising at the beginning of the cruise now seemed in almost total eclipse, there were still in the main saloon a few exciting or amusing moments, as when, for example, Edma tried to drag Elledocq out onto the floor, swearing to him that afterwards he could smoke his pipe all he wanted. There was a less funny but perhaps more exciting scene when Olga went running from the deck, in tears, shrieking at Simon with every sign of despair—without any lipstick on—that she didn't love him any more. But none of these incidents was able to dissipate the sadness, the sweetness, the charm of that evening that recalled so many others already so distant, both in time and space, those evenings perfumed with jasmine or *zeppole*, evenings never to return, evenings which winter—already in wait at the harbour—would quickly make them forget. La Doriacci sang some melodies by Debussy in a soft, sentimental voice whose sadness excluded all sensuality, a very mature, very young voice, slightly pleading, though still restrained—an intimate voice that made all the little secrets of the cruise, revealed or not, seem pointless and absurd. Everyone went to bed early, some with tears in their eyes without knowing why; and they were more numerous than one might have supposed.

425

Having completely gnawed through the bonds that confined him to his dungeon, Fuchsia, free at last, lay down for a few moments, relaxing a jaw pained by the effort, then set off again, on the rampage.

*S*o it was a bloodthirsty dog that
Julien encountered before dawn on his nocturnal stroll, a
longer stroll than usual. He was walking the deck alone, and
above the silken rustling of the bow cleaving water, he felt
as though his steps were enough to make the deck vibrate,
the planks shiver and creak, a creaking that reverberated all
the way down to the cabins, to Clarisse who would probably
not hear it as she slept calmly beneath the fake Marquet.
Clarisse, released from her cares and her loneliness, Clarisse
who had entrusted her life to a ship's pilot who might be
out to scuttle their craft before her very eyes. There had to
be some reason why Eric had bought the painting, Julien
knew that. And he wondered when and where he would
have to pay the penalty for it. Sheltered from his embezzle-
ments, unaware of the swindles that were her lover's livelihood, Clarisse slept on. Perhaps she saw him passing
through her dreams. Probably she would wake up happy,
not suspecting the brevity of her joy. And once again Julien
trembled for her, fearing for her disappointment much more

than he feared on his own account the prisons of the French Republic—cheerless as he had been told they were. Well, he loved her, and he derived a sort of masochistic pleasure from the fact that the first absolute love he had known in his life was going to be over before it had quite begun, that the one time he had loved 'well' would lead him straight to jail. As long as it was not right away, as long as he could still hold that trembling body to his, as long as he could smell her perfume, lay his cheek against her hair, talk to her as to a child or animal, see the wild joy on that beautiful face, so noble in its innocence, a face he couldn't help thinking of as a Delly or sometimes one of Laclos' heroines. If only fate would allow him one more time with that face, those shoulders, the neck beneath that mouth, Clarisse's tender hands in his hair, the supreme sweetness radiating from her that had turned a cynical gambler into a bashful lover. 'Clarisse,' he said three or four times into the dwindling night, into the white and downy-soft air, an air still without sun. The light on deck at that hour was beige, metallic and sad. We might be on an abandoned ship, on a wreck, Julien said to himself. On some Indian Ocean of great, unfathomable depths.

An animal that had clearly not arisen from the Indian Ocean suddenly impressed itself on Julien's retina and froze there for an instant—time enough for all the relays, circuits, paths and data-recall to unite in alerting Julien: this was Fuchsia, the dog that bit, advancing on him through the dawn, its hackles raised in rage, sneering and implacable. Julien barely had time to leap up on to a service ladder. And even in his haste he had the joy of hearing the monster's furious and disappointed growls. And shortly thereafter, the undeniable pleasure of spitting at him from a height of six feet, a perfect distance to aim from, given the absence of wind. It was not so uncomfortable after all up there on the rungs, and it took him a second to interpret the bewildered expression on la Doriacci's face as she emerged from the companionway. Draped in a burnous-jellaba affair in black-and-red silk that clashed with, but also brightened, the grey around her, la Doriacci gave him an inquisitive glance and signalled him to stop playing the sailor—until she caught sight of the cause of the whole performance.

'Well, well, well,' she said in her great stormy voice, 'here's my friend Fuchsia . . .'

And as the dog turned, Julien, with a sigh of resignation, got ready to leap upon him as onto a rugby ball. But, to his great astonishment, the animal came to her almost purring and then energetically licked her feet; she seemed not the least bit surprised.

'Hello, little Fuchsia . . .' she murmured. 'Hello, you good little dog . . . see, it recognises the hand that feeds it! Yes, that was me with the lovely chocolate. That was me, with the chicken bone . . . yes, that was me with the delicious custard. Little dog, horrid, nasty little dog, come say hello to Auntie Doria . . . what would little Fuchsia like for breakfast this morning? That awful Elledocq?

'Ah, no! It's Monsieur Peyrat that Fuchsia wants this morning,' she said, raising her eyes towards Julien and levelling an ironic look at him, or so Julien thought. 'But what is the matter, Monsieur Peyrat?' said the diva. 'You had better not lean down that way. You look as if you're about to fall, or your eyes are going to pop right out of your head . . .'

'You bet my eyes are bulging,' said Julien, placing a tentative foot on the deck. 'I tell you I haven't seen anything like this since Saint Blandine and the lions . . .'

'I am a lion tamer, don't you see, Monsieur Peyrat,' said la Doriacci with a derisive smile. 'And I'm wondering where my latest cub can have gone . . . I'm even anxious about him, which is a very bad sign. Don't move, Fuchsia. And leave Monsieur Peyrat alone,' she said in the same tone of voice.

'Not for him,' said Julien, now at the foot of the mast but with his eyes glued on Fuchsia. 'It's not a bad sign for him, I mean.'

'Oh yes it is!' said la Doriacci with conviction. 'Oh yes it is! That's all he needs, poor Andreas, for me to fall in love with him . . .'

'You're very hard on him. Isn't he a good lover, in addition to all his charm?'

'A good lover? Come on, Monsieur Peyrat! A good lover is one who tells his mistresses they are marvellous mistresses.'

She repeated this with sombre satisfaction, at the same time adjusting her scarf about her shoulders.

'You're going to catch cold,' said Julien, taking off his sweater to lay it across them. For a moment la Doriacci's perfume stopped him dead. It was the perfume of a woman he had dearly loved, or at least thought he had dearly loved before he met Clarisse. They had been greatly drawn to each other, Julien remembered, seeing again the chalet terrace under the snow, feeling again the tingling cold on his cheeks and the warmth of a naked stomach against his own. It had happened on leaving a casino in Austria, where his slightly mad way of playing had attracted sexual propositions from all sides. It must be said that he had won on the 'zero' three times in a row, and on the 'eight' four times, and . . .

'You were thinking about a casino, Monsieur Peyrat, if I'm not mistaken?' said la Doriacci, still with her back towards him, as though now that he had placed his sweater across her shoulders, she was waiting for him to arrange it or button it for her.

'That's really odd,' said Julien ingenuously, patting the sweater vaguely. 'How did you guess?'

'When you accuse a gambler of thinking of the game, you are rarely going to be very far from the truth.'

And she turned towards him, enveloping him in a cloud of perfume. She was looking at him with such open invitation written all across her face that Julien, hypnotised and incapable of retreating without crushing Fuchsia, who was circling him, leaned down to kiss her without knowing why, and probably without her knowing either, simply because at that precise moment it was the only thing to do.

There was a lifeboat two paces away, damp with dew, and presently Julien emerged from it laughing at la Doriacci's awful joke about the amorous exploits of Olga Lamouroux. He was astonished at the quasi-rape perpetrated upon him, but curiously enough not at all ashamed. It was the archetypal chance encounter, he reflected: a brutal ten minutes with a woman he had never really desired and who meant nothing to him, but who was out looking for a cub in the early morning, while he lurked under the porthole of a married woman. La Doriacci gaily put on her clothes, her face a bit puffy from the stolen pleasure, but already creased in laughter as if she had played a good trick on someone.

'Every time I hear one of your records,' Julien said gallantly, 'or every time I go to a concert, I'll have a terrible time not telling . . .'

'Go ahead, tell all, tell all,' said la Doriacci. 'It's not the story that is shameful. It's usually the people who tell it. I'd rather have you speak of my perversities than hear Kreuze speak of my voice . . . Well, that's that. I'm going to sleep now. All this makes me sleepy,' she said without the slightest tinge of romance.

Having kissed Julien on the cheek, and reassuming a certain hauteur in her looks and carriage, she disappeared, leaving him dumbfounded.

*A*t the stroke of noon the police came on board the *Narcissus*. The de luxe-class passengers who had stayed on board for the final night—that is, everyone except Andreas—and were sitting at the edge of the pool or paddling around in it, smiled at their arrival. In the midst of all these half-naked tanned bodies and wealthy vacationers, the three sombrely clad men, shod in heavy shoes that pounded the deck, seemed somehow unreal. They disappeared with Elledocq for fifteen minutes and for fifteen minutes they were forgotten, presumed to be occupied with some matter concerning cargo or administration. Julien alone followed them with a distrustful eye for a few minutes, then he, too, forgot them. But when Eric burst onto the deck surrounded by the four others, Julien became aware of the danger. He stood up instinctively, as though trying to escape Clarisse and the others, as though wanting to explain himself (if any explanation were possible) in some less public place. But Eric was not having it that way. Clarisse looked at him and was scared. He had turned pale, was laughing too loudly: in short he was jubilant, and Clarisse knew from experience that Eric's jubilation always depended on someone else's discomfort or misfortune. She too stood up and caught Julien by the hand. The eldest of the three officers stepped forward, and Julien prayed childishly that he might fall, raincoat, portfolio and all, right into the pool.

'Monsieur Peyrat, I believe?' the policeman said with a show of teeth. 'I am Commissioner Rivel, of the Municipality of Cannes. Here is my card. I am here with regard to charges made by Monsieur Eric Lethuillier.'

There was a sudden total silence around the pool. Edma closed her eyes, for once, and was saying to Armand in a strained voice, 'There we are, the axe is falling, this is it. What made you get mixed up in this?'

'But in what?' said Armand softly. 'What did I do?'

'Nothing,' said Edma. 'Nothing.' And she closed her eyes again.

Julien had unconsciously adopted a mocking pose, the amused expression with which he always confronted a blow of this sort. Just behind him he could feel Clarisse, feel her shivering in the warm air, in the sun beside him, and this time he was feeling her shiver with fright. He gave up trying to put himself at a discreet distance; it was better for her to learn the whole thing painfully and directly. Poor Clarisse . . . My poor dear, he was saying to himself, and a surge of tenderness made his heart sink.

'Now then, we are here because Monsieur Lethuillier wishes to press charges,' said Commissioner Rivel. 'You are accused of supplying to Monsieur Lethuillier, Eric, for the sum of two hundred fifty thousand francs, a painting of whose origin, in view of your professional expertise, you cannot be unaware. We have just examined this Marquet with Monsieur Plessis, an expert employed by the courts, who is quite categorical: this painting is a forgery. And so is the certificate that accompanies it.'

Julien listened to him and felt almost bored. He was smitten by a growing lethargy, almost a drowsiness. That was what he wished for above all else, that this drowsiness might take him away from these pompous individuals, their disagreeable pronouncements and the mass of red tape it was all going to entail.

'The law is quite clear on this,' continued the aforementioned Rivel. 'I am obliged to take you with me to the commissariat, where we will take a statement from you.'

'This whole thing is grotesque and ridiculous, and just as uninteresting as can be,' said la Doriacci, her eyes glinting in her rocking chair. 'Monsieur le Commissaire, I am surprised to see that in France . . .'

'No, don't bother, don't bother,' said Julien. 'It's all useless.'

He looked attentively at his feet and at the crease of his trousers. His one concern was to avoid Clarisse's eyes. Ever since the idiot facing him had begun to pontificate, Julien, every muscle in his body tensed, had been expecting Clarisse to run off to her cabin. She would pack her bags, go back home to Versailles, allow herself to be abused, and made miserable: everything she was used to when she boarded the ship. But he had had the cruelty to make her think all that was over. She would cry a little, she would send him a charming letter saying that she didn't hold it against him, and they would never see each other again. Or only by chance, and she would look away with compassion and sorrow, perhaps with relief that her husband had saved her from this cheat.

'You admit these facts to be true, I presume?' asked the chief official.

Julien saw Lethuillier's handsome face convulsed by a bitter joy that twisted his mouth and made him look like a fish. Behind him he could hear Clarisse's voice, but understood the words only a second later, after seeing the effect they had on Eric's face—the joy evaporating instantly and giving way to astonishment.

'But this is completely ridiculous,' Clarisse was saying in a gay voice, even laughing a little. 'Commissioner, you have been called out for nothing. You should have spoken to me, Eric, before you disturbed these gentlemen.'

'Talk to you, what about?' said Eric in a cold voice.

'Officer,' said Clarisse without looking at him. 'Monsieur le Commissaire, I am really sorry. Monsieur Peyrat and Madame Bautet-Lebreche and I had planned to play a trick on my husband. A few days ago he was being very pretentious on the subject of painting and we had found it rather annoying . . . Monsieur Peyrat had this fake in his baggage as a curiosity. And, just for fun, we thought we would persuade my husband to buy it, though with the proviso, of course, that we would tell him the truth once we reached Cannes. We were going to let him in on it during lunch, very soon . . .'

There was a brief silence, broken by Edma. 'I have to admit that all this is quite true, Eric. I am terribly sorry about this practical joke, which is no doubt in poor taste.'

'You are Madame Bautet-Lebreche, you say?' said the commissioner, now furious it seemed, and whose tone lacked the respect and deference Edma felt due her wherever she went.

Julien watched with delight as the bust of the aforementioned Edma expanded and her eyes grew sharp, as did her voice.

'I am indeed Madame Bautet-Lebreche. This is my husband, Armand Bautet-Lebreche, who is a commander of the Legion of Honour and president of the Paris Chamber of Commerce, and counsellor to the Court of Audits.'

Armand punctuated each of these titles with a little affirmative nod, which at any other time would have driven Julien into convulsions of laughter.

'Exactly,' he said, also looking indignant, though nobody could see why.

And then there was general pandemonium.

Julien felt Clarisse's hand on his arm, and turned to her almost regretfully. She looked at him, eyes dilated with relief, a tear poised between the lashes.

'Oh God,' she said softly. 'I was really scared, Julien. I thought they were going to arrest you for bigamy!'

And without seeming the slightest bit embarrassed, she put her arms around his neck and kissed him between the roots of his hair and the collar of his black polo shirt.

A little later the three officials, suffused with champagne, jokes and laughter, backed down the gangplank, waving. Clarisse, radiant as she leaned on the rail with the other passengers, murmured to Julien, 'My own dear forger, my gorgeous love, what difference did you think all that could possibly make for us?' And she laughed again with relief.

*C*larisse did not want to go down to her cabin. She had no wish to see Eric again. Every inch of her body held back, and Julien was partly surprised, partly amused and partly annoyed at this resistance, or rather cowardice.

'But you can't just leave without a word. You spent ten years with the man.'

'Yes,' said Clarisse, turning away. 'Yes, and that was ten years too many. I can't tell him to his face that I'm leaving. I'm too cowardly, I'm afraid . . .'

'But afraid of what?' said Julien. 'I'll be two steps away. If he's nasty, you can call me. I'll come right away and we can start up our little Wild West brawl again, for your lovely bright eyes!'

He was laughing and trying to defuse the situation. He saw Clarisse blush, then go pale, clutching his arm convulsively with her long fingers. He saw her eyes go dark with tears of anger, of fear.

'I've had too much emotion for one day,' she said in a

breathless voice. 'I thought that you weren't mine any more, that you were going to prison, that everything was ruined, finished . . . I thought everything was over, happiness, all that . . .'

'So did I,' said Julien, abandoning his moralising. 'So did I, I can tell you. And things could so easily have gone that way,' he added after a moment's silence.

'How do you mean?'

Clarisse looked surprised. Her calm seemed too perfect to Julien. He did not realise that a scrupulous honesty and respect for another's property were notions held by only certain members of the middle-ranking bourgeoisie and were practised only rarely in the higher echelons—that above a certain level the lack of scruples actually increased with the fortune.

'You know,' he said, 'when you realised that I was a low-down thief, a cheat and a forger, that might have disgusted you, mightn't it?'

'Don't use that language,' said Clarisse, smiling, as though he had wrongfully insulted himself. 'They're not important, those things you did. And anyway,' she concluded with a little laugh he found cynical, 'now you won't need all that.'

But what did she think? What did she mean? A tide of far-fetched ideas flooded through his head. 'What do you mean?' he was almost pleading. In fact he was pleading with her not to take him for a gigolo. Thief was enough. He was pleading with her not to underestimate him, a mistake that might some day oblige him to leave her, he realised, because he loved her.

'I mean that you can be an art appraiser without doing all that. We'll go everywhere together and buy paintings, we'll sell them and split the profits once you've paid back my bank, for your own peace of mind. For a forger you affect frightfully moralistic airs and graces,' she told him tenderly.

And Julien gave up for good all attempts to understand what she meant by 'moralistic'. He pushed her towards the stairs, gently, but firmly, and watched her go into her cabin, while he leaned against the wall in the corridor, torn between a desire to take on the lousy stool pigeon and the wish to have Clarisse back without her being drained, wounded and guilty.

Eric was packing, or rather repacking, since the steward had filled his bags without knowing that the publisher of *Forum* organised his belongings, everything in its place, with the same care he applied to laying out the articles in his paper. Clarisse closed the door and leaned against it, her heart pounding. It seemed to her that it could be heard all over the room, resounding and then slackening. Her heart seemed to flag by moments, slowed and was about to stop entirely when Eric suddenly turned, pale but determined, and seemingly affable. There was a resolute look on his face, and the haste in his gestures and voice confirmed her suppositions. He wasn't going to acknowledge what had occurred, he wasn't going to speak of it at all; he was going to act as if nothing had happened, as he always did in embarrassing situations.

'I am so very sorry,' he said with a slight grin. 'Sorry to have suspected good old Julien Peyrat. I should have guessed it was a prank, it's true. You have my cheque, I suppose?'

'Yes,' said Clarisse.

She handed him Armand's beautiful cheque, endorsed by Julien to the order of Monsieur Lethuillier.

'Good. I'll send a note to Monsieur Peyrat later—if you have his address, that is. Are you ready? We just have time to dash to Nice Airport, and I'll be back before the paper goes to press.'

And without seeming to notice her immobility and failure to obey, he went into the bathroom, swept up the brushes and combs and various tubes, even allowing some of them to fall into the bathtub with a clatter, the only thing to reveal his tension: Eric never let anything fall, nor broke anything, nor bumped into furniture, nor burnt himself on a hot potato, nor let champagne bubble over when he opened the bottle, nor . . . Clarisse tried to stop herself itemising this parade of virtues—or rather the absence of faults. It was true there was something negative about Eric, that everything he did was at someone else's expense, as a

439

rejection of someone. He had bumped into the dressing table as he passed, and in the mirror Clarisse saw herself as she was: standing there, pale, and ugly she thought, with a stupid tic she couldn't control that was making the right side of her mouth jump. The pale woman in the mirror was absolutely unable to tell the truth, to flee, to escape this handsome, tanned, determined man who was rapidly moving to and fro in front of this same mirror where sometimes his reflection symbolically hid her own.

'Eric . . .' the woman in the mirror said nevertheless, in a quavering voice. 'Eric, I'm going away . . . I'm not going with you, I'm not going back to Paris . . . I think we're leaving each other . . . I'm leaving you. It's . . . it's a pity,' she said in her bewilderment. 'But there's nothing else for us to do.'

Eric was there in front of her, and she saw him stop at her first words and remain there without moving, standing on his two feet almost like an athlete, a stance that did not go at all with the sense of her words. Out of the corner of her eye she could see him without actually looking at him openly. She saw, or guessed, or remembered an attentive, inscrutable face, drugged by the idea of what he was going to do, yes doped by this notion of himself, by his absolute assurance that any action, the instant he decided on it, was the only possible one to pursue. She could see him, arms at his sides, chest out, knees slightly flexed, eyes trained on her. Somehow he looked as though he were playing tennis. But the shots she had just delivered were all aces. Despite this, his voice was calm as he answered her.

'You mean to say that you're going off with that dime-store thief, that no-good nobody? That superannuated truant? You mean to say you find him interesting—his little poker games, his bad paintings and racetracks? That schoolboy? You, Clarisse?'

'Me, Clarisse,' she repeated dreamily, behind him. 'Me, Clarisse. You know very well that I'm alcoholic, spoiled, apathetic and stupid . . . and insipid,' she added with a sort of profoundly proud pleasure, a tone of deliverance in her voice, a tone Eric instantly recognised. He had heard it from

440

his chauffeur when he fired him three months earlier. And he had heard it from a great philosopher and writer, a former contributing editor of *Forum*, who had taken his name off the masthead, for good, in response to an innocent remark Eric had made about his articles just before he left on vacation. He had heard the same sharp note, almost a note of gaiety, from all three as they said goodbye. From all three: simple-minded, cultured or not, linked to him by such diverse feelings or hierarchies. Yes, it had been gaiety, and it was gaiety this time as well. And what he wanted to hear was shame. Suddenly he was overwhelmed at the idea that he would no longer be able to wrench that shame from Clarisse or the other two. This became so clear to him that it was he, and not she, who staggered and blushed at his powerlessness.

'You may be sure I will not hinder you,' he said, with a halting emphasis that reinforced the brutality of his words. 'I will not chain you to the door of the house in Versailles, or have you trailed by thugs, or put you under lock and key.'

And as he enumerated the measures he would not take, the things he pledged not to do, they seemed in fact to be the only solutions possible; and he immediately told himself that if he did ever get out of this bind, and managed to keep her, if he did get her back to Versailles, he would soon retract these stupid concessions dictated by fear. Clarisse must have sensed this, since she backed up to the door, seizing the knob behind her.

'I have no desire to kill you,' he said bitterly. 'Without wanting to be cruel, dear Clarisse, I must say that I shall not be expending tears of despair during the few days it will take you to discover what Monsieur Peyrat is.'

'I wasn't expecting you to,' said Clarisse in a muted voice. 'I was hoping *Forum* would keep you busy and take your mind off it at first.'

'You are thinking perhaps of reclaiming *Forum*?' he said.

Instantly the absurdity of the notion embarrassed him. After all, she knew very well the paper belonged to him,

441

despite all the Dureau investments, and he knew that Clarisse would not take it back.

'No, forget I said that,' he said sharply.

She blinked, as though in fact she hadn't heard. She looked calm even though her hands and lower lip were both trembling; she actually looked serene. No doubt she had rediscovered in herself the invisible thing, the secret defence that had always escaped him, that he had been unable to name. Now there was no doubt he would never be able to name it. That 'never' that he finally admitted to himself, was like being hit below the belt. She would never come back, he was sure of it now. And even if it had been her fault, even if it was nothing to do with him, still it was something decisive, something that escaped him, escaped his control, his will, his dominance. In one furious final outburst, he exclaimed, 'If you think I'm going to miss you, or repent for one single instant, my poor Clarisse, you are truly, truly mistaken.'

And he stared at her without seeing her, without even hearing her. Her answer did not really reach him until five minutes after she had gone.

'I know,' she said. 'And that's another reason why I'm going.'

'And I had to be the one to miss it,' whined Simon Béjard, with a reproachful look at Olga, whose slowness in packing had been, it seemed, the cause of their delay. 'I would have shown them! I don't know why, but I can't stand cops. As though Eric didn't already know that painting was a fake! He even said that Julien wouldn't have wanted to sell it to him, see what I mean? It looks as though your husband's a reformed character. I don't mean to offend you, but he's a real bore. The archetypal preacher . . .'

These various opinions, interrupted by the consumption of smoked salmon and caviar on toast, cascaded from the mouth of Simon Béjard, with no apparent logic, occasionally punctuated by a glance towards the person who had, or should have had, a close interest in the allusions. Olga was eating lunch with lowered eyes. She wore a little checked blouse and blue overalls and no make-up, to make herself look younger, but the costume only clashed with her woebegone expression and gave her the ambiguous air of an ageing and disgruntled little girl. She had missed the scene too, but just now she didn't give a damn. For all she cared, the Lethuilliers, Bautet-Lebreches, Peyrat and consort, could all kill one another or be thrown into jail. So long as she hadn't signed her movie contract with Simon, Olga had absolutely no interest in anything else. The world could blow up and the great powers smash each other to smithereens, Olga was persuaded that atomic fall-out wouldn't reach the Boulogne Studios, that the presidents of the USA and USSR would hold off launching their bombers until she had signed her contract and the last reel had rolled, as they say. For the time being she followed Simon around like a puppy, yapping cheerfully whenever he laughed, grumbling when he was put out, filling his bowl if he was hungry and accompanying all of his speeches with a howl of enthusiasm. Sometimes Simon looked at her with what she took for tenderness, but which was nothing but disgust. He had spoken to her sternly, and already Clarisse had gently intervened.

Clarisse was at the head of the table, beside Elledocq, who looked glum. Julien, next to her, was in a contented daze. She chattered on, laughing, seemingly overflowing with happiness, while Julien drank her in with his eyes. Simon looked at them for a moment and suddenly felt very old and very pompous. Perhaps she would go on drinking, and Julien would go on gambling, but she would not get drunk and he would no longer cheat, neither of them really having any more reason to do so. Her trousseau was that of a wealthy woman, his that of a happy man; Clarisse's contribution was surely the lesser. They suddenly looked like two children, Simon said to himself with nostalgia, like two carefree kids, though Clarisse undoubtedly seemed the more pensive, if only in response to misfortune. And Simon felt, as he saw this woman laughing and darting ardent looks at the man sitting next to her, that she could easily surrender herself to happiness and stop this thinking. Their happiness stood a good chance of enduring, since they were both ready to make concessions, to forgive, and because they both hated unhappiness. She from experience; in him it was instinctive.

'Good luck!' said Simon, suddenly raising his glass.

And everyone got up and clinked glasses with each other, with some emotion, as if bidding farewell to a former life, as if each was seeing part of his own existence disappear along with these fleeting nine days. They all smiled at their emotional behaviour, all except Eric, who was now ashore, and Charley, who sat there silently. He was undoubtedly too sentimental; he had had tears in his eyes since the day before. Poor Charley, thought Edma Bautet-Lebreche as she clinked her glass. He must be crying for poor Andreas, though he hadn't won him, Andreas who must have gone off in a rage, to Nantes or Nevers.

'Let's drink to Andreas,' she said. 'Even if he isn't here. I drink to his career.'

'And I drink to his happiness,' said la Doriacci with spirit.

'As for me,' said Simon, 'I drink to Andreas the actor.'

'Hear, hear,' they said one after the other, all of them, right down to Armand Bautet-Lebreche, whose toast was cut short by the precipitous exit of Charley Bollinger who knocked over his chair as he went. 'But what's the matter with him?' 'What's dear Charley up to?' 'What's got into him?' The various hypotheses were all swept aside by Elledocq, who always knew what was going on where his personnel were concerned.

'Charley Bollinger, liver problems,' he said with an altogether husbandly look of concern. 'Yesterday, three helpings floating island. Taking him see Cannes doctor.'

'That's very good, really it is,' said Edma. 'You must take care of Charley, Captain. After all, you are at once both his father and his . . .' She stopped short. 'And his alter ego.'

'Meaning what?' scolded Elledocq, so sensitive on the subject of his relationship with Charley.

'Alter ego—well, it means another self. Charley completes you, Captain. He has the femininity, the gentleness, the delicacy you, with your gruffness, won't allow. As for his liver trouble, I know what that is: if the air around poor Charley weren't polluted all the time by cigar and pipe smoke, he would breathe more easily and . . . ah hah, Captain, don't roll your eyes at me so furiously, I wasn't

445

necessarily talking about you. You aren't the only one who sends up clouds of smoke about this ship . . . Yes, yes, I know, we all know,' she continued wearily as Elledocq, bright red and pounding the table with his fist, exclaimed:

'But I don't smoke, for God's sake! I gave up smoking three years ago!'

No one would listen to him except Kreuze who, though he despised the captain, admired his concern for his position and his respect for hierarchy. 'On the contrary, I find Captain Elledocq very courageous,' he said in his staccato voice. 'So as not to set a bad example, no doubt he smokes alone in his cabin. That is very worthy, for the nicotine habit is very difficult to get rid of, is it not?' he asked of Elledocq, who had turned from red to crimson.

'No!' howled the captain. 'NO! I have not smoked once, not once! I have not smoked for three years. You have not seen me, Monsieur Kreuze, not even twice, not even once. Nobody has seen me smoke, nobody!' he hiccupped with despair, while Edma and la Doriacci hid their faces behind their napkins like two schoolgirls.

Then he rose, and having, through an enormous effort of self-control, resumed his telegraphic style, he bowed to the company, fingers raised to his peaked hat, heroic and scrupulous to the very end. 'Await departure everybody gangplank,' he said.

He bowed once more and was gone. Left at the table now were only the Bautet-Lebreches, la Doriacci, Béjard and Olga, Julien and Clarisse.

'It's very late,' said Edma, consulting her Cartier watch, deposited during the cruise in the safe of the *Narcissus* along with three or four baubles of similar value. 'We lunched at two, actually, thanks to you, Armand. What were you doing down on the dock all that time, if that's not an indiscreet question?'

'I went to get a few financial papers, my dear,' said Armand without raising his eyes from his plate.

'And of course brought back *Les Echos de la Bourse*, *Le Journal Financier*, etcetera. I don't even know whether the fashion openings have begun in Paris . . .'

'I brought you *Minute* to show you the photo of Mademoiselle Lamouroux and Monsieur Lethuillier,' said Armand, courageously defending himself. 'But Monsieur Lethuillier reached out and simply took it from my hands as he came by. Actually, I think that was when he decided to eat in town. He seemed to hate that photo, and yet he came out looking quite good . . .'

'My God . . .' said Edma. 'And I had to miss that! And to think how close I came to missing your arrest too, my dear Julien . . . that would have made me sick.'

'Well,' said Julien, 'I certainly do entertain you royally! I practically sell our publisher a fake, and I take him on at boxing, and so on,' he concluded rapidly, but not rapidly enough to forestall Simon Béjard's tasteful commentary.

'And stole his wife, made him look ridiculous, and the truth is he adores you,' Simon said, gleefully, and burst into laughter, followed by Olga's shrill, compliant giggle and the much more convincing guffaw of la Doriacci, who seemed to be in a very good mood after a day and night of solitude. She got up and moved towards the door with her royal gait and bright red shawl. On the way she went up to Clarisse and kissed her on both cheeks; then she kissed Edma and Olga, then Simon and Armand, who both turned red; she ended up with Julien, whom she kissed a bit longer than the rest.

'*Addio*,' she said at the door. 'I'm off. If I'm singing somewhere and you happen to be passing, come and see me, never mind a ticket. I owe you some Mahler *Lieder*, four Mozart pieces and a song by Reynaldo Hahn. Be happy!' she called out as she went through the doorway.

The rest looked at one another, got up and headed for the gangplank to make their farewells both to and in the presence of Elledocq and Charley.

Clarisse held Julien's hand and glanced anxiously towards the city. But he had taken no more than fifteen minutes to rent a car and load it with half her baggage.

'And how will I get the rest back?' she asked as she got into the hired car.

'Perhaps you never will,' Julien said as he kissed her. He backed up, turned around on the quay to take the road west, and stopped for an instant to face the *Narcissus*, where it rode in the harbour still purring and smoking peacefully, satisfied, its duties done; the *Narcissus* under a sun to equal the one that shone on the day of their departure; without the sound of the passengers' voices or the noise of the engines the *Narcissus* lay beneath a deafening silence, a silence that, as they went back up the gangway, Charley found excruciating, though Elledocq thought it restful.